THE FLAMING JEWEL

Deep in the woods of upsta
disreputable Mike Clinch a.... ... .g..... Lve.
Clinch possesses a case full of jewels which he
acquired, not entirely honestly, from the thief,
Quintana. Quintana wants them back. To that end, he
has assembled a gang to reacquire the jewels. But the
jewels really don't belong to Quintana either. He stole
them from Theodorica, Grand Duchess of Estonia. And
hot on Quintana's heel is James Darragh, posing as a
thief as well, who has pledged to return them to her.
Meanwhile, state trooper Stormand, having fallen for
Eve, also becomes involved. Together this motley group
will play out a deadly game in search of the purloined
treasure, and most especially, the Flaming Jewel!

THE TALKERS

From the moment when Sadoul first meets Gilda
Greenway, he becomes mad about her. Unfortunately,
she does not share the feeling. Then comes the masked
ball, when Gilda meets Stuart Sutton. The spark
between them is instant. Everything changes for her.
Then, too, that is the night that Gilda dies. Or does
she? Sutton certainly thinks she is dead. But then
Pockman performs an operation on her, and the girl
opens her eyes. Now Gilda seems in thrall to Sadoul.
She becomes the new after hours belle of the ball. But
she confesses to Sutton that another soul entered her
body when she died, and now wants control of her—
Sadoul exerts a hypnotic control over her and her
Other. It is up to Sutton to figure out how to save Gilda.
For not only is her life in danger, but quite possibly her
very soul.

THE FLAMING JEWEL

•••••••••••••

THE TALKERS

ROBERT W. CHAMBERS

INTRODUCTION BY MIKE ASHLEY

Stark House Press • Eureka California

THE FLAMING JEWEL / THE TALKERS

Published by Stark House Press
1315 H Street
Eureka, CA 95501, USA
griffinskye3@sbcglobal.net
www.starkhousepress.com

THE FLAMING JEWEL
Originally published and copyright © 1922 by George H. Doran Company, New York.

THE TALKERS
Originally published and copyright © 1923 by George H. Doran Company, New York; and copyright ©1921 by International Magazine Company.

This edition copyright © 2022 by Stark House Press. All rights reserved under International and Pan-American Copyright Conventions.

"The Other Ones" copyright © 2022 by Mike Ashley

ISBN: 978-1-951473-82-2

Book design by Mark Shepard, shepgraphics.com
Cover art by Rafael DeSoto
Proofreading by Bill Kelly

PUBLISHER'S NOTE
This is a work of fiction. Names, characters, places and incidents are either the products of the author's imagination or used fictionally, and any resemblance to actual persons, living or dead, events or locales, is entirely coincidental. Without limiting the rights under copyright reserved above, no part of this publication may be reproduced, stored, or introduced into a retrieval system or transmitted in any form or by any means (electronic, mechanical, photocopying, recording or otherwise) without the prior written permission of both the copyright owner and the above publisher of the book.

First Stark House Press Edition: February 2022

7
The Other Ones
By Mike Ashley

11
The Flaming Jewel
By Robert W. Chambers

177
The Talkers
By Robert W. Chambers

371
Robert W. Chambers
Bibliography

THE OTHER ONES
Introduction by Mike Ashley

The two books reprinted here—*The Flaming Jewel* and *The Talkers*—are as different as night and day, prison and freedom, cradle and grave—well, perhaps not the cradle! The point is that though they were written at the same time, Chambers created two very diverse adventures—the first a relentless chase for jewels, the second a dangerous dance with death. They show that even though nearly thirty years had passed since his first novel, Chambers still had the ability to switch atmosphere, pace and plot and still sustain the interest and intensity of two disparate books.

Both were even serialized at the same time, *The Flaming Jewel* in *McCall's Magazine* from August 1921 to July 1922 and *The Talkers* in *Hearst's International* from January to June 1922. What is surprising is that *The Flaming Jewel* actually lent itself to serialization, because the pace is such that readers would be left breathless at the end of each episode, and then at the start of the next fight to remember who was who. The book has a cast of thousands (well, maybe thirty), one with a hidden identity and change of name, and it is to Chambers's credit that he keeps all these balls juggled in the air at the same time. It is a book that once you start you daren't stop, for fear the balls come tumbling down.

Chambers's career had had its ups and downs, from the critical successes of the weirdly strange *The King in Yellow* (1895) and various historical novels including *Lorraine* (1898) and *Cardigan* (1901) through such society novels as *The Fighting Chance* (1906) and *The Firing Line* (1908). But critics also recognized that Chambers had developed a formula that allowed him to produce books on a Henry-Ford-like conveyer-belt following a popular pattern, tweaked and adjusted according to demand. The public still enjoyed his work, but critics grew more cynical and over time, and certainly since his death, much of his later work has been written off.

Such is fame.

But not all those works should be written off, and the two presented here are fine examples.

In the early part of the twentieth century there were countless novels and stories in which jewels—sacred, accursed, priceless—pay a central part and *The Flaming Jewel* is no exception. At the start of the novel Chambers goes so far as to list all manner of precious stones. Needless to say the most precious, along with a tray of lesser but still expensive jewels, has been stolen. From whom, by whom I'll leave you to discover. Various disparate groups seek to recover them from, of all places, the remote woods of northern New York state where the forest becomes as treacherous as any South American jungle.

There is much sleight of hand in this novel. You can't always be sure who is who. You soon get a reasonable idea about the villains, but those on the side of good don't always play their cards right. Throughout the book, with its villainy, treachery, deceit and death by numbers, one person stands out around whom the action revolves—Eve. She is the daughter—or rather step-daughter (well, even that's not quite right—just remember not everyone is quite who they seem) of Mike Clinch, a nasty piece of work who nevertheless will do whatever he must to protect Eve. He chooses to live in the North Woods of New York state and run a "hotel" which caters for all the vermin, low-life, and occasional State Trooper, who happen to be in the area.

In 1921 *McCall's Magazine* was undergoing a transformation. It had started as a fashion magazine nearly fifty years earlier and it was still seen as primarily a magazine for women, but new editor, Harry Payne Burton, building upon women having at last won the right to vote across the USA in August 1920, wanted *McCall's* to feature women in strong, enlightened roles. Eve's fight for survival in the darkest depths of murderous mayhem reflects this change.

There's another strong woman in *The Talkers*, Gilda, who needs to be strong because, unlike Eve, she dies at the start of chapter III. That's not a spoiler, because the rest of the novel is how she is brought back to life and copes with the consequences of having been dead for several hours. We learn how she was already under the influence of the sinister Casimir Sadoul, a Svengali-like character who has some form of psychic control over her. Because she had not responded to his advances, he has awoken within her a twin soul, known as the *Other One*. There is this constant battle for control between the two spirits. It's not as extreme as Jekyll and Hyde. There is no pure evil. In fact in one scene we see the two spirits standing together over the slumbering body of Gilda. The challenge for Gilda is how she wrests herself free of Sadoul who thwarts her every action and threatens her lover, Sutton. Sutton is himself restricted because, against her will, Gilda had gone through a marriage ceremony with Sadoul in Paris. The novel thereby allows Chambers the chance to explore women's liberation at all levels.

It's a shame Chambers called the novel *The Talkers*. The title refers to a group of individuals who feel that they are influencing the world and its future through their incessant talking about anything and everything but who actually achieve nothing. It's an opportunity for Chambers to satirise New York society as he had in previous novels. The Talkers themselves become something of an annoyance and are the one clumsy element in the book, because they have no idea what is going on. Perhaps because of this critic Everett Bleiler called the book "rubbish" in his *Guide to Supernatural Fiction* in 1983, but it's far from rubbish. It's a blend of the occult and science fiction and the most interesting discussions are between Sadoul, and his theories on the immortality of the human soul, and his colleague Pockman, a doctor who has been experimenting on rejuvenation through the transplant of glands, notably the nymphalic gland—an invention by Chambers. There are several scenes involving the spirits of Gilda and the *Other One*, and later of Sadoul, which are amongst Chambers's most atmospheric. *Hearst's International* went so far as to call it Chambers's best novel since *The King in Yellow*.

You'll have to decide for yourself, of course, but I believe these are two examples of where Chambers could demonstrate his abilities to continue to write tense, exciting and compelling fiction even late in his career.

—December 2021

THE FLAMING JEWEL

ROBERT W. CHAMBERS

TO
MY FRIEND
R. T. HAINES-HALSEY

WHO
UNRESERVEDLY BELIEVES
EVERYTHING I WRITE

To R. T.

I

Three Guests at dinner! That's the life!—
Wedgewood, Revere, and Duncan Phyfe!

II

You sit on Duncan—when you dare,—
And out of Wedgewood, using care,
With Paul Revere you eat your fare.

III

From Paul you borrow fork and knife
To wage a gastronomic strife
In porringers; and platters rare
Of blue Historic Willow-ware.

IV

Banquets with cymbal, drum and fife,
Or rose-wreathed feasts with riot rife
To your chaste suppers can't compare.

V

Let those deny the truth who dare!—
Paul, Duncan, Wedgewood! That's the life!
All else is bunk and empty air.

ENVOI

The Cordon-bleu has set the pace
With Goulash, Haggis, Bouillabaisse,
Curry, Chop-suey, Kous-Kous Stew—
I can not offer these to you,—
Being a plain, old-fashioned cook,—
So pray accept this scrambled book.

R. W. C.

Episode One
EVE

I

During the last two years Fate, Chance, and Destiny had been too busy to attend to Mike Clinch.

But now his turn was coming in the Eternal Sequence of things. The stars in their courses indicated the beginning of the undoing of Mike Clinch.

From Esthonia a refugee Countess wrote to James Darragh in New York:

"—After two years we have discovered that it was José Quintana's band of international thieves that robbed Ricca. Quintana has disappeared.

"A Levantine diamond broker in New York, named Emanuel Sard, may be in communication with him.

"Ricca and I are going to America as soon as possible.
"Valentine."

The day Darragh received the letter he started to look up Sard.

But that very morning Sard had received a curious letter from Rotterdam. This was the letter:

"Sardius — Tourmaline — Aragonite — Rhodonite * Porphyry — Obsidian — Nugget Gold — Diaspore * Novaculite * Yu * Nugget Silver — Amber — Matrix Turquoise — Elaeolite * Ivory — Sardonyx * Moonstone — Iceland Spar — Kalpa Zircon — Eye Agate * Celonite — Lapis — Iolite — Nephrite — Chalcedony — Hydrolite * Hegolite — Amethyst — Selenite * Fire Opal — Labradorite — Aquamarine — Malachite — Iris Stone — Natrolite — Garnet * Jade — Emerald — Wood Opal — Essonite — Lazuli * Epidote — Ruby — Onyx — Sapphire — Indicolite — Topaz — Euclase * Indian Diamond * Star Sapphire — African Diamond — Iceland Spar — Lapis Crucifer * Abalone — Turkish Turquoise * Old Mine Stone — Natrolite — Cats Eye — Electrum * * * ⅕ āā ."

That afternoon young Darragh located Sard's office and presented himself as a customer. The weasel-faced clerk behind the wicket laid a pistol handy and informed Darragh that Sard was away on a business trip.

Darragh looked cautiously around the small office:

"Can anybody hear us?"

"Nobody. Why?"

"I have important news concerning José Quintana," whispered Darragh; "Where is Sard?"

"Why, he had a letter from Quintana this very morning," replied the clerk in a low, uneasy voice. "Mr. Sard left for Albany on the one o'clock train. Is there any trouble?"

"Plenty," replied Darragh coolly; "do you know Quintana?"

"No. But Mr. Sard expects him here any day now."

Darragh leaned closer against the grille: "Listen very carefully; if a man comes here who calls himself José Quintana, turn him over to the police until Mr. Sard returns. No matter what he tells you, turn him over to the police. Do you understand?"

"Who are you?" demanded the worried clerk. "Are you one of Quintana's people?"

"Young man," said Darragh, "I'm close enough to Quintana to give *you* orders. And give Sard orders.... And Quintana, too!"

A great light dawned on the scared clerk:

"*You* are José Quintana!" he said hoarsely.

Darragh bored him through with his dark stare:

"Mind your business," he said.

That night in Albany Darragh picked up Sard's trail. It led to a dealer in automobiles. Sard had bought a Comet Six, paying cash, and had started north.

Through Schenectady, Fonda, and Mayfield, the following day, Darragh traced a brand new Comet Six containing one short, dark Levantine with a parrot nose. In Northville Darragh hired a Ford.

At Lake Pleasant Sard's car went wrong. Darragh missed him by ten minutes; but he learned that Sard had inquired the way to Ghost Lake Inn.

That was sufficient. Darragh bought an axe, drove as far as Harrod's Corners, dismissed the Ford, and walked into a forest entirely familiar to him.

He emerged in half an hour on a wood road two miles farther on. Here he felled a tree across the road and sat down in the bushes to await events.

Toward sunset, hearing a car coming, he tied his handkerchief over his face below the eyes, and took an automatic from his pocket.

Sard's car stopped and Sard got out to inspect the obstruction. Darragh sauntered out of the bushes, poked his pistol against Mr. Sard's fat abdomen, and leisurely and thoroughly robbed him.

In an agreeable spot near a brook Darragh lighted his pipe and sat him down to examine the booty in detail. Two pistols, a stiletto, and a blackjack composed the arsenal of Mr. Sard. A large wallet disclosed more than four thousand dollars in Treasury notes—something to reimburse Ricca when she arrived, he thought.

Among Sard's papers he discovered a cipher letter from Rotterdam—probably from Quintana. Cipher was rather in Darragh's line. All ciphers are solved by similar methods, unless the key is contained in a code book known only to sender and receiver.

But Quintana's cipher proved to be only an easy acrostic—the very simplest of secret messages. Within an hour Darragh had it pencilled out:

Cipher

"Take notice:
"Star Pond, N. Y.... Name is Mike Clinch.... Has Flaming Jewel.... Erosite.... I sail at once.
"Quintana."

Having served in Russia as an officer in the Military Intelligence Department attached to the American Expeditionary Forces, Darragh had little trouble with Quintana's letter. Even the signature was not difficult, the fraction $\frac{1}{5}$ was easily translated *Quint*; and the familiar prescription symbol āā spelled *ana*; which gave Quintana's name in full.

He had heard of Erosite as the rarest and most magnificent of all gems. Only three were known. The young Duchess Theodorica of Esthonia had possessed one.

Darragh was immensely amused to find that the chase after Emanuel Sard should have led him to the very borders of the great Harrod estate in the Adirondacks.

He gathered up his loot and walked on through the splendid forest which once had belonged to Henry Harrod of Boston, and which now was the property of Harrod's nephew, James Darragh.

When he came to the first trespass notice he stood a moment to read it. Then, slowly, he turned and looked toward Clinch's. An autumn sunset flared like a conflagration through the pines. There was a glimmer of water, too, where Star Pond lay.

Fate, Chance, and Destiny were becoming very busy with Mike Clinch.

They had started Quintana, Sard, and Darragh on his trail. Now they stirred up the sovereign State of New York.

That lank wolf, Justice, was afoot and sniffing uncomfortably close to the heels of Mike Clinch.

II

Two State Troopers drew bridles in the yellowing October forest. Their smart drab uniforms touched with purple blended harmoniously with the autumn woods. They were as inconspicuous as two deer in the dappled shadow. There was a sunny clearing just ahead. The wood road they had been travelling entered it. Beyond lay Star Pond.

Trooper Lannis said to Trooper Stormont: "That's Mike Clinch's clearing. Our man may be there. Now we'll see if anybody tips him off this time."

Forest and clearing were very still in the sunshine. Nothing stirred save gold leaves drifting down, and a hawk high in the deep blue sky turning in narrow circles.

Lannis was instructing Stormont, who had been transferred from the Long Island Troop, and who was unacquainted with local matters.

Lannis said: "Clinch's dump stands on the other edge of the clearing. Clinch owns five hundred acres in here. He's a rat."

"Bad?"

"Well, he's mean. I don't know how bad he is. But he runs a rotten dump. The forest has its slums as well as the city. This is the Hell's Kitchen of the North Woods."

Stormont nodded.

"All the scum of the wilderness gathers here," went on Lannis. "Here's where half the trouble in the North Woods hatches. We'll eat dinner at Clinch's. His stepdaughter is a peach."

The sturdy, sun-browned trooper glanced at his wrist watch, stretched his legs in his stirrups.

"Jack," he said, "I want you to get Clinch right, and I'm going to tell you about his outfit while we watch this road. It's like a movie. Clinch plays the lead. I'll dope out the scenario for you—"

He turned sideways in his saddle, freeing both spurred heels and lolled so, constructing a cigarette while he talked:

"Way back around 1900 Mike Clinch was a guide—a decent young fellow they say. He guided fishing parties in summer, hunters in fall and winter. He made money and built the house. The people he guided were wealthy. He made a lot of money and bought land. I understand he was square and that everybody liked him.

"About that time there came to Clinch's 'hotel' a Mr. and Mrs. Strayer. They were 'lungers.' Strayer seemed to be a gentleman; his wife was good looking and rather common. Both were very young. He had the consump bad—the galloping variety. He didn't last long. A month after he died his young wife had a baby. Clinch married her. She also died the same year. The baby's name was Eve. Clinch became quite crazy about her and started to make a lady of her. That was his mania."

Lannis leaned from his saddle and carefully dropped his cigarette end into a puddle of rain water. Then he swung one leg over and sat side saddle.

"Clinch had plenty of money in those days," he went on. "He could afford to educate the child. The kid had a governess. Then he sent her to a fancy boarding school. She had everything a young girl could want.

"She developed into a pretty young thing at fifteen.... She's eighteen now—and I don't know what to call her. She pulled a gun on me in July."

"What!"

"Sure. There was a row at Clinch's dump. A rum-runner called Jake Kloon got shot up. I came up to get Clinch. He was sick-drunk in his bunk. When I broke in the door Eve Strayer pulled a gun on me."

"What happened?" inquired Stormont.

"Nothing. I took Clinch.... But he got off as usual."

"Acquitted?"

Lannis nodded, rolling another cigarette:

"Now, I'll tell you how Clinch happened to go wrong," he said. "You see he'd always made his living by guiding. Well, some years ago Henry Harrod, of Boston, came here and bought thousands and thousands of acres of forest all around Clinch's—" Lannis half rose on one stirrup and, with a comprehensive sweep of his muscular arm, ending in a flourish: "—He bought everything for miles and miles. And that started Clinch down hill. Harrod tried to force Clinch to sell. The millionaire tactics you know. He was determined to oust him. Clinch got mad and wouldn't sell at any price. Harrod kept on buying all around Clinch and posted trespass notices. That meant ruin to Clinch. He was walled in. No hunters care to be restricted. Clinch's little property was no good. Business stopped. His stepdaughter's education became expensive. He was in a bad way. Harrod offered him a big price. But Clinch turned ugly and wouldn't budge. And that's how Clinch began to go wrong."

"Poor devil," said Stormont.

"Devil, all right. Poor, too. But he needed money. He was crazy to make a lady of Eve Strayer. And there are ways of finding money, you know."

Stormont nodded.

"Well, Clinch found money in those ways. The Conservation Commissioner in Albany began to hear about game law violations. The Revenue people heard of rum-running. Clinch lost his guide's license. But nobody could get the goods on him.

"There was a rough backwoods bunch always drifting about Clinch's place in those days. There were fights. And not so many miles from Clinch's there was highway robbery and a murder or two.

"Then the war came. The draft caught Clinch. Malone exempted him, he being the sole support of his stepchild.

"But the girl volunteered. She got to France, somehow—scrubbed in a hospital, I believe—anyway, Clinch wanted to be on the same side of the world she was on, and he went with a Forestry Regiment and cut trees for railroad ties in southern France until the war ended and they sent him home.

"Eve Strayer came back too. She's there now. You'll see her at dinner time. She sticks to Clinch. He's a rat. He's up against the dry laws and the game laws. Government enforcement agents, game protectors, State Constabulary, all keep an eye on Clinch. Harrod's trespass signs fence him in. He's like a rat in a trap. Yet Clinch makes money at law breaking and nobody can catch him red-handed.

"He kills Harrod's deer. That's certain. I mean Harrod's nephew's deer. Harrod's dead. Darragh's the young nephew's name. He's never been here—he was in the army—in Russia—I don't know what became of him—but he keeps up the Harrod preserve—game-wardens, patrols, watchers, trespass signs and all."

Lannis finished his second cigarette, got back into his stirrups and, gathering bridle, began leisurely to divide curb and snaffle.

"That's the layout, Jack," he said. "Yonder lies the Red Light district of the North Woods. Mike Clinch is the brains of all the dirty work that goes on. A floating population of crooks and bums—game violators, bootleggers, market hunters, pelt 'collectors,' rum-runners, hootch makers, do his dirty work—and I guess there are some who'll stick you up by starlight for a quarter and others who'll knock your block off for a dollar.... And there's the girl, Eve Strayer. I don't get her at all, except that she's loyal to Clinch.... And now you know what you ought to know about this movie called 'Hell in the Woods.' And it's up to us to keep a calm, impartial eye on the picture and try to follow the plot they're acting out—if there is any."

Stormont said: "Thanks, Bill; I'm posted.... And I'm getting hungry, too."

"I believe," said Lannis, "that you want to see that girl."

"I do," returned the other, laughing.

"Well, you'll see her. She's good to look at. But I don't get her at all."

"Why?"

"Because she *looks* right and yet she lives at Clinch's with him and his bunch of bums. Would you think a straight girl could stand it?"

"No man can tell what a straight girl can stand."

"Straight or crooked she stands for Mike Clinch," said Lannis, "and he's a ratty customer."

"Maybe the girl is fond of him. It's natural."

"I guess it's that. But I don't see how any young girl can stomach the life at Clinch's."

"It's a wonder what a decent woman will stand," observed Stormont. "Ninety-nine per cent. of all wives ought to receive the D. S. O."

"Do you think we're so rotten?" inquired Lannis, smiling.

"Not so rotten. No. But any man knows what men are. And it's a wonder women stick to us when they learn."

They laughed. Lannis glanced at his watch again.

"Well," he said, "I don't believe anybody has tipped off our man. It's noon. Come on to dinner, Jack."

They cantered forward into the sunlit clearing. Star Pond lay ahead. On its edge stood Clinch's.

III

Clinch, in his shirt sleeves, came out on the veranda. He had little light grey eyes, close-clipped grey hair, and was clean shaven.

"How are you, Clinch," inquired Lannis affably.

"All right," replied Clinch; "you're the same, I hope."

"Trooper Stormont, Mr. Clinch," said Lannis in his genial way.

"Pleased to know you," said Clinch, level-eyed, unstirring.

The troopers dismounted. Both shook hands with Clinch. Then Lannis led the way to the barn.

"We'll eat well," he remarked to his comrade. "Clinch cooks."

From the care of their horses they went to a pump to wash. One or two rough looking men slouched out of the house and glanced at them.

"Hallo, Jake," said Lannis cheerily.

Jake Kloon grunted acknowledgment.

Lannis said in Stormont's ear: "Here she comes with towels. She's pretty, isn't she?"

A young girl in pink gingham advanced toward them across the patch of grass.

Lannis was very polite and presented Stormont. The girl handed them two rough towels, glanced at Stormont again after the introduction, smiled slightly.

"Dinner is ready," she said.

They dried their faces and followed her back to the house.

It was an unpainted building, partly of log. In the dining room half a dozen men waited silently for food. Lannis saluted all, named his comrade, and seated himself.

A delicious odour of johnny-cake pervaded the room. Presently Eve Strayer appeared with the dinner.

There was dew on her pale forehead—the heat of the kitchen, no doubt. The girl's thick, lustrous hair was brownish gold, and so twisted up that it revealed her ears and a very white neck.

When she brought Stormont his dinner he caught her eyes a moment—experienced a slight shock of pleasure at their intense blue—the gentian-blue of the summer zenith at midday.

Lannis remained affable, even became jocose at moments:

"No hootch for dinner, Mike? How's that, now?"

"The Boot-leg Express is a day late," replied Clinch, with cold humour.

Around the table ran an odd sound—a company of catamounts feeding might have made such a noise—if catamounts ever laugh.

"How's the fur market, Jake?" inquired Lannis, pouring gravy over his mashed potato.

Kloon quoted prices with an oath.

A mean-visaged young man named Leverett complained of the price of traps.

"What do you care?" inquired Lannis genially. "The other man pays. What are you kicking about, anyway? It wasn't so long ago that muskrats were ten cents."

The trooper's good-humoured intimation that Earl Leverett took fur in other men's traps was not lost on the company. Leverett's fox visage reddened; Jake Kloon, who had only one eye, glared at the State Trooper but said nothing.

Clinch's pale gaze met the trooper's smiling one: "The jays and squirrels talk too," he said slowly. "It don't mean anything. Only the show-down counts."

"You're quite right, Clinch. The show-down is what we pay to see. But talk is the tune the orchestra plays before the curtain rises."

Stormont had finished dinner. He heard a low, charming voice from behind his chair:

"Apple pie, lemon pie, maple cake, berry roll."

He looked up into two gentian-blue eyes.

"Lemon pie, please," he said, blushing.

When dinner was over and the bare little dining room empty except for Clinch and the two State Troopers, the former folded his heavy, powerful hands on the table's edge and turned his square face and pale-eyed gaze on Lannis.

"Spit it out," he said in a passionless voice.

Lannis crossed one knee over the other, lighted a cigarette:

"Is there a young fellow working for you named Hal Smith?"

"No," said Clinch.

"Sure?"

"Sure."

"Clinch," continued Lannis, "have you heard about a stick-up on the wood-road out of Ghost Lake?"

"No."

"Well, a wealthy tourist from New York—a Mr. Sard, stopping at Ghost Lake Inn—was held up and robbed last Saturday toward sundown."

"Never heard of him," said Clinch, calmly.

"The robber took four thousand dollars in bills and some private papers from him."

"It's no skin off my shins," remarked Clinch.

"He's laid a complaint."

"Yes?"

"Have any strangers been here since Saturday evening?"

"No."

There was a pause.

"We heard you had a new man named Hal Smith working around your place."

"No."

"He came here Saturday night."

"Who says so?"

"A guide from Ghost Lake."

"He's a liar."

"You know," said Lannis, "it won't do you any good if hold-up men can hide here and make a getaway."

"G'wan and search," said Clinch, calmly.

They searched the "hotel" from garret to cellar. They searched the barn, boat-shed, out-houses.

While this was going on, Clinch went into the kitchen.

"Eve," he said coolly, "the State Troopers are after that fellow, Hal Smith, who came here Saturday night. Where is he?"

"He went into Harrod's to get us a deer," she replied in a low voice. "What has he done?"

"Stuck up a man on the Ghost Lake road. He ought to have told me.

Do you think you could meet up with him and tip him off?"

"He's hunting on Owl Marsh. I'll try."

"All right. Change your clothes and slip out the back door. And look out for Harrod's patrols, too."

"All right, dad," she said. "If I have to be out to-night, don't worry. I'll get word to Smith somehow."

Half an hour later Lannis and Stormont returned from a prowl around the clearing. Lannis paid the reckoning; his comrade led out the horses. He said again to Lannis:

"I'm sure it was the girl. She wore men's clothes and she went into the woods on a run."

As they started to ride away, Lannis said to Clinch, who stood on the veranda:

"It's still blue-jay and squirrel talk between us, Mike, but the showdown is sure to come. Better go straight while the going's good."

"I go straight enough to suit me," said Clinch.

"But it's the Government that is to be suited, Mike. And if it gets you right you'll be in dutch."

"Don't let that worry you," said Clinch.

About three o'clock the two State Troopers, riding at a walk, came to the forks of the Ghost Lake road.

"Now," said Lannis to Stormont, "if you really believe you saw the girl beat it out of the back door and take to the woods, she's probably somewhere in there—" he pointed into the western forest. "But," he added, "what's your idea in following her?"

"She wore men's clothes; she was in a hurry and trying to keep out of sight. I wondered whether Clinch might have sent her to warn this hold-up fellow."

"That's rather a long shot, isn't it?"

"Very long. I could go in and look about a bit, if you'll lead my horse."

"All right. Take your bearings. This road runs west to Ghost Lake. We sleep at the Inn there—if you mean to cross the woods on foot."

Stormont nodded, consulted his map and compass, pocketed both, unbuckled his spurs.

When he was ready he gave his bridle to Lannis.

"I'd just like to see what she's up to," he remarked.

"All right. If you miss me come to the Inn," said Lannis, starting on with the led horse.

The forest was open amid a big stand of white pine and hemlock, and Stormont travelled easily and swiftly. He had struck a line by compass that must cross the direction taken by Eve Strayer when she left Clinch's. But it was a wild chance that he would ever run across her.

And probably he never would have if the man that she was looking for had not fired a shot on the edge of that vast maze of stream, morass and dead timber called Owl Marsh.

Far away in the open forest Stormont heard the shot and turned in that direction.

But Eve already was very near when the young man who called himself Hal Smith fired at one of Harrod's deer—a three-prong buck on the edge of the dead water.

Smith had drawn and dressed the buck by the time the girl found him.

He was cleaning up when she arrived, squatting by the water's edge when he heard her voice across the swale:

"Smith! The State Troopers are looking for you!"

He stood up, dried his hands on his breeches. The girl picked her way across the bog, jumping from one tussock to the next.

When she told him what had happened he began to laugh.

"Did you really stick up this man?" she asked incredulously.

"I'm afraid I did, Eve," he replied, still laughing.

The girl's entire expression altered.

"So that's the sort you are," she said. "I thought you different. But you're all a rotten lot—"

"Hold on," he interrupted, "what do you mean by that?"

"I mean that the only men who ever come to Star Pond are crooks," she retorted bitterly. "I didn't believe you were. You look decent. But you're as crooked as the rest of them—and it seems as if I—I couldn't stand it—any longer—"

"If you think me so rotten, why did you run all the way from Clinch's to warn me?" he asked curiously.

"I didn't do it for *you*; I did it for my father. They'll jail him if they catch him hiding you. They've got it in for him. If they put him in prison he'll die. He couldn't stand it. I *know*. And that's why I came to find you and tell you to clear out—"

The distant crack of a dry stick checked her. The next instant she picked up his rifle, seized his arm, and fairly dragged him into a spruce thicket.

"Do you want to get my father into trouble!" she said fiercely.

The rocky flank of Star Peak bordered the marsh here.

"Come on," she whispered, jerking him along through the thicket and up the rocks to a cleft—a hole in the sheer rock overhung by shaggy hemlock.

"Get in there," she said breathlessly.

"Whoever comes," he protested, "will see the buck yonder, and will certainly look in here—"

"Not if I go down there and take your medicine. Creep into that cave and lie down."

"What do you intend to do?" he demanded, interested and amused.

"If it's one of Harrod's game-keepers," said the girl drily, "it only means a summons and a fine for me. And if it's a State Trooper, who is prowling in the woods yonder hunting crooks, he'll find nobody here but a trespasser. Keep quiet. I'll stand him off."

IV

When State Trooper Stormont came out on the edge of Owl Marsh, the girl was kneeling by the water, washing deer blood from her slender, suntanned fingers.

"What are you doing here?" she enquired, looking up over her shoulder with a slight smile.

"Just having a look around," he said pleasantly. "That's a nice fat buck you have there."

"Yes, he's nice."

"You shot him?" asked Stormont.

"Who else do you suppose shot him?" she enquired, smilingly. She rinsed her fingers again and stood up, swinging her arms to dry her hands—a lithe, grey-shirted figure in her boyish garments, straight, supple, and strong.

"I saw you hurrying into the woods," said Stormont.

"Yes, I was in a hurry. We need meat."

"I didn't notice that you carried a rifle when I saw you leave the house—by the back door."

"No; it was in the woods," she said indifferently.

"You have a hiding place for your rifle?"

"For other things, also," she said, letting her eyes of gentian-blue rest on the young man.

"You seem to be very secretive."

"Is a girl more so than a man?" she asked smilingly.

Stormont smiled too, then became grave.

"Who else was here with you?" he asked quietly.

She seemed surprised. "Did you see anybody else?"

He hesitated, flushed, pointed down at the wet sphagnum. Smith's foot-prints were there in damning contrast to her own. Worse than that, Smith's pipe lay on an embedded log, and a rubber tobacco pouch beside it.

She said with a slight catch in her breath: "It seems that somebody has been here.... Some hunter, perhaps—or a game warden...."

"Or Hal Smith," said Stormont.

A painful colour swept the girl's face and throat. The man, sorry for her, looked away.

After a silence: "I know something about you," he said gently. "And now that I've seen you—heard you speak—met your eyes—I know enough about you to form an opinion.... So I don't ask you to turn informer. But the law won't stand for what Clinch is doing—whatever provocation he has had. And he must not aid or abet any criminal, or harbour any malefactor."

The girl's features were expressionless. The passive, sullen beauty of her troubled the trooper.

"Trouble for Clinch means sorrow for you," he said. "I don't want you to be unhappy. I bear Clinch no ill will. For this reason I ask him, and I ask you too, to stand clear of this affair.

"Hal Smith is wanted. I'm here to take him."

As she said nothing, he looked down at the foot-print in the sphagnum. Then his eyes moved to the next imprint; to the next. Then he moved slowly along the water's edge, tracking the course of the man he was following.

The girl watched him in silence until the plain trail led him to the spruce thicket.

"Don't go in there!" she said sharply, with an odd tremor in her voice.

He turned and looked at her, then stepped calmly into the thicket. And the next instant she was among the spruces, too, confronting him with her rifle.

"Get out of these woods!" she said.

He looked into the girl's deathly white face.

"Eve," he said, "it will go hard with you if you kill me. I don't want you to live out your life in prison."

"I can't help it. If you send my father to prison he'll die. I'd rather die myself. Let us alone, I tell you! The man you're after is nothing to us. We didn't know he had stuck up anybody!"

"If he's nothing to you, why do you point that rifle at me?"

"I tell you he is nothing to us. But my father wouldn't betray a dog. And I won't. That's all. Now get out of these woods and come back to-morrow. Nobody'll interfere with you then."

Stormont smiled: "Eve," he said, "do you really think me as yellow as that?"

Her blue eyes flashed a terrible warning, but, in the same instant, he had caught her rifle, twisting it out of her grasp as it exploded.

The detonation dazed her; then, as he flung the rifle into the water, she caught him by neck and belt and flung him bodily into the spruces.

But she fell with him; he held her twisting and struggling with all her superb and supple strength; staggered to his feet, still mastering her; and, as she struggled, sobbing, locked hot and panting in his arms, he snapped a pair of handcuffs on her wrists and flung her aside.

She fell on both knees, got up, shoulder deep in spruce, blood running from her lip over her chin.

The trooper took her by the arm. She was trembling all over. He took a thin steel chain and padlock from his pocket, passed the links around her steel-bound wrists, and fastened her to a young birch tree.

Then, drawing his pistol from its holster, he went swiftly forward through the spruces.

When he saw the cleft in the rocky flank of Star Peak, he walked straight to the black hole which confronted him.

"Come out of there," he said distinctly.

After a few seconds Smith came out.

"Good God!" said Stormont in a low voice. "What are you doing here, Darragh?"

Darragh came close and rested one hand on Stormont's shoulder:

"Don't crab my game, Stormont. I never dreamed you were in the Constabulary or I'd have let you know."

"Are *you* Hal Smith?"

"I sure am. Where's that girl?"

"Handcuffed out yonder."

"Then for God's sake go back and act as if you hadn't found me. Tell Mayor Chandler that I'm after bigger game than he is."

"Clinch?"

"Stormont, I'm here to *protect* Mike Clinch. Tell the Mayor not to touch him. The men I'm after are going to try to rob him. I don't want them to because—well, I'm going to rob him myself."

Stormont stared.

"You must stand by me," said Darragh. "So must the Mayor. He knows me through and through. Tell him to forget that hold-up. I stopped that man Sard. I frisked him. Tell the Mayor. I'll keep in touch with him."

"Of course," said Stormont, "that settles it."

"Thanks, old chap. Now go back to that girl and let her believe that you never found me."

A slight smile touched their eyes. Both instinctively saluted. Then they shook hands; Darragh, alias Hal Smith, went back into the hemlock-shaded hole in the rocks; Trooper Stormont walked slowly down through the spruces.

When Eve saw him returning empty handed, something flashed in her pallid face like sunlight across snow.

Stormont passed her, went to the water's edge, soaked a spicy handful of sphagnum moss in the icy water, came back and wiped the blood from her face.

The girl seemed astounded; her face surged in vivid colour as he unlocked the handcuffs and pocketed them and the little steel chain.

Her lip was bleeding again. He washed it with wet moss, took a clean handkerchief from the breast of his tunic and laid it against her mouth.

"Hold it there," he said.

Mechanically she raised her hand to support the compress. Stormont went back to the shore, recovered her rifle from the shallow water, and returned with it.

As she made no motion to take it, he stood it against the tree to which he had tied her.

Then he came close to her where she stood holding his handkerchief against her mouth and looking at him out of steady eyes as deeply blue as gentian blossoms.

"Eve," he said, "you win. But you won't forgive me.... I wish we could be friends, some day.... We never can, now.... Good-bye."

Neither spoke again. Then, of a sudden, the girl's eyes filled; and Trooper Stormont caught her free hand and kissed it;—kissed it again and again—dropped it and went striding away through the underbrush which was now all rosy with the rays of sunset.

After he had disappeared, the girl, Eve, went to the cleft in the rocks above.

"Come out," she said contemptuously. "It's a good thing you hid, because there was a real man after you; and God help you if he ever finds you!"

Hal Smith came out.

"Pack in your meat," said the girl curtly, and flung his rifle across her shoulder.

Through the ruddy afterglow she led the way homeward, a man's handkerchief pressed to her wounded mouth, her eyes preoccupied with the strangest thoughts that ever had stirred her virgin mind.

Behind her walked Darragh with his load of venison and his alias—and his tongue in his cheek.

Thus began the preliminaries toward the ultimate undoing of Mike Clinch. Fate, Chance, and Destiny had undertaken the job in earnest.

Episode Two
THE RULING PASSION

I

Nobody understood how José Quintana had slipped through the Secret Service net spread for him at every port.

The United States authorities did not know why Quintana had come to America. They realised merely that he arrived for no good purpose; and they had meant to arrest and hold him for extradition if requested; for deportation as an undesirable alien anyway.

Only two men in America knew that Quintana had come to the United States for the purpose of recovering the famous "Flaming Jewel," stolen by him from the Grand Duchess Theodorica of Esthonia; and stolen from Quintana, in turn, by a private soldier in an American Forestry Regiment, on leave in Paris. This soldier's name, probably, was Michael Clinch.

One of the men who knew why Quintana might come to America was James Darragh, recently of the Military Intelligence, but now passing as a hold-up man under the name of Hal Smith, and actually in the employment of Clinch at his disreputable "hotel" at Star Pond in the North Woods.

The other man who knew why Quintana had come to America was Emanuel Sard, a Levantine diamond broker of New York, Quintana's agent in America.

Now, as the October days passed without any report of Quintana's detention, Darragh, known as Hal Smith at Clinch's dump, began to suspect that Quintana had already slid into America through the meshes of the police.

If so, this desperate international criminal could be expected at Clinch's under some guise or other, piloted thither by Emanuel Sard.

So Hal Smith, whose duty was to wash dishes, do chores, and also to supply Clinch's with "mountain beef"—or deer taken illegally—made it convenient to prowl every day in the vicinity of the Ghost Lake road.

He was perfectly familiar with Emanuel Sard's squat features and parrot nose, having robbed Mr. Sard of Quintana's cipher and of $4,000 at pistol point. And one morning, while roving around the guide's quarters at Ghost Lake Inn, Smith beheld Sard himself on the hotel veranda, in company with five strangers of foreign aspect.

During the midday dinner Smith, on pretense of enquiring for a guide's license, got a look at the Inn ledger. Sard's signature was on it, followed by the names of Henri Picquet, Nicolas Salzar, Victor Georgiades, Harry Beck, and José Sanchez. And Smith went back through the wilderness to Star Pond, convinced that one of these gentlemen was Quintana, and the remainder, Quintana's gang; and that they were here to do murder if necessary in their remorseless quest of "The Flaming Jewel." Two million dollars once had been offered for the Flaming Jewel; and had been refused.

Clinch probably possessed it. Smith was now convinced of that. But he was there to rob Clinch of it himself. For he had promised the little Grand Duchess to help recover her Erosite jewel; and now that he had finally traced its probable possession to Clinch, he was wondering how this recovery was to be accomplished.

To arrest Clinch meant ruin to Eve Strayer. Besides he knew now that Clinch would die in prison before revealing the hiding place of the Flaming Jewel.

Also, how could it be proven that Clinch had the Erosite gem? The cipher from Quintana was not sufficient evidence.

No; the only way was to watch Clinch, prevent any robbery by Quintana's gang, somehow discover where the Flaming Jewel had been concealed, take it, and restore it to the beggared young girl whose only financial resource now lay in the possible recovery of this almost priceless gem.

Toward evening Hal Smith shot two deer near Owl Marsh. To poach on his own property appealed to his sense of humour. And Clinch, never dreaming that Hal Smith was the James Darragh who had inherited Harrod's vast preserve, damned all millionaires for every buck brought in, and became friendlier to Smith.

II

Clinch's dump was the disposal plant in which collected the human sewage of the wilderness.

It being Saturday, the scum of the North Woods was gathering at the Star Pond resort. A venison and chicken supper was promised—and a dance if any women appeared.

Jake Kloon had run in some Canadian hooch; Darragh, alias Hal Smith, contributed two fat deer and Clinch cooked them. By ten o'clock that morning many of the men were growing noisy; some were already drunk by noon. Shortly after midday dinner the first fight started—

extinguished only after Clinch had beaten several of the backwoods aristocracy insensible.

Towering amid the wreck of battle, his light grey eyes a-glitter, Clinch dominated, swinging his iron fists.

When the combat ended and the fallen lay starkly where they fell, Clinch said in his pleasant, level voice:

"Take them out and stick their heads in the pond. And don't go for to get me mad, boys, or I'm liable to act up rough."

They bore forth the sleepers for immersion in Star Pond. Clinch relighted his cigar and repeated the rulings which had caused the fracas:

"You gotta play square cards here or you don't play none in my house. No living thumb-nail can nick no cards in my place and get away with it. Three kings and two trays is better than three chickens and two eggs. If you don't like it, g'wan home."

He went out in his shirt sleeves to see how the knock-outs were reviving, and met Hal Smith returning from the pond, who reported progress toward consciousness. They walked back to the "hotel" together.

"Say, young fella," said Clinch in his soft, agreeable way, "you want to keep your eye peeled to-night."

"Why?" inquired Smith.

"Well, there'll be a lot o' folks here. There'll be strangers, too.... Don't forget the State Troopers are looking for you."

"Do the State Troopers ever play detective?" asked Smith, smiling.

"Sure. They've been in here rigged out like peddlers and lumber-jacks and timber lookers."

"Did they ever get anything on you?"

"Not a thing."

"Can you always spot them, Mike?"

"No. But when a stranger shows up here who don't know nobody, he never sees nothing and he don't never learn nothing. He gets no hootch outa me. No, nor no craps and no cards. He gets his supper; that's what he gets ... and a dance, if there's ladies—and if any girl favours him. That's all the change any stranger gets out of Mike Clinch."

They had paused on the rough veranda in the hot October sunshine.

"Mike," suggested Smith carelessly, "wouldn't it pay you better to go straight?"

Clinch's small grey eyes, which had been roaming over the prospect of lake and forest, focussed on Smith's smiling features.

"What's that to you?" he asked.

"I'll be out of a job," remarked Smith, laughing, "if they ever land you."

Clinch's level gaze measured him; his mind was busy measuring him, too.

"Who the hell are you, anyway?" he asked. "*I* don't know. You stick up a man on the Ghost Lake Road and hide out here when the State Troopers come after you. And now you ask me if it pays better to go straight. Why didn't *you* go straight if you think it pays?"

"I haven't got a daughter to worry about," explained Smith. "If they get me it won't hurt anybody else."

A dull red tinge came out under Clinch's tan:

"Who asked *you* to worry about Eve?"

"She's a fine girl: that's all."

Clinch's steely glare measured the young man:

"You trying to make up to her?" he enquired gently.

"No. She has no use for me."

Clinch reflected, his cold tiger-gaze still fastened on Smith.

"You're right," he said after a moment. "Eve is a good girl. Some day I'll make a lady of her."

"She *is* one, Clinch."

At that Clinch reddened heavily—the first finer emotion ever betrayed before Smith. He did not say anything for a few moments, but his grim mouth worked. Finally:

"I guess you was a gentleman once before you went crooked, Hal," he said. "You act up like you once was.... Say; there's only one thing on God's earth I care about. You've guessed it, too." He was off again upon his ruling passion.

"Eve," nodded Smith.

"Sure. She isn't my flesh and blood. But it seems like she's more, even. I want she should be a lady. It's *all* I want. That damned millionaire Harrod bust me. But he couldn't stop me giving Eve her schooling. And now all I'm livin' for is to be fixed so's to give her money to go to the city like a lady. I don't care how I make money; all I want is to make it. And I'm a-going to."

Smith nodded again.

Clinch, now obsessed by his monomania, went on with an oath:

"I can't make no money on the level after what Harrod done to me. And I gotta fix up Eve. What the hell do you mean by asking me would it pay me to travel straight I dunno."

"I was only thinking of Eve. A lady isn't supposed to have a crook for a father."

Clinch's grey eyes blazed for a moment, then their menacing glare dulled, died out into wintry fixity.

"I wan't born a crook," he said. "I ain't got no choice. And don't worry, young fella; they ain't a-going to get me."

"You can't go on beating the game forever, Clinch."

"I'm beating it—" he hesitated—"and it won't be so long, neither, before I turn over enough to let Eve live in the city like any lady, with her autymobile and her own butler and all her swell friends, in a big house like she is educated for—"

He broke off abruptly as a procession approached from the lake, escorting the battered gentry who now were able to wabble about a little.

One of them, a fox-faced trap thief named Earl Leverett, slunk hastily by as though expecting another kick from Clinch.

"G'wan inside, Earl, and act up right," said Clinch pleasantly. "You oughter have more sense than to start a fight in my place—you and Sid Hone and Harvey Chase. G'wan in and behave."

He and Smith followed the procession of damaged ones into the house.

The big unpainted room where a bar had once been was blue with cheap cigar smoke; the air reeked with the stench of beer and spirits. A score or more shambling forest louts in their dingy Saturday finery were gathered there playing cards, shooting craps, lolling around tables and tilting slopping glasses at one another.

Heavy pleasantries were exchanged with the victims of Clinch's ponderous fists as they re-entered the room from which they had been borne so recently, feet first.

"Now, boys," said Clinch kindly, "act up like swell gents and behave friendly. And if any ladies come in for the chicken supper, why, gol dang it, we'll have a dance!"

III

Toward sundown the first woodland nymph appeared—a half-shy, half-bold, willowy thing in the rosy light of the clearing.

Hal Smith, washing glasses and dishes on the back porch for Eve Strayer to dry, asked who the rustic beauty might be.

"Harvey Chase's sister," said Eve. "She shouldn't come here, but I can't keep her away and her brother doesn't care. She's only a child, too."

"Is there any harm in a chicken supper and a dance?"

Eve looked gravely at young Smith without replying.

Other girlish shapes loomed in the evening light. Some were met by gallants, some arrived at the veranda unescorted.

"Where do they all come from? Do they live in trees like dryads?" asked Smith.

"There are always squatters in the woods," she replied indifferently. "Some of these girls come from Ghost Lake, I suppose."

"Yes; waitresses at the Inn."

"What music is there?"

"Jim Hastings plays a fiddle. I play the melodeon if they need me."

"What do you do when there's a fight?" he asked, with a side glance at her pure profile.

"What do you suppose I do? Fight, too?"

He laughed—mirthlessly—conscious always of his secret pity for this girl.

"Well," he said, "when your father makes enough to quit, he'll take you out of this. It's a vile hole for a young girl—"

"See here," she said, flushing; "you're rather particular for a young man who stuck up a tourist and robbed him of four thousand dollars."

"I'm not complaining on my own account," returned Smith, laughing; "Clinch's suits me."

"Well, don't concern yourself on my account, Hal Smith. And you'd better keep out of the dance, too, if there are any strangers there."

"You think a State Trooper may happen in?"

"It's likely. A lot of people come and go. We don't always know them." She opened a sliding wooden shutter and looked into the bar room. After a moment she beckoned him to her side.

"There are strangers there now," she said, "—that thin, dark man who looks like a Kanuk. And those two men shaking dice. I don't know who they are. I never before saw them."

But Smith had seen them at Ghost Lake Inn. One of them was Sard. Quintana's gang had arrived at Clinch's dump.

A moment later Clinch came through the pantry and kitchen and out onto the rear porch where Smith was washing glasses in a tub filled from an ever-flowing spring.

"I'm a-going to get supper," he said to Eve. "There'll be twenty-three plates." And to Smith: "Hal—you help Eve wait on the table. And if anybody acts up rough you slam him on the jaw—don't argue, don't wait—just slam him good, and I'll come on the hop."

"Who are the strangers, dad?" asked Eve.

"Don't nobody know 'em none, girlie. But they ain't State Troopers. They talk like they was foreign. One of 'em's English—the big, bony one with yellow hair and mustache."

"Did they give any names?" asked Smith.

"You bet. The stout, dark man calls himself Hongri Picket. French, I guess. The fat beak is a fella named Sard. Sanchez is the guy with a face like a Canada priest—José Sanchez—or something on that style. And then the yellow skinned young man is Nicole Salzar; the Britisher, Harry Beck; and that good lookin' dark gent with a little black Charlie

Chaplin, he's Victor Georgiades."

"What are those foreigners doing in the North Woods, Clinch?" enquired Smith.

"Oh, they all give the same spiel—hire out in a lumber camp. But *they* ain't no lumberjacks," added Clinch contemptuously. "I don't know what they be—hootch runners maybe—or booze bandits—or they done something crooked som'ers r'other. It's safe to serve 'em drinks."

Clinch himself had been drinking. He always drank when preparing to cook.

He turned and went into the kitchen now, rolling up his shirt sleeves and relighting his clay pipe.

IV

By nine o'clock the noisy chicken supper had ended; the table had been cleared; Jim Hastings was tuning his fiddle in the big room; Eve had seated herself before the battered melodeon.

"Ladies and gents," said Clinch in his clear, pleasant voice, which carried through the hubbub, "we're a-going to have a dance—thanks and beholden to Jim Hastings and my daughter Eve. Eve, she don't drink and she don't dance, so no use askin' and no hard feelin' toward nobody.

"So act up pleasant to one and all and have a good time and no rough stuff in no form, shape or manner, but behave like gents all and swell dames, like you was to a swarry on Fifth Avenue. Let's go!"

He went back to the pantry, taking no notice of the cheering. The fiddler scraped a fox trot, and Eve's melodeon joined in. A vast scuffling of heavily shod feet filled the momentary silence, accented by the shrill giggle of young girls.

"They're off," remarked Clinch to Smith, who stood at the pantry shelf prepared to serve whiskey or beer upon previous receipt of payment.

In the event of a sudden raid, the arrangements at Clinch's were quite simple. Two large drain pipes emerged from the kitchen floor beside Smith, and ended in Star Pond. In case of alarm the tub of beer was poured down one pipe; the whiskey down the other.

Only the trout in Star Pond would ever sample that hootch again.

Clinch, now slightly intoxicated, leaned heavily on the pantry shelf beside Smith, adjusting his pistol under his suspenders.

"Young fella," he said in his agreeable voice, "you're dead right. You sure said a face-full when you says to me, 'Eve's a lady, by God!' *You* oughta know. You was a gentleman yourself once. Even if you take to stickin' up tourists you know a lady when you see one. And you called the turn. She *is* a lady. All I'm livin' for is to get her down to the city and give her money to live like a lady. I'll do it yet.... Soon!... I'd do it to-morrow—to-night—if I dared.... If I thought it sure fire.... If I was dead certain I could get away with it.... I've *got* the money. *Now!* ... Only it ain't in *money*.... Smith?"

"Yes, Mike."

"You know me?"

"Sure."

"You size me up?"

"I do."

"All right. If you ever tell anyone I got money that ain't money I'll shoot you through the head."

"Don't worry, Clinch."

"I ain't. You're a crook; you won't talk. You're a gentleman, too. *They* don't sell out a pal. Say, Hal, there's only one fella I don't want to meet."

"Who's that, Mike?"

"Lemme tell you," continued Clinch, resting more heavily on the shelf while Smith, looking out through the pantry shutter at the dancing, listened intently.

"When I was in France in a Forestry Rig'ment," went on Clinch, lowering his always pleasant voice, "I was to Paris on leave a few days before they sent us home.

"I was in the washroom of a caffy—a-cleanin' up for supper, when dodbang! into the place comes a-tumblin' a man with two cops pushing and kickin' him.

"They didn't see me in there for they locked the door on the man. He was a swell gent, too, in full dress and silk hat and all like that, and a opry cloak and white kid gloves, and mustache and French beard.

"When they locked him up he stood stock still and lit a cigarette, as cool as ice. Then he begun walkin' around looking for a way to get out; but there wasn't no way.

"Then he seen me and over he comes and talks English right away: 'Want to make a thousand francs, soldier?' sez he in a quick whisper. 'You're on,' sez I; 'show your dough.' 'Them Flics has went to get the Commissaire for to frisk me,' sez he. 'If they find this parcel on me I do twenty years in Noumea. Five years kills anybody out there.' 'What do you want I should do?' sez I, havin' no love for no cops, French or other. 'Take this packet and stick it in your overcoat,' sez he. 'Go to 13 roo Quinze Octobre and give it to the concierge for José Quintana.' And he shoves the packet on me and a thousand-franc note.

"Then he grabs me sudden and pulls open my collar. God, he was strong.

"'What's the matter with you?' says I. 'Lemme go or I'll mash your mug flat.' 'Lemme see your identification disc,' he barks.

"Bein' in Paris for a bat, I had exchanged with my bunkie, Bill Hanson. 'Let him look,' thinks I; and he reads Bill's check.

"'If you fool me,' says he, 'I'll folly ye and I'll do you in if it takes the rest of my life. You understand?' 'Sure,' says I, me tongue in me cheek. 'Bong! Allez vous en!' says he.

"'How the hell,' sez I, 'do I get out of here?' 'You're a Yankee soldier. The Flics don't know you were in here. You go and kick on that door and make a holler.'

"So I done it good; and a cop opens and swears at me, but when he sees a Yankee soldier was locked in the wash-room by mistake, he lets me out, you bet."

Clinch smiled a thin smile, poured out three fingers of hooch.

"What else?" asked Smith quietly.

"Nothing much. I didn't go to no roo Quinze Octobre. But I don't never want to see that fella Quintana. I've been waiting till it's safe to sell—what was in that packet."

"Sell what?"

"What was in that packet," replied Clinch thickly.

"What was in it?"

"Sparklers—since you're so nosey."

"Diamonds?"

"And then some. I dunno what they're called. All I know is I'll croak Quintana if he even turns up askin' for 'em. He frisked somebody. I frisked him. I'll kill anybody who tries to frisk me."

"Where do you keep them?" enquired Smith naïvely.

Clinch looked at him, very drunk: "None o' your dinged business," he said very softly.

The dancing had become boisterous but not unseemly, although all the men had been drinking too freely.

Smith closed the pantry bar at midnight, by direction of Eve. Now he came out into the ballroom and mixed affably with the company, even dancing with Harvey Chase's sister once—a slender hoyden, all flushed and dishevelled, with a tireless mania for dancing which seemed to intoxicate her.

She danced, danced, danced, accepting any partner offered. But Smith's skill enraptured her and she refused to let him go when her beau, a late arrival, one Charlie Berry, slouched up to claim her.

Smith, always trying to keep Clinch and Quintana's men in view, took no part in the discussion; but Berry thought he was detaining Lily Chase and pushed him aside.

"Hold on, young man!" exclaimed Smith sharply. "Keep your hands to yourself. If your girl don't want to dance with you she doesn't have to."

Some of Quintana's gang came up to listen. Berry glared at Smith.

"Say," he said, "I seen you before somewhere. Wasn't you in Russia?"

"What are you talking about?"

"Yes, you was. You was an officer! What you doing at Clinch's?"

"What's that?" growled Clinch, shoving his way forward and shouldering the crowd aside.

"Who's this man, Mike?" demanded Berry.

"Well, who do you think he is?" asked Clinch thickly.

"I think he's gettin' the goods on you, that's what I think," yelled Berry.

"G'wan home, Charlie," returned Clinch. "G'wan, all o' you. The dance is over. Go peaceable, every one. Stop that fiddle!"

The music ceased. The dance was ended; they all understood that; but there was grumbling and demands for drinks.

Clinch, drunk but impassive, herded them through the door out into the starlight. There was scuffling, horse-play, but no fighting.

The big Englishman, Harry Beck, asked for accommodations for his party over night.

"Naw," said Clinch, "g'wan back to the Inn. I can't bother with you folks to-night." And as the others, Salzar, Georgiades, Picquet and Sanchez gathered about to insist, Clinch pushed them all out of doors in a mass.

"Get the hell out o' here!" he growled; and slammed the door.

He stood for a moment with head lowered, drunk, but apparently capable of reflection. Eve came from the melodeon and laid one slim hand on his arm.

"Go to bed, girlie," he said, not looking at her.

"You also, dad."

"No.... I got business with Hal Smith."

Passing Smith, the girl whispered: "You look out for him and undress him."

Smith nodded, gravely preoccupied with coming events, and nerving himself to meet them.

He had no gun. Clinch's big automatic bulged under his armpit.

When the girl had ascended the creaking stairs and her door, above, closed, Clinch walked unsteadily to the door, opened it, fished out his pistol.

"Come on out," he said without turning.

"Where?" enquired Smith.

Clinched turned, lifted his square head; and the deadly glare in his eyes left Smith silent.

"You comin'?"

"Sure," said Smith quietly.

But Clinch gave him no chance to close in: it was death even to swerve. Smith walked slowly out into the starlight, ahead of Clinch—slowly forward in the luminous darkness.

"Keep going," came Clinch's quiet voice behind him. And, after they had entered the woods—"Bear to the right."

Smith knew now. The low woods were full of sink-holes. They were headed for the nearest one.

On the edge of the thing they halted. Smith turned and faced Clinch.

"What's the idea?" he asked without a quaver.

"Was you in Roosia?"

"Yes."

"Was you an officer?"

"I was."

"Then you're spyin'. You're a cop."

"You're mistaken."

"Ah, don't hand me none like that! You're a State Trooper or a Secret Service guy, or a plain, dirty cop. And I'm a-going to croak you."

"I'm not in any service, now."

"Wasn't you an army officer?"

"Yes. Can't an officer go wrong?"

"Soft stuff. Don't feed it to me. I told you too much anyway. I was babblin' drunk. I'm drunk now, but I got sense. D'you think I'll run chances of sittin' in State's Prison for the next ten years and leave Eve out here alone? No. I gotta shoot you, Smith. And I'm a-going to do it. G'wan and say what you want ... if you think there's some kind o' god you can square before you croak."

"If you go to the chair for murder, what good will it do Eve?" asked Smith. His lips were crackling dry; he moistened them.

"Sink holes don't talk," said Clinch. "G'wan and square yourself, if you're the church kind."

"Clinch," said Smith unsteadily, "if you kill me now you're as good as dead yourself. Quintana is here."

"Say, don't hand me that," retorted Clinch. "Do you square yourself or no?"

"I tell you Quintana's gang were at the dance to-night—Picquet, Salzar, Georgiades, Sard, Beck, José Sanchez—the one who looks like a French priest. Maybe he had a beard when you saw him in that café wash-room—"

"What!" shouted Clinch in sudden fury. "What yeh talkin' about, you poor dumb dingo! Yeh fixin' to scare me? What do *you* know about

Quintana? Are you one of Quintana's gang, too? Is that what you're up to, hidin' out at Star Pond. Come on, now, out with it! I'll have it all out of you now, Hal Smith, before I plug you—"

He came lurching forward, swinging his heavy pistol as though he meant to brain his victim, but he halted after the first step or two and stood there, a shadowy bulk, growling, enraged, undecided.

And, as Smith looked at him, two shadows detached themselves from the trees behind Clinch—silently—silently glided behind—struck in utter silence.

Down crashed Clinch, black-jacked, his face in the ooze. His pistol flew from his hand, struck Smith's leg; and Smith had it at the same instant and turned it like lightning on the murderous shadows.

"Hands up! Quick!" he cried, at bay now, and his back to the sink-hole.

Pistol levelled, he bent one knee, pushed Clinch over on his back, lest the ooze suffocate him.

"Now," he said coolly, "what do you bums want of Mike Clinch?"

"Who are you?" came a sullen voice. "This is none o' your bloody business. We want Clinch, not you."

"What do you want of Clinch?"

"Take your gun off us!"

"Answer, or I'll let go at you. What do you want of Clinch?"

"Money. What do you think?"

"You're here to stick up Clinch?" enquired Smith.

"Yes. What's that to you?"

"What has Clinch done to you?"

"He stuck *us* up, that's what! Now, are you going to keep out of this?"

"No."

"We ain't going to hurt Clinch."

"You bet you're not. Where's the rest of your gang?"

"What gang?"

"Quintana's," said Smith, laughing. A wild exhilaration possessed him. His flanks and rear were protected by the sink-hole. He had Quintana's gang—two of them—over his pistol.

"Turn your backs and sit down," he said. As the shadowy forms hesitated, he picked up a stick and hurled it at them. They sat down hastily, hands up, backs toward him.

"You'll both die where you sit," remarked Smith, "if you yell for help."

Clinch sighed heavily, stirred, groped on the damp leaves with his hands.

"I say," began the voice which Smith identified as Harry Beck's, "if you'll come in with us on this it will pay you, young man."

"No," drawled Smith, "I'll go it alone."

"It can't be done, old dear. You'll see if you try it on."

"Who'll stop me? Quintana?"

"Come," urged Beck, "and be a good pal. You can't manage it alone. We've got all night to make Clinch talk. We know how, too. You'll get your share—"

"Oh, stow it," said Smith, watching Clinch, who was reviving. He sat up presently, and put both hands over his head. Smith touched him silently on the shoulder and he turned his heavy, square head in a dazed way. Blood striped his visage. He gazed dully at Smith for a little while, then, seeming to recollect, the old glare began to light his pale eyes.

The next instant, however, Beck spoke again, and Clinch turned in astonishment and saw the two figures sitting there with backs toward Smith and hands up.

Clinch stared at the squatting forms, then slowly moved his head and looked at Smith and his levelled pistol.

"We know how to make a man squeal," said Harry Beck suddenly. "He'll talk. We can make Clinch talk, no fear! Leave it to us, old pal. Are you with us?" He started to look around over his shoulder and Smith hurled another stick and hit him in the face.

"Quiet there, Harry," he said. "What's my share if I go in with you?"

"One sixth, same's we all get."

"What's it worth?" asked Smith, with a motion of caution toward Clinch.

"If I say a million you'll tell me I lie. But it's nearer three—or you can have my share. Is it a go?"

"You'll not hurt Clinch when he comes to?"

"We'll make him talk, that's all. It may hurt him some."

"You won't kill him?"

"I swear by God—"

"Wait! Isn't it better to shoot him after he squeals? Here's a lovely sink-hole handy."

"Right-o! We'll make him talk first and then shove him in. Are you with us?"

"If you turn your head I'll blow the face off you, Harry," said Smith, cautioning Clinch to silence with a gesture.

"All right. Only you better make up your mind. That cove is likely to wake up now at any time," grumbled Beck.

Clinch looked at Smith. The latter smiled, leaned over, and whispered:

"Can you walk all right?"

Clinch nodded.

"Well, we'd better beat it. Quintana's whole gang is in these woods, somewhere, hunting for you, and they might stumble on us here, at any moment." And, to the two men in front: "Lie down flat on your faces. Don't stir; don't speak; or it's you for the sink-hole.... Lie down, I tell you! That's it. Don't move till I tell you to."

Clinch got up from where he was sitting, cast one murderous glance at the prostrate forms, then followed Smith, noiselessly, over the stretch of sphagnum moss.

When they reached the house they saw Eve standing on the steps in her night-dress and bare feet, holding a lantern.

"Daddy," she whimpered, "I was frightened. I didn't know where you had gone—"

Clinch put his arm around her, turned his bloody face and looked at Smith.

"It's *this*," he said, "that I ain't forgetting, young fella. What you done for me you done for *her*.

"I gotta live to make a lady of her. That's why," he added thickly, "I'm much obliged to you, Hal Smith.... Go to bed, girlie—"

"You're bleeding, dad?"

"Aw, a twig scratched me. I been in the woods with Hal. G'wan to bed."

He went to the sink and washed his face, dried it, kissed the girl, and gave her a gentle shove toward the stairs.

"Hal and I is sittin' up talkin' business," he remarked, bolting the door and all the shutters.

When the girl had gone, Clinch went to a closet and brought back two Winchester rifles, two shot guns, and a box of ammunition.

"Goin' to see it out with me, Hal?"

"Sure," smiled Smith.

"Aw' right. Have a drink?"

"No."

"Aw' right. Where'll you set?"

"Anywhere."

"Aw' right. Set over there. They may try the back porch. I'll jest set here a spell, n'then I'll kind er mosey 'round.... Plug the first fella that tries a shutter, Hal."

"You bet."

Clinch came over and held out his hand.

"You said a face-full that time when you says to me, 'Clinch,' you says, 'Eve *is* a lady.' ... I gotta fix her up. I gotta be alive to do it.... That's why I'm greatly obliged to yeh, Hal."

He took his rifle and walked slowly toward the pantry.

"You bet," he muttered, "she *is* a lady, so help me God."

Episode Three
ON STAR PEAK

I

Mike Clinch regarded the jewels taken from José Quintana as legitimate loot acquired in war.

He was prepared to kill anybody who attempted to take the gems from him.

At the very possibility his ruling passion blazed—his mania to make of Eve Strayer a grand lady.

But now, what he had feared for years had happened. Quintana had found him—Quintana, after all these years, had discovered the identity and dwelling place of the obscure American soldier who had robbed him in the wash-room of a Paris café. And Quintana was now in America, here in this very wilderness, tracking the man who had despoiled him.

Clinch, in his shirt-sleeves, carrying a rifle, came out on the log veranda and sat down to think it over.

He began to realise that he was likely to have trouble with a man as cold-blooded and as dogged as himself.

Nor did he doubt that those with Quintana were desperate men.

On whom could he count? On nobody unless he paid their hire. None among the lawless men who haunted his backwoods "hotel" at Star Pond would lift a finger to help him. Almost any among them would have robbed him—murdered him, probably—if it were known that jewels were hidden in the house.

He could not trust Jake Kloon; Leverett was as treacherous as only a born coward can be; Sid Hone, Harvey Chase, Blommers, Byron Hastings—he knew them all too well to trust them—a sullen, unscrupulous pack, partly cowardly, always fierce—as are any creatures that live furtively, feed only by their wits, and slink through life just outside the frontiers of law.

And yet, one of this gang had stood by him—Hal Smith—the man he himself had been about to slay.

Clinch got up from the bench where he had been sitting and walked down to the pond where Hal Smith sat cleaning trout.

"Hal," he said, "I been figuring some. Quintana don't dare call in the constables. I can't afford to. Quintana and I've got to settle this on our own."

Smith slit open a ten-inch trout, stripped it, flung the entrails out into the pond, soused the fish in water, and threw it into a milk pan.

"Whose jewels were they in the beginning?" he enquired carelessly.

"How do I know?"

"If you ever found out—"

"I don't want to. I got them in the war, anyway. And it don't make no difference how I got 'em; Eve's going to be a lady if I go to the chair for it. So that's that."

Smith slit another trout, gutted it, flung away the viscera but laid back the roe.

"Shame to take them in October," he remarked, "but people must eat."

"Same's me," nodded Clinch; "I don't want to kill no one, but Eve she's gotta be a lady and ride in her own automobile with the proudest."

"Does Eve know about the jewels?"

Clinch's pale eyes, which had been roving over the wooded shores of Star Pond, reverted to Smith.

"I'd cut my throat before I'd tell her," he said softly.

"She wouldn't stand for it?"

"Hal, when you said to me, 'Eve's a lady, by God!' you swallowed the hull pie. That's the answer. A lady don't stand for what you and I don't bother about."

"Suppose she learns that you robbed the man who robbed somebody else of these jewels."

Clinch's pale eyes were fixed on him: "Only you and me know," he said in his pleasant voice.

"Quintana knows. His gang knows."

Clinch's smile was terrifying. "I guess she ain't never likely to know nothing, Hal."

"What do you purpose to do, Mike?"

"Still hunt."

"For Quintana?"

"I might mistake him for a deer. Them accidents is likely, too."

"If Quintana catches you it will go hard with you, Mike."

"Sure. I know."

"He'll torture you to make you talk."

"You think I'd talk, Hal?"

Smith looked up into the light-coloured eyes. The pupils were pin points. Then he went on cleaning fish.

"Hal?"

"What?"

"If they get me—but no matter; they ain't a-going to get me."

"Were you going to tell me where those jewels are hidden, Mike?"

enquired the young man, still busy with his fish. He did not look around when he spoke. Clinch's murderous gaze was fastened on the back of his head.

"Don't go to gettin' too damn nosey, Hal," he said in his always agreeable voice.

Smith soused all the fish in water again: "You'd better tell somebody if you go gunning for Quintana."

"Did I ask your advice?"

"You did not," said the young man, smiling.

"All right. Mind your business."

Smith got up from the water's edge with his pan of trout:

"That's what I shall do, Mike," he said, laughing. "So go on with your private war; it's no button off *my* pants if Quintana gets you."

He went away toward the ice-house with the trout. Eve Strayer, doing chamber work, watched the young man from an upper room.

The girl's instinct was to like Smith—but that very instinct aroused her distrust. What was a man of his breeding and education doing at Clinch's dump? Why was he content to hang around and do chores? A man of his type who has gone crooked enough to stick up a tourist in an automobile nourishes higher—though probably perverted—ambitions than a dollar a day and board.

She heard Clinch's light step on the uncarpeted stair; went on making up Smith's bed; and smiled as her step-father came into the room, still carrying his rifle.

He had something else in his hand, too—a flat, thin packet wrapped in heavy paper and sealed all over with black wax.

"Girlie," he said, "I want you should do a little errand for me this morning. If you're spry it won't take long—time to go there and get back to help with noon dinner."

"Very well, dad."

"Go git your pants on, girlie."

"You want me to go into the woods?"

"I want you to go to the hole in the rocks under Star Peak and lay this packet in the hootch cache."

She nodded, tucked in the sheets, smoothed blanket and pillow with deft hands, went out to her own room. Clinch seated himself and turned a blank face to the window.

It was a sudden decision. He realised now that he couldn't keep the jewels in his house. War was on with Quintana. The "hotel" would be the goal for Quintana and his gang. And for Smith, too, if ever temptation overpowered him. The house was liable to an attempt at robbery any night, now;—any day, perhaps. It was no place for the packet he had taken from José Quintana.

Eve came in wearing grey shirt, breeches, and puttees. Clinch gave her the packet.

"What's in it, dad?" she asked smilingly.

"Don't you get nosey, girlie. Come here."

She went to him. He put his left arm around her.

"You like me some, don't you, girlie?"

"You know it, dad."

"All right. You're all that matters to me ... since your mother went and died ... after a year.... That was crool, girlie. Only a year. Well, I ain't cared none for nobody since—only you, girlie."

He touched the packet with his forefinger:

"If I step out, that's yours. But I ain't a-going to step out. Put it with the hootch. You know how to move that keystone?"

"Yes, dad."

"And watch out that no game protector and none of that damn millionaire's wardens see you in the woods. No, nor none o' these here fancy State Troopers. You gotta watch out *this* time, Eve. It means everything to us—to you, girlie—and to me. Go tip-toe. Lay low, coming and going. Take a rifle."

Eve ran to her bed-room and returned with her Winchester and belt.

"You shoot to kill," said Clinch grimly, "if anyone wants to stop you. But lay low and you won't need to shoot nobody, girlie. G'wan out the back way; Hal's in the ice house."

II

Slim and straight as a young boy in her grey shirt and breeches, Eve continued on lightly through the woods, her rifle over her shoulder, her eyes of gentian-blue always alert.

The morning turned warm; she pulled off her soft felt hat, shook out her clipped curls, stripped open the shirt at her snowy throat where sweat glimmered like melted frost.

The forest was lovely in the morning sunlight—lovely and still—save for the blue-jays—for the summer birds had gone and only birds destined to a long Northern winter remained.

Now and then, ahead of her, she saw a ruffed grouse wandering in the trail. These, and a single tiny grey bird with a dreary note interminably repeated, were the only living things she saw except here and there a summer-battered butterfly of the Vanessa tribe flitting in some stray sunbeam.

The haunting odour of late autumn was in the air—delicately acrid—

the scent of frost-killed brake and ripening wild grasses, of brilliant dead leaves and black forest loam pungent with mast from beech and oak.

Eve's tread was light on the moist trail; her quick eyes missed nothing—not the dainty imprint of deer, fresh made, nor the sprawling insignia of rambling raccoons—nor the big barred owl huddled on a pine limb overhead, nor, where the swift gravelly reaches of the brook caught sunlight, did she miss the swirl and furrowing and milling of painted trout on the spawning beds.

Once she took cover, hearing something stirring; but it was only a yearling buck that came out of the witch-hazel to stare, stamp, then wheel and trot away, displaying the danger signal.

In her cartridge-pouch she carried the flat, sealed packet which Clinch had trusted to her. The sack swayed gently as she strode on, slapping her left hip at every step; and always her subconscious mind remained on guard and aware of it; and now and then she dropped her hand to feel of the pouch and strap.

The character of the forest was now changing as she advanced. The first tamaracks appeared, slim, silvery trunks, crowned with the gold of autumn foliage, outer sentinels of that vast maze of swamp and stream called Owl Marsh, the stronghold and refuge of forest wild things—sometimes the sanctuary of hunted men.

From Star Peak's left flank an icy stream clatters down to the level floor of the woods, here; and it was here that Eve had meant to quench her thirst with a mouthful of sweet water.

But as she approached the tiny ford, warily, she saw a saddled horse tied to a sapling and a man seated on a mossy log.

The trappings of horse, the grey-green uniform of the man, left no room for speculation; a trooper of the State Constabulary was seated there.

His cap was off; his head rested on his palm. Elbow on knee, he sat there gazing at the water—watching the slim fish, perhaps, darting up stream toward their bridal-beds hidden far away at the headwaters.

A detour was imperative. The girl, from the shelter of a pine, looked out cautiously at the trooper. The sudden sight of him had merely checked her; now the recognition of his uniform startled her heart out of its tranquil rhythm and set the blood burning in her cheeks.

There was a memory of such a man seared into the girl's very soul;—a man whose head and shoulders resembled this man's—who had the same bright hair, the same slim and powerful body—and who moved, too, as this young man moved.

The trooper stirred, lifted his head to relight his pipe.

The girl knew him. Her heart stood still; then heart and blood ran riot and she felt her knees tremble—felt weak as she rested against the pine's huge trunk and covered her face with unsteady fingers.

Until the moment, Eve had never dreamed what the memory of this man really meant to her—never dreamed that she had capacity for emotion so utterly overwhelming.

Even now confusion, shame, fear were paramount. All she wanted was to get away—get away and still her heart's wild beating—control the strange tremor that possessed her, recover mind and sense and breath.

She drew her hand from her eyes and looked upon the man she had attempted to kill—upon the young man who had wrestled her off her feet and handcuffed her—and who had bathed her bleeding mouth with sphagnum—and who had kissed her hands—

She was trembling so that she became frightened. The racket of the brook in his ears safeguarded her in a measure. She bent over nearly double, her rifle at a trail, and cautiously began the detour.

When at length the wide circle through the woods had been safely accomplished and Eve was moving out through the thickening ranks of tamarack, her heart, which seemed to suffocate her, quieted; and she leaned against a shoulder of rock, strangely tired.

After a while she drew from her pocket *his* handkerchief, and looked at it. The square of cambric bore his initials, J. S. Blood from her lip remained on it. She had not washed out the spots.

She put it to her lips again, mechanically. A faint odour of tobacco still clung to it.

By every law of loyalty, pride, self-respect, she should have held this man her enemy. Instead, she held his handkerchief against her lips— crushed it there suddenly, closing her eyes while the colour surged and surged through her skin from throat to hair.

Then, wearily, she lifted her head and looked out into the grey and empty vista of her life, where the dreary years seemed to stretch like milestones away, away into an endless waste.

She put the handkerchief into her pocket, shouldered her rifle, moved on without looking about her—a mistake which only the emotion of the moment could account for in a girl so habituated to caution—for she had gone only a few rods before a man's strident voice halted her:

"*Halte là! Crosse en air!* "

"Drop that rifle!" came another voice from behind her. "You're covered! Throw your gun on the ground!"

She stood as though paralysed. To the right and left she heard people trampling through the thicket toward her.

"Down with that gun, damn you!" repeated the voice, breathless from running. All around her men came floundering and crashing toward her through the undergrowth. She could see some of them.

As she stooped to place her rifle on the dead leaves, she drew the flat packet from her cartridge sack at the same time and slid it deftly under a rotting log. Then, calm but very pale, she stood upright to face events.

The first man wore a red and yellow bandanna handkerchief over the lower half of his face, pulled tightly across a bony nose. He held a long pistol nearly parallel to his own body; and when he came up to where she was standing he poked the muzzle into her stomach.

She did not flinch; he said nothing; she looked intently into the two ratty eyes fastened on her over the edge of his bandanna.

Five other men were surrounding her, but they all wore white masks of vizard shape, revealing chin and mouth.

They were different otherwise, also, wearing various sorts and patterns of sport clothes, brand new, and giving them an odd, foreign appearance.

What troubled her most was the silence they maintained. The man wearing the bandanna was the only one who seemed at all a familiar figure—merely, perhaps, because he was American in build, clothing, and movement.

He took her by the shoulder, turned her around and gave her a shove forward. She staggered a step or two; he gave her another shove and she comprehended that she was to keep on going.

Presently she found herself in a steep, wet deer-trail rising upward through a gully. She knew that runway. It led up Star Peak.

Behind her as she climbed she heard the slopping, panting tread of men; her wind was better than theirs; she climbed lithely upward, setting a pace which finally resulted in a violent jerk backward—a savage, wordless admonition to go more slowly.

As she climbed she wondered whether she should have fired an alarm shot on the chance of the State Trooper, Stormont, hearing it.

But she had thought only of the packet at the moment of surprise. And now she wondered whether, when freed, she could ever again find that rotting log.

Up, up, always up along the wet gully, deep with silt and frost-splintered rock, she toiled, the heavy gasping of men behind her. Twice she was jerked to a halt while her escort rested.

Once, without turning, she said unsteadily: "Who are you? What have I done to you?"

There was no reply.

"What are you going to do to me—" she began again, and was shaken by the shoulder until silent.

At last the vast arch of the eastern sky sprang out ahead, where stunted spruces stood out against the sunshine and the intense heat of midday fell upon a bare table-land of rock and moss and fern.

As she came out upon the level, the man behind her took both her arms and pulled them back and somebody bandaged her eyes. Then a hand closed on her left arm and, so guided, she stumbled and crept forward across the rocks for a few moments until her guide halted her and forced her into a sitting position on a smooth, flat boulder.

She heard the crunching of heavy feet all around her, whispering made hoarse by breath exhausted, movement across rock and scrub, retreating steps.

For an interminable time she sat there alone in the hot sun, drenched to the skin in sweat, listening, thinking, striving to find a reason for this lawless outrage.

After a long while she heard somebody coming across the rocks, stiffened as she listened with some vague presentiment of evil.

Somebody had halted beside her. After a pause she was aware of nimble fingers busy with the bandage over her eyes.

At first, when freed, the light blinded her. By degrees she was able to distinguish the rocky crest of Star Peak, with the tops of tall trees appearing level with the rocks from depths below.

Then she turned, slowly, and looked at the man who had seated himself beside her.

He wore a white mask over a delicate, smoothly shaven face.

His soft hat and sporting clothes were dark grey, evidently new. And she noticed his hands—long, elegantly made, smooth, restless, playing with a pencil and some sheets of paper on his knees.

As she met his brilliant eyes behind the mask, his delicate, thin lips grew tense in what seemed to be a smile—or a soundless sort of laugh.

"Veree happee," he said, "to make the acquaintance. Pardon my unceremony, miss, but onlee necissitee compels. Are you, perhaps, a little rested?"

"Yes."

"Ah! Then, if you permit, we proceed with affairs of moment. You will be sufficiently kind to write down what I say. Yes?"

He placed paper and pencil in Eve's hand. Without demurring or hesitation she made ready to write, her mind groping wildly for the reason of it all.

"Write," he said, with his silent laugh which was more like the soundless snarl of a lynx unafraid:

"To Mike Clinch, my fathaire, from his child, Eve.... I am hostage, held by José Quintana. Pay what you owe him and I go free.

"For each day delay he sends to you one finger which will be severed from my right hand—"

Eve's slender fingers trembled; she looked up at the masked man, stared steadily into his brilliant eyes.

"Proceed miss, if you are so amiable," he said softly.

She wrote on: "—One finger for every day's delay. The whole hand at the week's end. The other hand then, finger by finger. Then, alas! the right foot—"

Eve trembled.

"Proceed," he said softly.

She wrote: "If you agree you shall pay what you owe to José Quintana in this manner: you shall place a stick at the edge of the Star Pond where the Star rivulet flows out. Upon this stick you shall tie a white rag. At the foot of the stick you shall lay the parcel which contains your indebt to José Quintana.

"Failing this, by to-night *one finger* at sunset."

The man paused: Eve waited, dumb under the surging confusion in her brain. A sort of incredulous horror benumbed her, through which she still heard and perceived.

"Be kind enough to sign it with your name," said the man pleasantly. Eve signed.

Then the masked man took the letter, got up, removed his hat.

"I am Quintana," he said. "I keep my word. A thousand thanks and apologies, miss. I trust that your detention may be brief and not too disagreeable. I place at your feet my humble respects."

He bowed, put on his hat, and walked quickly away. And she saw him descend the rocks to the eastward, where the peak slopes.

When Quintana had disappeared behind the summit scrub and rocks, Eve slowly stood up and looked about her at the rocky pulpit so familiar.

There was only one way out. Quintana had gone that way. His men no doubt guarded it. Otherwise, sheer precipices confronted her.

She walked to the western edge where a sheet of slippery reindeer moss clothed the rock. Below the mountain fell away to the valley where she had been made prisoner.

She looked out over the vast panorama of wilderness and mountain, range on range stretching blue to the horizon. She looked down into the depths of the valley where deep under the flaming foliage of October, somewhere, a State Trooper was sitting, cheek on hand, beside a waterfall—or, perhaps, riding slowly through a forest which she might never gaze upon again.

There was a noise on the rocks behind her. A masked man came out of the spruce scrub, laid a blanket on the rocks, placed a loaf of bread, some cheese, and a tin pail full of water upon it, motioned her, and went away through the dwarf spruces.

Eve walked slowly to the blanket. She drank out of the tin pail. Then she set aside the food, lay down, and buried her quivering face in her arms.

The sun was half way between zenith and horizon when she heard somebody coming, and rose to a sitting posture. Her visitor was Quintana.

He came up to her quite close, stood with glittering eyes intent upon her.

After a moment he handed her a letter.

She could scarcely unfold it, she trembled so:

> "Girlie, for God's sake give that packet to Quintana and come on home. I'm near crazy with it all. What the hell's anything worth beside you girlie. I don't give a damn for nothing only you, so come on quick. Dad."

After a little while she lifted her eyes to Quintana.

"So," he said quietly, "you are the little she-fox that has learned tricks already."

"What do you mean?"

"Where is that packet?"

"I haven't it."

"Where is it?"

She shook her head slightly.

"You had a packet," he insisted fiercely. "Look here! Regard!" and he spread out a penciled sheet in Clinch's hand:

> "José Quintana:
> "You win. She's got that stuff with her. Take your damn junk and let my girl go.
> "Mike Clinch."

"Well," said Quintana, a thin, strident edge to his tone.

"My father is mistaken. I haven't any packet."

The man's visage behind his mask flushed darkly. Without warning or ceremony he caught Eve by the throat and tore open her shirt. Then, hissing and cursing and panting with his own violence, he searched her brutally and without mercy—flung her down and tore off her spiral puttees and even her shoes and stockings, now apparently beside himself with fury, puffing, gasping, always with a fierce, nasal sort of whining undertone like an animal worrying its kill.

"Cowardly beast!" she panted, fighting him with all her strength—"filthy, cowardly beast!—" striking at him, wrenching his grasp away, snatching at the disordered clothing half stripped from her.

His hunting knife fell clattering and she fought to get it, but he struck her with his open hand, knocking her down at his feet, and stood glaring at her with every tooth bared.

"So," he cried, "I give you ten minutes, make up your mind, tell me what you do with that packet."

He wiped the blood from his face where she had struck him.

"You don't know José Quintana. No! You shall make his acquaintance. Yes!"

Eve got up on naked feet, quivering from head to foot, striving to button the grey shirt at her throat.

"Where?" he demanded, beside himself.

Her mute lips only tightened.

"Ver' well, by God!" he cried. "I go make me some fire. You like it, eh? We shall put one toe in the fire until it burn off. Yes? Eh? How you like it? Eh?"

The girl's trembling hands continued busy with her clothing.

"So!" he said, hoarsely, "you remain dumb! Well, then, in ten minutes you shall talk!"

He walked toward her, pushed her savagely aside, and strode on into the spruce thicket.

The instant he disappeared Eve caught up the knife he had dropped, knelt down on the blanket and fell to cutting it into strips.

The hunting knife was like a razor; the feverish business was accomplished in a few moments, the pieces knotted, the cord strained in a desperate test over her knee.

And now she ran to the precipice where, ten feet below, the top of a great pine protruded from the gulf.

On the edge of the abyss was a spruce root. It looked dead, wedged deep between two rocks; but with all her strength she could not pull it out.

Sobbing, breathless, she tied her blanket rope to this, threw the other end over the cliff's edge, and, not giving herself time to think, lay flat, grasped the knotted line, swung off.

Knot by knot she went down. Half-way her naked feet brushed the needles. She looked over her shoulder, behind and down. Then, teeth clenched, she lowered herself steadily as she had learned to do in the school gymnasium, down, down, until her legs came astride of a pine limb.

It bent, swayed, gave with her, letting her sag to a larger limb below. This she clasped, letting go her rope.

Already, from the mountain's rocky crest above, she heard excited cries. Once, on her breakneck descent, she looked up through the foliage of the pine; and she saw, far up against the sky, a white-masked face looking over the edge of the precipice.

But if it were Quintana or another of his people she could not tell. And, again looking down, she began again the terrible descent.

An hour later, Trooper Stormont of the State Constabulary sat his horse in amazement to see a ragged, breathless, boyish figure speeding toward him among the tamaracks, her naked feet splashing through pool and mire and sphagnum.

"Good heavens!" he exclaimed as she flung herself against his stirrup, sobbing, hysterical, and clinging to his knee.

"Take me back," she stammered, "—take me back to daddy! I can't—go on—another step—"

He leaned down, swung her up to his saddle in front, holding her cradled in his arms.

"Lie still," he said coolly; "you're all right now."

For another second he sat looking down at her, at the dishevelled hair, the gasping mouth—at the rags clothing her, and at the flat packet clasped convulsively to her breast.

Then he spoke in a low voice to his horse, guiding left with one knee.

Episode Four
A PRIVATE WAR

I

When State Trooper Stormont rode up to Clinch's with Eve Strayer lying in his arms, Mike Clinch strode out of the motley crowd around the tavern, laid his rifle against a tree, and stretched forth his powerful hands to receive his stepchild.

He held her, cradled, looking down at her in silence as the men clustered around.

"Eve," he said hoarsely, "be you hurted?"

The girl opened her sky-blue eyes.

"I'm all right, dad.... just tired.... I've got your parcel ... safe...."

"To hell with the gol-dinged parcel," he almost sobbed; "—did Quintana harm you?"

"No, dad."

As he carried her to the veranda the packet fell from her cramped fingers. Clinch kicked it under a chair and continued on into the house and up the stairs to Eve's bedroom.

Flat on the bed, the girl opened her drowsy eyes again, unsmiling.

"Did that dirty louse misuse you?" demanded Clinch unsteadily. "G'wan tell me, girlie."

"He knocked me down.... He went away to get fire to make me talk. I cut up the blanket they gave me and made a rope. Then I went over the cliff into the big pine below. That was all, dad."

Clinch filled a tin basin and washed the girl's torn feet. When he had dried them he kissed them. She felt his unshaven lips trembling, heard him whimper for the first time in his life.

"Why the hell didn't you give Quintana the packet?" he demanded. "What does that count for—what does any damn thing count for against you, girlie?"

She looked up at him out of heavy-lidded eyes: "You told me to take good care of it."

"It's only a little truck I'd laid by for you," he retorted unsteadily, "— a few trifles for to make a grand lady of you when the time's ripe. 'Tain't worth a thorn in your little foot to me.... The hull gol-dinged world full o' money ain't worth that there stone-bruise onto them little white feet o' yourn, Eve.

"Look at you now—my God, look at you there, all peaked an' scairt an' bleedin'—plum tuckered out, 'n' all ragged 'n' dirty—"

A blaze of fury flared in his small pale eyes: "—And he hit you, too, did he?—that skunk! Quintana done that to my little girlie, did he?"

"I don't know if it was Quintana. I don't know who he was, dad," she murmured drowsily.

"Masked, wa'n't he?"

"Yes."

Clinch's iron visage twitched and quivered. He gnawed his thin lips into control:

"Girlie, I gotta go out a spell. But I ain't a-leavin' you alone here. I'll git somebody to set up with you. You jest lie snug and don't think about nothin' till I come back."

"Yes, dad," she sighed, closing her eyes.

Clinch stood looking at her for a moment, then he went downstairs heavily, and out to the veranda where State Trooper Stormont still sat his saddle, talking to Hal Smith. On the porch a sullen crowd of backwoods riff-raff lounged in silence, awaiting events.

Clinch called across to Smith: "Hey, Hal, g'wan up and set with Eve a spell while she's nappin'. Take a gun."

Smith said to Stormont in a low voice: "Do me a favour, Jack?"

"You bet."

"That girl of Clinch's is in real danger if left here alone. But I've got another job on my hands. Can you keep a watch on her till I return?"

"Can't you tell me a little more, Jim?"

"I will, later. Do you mind helping me out now?"

"All right."

Trooper Stormont swung out of his saddle and led his horse away toward the stable.

Hal Smith went into the bar where Clinch stood, oiling a rifle.

"G'wan upstairs," he muttered. "I got a private war on. It's me or Quintana, now."

"You're going after Quintana?" inquired Smith, carelessly.

"I be. And I want you should git your gun and set up by Evie. And I want you should kill any living human son of a slut that comes botherin' around this here hotel."

"I'm going after Quintana with you, Mike."

"B'gosh, you ain't. You're a-goin' to keep watch here."

"No. Trooper Stormont has promised to stay with Eve. You'll need every man to-day, Mike. This isn't a deer drive."

Clinch let his rifle sag across the hollow of his left arm.

"Did you beef to that trooper?" he demanded in his pleasant, misleading way.

"Do you think I'm crazy?" retorted Smith.

"Well, what the hell—"

"They all know that some man used your girl roughly. That's all I said to him—'keep an eye on Eve until we can get back.' And I tell you, Mike, if we drive Star Peak we won't be back till long after sundown."

Clinch growled: "I ain't never asked no favours of no State Trooper—"

"He did you a favour, didn't he? He brought your daughter in."

"Yes, 'n' he'd jail us all if he got anything on us."

"Yes; and he'll shoot to kill if any of Quintana's people come here and try to break in."

Clinch grunted, peeled off his coat and got into a leather vest bristling with cartridge loops.

Trooper Stormont came in the back door, carrying his rifle.

"Some rough fellow been bothering your little daughter, Clinch?" he inquired. "The child was nearly all in when she met me out by Owl Marsh—clothes half torn off her back, bare-foot and bleeding. She's a plucky youngster. I'll say so, Clinch. If you think the fellow may come here to annoy her I'll keep an eye on her till you return."

Clinch went up to Stormont, put his powerful hands on the young fellow's shoulders.

After a moment's glaring silence: "You *look* clean. I guess you be, too. I wanta tell you I'll cut the guts outa any guy that lays the heft of a single finger onto Eve."

"I'd do so, too, if I were you," said Stormont.

"Would ye? Well, I guess you're a real man, too, even if you're a State Trooper," growled Clinch. "G'wan up. She's a-nappin'. If she wakes up you kinda talk pleasant to her. You act kind pleasant and cosy. She ain't had no ma. You tell her to set snug and ca'm. Then you cook her a egg if she wants it. There's pie, too. I cal'late to be back by sundown."

"Nearer morning," remarked Smith.

Stormont shrugged. "I'll stay until you show up, Clinch."

The latter took another rifle from the corner and handed it to Smith with a loop of ammunition.

"Come on," he grunted.

On the veranda he strode up to the group of sullen, armed men who regarded his advent in expressionless silence.

Sid Hone was there, and Harvey Chase, and the Hastings boys, and Cornelius Blommers.

"You fellas comin'?" inquired Clinch.

"Where?" drawled Sid Hone.

"Me an' Hal Smith is cal'kalatin' to drive Star Peak. It ain't a deer, neither."

There ensued a grim interval. Clinch's wintry smile began to glimmer.

"Booze agents or game protectors? Which?" asked Byron Hastings. "They both look like deer—if a man gits mad enough."

Clinch's smile became terrifying. "I shell out five hundred dollars for every *deer* that's dropped on Star Peak to-day," he said. "And I hope there won't be no accidents and no mistakin' no *stranger* for a deer," he added, wagging his great, square head.

"Them accidents is liable to happen," remarked Hone, reflectively.

After another pause: "Where's Jake Kloon?" inquired Smith.

Nobody seemed to know.

"He was here when Mike called me into the bar," insisted Smith. "Where'd he go?"

Then, of a sudden, Clinch recollected the packet which he had kicked under a veranda chair. It was no longer there.

"Any o' you fellas seen a package here on the pyazza?" demanded Clinch harshly.

"Jake Kloon, he had somethin'," drawled Chase. "I supposed it was his lunch. Mebbe 'twas, too."

In the intense stillness Clinch glared into one face after another.

"Boys," he said in his softly modulated voice, "I kinda guess there's a rat amongst us. I wouldn't like for to be that there rat—no, not for a billion hundred dollars. No, I wouldn't. Becuz that there rat has bit my little girlie, Eve—like that there deer bit her up onto Star Peak.... No, I wouldn't like for to be that there rat. Fer he's a-goin' to die like a rat, same's that there deer is a-goin' to die like a deer.... Anyone seen which way Jake Kloon went?"

"Now you speak of it," said Byron Hastings, "seems like I noticed Jake and Earl Leverett down by the woods near the pond. I kinda disremembered when you asked, but I guess I seen them."

"Sure," said Sid Hone. "Now you mention it, I seen 'em, too. Thinks I to m'self, they is pickin' them blackberries down to the crick. Yas, I seen 'em."

Clinch tossed his rifle across his left shoulder.

"Rats an' deer," he said pleasantly. "Them's the articles we're lookin' for. Only for God's sake be careful you don't mistake a *man* for 'em in the woods."

One or two men laughed.

On the edge of Owl Marsh Clinch halted in the trail, and, as his men came up, he counted them with a cold eye.

"Here's the runway and this here hazel bush is my station," he said. "You fellas do the barkin'. You, Sid Hone, and you, Corny, start drivin' from the west. Harve, you yelp 'em from the north by Lynx Brook. Jim and Byron, you get twenty minutes to go 'round to the eastward and drive by the Slide. And you, Hal Smith,"—he looked around—"where 'n hell be you, Hal?—"

Smith came up from the bog's edge.

"Send 'em out," he said in a low voice. "I've got Jake's tracks in the bog."

Clinch motioned his beaters to their duty. "Twenty minutes," he reminded Hone, Chase, and Blommers, "before you start drivin'." And, to the Hastings boys: "If you shoot, aim low for their bellies. Don't leave no blood around. Scrape it up. We bury what we get."

He and Smith stood looking after the five slouching figures moving away toward their blind trails. When all had disappeared:

"Show me Jake's mark," he said calmly.

Smith led him to the edge of the bog, knelt down, drew aside a branch of witch-hopple. A man's footprint was plainly visible on the mud.

"That's Jake," said Clinch slowly. "I know them half-soled boots o' hisn." He lifted another branch. "There's another man's track!"

"The other is probably Leverett's."

"Likely. He's got thin feet."

"I think I'd better go after them," said Smith, reflectively.

"They'll plug you, you poor jackass—two o' them like that, and one a-settin' up to watch out. Hell! Be you tired o' bed an' board?"

Smith smiled: "Don't you worry, Mike."

"Why? You think you're that smart? Jest becuz you stuck up a tourist you think you're cock o' the North Woods—with them two foxes lyin' out for to snap you up? Hey? Why, you poor dumb thing, Jake runs Canadian hootch for a livin' and Leverett's a trap thief! What could *you* do with a pair o' foxes like that?"

"Catch 'em," said Smith, coolly. "You mind your business, Mike."

As he shouldered his rifle and started into the marsh, Clinch dropped a heavy hand on his shoulder; but the young man shook it off.

"Shut up," he said sharply. "You've a private war on your hands. So have I. I'll take care of my own."

"What's *your* grievance?" demanded Clinch, surprised.

"Jake Kloon played a dirty trick on me."

"When was that?"

"Not very long ago."

"I hadn't heard," said Clinch.

"Well, you hear it now, don't you? All right. All right; I'm going after him."

As he started again across the marsh, Clinch called out in a guarded voice: "Take good care of that packet if you catch them rats. It belongs to Eve."

"I'll take such good care of it," replied Smith, "that its proper owner need not worry."

II

The "proper owner" of the packet was, at that moment, on the Atlantic Ocean, travelling toward the United States.

Four other pretended owners of the Grand Duchess Theodorica's jewels, totally unconscious of anything impending which might impair their several titles to the gems, were now gathered together in a wilderness within a few miles of one another.

José Quintana lay somewhere in the forests with his gang, fiercely planning the recovery of the treasure of which Clinch had once robbed him. Clinch squatted on his runway, watching the mountain flank with murderous eyes. It was no longer the Flaming Jewel which mattered. His master passion ruled him now. Those who had offered violence to Eve must be reckoned with first of all. The hand that struck

Eve Strayer had offered mortal insult to Mike Clinch.

As for the third pretender to the Flaming Jewel, Jake Kloon, he was now travelling in a fox's circle toward Drowned Valley—that shaggy wilderness of slime and tamarack and depthless bog which touches the northwest base of Star Peak. He was not hurrying, having no thought of pursuit. Behind him plodded Leverett, the trap thief, very, very busy with his own ideas.

To Leverett's repeated requests that Kloon halt and open the packet to see what it contained, Kloon gruffly refused.

"What do we care what's in it?" he said. "We get ten thousand apiece over our rifles for it from them guys. Ain't it a good enough job for you?"

"Maybe we make more if we take what's inside it for ourselves," argued Leverett. "Let's take a peek, anyway."

"Naw. I don't want no peek nor nothin'. The ten thousand comes too easy. More might scare us. Let that guy, Quintana, have what's his'n. All I ask is my rake-off. You allus was a dirty, thieving mink, Earl. Let's give him his and take ours and git. I'm going to Albany to live. You bet I don't stay in no woods where Mike Clinch dens."

They plodded on, arguing, toward their rendezvous with Quintana's outpost on the edge of Drowned Valley.

The fourth pretender to the pearls, rubies, and great gem called the Flaming Jewel, stolen from the young Grand Duchess Theodorica of Esthonia by José Quintana, was an unconscious pretender, entirely innocent of the rôle assigned her by Clinch.

For Eve Strayer had never heard where the packet came from or what it contained. All she knew was that her stepfather had told her that it belonged to her. And the knowledge left her incurious.

III

Eve slept the sleep of mental and physical exhaustion. Reaction from fear brings a fatigue more profound than that which follows physical overstrain. But the healthy mind, like the healthy body, disposes very thoroughly of toxics which arise from terror and exhaustion.

The girl slept profoundly, calmly. Her bruised young mind and body left her undisturbed. There was neither restlessness nor fever. Sleep swept her with its clean, sweet tide, cleansing the superb youth and health of her with the most wonderful balm in the Divine pharmacy.

She awoke late in the afternoon, opened her flower-blue eyes, and saw State Trooper Stormont sitting by the window, and gazing out.

Perhaps Eve's confused senses mistook the young man for a vision; for she lay very still, nor stirred even her little finger.

After a while Stormont glanced around at her. A warm, delicate colour stained her skin slowly, evenly, from throat to hair.

He got up and came over to the bed.

"How do you feel?" he asked, awkwardly.

"Where is dad?" she managed to inquire in a steady voice.

"He won't be back till late. He asked me to stick around—in case you needed anything—"

The girl's clear eyes searched his.

"Trooper Stormont?"

"Yes, Eve."

"Dad's gone after Quintana."

"Is he the fellow who misused you?"

"I think so."

"Who is he?"

"I don't know."

"Is he your enemy or your stepfather's?"

But the girl shook her head: "I can't discuss dad's affairs with—with—"

"With a State Trooper," smiled Stormont. "That's all right, Eve. You don't have to."

There was a pause; Stormont stood beside the bed, looking down at her with his diffident, boyish smile. And the girl gazed back straight into his eyes—eyes she had so often looked into in her dreams.

"I'm to cook you an egg and bring you some pie," he remarked, still smiling.

"Did dad say I am to stay in bed?"

"That was my inference. Do you feel very lame and sore?"

"My feet burn."

"You poor kid!... Would you let me look at them? I have a first-aid packet with me."

After a moment she nodded and turned her face on the pillow. He drew aside the cover a little, knelt down beside the bed.

Then he rose and went downstairs to the kitchen. There was hot water in the kettle. He fetched it back, bathed her feet, drew out from cut and scratch the flakes of granite-grit and brier-points that still remained there.

From his first-aid packet he took a capsule, dissolved it, sterilized the torn skin, then bandaged both feet with a deliciously cool salve, and drew the sheets into place.

Eve had not stirred nor spoken. He washed and dried his hands and came back, drawing his chair nearer to the bedside.

"Sleep, if you feel like it," he said pleasantly.

As she made no sound or movement he bent over to see if she had already fallen asleep. And noticed that her flushed cheeks were wet with tears.

"Are you suffering?" he asked gently.

"No.... You are so wonderfully kind...."

"Why shouldn't I be kind?" he said, amused and touched by the girl's emotion.

"I tried to shoot you once. That is why you ought to hate me."

He began to laugh: "Is *that* what you're thinking about?"

"I—never can—forget—"

"Nonsense. We're quits anyway. Do you remember what I did to *you*?"

He was thinking of the handcuffs. Then, in her vivid blush he read what she was thinking. And he remembered his lips on her palms.

He, too, now was blushing brilliantly at memory of that swift, sudden rush of romantic tenderness which this girl had witnessed that memorable day on Owl Marsh.

In the hot, uncomfortable silence, neither spoke. He seated himself after a while. And, after a while, she turned on her pillow part way toward him.

Somehow they both understood that it was friendship which had subtly filled the interval that separated them since that amazing day.

"I've often thought of you," he said—as though they had been discussing his absence.

No hour of the waking day that she had not thought of him. But she did not say so now. After a little while:

"Is yours a lonely life?" she asked in a low voice.

"Sometimes. But I love the forest."

"Sometimes," she said, "the forest seems like a trap that I can't escape. Sometimes I hate it."

"Are you lonely, Eve?"

"As you are. You see I know what the outside world is. I miss it."

"You were in boarding school and college."

"Yes."

"It must be hard for you here at Star Pond."

The girl sighed, unconsciously:

"There are days when I—can scarcely—stand it.... The wilderness would be more endurable if dad and I were all alone.... But even then—"

"You need young people of your own age—educated companions—"

"I need the city, Mr. Stormont. I need all it can give: I'm starving for it. That's all."

She turned on her pillow, and he saw that she was smiling faintly. Her face bore no trace of the tragic truth she had uttered. But the tragedy was plain enough to him, even without her passionless words of revolt. The situation of this young, educated girl, aglow with youth, fettered, body and mind, to the squalor of Clinch's dump, was perfectly plain to anybody.

She said, seeing his troubled expression: "I'm sorry I spoke that way."

"I knew how you must feel, anyway."

"It seems ungrateful," she murmured. "I love my step-father."

"You've proven that," he remarked with a dry humour that brought the hot flush to her face again.

"I must have been crazy that day," she said. "It scares me to remember what I tried to do.... What a frightful thing—if I had killed you—How *can* you forgive me?"

"How can you forgive *me*, Eve?"

She turned her head: "I do."

"Entirely?"

"Yes."

He said—a slight emotion noticeable in his voice: "Well, I forgave you before the darned gun exploded in our hands."

"How *could* you?" she protested.

"I was thinking all the while that you were acting as I'd have acted if anything threatened *my* father."

"Were you thinking of *that*?"

"Yes—and also how to get hold of you before you shot me." He began to laugh.

After a moment she turned her head to look at him, and her smile glimmered, responsive to his amusement. But she shivered slightly, too.

"How about that egg?" he inquired.

"I can get up—"

"Better keep off your feet. What is there in the pantry? You must be starved."

"I could eat a little before supper time," she admitted. "I forgot to take my lunch with me this morning. It is still there in the pantry on the bread box, wrapped up in brown paper, just as I left it—"

She half rose in bed, supported on one arm, her curly brown-gold hair framing her face:

"—Two cakes of sugar-milk chocolate in a flat brown packet tied with a string," she explained, smiling at his amusement.

So he went down to the pantry and discovered the parcel on the bread box where she had left it that morning before starting for the cache on Owl Marsh.

He brought it to her, placed both pillows upright behind her, stepped back gaily to admire the effect. Eve, with her parcel in her hands, laughed shyly at his comedy.

"Begin on your chocolate," he said. "I'm going back to fix you some bread and butter and a cup of tea."

When again he had disappeared, the girl, still smiling, began to untie her packet, unhurriedly, slowly loosening string and wrapping.

Her attention was not fixed on what her slender fingers were about.

She drew from the parcel a flat morocco case with a coat of arms and crest stamped on it in gold, black, and scarlet.

For a few moments she stared at the object stupidly. The next moment she heard Stormont's spurred tread on the stairs; and she thrust the morocco case and the wrapping under the pillows behind her.

She looked up at him in a dazed way when he came in with the tea and bread. He set the tin tray on her bureau and came over to the bedside.

"Eve," he said, "you look very white and ill. Have you been hurt somewhere, and haven't you admitted it?"

She seemed unable to speak, and he took both her hands and looked anxiously into the lovely, pallid features.

After a moment she turned her head and buried her face in the pillow, trembling now in overwhelming realization of what she had endured for the sake of two cakes of sugar-milk chocolate hidden under a bush in the forest.

For a long while the girl lay there, the feverish flush of tears on her partly hidden face, her nervous hands tremulous, restless, now seeking his, convulsively, now striving to escape his clasp—eloquent, uncertain little hands that seemed to tell so much and yet were telling him nothing he could understand.

"Eve, dear," he said, "are you in pain? What is it that has happened to you? I thought you were all right. You seemed all right—"

"I am," she said in a smothered voice. "You'll stay here with me, won't you?"

"Of course I will. It's just the reaction. It's all over. You're relaxing. That's all, dear. You're safe. Nothing can harm you now—"

"Please don't leave me."

After a moment: "I won't leave you.... I wish I might never leave you."

In the tense silence that followed her trembling ceased. Then his heart, heavy, irregular, began beating so that the startled pulses in her body awoke, wildly responsive.

Deep emotions, new, unfamiliar, were stirring, awaking, confusing them both. In a sudden instinct to escape, she turned and partly rose on one elbow, gazing blindly about her out of tear-marred eyes.

"I want my room to myself," she murmured in a breathless sort of way, "—I want you to go out, please—"

A boyish flush burnt his face. He got up slowly, took his rifle from the corner, went out, closing the door, and seated himself on the stairs.

And there, on guard, sat Trooper Stormont, rigid, unstirring, hour after hour, facing the first great passion of his life, and stunned by the impact of its swift and unexpected blow.

In her chamber, on the bed's edge, sat Eve Strayer, her deep eyes fixed on space. Vague emotions, exquisitely recurrent, new born, possessed her. The whole world, too, all around her seemed to have become misty and golden and all pulsating with a faint, still rhythm that indefinably thrilled her pulses to response.

Passion, full-armed, springs flaming from the heart of man. Woman is slow to burn. And it was the delicate phantom of passion that Eve gazed upon, there in her unpainted chamber, her sun-tanned fingers linked listlessly in her lap, her little feet like bruised white flowers drooping above the floor.

Hour after hour she sat there dreaming, staring at the tinted ghost of Eros, rose-hued, near-smiling, unreal, impalpable as the dusty sunbeam that slanted from her window, gilding the boarded floor.

Three spectres, gliding near, paused to gaze at State Trooper Stormont, on guard by the stairs. Then they looked at the closed door of Eve's chamber.

Then the three spectres, Fate, Chance and Destiny, whispering together, passed on toward the depths of the sunset forest.

EPISODE FIVE
DROWNED VALLEY

I

The soft, bluish forest shadows had lengthened, and the barred sun-rays, filtering through, were tinged with a rosy hue before Jake Kloon, the hootch runner, and Earl Leverett, trap thief, came to Drowned Valley.

They were still a mile distant from the most southern edge of that vast desolation, but already tamaracks appeared in the beauty of their burnt gold; little pools glimmered here and there; patches of amber sphagnum and crimson pitcher-plants became frequent; and once or twice Kloon's big boots broke through the crust of fallen leaves, soaking him to the ankles with black silt.

Leverett, always a coward, had pursued his devious and larcenous way through the world, always in deadly fear of sink holes.

His movements and paths were those of a weasel, preferring always solid ground; but he lacked the courage of that sinuous little beast, though he possessed all of its ferocity and far more cunning.

Now trotting lightly and tirelessly in the broad and careless spoor of Jake Kloon, his narrow, pointed head alert, and every fear-sharpened instinct tensely observant, the trap-thief continued to meditate murder.

Like all cowards, he had always been inclined to bold and ruthless action; but inclination was all that ever had happened.

Yet, even in his pitiable misdemeanours he slunk through life in terror of that strength which never hesitates at violence. In his petty pilfering he died a hundred deaths for every trapped mink or otter he filched; he heard the game protector's tread as he slunk from the bagged trout brook or crawled away, belly dragging, and pockets full of snared grouse.

Always he had dreamed of the day when, through some sudden bold and savage stroke, he could deliver himself from a life of fear and live in a city, grossly, replete with the pleasures of satiation, never again to see a tree or a lonely lake or the blue peaks which, always, he had hated because they seemed to spy on him from their sky-blue heights.

They were spying on him now as he moved lightly, furtively at Jake Kloon's heels, meditating once more that swift, bold stroke which forever would free him from all care and fear.

He looked at the back of Kloon's massive head. One shot would blow that skull into fragments, he thought, shivering.

One shot from behind—and twenty thousand dollars—or, if it proved a better deal, the contents of the packet. For, if Quintana's bribery had dazzled them, what effect might the contents of that secret packet have if revealed?

Always in his mean and busy brain he was trying to figure to himself what that packet must contain. And, to make the bribe worth while, Leverett had concluded that only a solid packet of thousand-dollar bills could account for the twenty thousand offered.

There might easily be half a million in bills pressed together in that heavy, flat packet. Bills were absolutely safe plunder. But Kloon had turned a deaf ear to his suggestions—Kloon, who never entertained ambitions beyond his hootch rake-off—whose miserable imagination stopped at a wretched percentage, satisfied.

One shot! There was the back of Kloon's bushy head. One shot!—and fear, which had shadowed him from birth, was at an end forever. Ended, too, privation—the bitter rigour of black winters; scorching days; bodily squalor; ills that such as he endured in a wilderness where, like other creatures of the wild, men stricken died or recovered by chance alone.

A single shot would settle all problems for him.... But if he missed? At the mere idea he trembled as he trotted on, trying to tell himself that he couldn't miss. No use; always the coward's "if" blocked him; and the coward's rage—fiercest of all fury—ravaged him, almost crazing him with his own impotence.

Tamaracks, sphagnum, crimson pitcher-plants grew thicker; wet woods set with little black pools stretched away on every side.

It was still nearly a mile from Drowned Valley when Jake Kloon halted in his tracks and seated himself on a narrow ridge of hard ground. And Leverett came lightly up and, after nosing the whole vicinity, sat down cautiously where Kloon would have to turn partly around to look at him.

"Where the hell do we meet up with Quintana?" growled Kloon, tearing a mouthful from a gnawed tobacco plug and shoving the remainder deep into his trousers pocket.

"We gotta travel a piece, yet.... Say, Jake, be you a man or be you a poor dumb critter what ain't got no spunk?"

Kloon, chewing on his cud, turned and glanced at him. Then he spat, as answer.

"If you got the spunk of a chipmunk you and me'll take a peek at that there packet. I bet you it's thousand-dollar bills—more'n a billion million dollars, likely."

Kloon's dogged silence continued. Leverett licked his dry lips. His rifle lay on his knees. Almost imperceptibly he moved it, moved it again, froze stiff as Kloon spat, then, by infinitesimal degrees, continued to edge the muzzle toward Kloon.

"Jake?"

"Aw, shut your head," grumbled Kloon disdainfully. "You allus was a dirty rat—you sneakin' trap robber. Enough's enough. I ain't got no use for no billion million dollar bills. Ten thousand'll buy me all I cal'late to need till I'm planted. But you're like a hawg; you ain't never had enough o' nothin' and you won't never git enough, neither—not if you wuz God a'mighty you wouldn't."

"Ten thousand dollars hain't nothin' to a billion million, Jake."

Kloon squirted a stream of tobacco at a pitcher plant and filled the cup. Diverted and gratified by the accuracy of his aim, he took other shots at intervals.

Leverett moved the muzzle of his rifle a hair's width to the left, shivered, moved it again. Under his soggy, sun-tanned skin a pallour made his visage sickly grey.

"Jake?"

No answer.

"Say, Jake?"

No notice.

"Jake, I wanta take a peek at them bills."

Merely another stream of tobacco soiling the crimson pitcher.

"I'm—I'm desprit. I gotta take a peek. I gotta—gotta—"

Something in Leverett's unsteady voice made Kloon turn his head.

"You gol rammed fool," he said, "what you doin' with your—"

The loud detonation of the rifle punctuated Kloon's inquiry with a final period. The big, soft-nosed bullet struck him full in the face, spilling his brains and part of his skull down his back, and knocking him flat as though he had been clubbed.

Leverett, stunned, sat staring, motionless, clutching the rifle from the muzzle of which a delicate stain of vapour floated and disappeared through a rosy bar of sunshine.

In the intense stillness of the place, suddenly the dead man made a sound; and the trap-robber nearly fainted.

But it was only air escaping from the slowly collapsing lungs; and Leverett, ashy pale, shaking, got to his feet and leaned heavily against an oak tree, his eyes never stirring from the sprawling thing on the ground.

If it were a minute or a year he stood there he could never have reckoned the space of time. The sun's level rays glimmered ruddy through the woods. A green fly appeared, buzzing about the dead man. Another zig-zagged through the sunshine, lacing it with streaks of greenish fire. Others appeared, whirling, gyrating, filling the silence with their humming. And still Leverett dared not budge, dared not search the dead and take from it that for which the dead had died.

A little breeze came by and stirred the bushy hair on Kloon's head and fluttered the ferns around him where he lay.

Two delicate, pure-white butterflies—rare survivors of a native species driven from civilization into the wilderness by the advent of the foreign white—fluttered in airy play over the dead man, drifting away into the woodland at times, yet always returning to wage a fairy combat above the heap of soiled clothing which once had been a man.

Then, near in the ferns, the withering fronds twitched, and a red squirrel sprung his startling alarm, squeaking, squealing, chattering his opinion of murder; and Leverett, shaking with the shock, wiped icy sweat from his face, laid aside his rifle, and took his first stiff step toward the dead man.

But as he bent over he changed his mind, turned, reeling a little, then crept slowly out among the pitcher-plants, searching about him as though sniffing.

In a few minutes he discovered what he was looking for; took his bearings; carefully picked his way back over a leafy crust that trembled under his cautious tread.

He bent over Kloon and, from the left inside coat pocket, he drew the packet and placed it inside his own flannel shirt.

Then, turning his back to the dead, he squatted down and clutched Kloon's burly ankles, as a man grasps the handles of a wheelbarrow to draw it after him.

Dragging, rolling, bumping over roots, Jake Kloon took his last trail through the wilderness, leaving a redder path than was left by the setting sun through fern and moss and wastes of pitcher-plants.

Always, as Leverett crept on, pulling the dead behind him, the floor of the woods trembled slightly, and a black ooze wet the crust of withered leaves.

At the quaking edge of a little pool of water, Leverett halted. The water was dark but scarcely an inch deep over its black bed of silt.

Beside this sink hole the trap-thief dropped Kloon. Then he drew his hunting knife and cut a tall, slim swamp maple. The sapling was about twenty feet in height. Leverett thrust the butt of it into the pool. Without any effort he pushed the entire sapling out of sight in the depthless silt.

He had to manœuvre very gingerly to dump Kloon into the pool and keep out of it himself. Finally he managed it.

To his alarm, Kloon did not sink far. He cut another sapling and pushed the body until only the shoes were visible above the silt.

These, however, were very slowly sinking, now. Bubbles rose, dully iridescent, floated, broke. Strings of blood hung suspended in the clouding water.

Leverett went back to the little ridge and covered with dead leaves the spot where Kloon had lain. There were broken ferns, but he could not straighten them. And there lay Kloon's rifle.

For a while he hesitated, his habits of economy being ingrained; but he remembered the packet in his shirt, and he carried the rifle to the little pool and shoved it, muzzle first, driving it downward, out of sight.

As he rose from the pool's edge, somebody laid a hand on his shoulder.

That was the most real death that Leverett ever had died.

II

A coward dies many times before Old Man Death really gets him. The swimming minutes passed; his mind ceased to live for a space. Then, as through the swirling waters of the last dark whirlpool, a dulled roar of returning consciousness filled his being.

Somebody was shaking him, shouting at him. Suddenly instinct resumed its function, and he struggled madly to get away from the edge of the sink-hole—fought his way, blindly, through tangled undergrowth toward the hard ridge. No human power could have blocked the frantic creature thrashing toward solid ground.

But there Quintana held him in his wiry grip.

"Fool! Mule! Crazee fellow! What you do, eh? For why you make jumps like rabbits! Eh? You expec' Quintana? Yes? Alors!"

Leverett, in a state of collapse, sagged back against an oak tree. Quintana's nervous grasp fell from his arms and they swung, dangling.

"What you do by that pond-hole? Eh? I come and touch you, and, my God!—one would think I have stab you. Such an ass!"

The sickly greenish hue changed in Leverett's face as the warmer tide stirred from its stagnation. He lifted his head and tried to look at Quintana.

"Where Jake Kloon?" demanded the latter.

At that the weasel wits of the trap-robber awoke to the instant crisis. Blood and pulse began to jump. He passed one dirty hand over his mouth to mask any twitching.

"Where my packet, eh?" inquired Quintana.

"Jake's got it." Leverett's voice was growing stronger. His small eyes switched for an instant toward his rifle, where it stood against a tree behind Quintana.

"Where is he, then, this Jake?" repeated Quintana impatiently.

"He got bogged."

"Bogged? What is that, then?"

"He got into a sink-hole."

"What!"

"That's all I know," said Leverett, sullenly. "Him and me was travellin' hell-bent to meet up with you—Jake, he was for a short cut to Drowned Valley—but 'no,' sez I, 'gimme a good hard ridge an' a long deetoor when there's sink-holes into the woods—'"

"What is it the talk you talk to me?" asked Quintana, whose perplexed features began to darken. "Where is it, my packet?"

"I'm tellin' you, ain't I?" retorted the other, raising a voice now shrill with the strain of this new crisis rushing so unexpectedly upon him: "I heard Jake give a holler. 'What the hell's the trouble?' I yells. Then he lets out a beller, 'Save me!' he screeches, 'I'm into a sink-hole! The quicksand's got me,' sez he. So I drop my rifle, I did—there she stands against that birch sapling!—and I run down into them there pitcher-plants.

"'Whar be ye!' I yells. Then I listens, and don't hear nothin' only a kina wallerin' noise an' a slobber like he was gulpin' mud.

"Then I foller them there sounds and I come out by that sink-hole. The water was a-shakin' all over it but Jake he had went down plum out o' sight. T'want no use. I cut a sapling an' I poked down. I was sick and scared like, so when you come up over the moss, not makin' no noise, an' grabbed me—God!—I guess you'd jump, too."

Quintana's dark, tense face was expressionless when Leverett ventured to look at him. Like most liars he realised the advisability of looking his victim straight in the eyes. This he managed to accomplish, sustaining the cold intensity of Quintana's gaze as long as he deemed it necessary. Then he started toward his rifle. Quintana blocked his way.

"Where my packet?"

"Gol ram it! Ain't I told you? Jake had it in his pocket."

"My packet?"

"Yaas, yourn."

"My packet, it is down in thee sink 'ole?"

"You think I'm lyin'?" blustered Leverett, trying to move around Quintana's extended arm. The arm swerved and clutched him by the collar of his flannel shirt.

"Wait, my frien'," said Quintana in a soft voice. "You shall explain to me some things before you go."

"Explain what!—you gol dinged—"

Quintana shook him into speechlessness.

"Listen, my frien'," he continued with a terrifying smile, "I mus' ask you what it was, that gun-shot, which I hear while I await at Drown' Vallee. Eh? Who fire a gun?"

"I ain't heard no gun," replied Leverett in a strangled voice.

"You did not shoot? No?"

"No!—damn it all—"

"And Jake? He did not fire?"

"No, I tell yeh—"

"Ah! Someone lies. It is not me, my frien'. No. Let us examine your rifle—"

Leverett made a rush for the gun; Quintana slung him back against the oak tree and thrust an automatic pistol against his chin.

"Han's up, my frien'," he said gently, "—up! high up!—or someone will fire another shot you shall never hear.... So!... Now I search the other pocket.... So!... Still no packet. Bah! Not in the pants, either? Ah, bah! But wait! Tiens! What is this you hide inside your shirt—?"

"I was jokin'," gasped Leverett; "—I was jest a-goin' to give it to you—"

"Is that my packet?"

"Yes. It was all in fun; I wan't a-going to steal it—"

Quintana unbuttoned the grey wool shirt, thrust in his hand and drew forth the packet for which Jake Kloon had died within the hour.

Suddenly Leverett's knees gave way and he dropped to the ground, grovelling at Quintana's feet in an agony of fright:

"Don't hurt me," he screamed, "—I didn't meant no harm! Jake, he wanted me to steal it. I told him I was honest. I fired a shot to scare him, an' he tuk an' run off! I wan't a-goin' to steal it off you, so help me God! I was lookin' for you—as God is my witness—"

He got Quintana by one foot. Quintana kicked him aside and backed away.

"Swine," he said, calmly inspecting the whimpering creature who had started to crawl toward him.

He hesitated, lifted his automatic, then, as though annoyed by Leverett's deafening shriek, shrugged, hesitated, pocketed both pistol and packet, and turned on his heel.

By the birch sapling he paused and picked up Leverett's rifle. Something left a red smear on his palm as he worked the ejector. It was blood.

Quintana gazed curiously at his soiled hand. Then he stooped and picked up the empty cartridge case which had been ejected. And, as he stooped, he noticed more blood on a fallen leaf.

With one foot, daintily as a game-cock scratches, he brushed away the fallen leaves, revealing the mess underneath.

After he had contemplated the crimson traces of murder for a few moments, he turned and looked at Leverett with faint curiosity.

"So," he said in his leisurely, emotionless way, "you have fight with my frien' Jake for thee packet. Yes? Ver' amusing." He shrugged his indifference, tossed the rifle to his shoulder and, without another glance at the cringing creature on the ground, walked away toward Drowned Valley, unhurriedly.

III

When Quintana disappeared among the tamaracks, Leverett ventured to rise to his knees. As he crouched there, peering after Quintana, a man came swiftly out of the forest behind him and nearly stumbled over him.

Recognition was instant and mutual as the man jerked the trap-robber to his feet, stifling the muffled yell in his throat.

"I want that packet you picked up on Clinch's veranda," said Hal Smith.

"M-my God," stammered Leverett, "Quintana just took it off me. He ain't been gone a minute—"

"You lie!"

"I ain't lyin'. Look at his foot-marks there in the mud!"

"Quintana!"

"Yaas, Quintana! He tuk my gun, too—"

"Which way!" whispered Smith fiercely, shaking Leverett till his jaws wagged.

"Drowned Valley.... Lemme loose!—I'm chokin'—"

Smith pushed him aside.

"You rat," he said, "if you're lying to me I'll come back and settle your affair. And Kloon's, too!"

"Quintana shot Jake and stuck him into a sink-hole!" snivelled Leverett, breaking down and sobbing; "—oh, Gawd—Gawd—he's down under all that black mud with his brains spillin' out—"

But Smith was already gone, running lightly along the string of footprints which led straight away across slime and sphagnum toward the head of Drowned Valley.

In the first clump of hard-wood trees Smith saw Quintana. He had halted and he was fumbling at the twine which bound a flat, paper-wrapped packet.

He did not start when Smith's sharp warning struck his ear: "Don't move! I've got you over my rifle, Quintana!"

Quintana's fingers had instantly ceased operations. Then, warily, he lifted his head and looked into the muzzle of Smith's rifle.

"Ah, bah!" he said tranquilly. "There were three of you, then."

"Lay that packet on the ground."

"My frien'—"

"Drop it or I'll drop *you!*"

Quintana carefully placed the packet on a bed of vivid moss.

"Now your gun!" continued Smith.

Quintana shrugged and laid Leverett's rifle beside the packet.

"Kneel down with your hands up and your back toward me!" said Smith.

"My frien'—"

"Down with you!"

Quintana dropped gracefully into the humiliating attitude popularly indicative of prayerful supplication. Smith walked slowly up behind him, relieved him of two automatics and a dirk.

"Stay put," he said sharply, as Quintana started to turn his head. Then he picked up the packet with its loosened string, slipped it into his side pocket, gathered together the arsenal which had decorated Quintana, and so, loaded with weapons, walked away a few paces and seated himself on a fallen log.

Here he pocketed both automatics, shoved the sheathed dirk into his belt, placed the captured rifle handy, after examining the magazine, and laid his own weapon across his knees.

"You may turn around now, Quintana," he said amiably.

Quintana lowered his arms and started to rise.

"Sit down!" said Smith.

Quintana seated himself on the moss, facing Smith.

"Now, my gay and nimble thimble-rigger," said Smith genially, "while I take ten minutes' rest we'll have a little polite conversation. Or, rather, a monologue. Because I don't want to hear anything from you."

He settled himself comfortably on the log:

"Let me assemble for you, Señor Quintana, the interesting history of the jewels which so sparklingly repose in the packet in my pocket.

"In the first place, as you know, Monsieur Quintana, the famous Flaming Jewel and the other gems contained in this packet of mine, belonged to Her Highness the Grand Duchess Theodorica of Esthonia.

"Very interesting. More interesting still—along comes Don José Quintana and his celebrated gang of international thieves, and steals from the Grand Duchess of Esthonia the Flaming Jewel and all her rubies, emeralds and diamonds. Yes?"

"Certainly," said Quintana, with a polite inclination of acknowledgment.

"Bon! Well, then, still more interesting to relate, a gentleman named Clinch helps himself to these famous jewels. How very careless of you, Mr. Quintana."

"Careless, certainly," assented Quintana politely.

"Well," said Smith, laughing, "Clinch was more careless still. The robber baron, Sir Jacobus Kloon, swiped—as Froissart has it—the Esthonian gems, and, under agreement to deliver them to you, I suppose, thought better of it and attempted to abscond. Do you get me,

Herr Quintana?"

"Gewiss."

"Yes, and you got Jake Kloon, I hear," laughed Smith.

"No."

"Didn't you kill Kloon?"

"No."

"Oh, pardon. The mistake was natural. You merely robbed Kloon and Leverett. You should have killed them."

"Yes," said Quintana slowly, "I should have. It was my mistake."

"Signor Quintana, it is human for the human crook to err. Sooner or later he always does it. And then the Piper comes around holding out two itching palms."

"Mr. Smith," said Quintana pleasantly, "you are an unusually agreeable gentleman for a thief. I regret that you do not see your way to an amalgamation of interests with myself."

"As you say, Quintana mea, I am somewhat unusual. For example, what do you suppose I am going to do with this packet in my pocket?"

"Live," replied Quintana tersely.

"Live, certainly," laughed Smith, "but not on the proceeds of this coup-de-main. Non pas! I am going to return this packet to its rightful owner, the Grand Duchess Theodorica of Esthonia. And what do you think of that, Quintana?"

Quintana smiled.

"You do not believe me?" inquired Smith.

Quintana smiled again.

"Allons, bon!" exclaimed Smith, rising. "It's the unusual that happens in life, my dear Quintana. And now we'll take a little inventory of these marvellous gems before we part.... Sit very, very still, Quintana—unless you want to lie stiller still.... I'll let you take a modest peep at the Flaming Jewel—" busily unwrapping the packet—"just one little peep, Quintana—"

He unwrapped the paper. Two cakes of sugar-milk chocolate lay within.

Quintana turned white, then deeply, heavily red. Then he smiled in ghastly fashion:

"Yes," he said hoarsely, "as you have just said, sir, it is usually the unusual which happens in the world."

Episode Six
THE JEWEL AFLAME

I

Mike Clinch and his men "drove" Star Peak, and drew a blanket covert.

There was a new shanty atop, camp débris, plenty of signs of recent occupation everywhere—hot embers in which offal still smouldered, bottles odorous of claret dregs, and an aluminum culinary outfit, unwashed, as though Quintana and his men had departed in haste.

Far in the still valley below, Mike Clinch squatted beside the runway he had chosen, a cocked rifle across his knees.

The glare in his small, pale eyes waned and flared as distant sounds broke the forest silence, grew vague, died out—the fairy clatter of a falling leaf, the sudden scurry of a squirrel, a feathery rustle of swift wings in play or combat, the soft crash of a rotten bough sagging earthward to enrich the soil that grew it.

And, as Clinch squatted there, murderously intent, ever the fixed obsession burned in his fever brain, stirring his thin lips to incessant muttering—a sort of soundless invocation, part chronicle, part prayer:

"O God A'mighty, in your big, swell mansion up there, all has went contrary with me sence you let that there damn millionaire, Harrod, come into this here forest.... He went and built unto hisself an habitation, and he put up a wall of law all around me where I was earnin' a lawful livin' in Thy nice, clean wilderness.... And now comes this here Quintana and robs my girlie.... I promised her mother I'd make a lady of her little Eve.... I loved my wife, O Lord.... Once she showed me a piece in the Bible—I ain't never found it sence—but it said: 'And the woman she fled into the wilderness where there was a place prepared for her of God.' ... That's what *you* wrote into your own Bible, O God! You can't go back on it. I seen it.

"And now I wanta to ask, What place did you prepare for my Eve? What spot have you reference to? You didn't mean my 'Dump,' did you? Why, Lord, that ain't no place for no lady.... And now Quintana has went and robbed me of what I'd saved up for Eve.... Does that go with Thee, O Lord? No, it don't. And it don't go with me, neither. I'm a-goin' to git Quintana. Then I'm a-goin' to git them two minks that robbed my girlie—I am!... Jake Kloon, he done it in cahoots with Earl Leverett; and Quintana set 'em on. And they gotta die, O Lord of Israel, them there Egyptians is about to hop the twig.... I ain't aimin' to be mean to nobody.

I buy hootch of them that runs it. I eat mountain mutton in season and out. I trade with law-breakers, I do. But, Lord, I gotta get my girlie outa here; and Harrod he walled me in with the chariots and spears of Egypt, till I nigh went wild.... And now comes Quintana, and here I be a-lyin' out to get him so's my girlie can become a lady, same's them fine folks with all their butlers and automobiles and what-not—"

A far crash in the forest stilled his twitching lips and stiffened every iron muscle.

As he lifted his rifle, Sid Hone came into the glade.

"Yahoo! Yahoo!" he called. "Where be you, Mike?"

Clinch slowly rose, grasping his rifle, his small, grey eyes ablaze.

"Where's Quintana?" he demanded.

"H'ain't you seen nobody?"

"No."

In the intense silence other sounds broke sharply in the sunset forest; Harvey Chase's halloo rang out from the rocks above; Blommers and the Hastings boys came slouching through the ferns.

Byron Hastings greeted Clinch with upflung gun: "Me and Jim heard a shot away out on Drowned Valley," he announced. "Was you out that way, Mike?"

"No."

One by one the men who had driven Star Peak lounged up in the red sunset light, gathering around Clinch and wiping the sweat from sun-reddened faces.

"Someone's in Drowned Valley," repeated Byron. "Them minks slid off'n Star in a hurry, I reckon, judgin' how they left their shanty. Phew! It stunk! They had French hootch, too."

"Mebby Leverett and Kloon told 'em we was fixin' to visit them," suggested Blommers.

"They didn't know," said Clinch.

"Where's Hal Smith?" inquired Hone.

Clinch made no reply. Blommers silently gnawed a new quid from the remains of a sticky plug.

"Well," inquired Jim Hastings finally, "do we quit, Mike, or do we still-hunt in Drowned Valley?"

"Not me, at night," remarked Blommers drily.

"Not amongst them sink-holes," added Hone.

Suddenly Clinch turned and stared at him. Then the deadly light from his little eyes shone on the others one by one.

"Boys," he said, "I gotta get Quintana. I can't never sleep another wink till I get that man. Come on. Act up like gents all. Let's go."

Nobody stirred.

"Come on," repeated Clinch softly. But his lips shrank back, twitching. As they looked at him they saw his teeth.

"All right, all right," growled Hone, shouldering his rifle with a jerk.

The Hastings boys, young and rash, shuffled into the trail. Blommers hesitated, glanced askance at Clinch, and instantly made up his mind to take a chance with the sink-holes rather than with Clinch.

"God A'mighty, Mike, what be you aimin' to do?" faltered Harvey.

"I'm aimin' to stop the inlet and outlet to Drowned Valley, Harve," replied Clinch in his pleasant voice. "God is a-goin' to deliver Quintana into my hands."

"All right. What next?"

"Then," continued Clinch, "I cal'late to set down and wait."

"How long?"

"Ask God, boys. I don't know. All I know is that whatever is livin' in Drowned Valley at this hour has gotta live and die there. For it can't never live to come outen that there morass walkin' onto two legs like a real man."

He moved slowly along the file of sullen men, his rifle a-trail in one huge fist.

"Boys," he said, "I got first. There ain't no sink-hole deep enough to drowned me while Eve needs me.... And my little girlie needs me bad.... After she gits what's her'n, then I don't care no more...." He looked up into the sky, where the last ashes of sunset faded from the zenith.... "Then I don't care," he murmured. "Like's not I'll creep away like some shot-up critter, n'kinda find some lone, safe spot, n'kinda fix me f'r a long nap.... I guess that'll be the way ... when Eve's a lady down to Noo York 'r'som'ers—" he added vaguely.

Then, still looking up at the fading heavens, he moved forward, head lifted, silent, unhurried, with the soundless, stealthy, and certain tread of those who walk unseeing and asleep.

II

Clinch had not taken a dozen strides before Hal Smith loomed up ahead in the rosy dusk, driving in Leverett before him.

An exclamation of fierce exultation burst from Clinch's thin lips as he flung out one arm, indicating Smith and his clinking prisoner:

"Who was that gol-dinged catamount that suspicioned Hal? I wa'nt worried none, neither. Hal's a gent. Mebbe he sticks up folks, too, but he's a gent. And gents is honest or they ain't gents."

Smith came up at his easy, tireless gait, hustling Leverett along with prods from gun-butt or muzzle, as came handiest.

The prisoner turned a ghastly visage on Clinch, who ignored him.

"Got my packet, Hal?" he demanded.

Smith poked Leverett with his rifle: "Tune up," he said; "tell Clinch your story."

As a caged rat looks death in the face, his ratty wits working like lightning and every atom of cunning and ferocity alert for attack or escape, so the little, mean eyes of Earl Leverett became fixed on Clinch like two immobile and glassy beads of jet.

"G'wan," said Clinch softly, "spit it out."

"Jake done it," muttered Leverett, thickly.

"Done what?"

"Stole that there packet o' yourn—whatever there was into it."

"Who put him up to it?"

"A fella called Quintana."

"What was there in it for Jake?" inquired Clinch pleasantly.

"Ten thousand."

"How about you?"

"I told 'em I wouldn't touch it. Then they pulled their guns on me, and I was scared to squeal."

"So that was the way?" asked Clinch in his even, reassuring voice.

Leverett's eyes travelled stealthily around the circle of men, then reverted to Clinch.

"I dassn't touch it," he said, "but I dassn't squeal.... I was huntin' onto Drowned Valley when Jake meets up with me."

"'I got the packet,' he sez, 'and I'm a-going to double criss-cross Quintana, I am, and beat it. Don't you wish you was whacks with me?'

"'No,' sez I, 'honesty is my policy, no matter what they tell about me. S'help me God, I ain't never robbed no trap and I ain't no skin thief, whatever lies folks tell. All I ever done was run a little hootch, same's everybody.'"

He licked his lips furtively, his cold, bright eyes fastened on Clinch.

"G'wan, Earl," nodded the latter, "heave her up."

"That's all. I sez, 'Good-bye, Jake. An' if you heed my warnin', ill-gotten gains ain't a-going to prosper nobody.' That's what I said to Jake Kloon, the last solemn words I spoke to that there man now in his bloody grave—"

"Hey?" demanded Clinch.

"That's where Jake is," repeated Leverett. "Why, so help me, I wa'nt gone ten yards when, bang! goes a gun, and I see this here Quintana come outen the bush, I do, and walk up to Jake and frisk him, and Jake still a-kickin' the moss to slivers. Yessir, that's what I seen."

"G'wan."

"Yessir.... 'N'then Quintana he shoved Jake into a sink-hole. Thaswot I seen with my two eyes. Yessir. 'N'then Quintana he run off, 'n'I jest set down in the trail, I did; 'n'then Hal come up and acted like I had stole your packet, he did; 'n'then I told him what Quintana done. 'N'Hal, he takes after Quintana, but I don't guess he meets up with him, for he come back and ketched holt o' me, 'n'he druv me in like I was a caaf, he did. 'N'here I be."

The dusk in the forest had deepened so that the men's faces had become mere blotches of grey.

Smith said to Clinch: "That's his story, Mike. But I preferred he should tell it to you himself, so I brought him along.... Did you drive Star Peak?"

"There wa'nt nothin' onto it," said Clinch very softly. Then, of a sudden, his shadowy visage became contorted and he jerked up his rifle and threw a cartridge into the magazine.

"You dirty louse!" he roared at Leverett, "you was into this, too, a-robbin' my little Eve—"

"Run!" yelled somebody, giving Leverett a violent shove into the woods.

In the darkness and confusion, Clinch shouldered his way out of the circle and fired at the crackling noise that marked Leverett's course—fired again, lower, and again as a distant crash revealed the frenzied flight of the trap-robber. After he had fired a fourth shot, somebody struck up his rifle.

"Aw," said Jim Hastings, "that ain't no good. You act up like a kid, Mike. 'Tain't so far to Ghost Lake, n'them Troopers might hear you."

After a silence, Clinch spoke, his voice heavy with reaction:

"Into that there packet is my little girl's dower. It's all I got to give her. It's all she's got to make her a lady. I'll kill any man that robs her or that helps rob her. 'N'that's that."

"Are you going on after Quintana?" asked Smith.

"I am. 'N'these fellas are a-going with me. N' I want you should go back to my Dump and look after my girlie while I'm gone."

"How long are you going to be away?"

"I dunno."

There was a silence. Then,

"All right," said Smith, briefly. He added: "Look out for sink-holes, Mike."

Clinch tossed his heavy rifle to his shoulder: "Let's go," he said in his pleasant, misleading way, "—and I'll shoot the guts outa any fella that don't show up at roll call."

III

For its size there is no fiercer animal than a rat.

Rat-like rage possessed Leverett. In his headlong flight through the dusk, fear, instead of quenching, added to his rage; and he ran on and on, crashing through the undergrowth, made wilder by the pain of vicious blows from branches which flew back and struck him in the dark.

Thorns bled him; unseen logs tripped him; he heard Clinch's bullets whining around him; and he ran on, beginning to sob and curse in a frenzy of fury, fear, and shame.

Shots from Clinch's rifle ceased; the fugitive dropped into a heavy, shuffling walk, slavering, gasping, gesticulating with his weaponless fists in the darkness.

"Gol ram ye, I'll fix ye!" he kept stammering in his snarling, jangling voice, broken by sobs. "I'll learn ye, yeh poor danged thing, gol ram ye—"

An unseen limb struck him cruelly across the face, and a moose-bush tripped him flat. Almost crazed, he got up, yelling in his pain, one hand wet and sticky from blood welling up from his cheek-bone.

He stood listening, infuriated, vindictive, but heard nothing save the panting, animal sounds in his own throat.

He strove to see in the ghostly obscurity around him, but could make out little except the trees close by.

But wood-rats are never completely lost in their native darkness; and Leverett presently discovered the far stars shining faintly through rifts in the phantom foliage above.

These heavenly signals were sufficient to give him his directions. Then the question suddenly came, *which* direction?

To his own shack on Stinking Lake he dared not go. He tried to believe that it was fear of Clinch that made him shy of the home shanty; but, in his cowering soul, he knew it was fear of another kind—the deep, superstitious horror of Jake Kloon's empty bunk—the repugnant sight of Kloon's spare clothing hanging from its peg—the dead man's shoes—

No, he could not go to Stinking Lake and sleep.... And wake with the faint stench of sulphur in his throat.... And see the worm-like leeches unfolding in the shallows, and the big, reddish water-lizards, livid as skinned eels, wriggling convulsively toward their sunless lairs....

At the mere thought of his dead bunk-mate he sought relief in vindictive rage—stirred up the smouldering embers again, cursed Clinch and Hal Smith, violently searching in his inflamed brain some instant vengeance upon these men who had driven him out from the only place on earth where he knew how to exist—the wilderness.

All at once he thought of Clinch's step-daughter. The thought instantly scared him. Yet—what a revenge!—to strike Clinch through the only creature he cared for in all the world!... What a revenge!... Clinch was headed for Drowned Valley. Eve Strayer was alone at the Dump.... Another thought flashed like lightning across his turbid mind;—*the packet!*

Bribed by Quintana, Jake Kloon, lurking at Clinch's door, had heard him direct Eve to take a packet to Owl Marsh, and had notified Quintana.

Wittingly or unwittingly, the girl had taken a packet of sugar-milk chocolate instead of the priceless parcel expected.

Again, carried in, exhausted, by a State Trooper, Jake Kloon had been fooled; and it was the packet of sugar-milk chocolate that Jake had purloined from the veranda where Clinch kicked it. For two cakes of chocolate Kloon had died. For two cakes of chocolate he, Earl Leverett, had become a man-slayer, a homeless fugitive in peril of his life.

He stood licking his blood-dried lips there in the darkness, striving to hatch courage out of the dull fury eating at a coward's heart.

Somewhere in Clinch's Dump was the packet that would make him rich.... Here was his opportunity. He had only to dare; and pain and poverty and fear—above all else *fear* —would end forever!...

When, at last, he came out to the edge of Clinch's clearing, the dark October heavens were but a vast wilderness of stars.

Star Pond, set to its limpid depths with the heavenly gems, glittered and darkled with its million diamond incrustations. The humped-up lump of Clinch's Dump crouched like some huge and feeding night-beast on the bank, ringed by the solemn forest.

There was a kerosene lamp burning in Eve Strayer's rooms. Another light—a candle—flickered in the kitchen.

Leverett, crouching, ran rat-like down to the barn, slid in between the ice house and corn-crib, crawled out among the wilderness of weeds and lay flat.

The light burned steadily from Eve's window.

IV

From his form among frost-blackened rag-weeds, the trap-robber could see only the plastered ceiling of the bed chamber.

But the kerosene lamp cast two shadows on that—tall shadows of human shapes that stirred at times.

The trap-robber, scared, stiffened to immobility, but his little eyes remained fastened on the camera obscura above. All the cunning, patience, and murderous immobility of the rat were his.

Not a weed stirred under the stars where he lay with tiny, unwinking eyes intent upon the shadows on the ceiling.

The shadows on the ceiling were cast by Eve Strayer and her State Trooper.

Eve sat on her bed's edge, swathed in a lilac silk kimona—delicate relic of school days. Her bandaged feet, crossed, dangled above the rag-rug on the floor; her slim, tanned fingers were interlaced over the book on her lap.

Near the door stood State Trooper Stormont, spurred, booted, trig and trim, an undecided and flushed young man, fumbling irresolutely with the purple cord on his campaign-hat.

The book on Eve's knees—another relic of the past—was *Sigurd the Volsung* . Stormont had been reading to her—they having found, after the half shy tentatives of new friends, a point d'appui in literature. And the girl, admitting a passion for the poets, invited him to inspect the bookcase of unpainted pine which Clinch had built into her bedroom wall.

Here it was he discovered mutual friends among the nobler Victorians—surprised to discover *Sigurd* there—and, carrying it to her bedside, looked leisurely through the half forgotten pages.

"Would you read a little?" she ventured.

He blushed but did his best. His was an agreeable, boyish voice, betraying taste and understanding. Time passed quickly—not so much in the reading but in the conversations intervening.

And now, made uneasy by chance consultation with his wrist-watch, and being rather a conscientious young man, he had risen and had informed Eve that she ought to go to sleep.

And she had denounced the idea, almost fretfully.

"Even if you go I shan't sleep till daddy comes," she said. "Of course," she added, smiling at him out of gentian-blue eyes, "if *you* are sleepy I shouldn't dream of asking you to stay."

"I'm not intending to sleep."

"What are you going to do?"

"Take a chair on the landing outside your door."

"What!"

"Certainly. What did you expect me to do, Eve?"

"Go to bed, of course. The beds in the guest rooms are all made up."

"Your father didn't expect me to do that," he said, smiling.

"I'm not afraid, as long as you're in the house," she said.

She looked up at him again, wistfully. Perhaps he was restless, bored, sitting there beside her half the day, and, already, half the night. Men of that kind—active, nervous young men accustomed to the open, can't stand caging.

"I want you to go out and get some fresh air," she said. "It's a wonderful night. Go and walk a while. And—if you feel like—coming back to me—"

"Will you sleep?"

"No, I'll wait for you."

Her words were natural and direct, but in their simplicity there seemed a delicate sweetness that stirred him.

"I'll come back to you," he said.

Then, in his response, the girl in her turn became aware of something beside the simple words—a vague charm about them that faintly haunted her after he had gone away down the stairs.

That was the man she had once tried to kill! At the sudden and terrible recollection she shivered from curly head to bandaged feet. Then she trembled a little with the memory of his lips against her bruised hands—bruised by handcuffs which he had fastened upon her.

She sat very, very still now, huddled on the bed's edge, scarcely breathing.

For the girl was beginning to dare formulate the deepest of any thoughts that ever had stirred her virgin mind and body.

If it was love, then it had come suddenly, and strangely. It had come on that day—at the very moment when he flung her against the tree and handcuffed her—that terrible instant—if it were love.

Or—what was it that so delicately overwhelmed her with pleasure in his presence, in his voice, in the light, firm sound of his spurred tread on the veranda below?

Friendship? A lonely passion for young and decent companionship? The clean youth of him in contrast to the mangy, surly louts who haunted Clinch's Dump—was that the appeal?

Listening there where she sat clasping the book, she heard his steady tread patrolling the veranda; caught the faint fragrance of his brier pipe in the still night air.

"I think—I think it's—love," she said under her breath.... "But he couldn't ever think of me—" always listening to his spurred tread below.

After a while she placed both bandaged feet on the rug. It hurt her, but she stood up, walked to the open window. She wanted to look at him—just a moment—

By chance he looked up at that instant, and saw her pale face, like a flower in the starlight.

"Why, Eve," he said, "you ought not to be on your feet."

"Once," she said, "you weren't so particular about my bruises."

Her breathless little voice coming down through the starlight thrilled him.

"Do you remember what I did?" he asked.

"Yes. You bruised my hands and made my mouth bleed."

"I did penance—for your hands."

"Yes, you kissed *them!*"

What possessed her—what irresponsible exhilaration was inciting her to a daring utterly foreign to her nature? She heard herself laugh, knew that she was young, pretty, capable of provocation. And in a sudden, breathless sort of way an overwhelming desire seized her to please, to charm, to be noticed by such a man—whatever, on afterthought, he might think of the step-child of Mike Clinch.

Stormont had come directly under her window and stood looking up.

"I dared not offer further penance," he said.

The emotion in his voice stirred her—but she was still laughing down at him.

She said: "You *did* offer further penance—you offered your handkerchief. So—as that was *all* you offered as reparation for—my lips—"

"Eve! I could have taken you into my arms—"

"You *did!* And threw me down among the spruces. You really did everything that a contrite heart could suggest—"

"Good heavens!" said that rather matter-of-fact young man, "I don't believe you have forgiven me after all."

"I have—everything except the handkerchief—"

"Then I'm coming up to complete my penance—"

"I'll lock my door!"

"Would you?"

"I ought to.... But if you are in great spiritual distress, and if you really and truly repent, and if you humbly desire to expiate your sin by doing—penance—" And hesitated: "Do you so desire?"

"Yes, I do."

"Humbly? Contritely?"

"Yes."

"Very well. Say 'Mea culpa, mea maxima culpa.'"

"Mea maxima culpa," he said so earnestly, looking up into her face that she bent lower over the sill to see him.

"Let me come up, Eve," he said.

She strove to laugh, gazing down into his shadowy face—but suddenly the desire had left her—and all her gaiety left her, too, suddenly, leaving only a still excitement in her breast.

"You—you knew I was just laughing," she said unsteadily. "You understood, didn't you?"

"I don't know."

After a silence: "I didn't mean you to take me seriously," she said. She tried to laugh. It was no use. And, as she leaned there on the sill, her heart frightened her with its loud beating.

"Will you let me come up, Eve?"

No answer.

"Would you lock your door?"

"What do you think I'd do?" she asked tremulously.

"You know; I don't."

"Are you so sure I know what I'd do? I don't think either of us know our own minds.... I seem to have lost some of my wits.... Somehow...."

"If you are not going to sleep, let me come up."

"I want you to take a walk down by the pond. And while you're walking there all by yourself, I want you to think very clearly, very calmly, and make up your mind whether I should remain awake tonight, or whether, when you return, I ought to be asleep and—and my door bolted."

After a long pause: "All right," he said in a low voice.

V

She saw him walk away—saw his shadowy, well-built form fade into the starlit mist.

An almost uncontrollable impulse set her throat and lips quivering with desire to call to him through the night, "I do love you! I do love you! Come back quickly, quickly!—"

Fog hung over Star Pond, edging the veranda, rising in frail shreds to her window. The lapping of the water sounded very near. An owl was very mournful in the hemlocks.

The girl turned from the window, looked at the door for a moment, then her face flushed and she walked toward a chair and seated herself, leaving the door unbolted.

For a little while she sat upright, alert, as though a little frightened. After a few moments she folded her hands and sat unstirring, with lowered head, awaiting Destiny.

It came, noiselessly. And so swiftly that the rush of air from her violently opened door was what first startled her.

For in the same second Earl Leverett was upon her in his stockinged feet, one bony hand gripping her mouth, the other flung around her, pinning both arms to her sides.

"The packet!" he panted, "—quick, yeh dirty little cat, 'r'I'll break yeh head off'n yeh damn neck!"

She bit at the hand that he held crushed against her mouth. He lifted her bodily, flung her onto the bed, and, twisting sheet and quilt around her, swathed her to the throat.

Still controlling her violently distorted lips with his left hand and holding her so, one knee upon her, he reached back, unsheathed his hunting knife, and pricked her throat till the blood spurted.

"Now, gol ram yeh!" he whispered fiercely, "where's Mike's packet? Yell, and I'll hog-stick yeh fur fair! Where is it, you dum thing!"

He took his left hand from her mouth. The distorted, scarlet lips writhed back, displaying her white teeth clenched.

"Where's Mike's bundle!" he repeated, hoarse with rage and fear.

"You rat!" she gasped.

At that he closed her mouth again, and again he pricked her with his knife, cruelly. The blood welled up onto the sheets.

"Now, by God!" he said in a ghastly voice, "answer or I'll hog-stick yeh next time! Where is it? Where! Where!"

She only showed her teeth in answer. Her eyes flamed.

"Where! Quick! Gol ding yeh, I'll shove this knife in behind your ear if you don't tell! Go on. Where is it? It's in this Dump som'ers. I know it is—don't lie! You want that I should stick you good? That what you want—you dirty little dump-slut? Well, then, gol ram yeh—I'll fix yeh like Quintana was aimin' at—"

He slit the sheet downward from her imprisoned knees, seized one wounded foot and tried to slash the bandages.

"I'll cut a coupla toes off'n yeh," he snarled, "—I'll hamstring yeh fur keeps!"—struggling to mutilate her while she flung her helpless and entangled body from side to side and bit at the hand that was almost suffocating her.

Unable to hold her any longer, he seized a pillow, to bury the venomous little head that writhed, biting, under his clutch.

As he lifted it he saw a packet lying under it.

"By God!" he panted.

As he seized it she screamed for the first time: "Jack! Jack Stormont!"—and fairly hurled her helpless little body at Leverett, striking him full in the face with her head.

Half stunned, still clutching the packet, he tried to stab her in the stomach; but the armour of bed-clothes turned the knife, although his violence dashed all breath out of her.

Sick with the agony of it, speechless, she still made the effort; and, as he stumbled to his feet and turned to escape, she struggled upright, choking, blood running from the knife pricks in her neck.

With the remnant of her strength, and still writhing and gasping for breath, she tore herself from the sheets and blankets, reeled across the room to where Stormont's rifle stood, threw in a cartridge, dragged herself to the window.

Dimly she saw a running figure in the night mist, flung the rifle across the window sill and fired. Then she fired again—or thought she did. There were two shots.

"Eve!" came Stormont's sharp cry, "what the devil are you trying to do to me?"

His cry terrified her; the rifle clattered to the floor.

The next instant he came running up the stairs, bare headed, heavy pistol swinging, and halted, horrified at sight of her.

"Eve! My God!" he whispered, taking her blood-wet body into his arms.

"Go after Leverett," she gasped. "He's robbed daddy. He's running away—out there—somewhere—"

"Where did he hurt you, Eve—my little Eve—"

"Oh, go! go!" she wailed—"I'm not hurt. He only pricked me with his knife. I'm not hurt, I tell you. Go after him! Take your pistol and follow him and kill him!"

"Oh," she cried hysterically, twisting and sobbing in his arms, "don't lose time here with me! Don't stand here while he's running away with dad's money!" And, "Oh—oh—*oh!!*" she sobbed, collapsing in his arms and clinging to him convulsively as he carried her to her tumbled bed and laid her there.

He said: "I couldn't risk following anybody now, after what has happened to you. I can't leave you alone here! Don't cry, Eve. I'll get your man for you, I promise! Don't cry, dear. It was all my fault for leaving this room even for a minute—"

"No, no, no! It's my fault. I sent you away. Oh, I wish I hadn't. I wish I had let you come back when you wanted to.... I was waiting for you.... I left the door unbolted for you. When it opened I thought it was you. And it was Leverett!—it was Leverett!—"

Stormont's face grew very white: "What did he do to you, Eve? Tell me, darling. What did he do to you?"

"Dad's money was under my pillow," she wailed. "Leverett tried to make me tell where it was. I wouldn't, and he hurt me—"

"How?"

"He pricked me with his knife. When I screamed for you he tried to choke me with the pillow. Didn't you hear me scream?"

"Yes. I came on the jump."

"It was too late," she sobbed; "—too late! He saw the money packet under my pillow and he snatched it and ran. Somehow I found your rifle and fired. I fired twice."

Her only bullet had torn his campaign hat from his head. But he did not tell her.

"Let me see your neck," he said, bending closer.

She bared her throat, making a soft, vague complaint like a hurt bird—lay there whimpering under her breath while he bathed the blood away with lint, sterilised the two cuts from his emergency packet, and bound them.

He was still bending low over her when her blue eyes unclosed on his.

"That is the second time I've tried to kill you," she whispered. "I thought it was Leverett.... I'd have died if I had killed you."

There was a silence.

"Lie very still," he said huskily. "I'll be back in a moment to rebandage your feet and make you comfortable for the night."

"I can't sleep," she repeated desolately. "Dad trusted his money to me and I've let Leverett rob me. How can I sleep?"

"I'll bring you something to make you sleep."

"I can't!"

"I promise you you will sleep. Lie still."

He rose, went away downstairs and out to the barn, where his campaign hat lay in the weed, drilled through by a bullet.

There was something else lying there in the weeds—a flat, muddy, shoeless shape sprawling grotesquely in the foggy starlight.

One hand clutched a hunting knife; the other a packet.

Stormont drew the packet from the stiff fingers, then turned the body over, and, flashing his electric torch, examined the ratty visage—what remained of it—for his pistol bullet had crashed through from ear to cheek-bone, almost obliterating the trap-robber's features.

Stormont came slowly into Eve's room and laid the packet on the sheet beside her.

"Now," he said, "there is no reason for you to lie awake any longer. I'll fix you up for the night."

Deftly he unbandaged, bathed, dressed, and rebandaged her slim white feet—little wounded feet so lovely, so exquisite that his hand trembled as he touched them.

"They're doing fine," he said cheerily. "You've half a degree of fever and I'm going to give you something to drink before you go to sleep—"

He poured out a glass of water, dissolved two tablets, supported her shoulders while she drank in a dazed way, looking always at him over the glass.

"Now," he said, "go to sleep. I'll be on the job outside your door until your daddy arrives."

"How did you get back dad's money?" she asked in an odd, emotionless way as though too weary for further surprises.

"I'll tell you in the morning."

"Did you kill him? I didn't hear your pistol."

"I'll tell you all about it in the morning. Good night, Eve."

As he bent over her, she looked up into his eyes and put both arms around his neck.

It was her first kiss given to any man, except Mike Clinch.

After Stormont had gone out and closed the door, she lay very still for a long while.

Then, instinctively, she touched her lips with her fingers; and, at the contact, a blush clothed her from brow to ankle.

The Flaming Jewel in its morocco casket under her pillow burned with no purer fire than the enchanted flame glowing in the virgin heart of Eve Strayer of Clinch's Dump.

Thus they lay together, two lovely flaming jewels burning softly, steadily through the misty splendour of the night.

Under a million stars, Death sprawled in squalor among the trampled weeds. Under the same high stars dark mountains waited; and there was a silvery sound of waters stirring somewhere in the mist.

EPISODE SEVEN
CLINCH'S DUMP

I

When Mike Clinch bade Hal Smith return to the Dump and take care of Eve, Smith already had decided to go there.

Somewhere in Clinch's Dump was hidden the Flaming Jewel. Now was his time to search for it.

There were two other reasons why he should go back. One of them was that Leverett was loose. If anything had called Trooper Stormont away, Eve would be alone in the house. And nobody on earth could forecast what a coward like Leverett might attempt.

But there was another and more serious reason for returning to Clinch's. Clinch, blood-mad, was headed for Drowned Valley with his men, to stop both ends of that vast morass before Quintana and his gang could get out.

It was evident that neither Clinch nor any of his men—although their very lives depended upon familiarity with the wilderness—knew that a third exit from Drowned Valley existed.

But the nephew of the late Henry Harrod knew.

When Jake Kloon was a young man and Darragh was a boy, Kloon had shown him the rocky, submerged game trail into Drowned Valley. Doubtless Kloon had used it in hootch running since. If ever he had told anybody else about it, probably he had revealed the trail to Quintana.

And that was why Darragh, or Hal Smith, finally decided to return to Star Pond;—because if Quintana had been told or had discovered that circuitous way out of Drowned Valley, he might go straight to Clinch's Dump.... And, supposing Stormont was still there, how long could one State Trooper stand off Quintana's gang?

No sooner had Clinch and his motley followers disappeared in the dusk than Smith unslung his basket-pack, fished out a big electric torch, flashed it tentatively, and then, reslinging the pack and taking his rifle in his left hand, he set off at an easy swinging stride.

His course was not toward Star Pond; it was at right angles with that trail. For he was taking no chances. Quintana might already have left Drowned Valley by that third exit unknown to Clinch.

Smith's course would now cut this unmarked trail, trodden only by game that left no sign in the shallow mountain rivulet which was the path.

The trail lay a long way off through the night. But if Quintana had discovered and taken that trail, it would be longer still for him—twice as long as the regular trail out.

For a mile or two the forest was first growth pine, and sufficiently open so that Smith might economise on his torch.

He knew every foot of it. As a boy he had carried a jacob-staff in the Geological Survey. Who better than the forest-roaming nephew of Henry Harrod should know this blind wilderness?

The great pines towered on every side, lofty and smooth to the feathery canopy that crowned them under the high stars.

There was no game here, no water, nothing to attract anybody except the devastating lumberman. But this was a five thousand acre patch of State land. The ugly whine of the steam-saw would never be heard here.

On he walked at an easy, swinging stride, flashing his torch rarely, feeling no concern about discovery by Quintana's people.

It was only when he came into the hardwoods that the combined necessity for caution and torch perplexed and worried him.

Somewhere in here began an outcrop of rock running east for miles. Only stunted cedar and berry bushes found shallow nourishment on this ridge.

When at last he found it he travelled upon it, more slowly, constantly obliged to employ the torch.

After an hour, perhaps, his feet splashed in shallow water. *That* was what he was expecting. The water was only an inch or two deep; it was ice cold and running north.

Now, he must advance with every caution. For here trickled the thin flow of that rocky rivulet which was the other entrance and exit penetrating that immense horror of marsh and bog and depthless sink-hole known as Drowned Valley.

For a long while he did not dare to use his torch; but now he was obliged to.

He shined the ground at his feet, elevated the torch with infinite precaution, throwing a fan-shaped light over the stretch of sink he had suspected and feared. It flanked the flat, wet path of rock on either side. Here Death spread its slimy trap at his very feet.

Then, as he stood taking his bearings with burning torch, far ahead in the darkness a light flashed, went out, flashed twice more, and was extinguished.

Quintana!

Smith's wits were working like lightning, but instinct guided him before his brain took command. He levelled his torch and repeated the three signal flashes. Then, in darkness, he came to swift conclusion.

There were no other signals from the unknown. The stony bottom of the rivulet was his only aid.

In his right hand the torch hung almost touching the water. At times he ventured sufficient pressure for a feeble glimmer, then again trusted to his sense of contact.

For three hundred yards, counting his strides, he continued on. Then, in total darkness, he pocketed the torch, slid a cartridge into the breech of his rifle, slung the weapon, pulled out a handkerchief, and tied it across his face under the eyes.

Now, he drew the torch from his pocket, levelled it, sent three quick flashes out into darkness.

Instantly, close ahead, three blinding flashes broke out.

For Hal Smith it all had become a question of seconds.

Death lay depthless on either hand; ahead Death blocked the trail in silence.

Out of the dark some unseen rifle might vomit death in his very face at any moment.

He continued to move forward. After a little while his ear caught a slight splash ahead. Suddenly a glare of light enveloped him.

"Is it you, Harry Beck?"

Instinct led again while wits worked madly: "Harry Beck is two miles back on guard. Where is Sard?"

The silence became terrible. Once the glaring light in front moved, then become fixed. There was a light splashing. Instantly Smith realised that the man in front had set his torch in a tree-crotch and was now cowering somewhere behind a levelled weapon. His voice came presently:

"Hé! Drap-a that-a gun damn quick!"

Smith bent, leisurely, and laid his rifle on a mossy rock.

"Now! You there! Why you want Sard! Eh?"

"I'll tell Sard, not you," retorted Smith coolly. "You listen to me, whoever you are. I'm from Sard's office in New York. I'm Abrams. The police are on their way here to find Quintana."

"How I know? Eh? Why shall I believe that? You tell-a me queeck or I blow-a your damn head off!"

"Quintana will blow-a *your* head off unless you take me to Sard," drawled Smith.

A movement might have meant death, but he calmly rummaged for a cigarette, lighted it, blew a cloud insolently toward the white glare ahead. Then he took another chance:

"I guess you're Nick Salzar, aren't you?"

"Si! I am Salzar. Who the dev' are you?"

"I'm Eddie Abrams, Sard's lawyer. My business is to find my client. If you stop me you'll go to prison—the whole gang of you—Sard, Quintana, Picquet, Sanchez, Georgiades and Harry Beck—and *you!*"

After a dead silence: "Maybe *you'll* go to the chair, too!"

It was the third chance he took.

There was a dreadful stillness in the woods. Finally came a slight series of splashes; the crunch of heavy boots on rock.

"For why you com-a here, eh?" demanded Salzar, in a less aggressive manner. "What-a da matt', eh?"

"Well," said Smith, "if you've got to know, there are people from Esthonia in New York.... If you understand that."

"Christi! When do they arrive?"

"A week ago. Sard's place is in the hands of the police. I couldn't stop them. They've got his safe and all his papers. City, State, and Federal officers are looking for him. The Constabulary rode into Ghost Lake yesterday. Now, don't you think you'd better lead me to Sard?"

"Cristi!" exclaimed Salzar. "Sard he is a mile ahead with the others. Damn! Damn! Me, how should I know what is to be done? Me, I have my orders from Quintana. What I do, eh? Cristi! What to do? What you say I should do, eh, Abrams?"

A new fear had succeeded the old one—that was evident—and Salzar came forward into the light of his own fixed torch—a well-knit figure in slouch hat, grey shirt, and grey breeches, and wearing a red bandanna over the lower part of his face. He carried a heavy rifle.

He came on, sturdily, splashing through the water, and walked up to Smith, his rifle resting on his right shoulder.

"For me," he said excitedly, "long time I have worry in this-a damn wood! Si! Where you say those carbinieri? Eh?"

"At Ghost Lake. *Your* signature is in the hotel ledger."

"Cristi! You know where Clinch is?"

"You know, too. He is on the way to Drowned Valley."

"Damn! I knew it. Quintana also. You know where is Quintana? And Sard? I tell-a you. They march ver' fast to the Dump of Clinch. Si! And there they would discover these-a beeg-a dimon'—these-a Flame-Jewel. Si! *Now*, you tell-a me what I do?"

Smith said slowly: "If Quintana is marching on Clinch's he's marching into a trap!"

Salzar blanched above his bandanna.

"The State Troopers are there," said Smith. "They'll get him sure."

"Cristi," faltered Salzar, "—then they are gobble—Quintana, Sard, everybody! Si?"

Smith considered the man: "You can save *your* skin anyway. You can go back and tell Harry Beck. Then both of you can beat it for Drowned Valley."

He picked up his rifle, stood a moment in troubled reflection:

"If I could overtake Quintana I'd do it," he said. "I think I'll try. If I can't, he's done for. You tell Harry Beck that Eddie Abrams advises him to beat it for Drowned Valley."

Suddenly Salzar tore the bandanna from his face, flung it down and stamped on it.

"What I tell Quintana!" he yelled, his features distorted with rage. "I don't-a like!—no, not me!—no, I tell-a heem, stay at those Ghost-a Lake and watch thees-a fellow Clinch. Si! Not for me thees-a wood. No! I spit upon it! I curse like hell! I tell Quintana I don't-a like. Now, eet is trouble that comes and we lose-a out! Damn! *Damn!* Me, I find me Beck. You shall say to José Quintana how he is a damfool. Me, I am finish—

me, Nick Salzar! You hear me, Abrams! I am through! I go!"

He glared at Smith, started to move, came back and took his torch, made a violent gesture with it which drenched the woods with goblin light.

"You stop-a Quintana, maybe. You tell-a heem he is the bigg-a fool! You tell-a heem Nick Salzar is no damn fool. No! Adios, my frien' Abrams. I beat it. I save my skin!"

Once more Salzar turned and headed for Drowned Valley.... Where Clinch would not fail to kill him.... The man was going to his death.... And it was Smith who sent him.

Suddenly it came to Smith that he could not do this thing; that this man had no chance; that he was slaying a human being with perfect safety to himself and without giving him a chance.

"Salzar!" he called sharply.

The man halted and looked around.

"Come back!"

Salzar hesitated, turned finally, slouched toward him.

Smith laid aside his pack and rifle, and, as Salzar came up, he quietly took his weapon from him and laid it beside his own.

"What-a da matt'?" demanded Salzar, astonished. "Why you taka my gun?"

Smith measured him. They were well matched.

"Set your torch in that crotch," he said.

Salzar, puzzled and impatient, demanded to know why. Smith took both torches, set them opposite each other and drew Salzar into the white glare.

"Now," he said, "you dirty desperado, I am going to try to kill you clean. Look out for yourself!"

For a second Salzar stood rooted in blank astonishment.

"I'm one of Clinch's men," said Smith, "but I can't stick a knife in your back, at that! Now, take care of yourself if you can—"

His voice died in his throat; Salzar was on him, clawing, biting, kicking, striving to strangle him, to wrestle him off his feet. Smith reeled, staggering under the sheer rush of the man, almost blinded by blows, clutched, bewildered in Salzar's panther grip.

For a moment he writhed there, searching blindly for his enemy's wrist, striving to avoid the teeth that snapped at his throat, stifled by the hot stench of the man's breath in his face.

"I keel you! I keel you! Damn! Damn!" panted Salzar, in convulsive fury as Smith freed his left arm and struck him in the face.

Now, on the narrow, wet and slippery strip of rock they swayed to and fro, murderously interlocked, their heavy boots splashing, battling with limb and body.

Twice Salzar forced Smith outward over the sink, trying to end it, but could not free himself.

Once, too, he managed to get at a hidden knife, drag it out and stab at head and throat; but Smith caught the fist that wielded it, forced back the arm, held it while Salzar screamed at him, lunging at his face with bared teeth.

Suddenly the end came: Salzar's body heaved upward, sprawled for an instant in the dazzling glare, hurtled over Smith's head and fell into the sink with a crashing splash.

Frantically he thrashed there, spattering and floundering in darkness. He made no outcry. Probably he had landed head first.

In a moment only a vague heaving came from the unseen ooze.

Smith, exhausted, drenched with sweat, leaned against a tamarack, sickened.

After all sound had ceased he straightened up with an effort. Presently he bent and recovered Salzar's red bandanna and his hat, lifted his own rifle and pack and struggled into the harness. Then, kicking Salzar's rifle overboard, he unfastened both torches, pocketed one, and started on in a flood of ghostly light.

He was shaking all over and the torch quivered in his hand. He had seen men die in the Great War. He had been near death himself. But never before had he been near death in so horrible a form. The sodden noises in the mud, the deadened flopping of the sinking body—mud-plastered hands beating frantically on mud, spattering, agonising in darkness—"My God," he breathed, "anything but that—anything but that!—"

II

Before midnight he struck the hard forest. Here there was no trail at all, only spreading outcrop of rock under dying leaves.

He could see a few stars. Cautiously he ventured to shine his compass close to the ground. He was still headed right. The ghastly sink country lay behind him.

Ahead of him, somewhere in darkness—but how far he did not know—Quintana and his people were moving swiftly on Clinch's Dump.

It may have been an hour later—two hours, perhaps—when from far ahead in the forest came a sound—the faint clink of a shod heel on rock.

Now, Smith unslung his pack, placed it between two rocks where laurel grew.

Salzar's red bandanna was still wet, but he tied it across his face, leaving his eyes exposed. The dead man's hat fitted him. His own hat and the extra torch he dropped into his basket-pack.

Ready, now, he moved swiftly forward, trailing his rifle. And very soon it became plain to him that the people ahead were moving without much caution, evidently fearing no unfriendly ear or eye in that section of the wilderness.

Smith could hear their tread on rock and root and rotten branch, or swishing through frosted fern and brake, or louder on newly fallen leaves.

At times he could even see the round white glare of a torch on the ground—see it shift ahead, lighting up tree trunks, spread out, fanlike, into a wide, misty glory, then vanish as darkness rushed in from the vast ocean of the night.

Once they halted at a brook. Their torches flashed it; he heard them sounding its depths with their gun-butts.

Smith knew that brook. It was the east branch of Star Brook, the inlet to Star Pond.

Far ahead above the trees the sky seemed luminous. It was star lustre over the pond, turning the mist to a silvery splendour.

Now the people ahead of him moved with more caution, crossing the brook without splashing, and their boots made less noise in the woods.

To keep in touch with them Smith hastened his pace until he drew near enough to hear the low murmur of their voices.

They were travelling in single file; he had a glimpse of them against the ghostly radiance ahead. Indeed, so near had he approached that he could hear the heavy, laboured breathing of the last man in the file—some laggard who dragged his feet, plodding on doggedly, panting, muttering. Probably the man was Sard.

Already the forest in front was invaded by the misty radiance from the clearing. Through the trees starlight glimmered on water. The perfume of the open land grew in the night air—the scent of dew-wet grass, the smell of still water and of sedgy shores.

Lying flat behind a rotting log, Smith could see them all now—spectral shapes against the light. There were five of them at the forest's edge.

They seemed to know what was to be done and how to do it. Two went down among the ferns and stunted willows toward the west shore of the pond; two sheered off to the southwest, shoulder deep in blackberry and sumac. The fifth man waited for a while, then ran down across the open pasture.

Scarcely had he started when Smith glided to the wood's edge, crouched, and looked down.

Below stood Clinch's Dump, plain in the starlight, every window dark. To the west the barn loomed, huge with its ramshackle outbuildings straggling toward the lake.

Straight down the slope toward the barn ran the fifth man of Quintana's gang, and disappeared among the out-buildings.

Smith crept after him through the sumacs; and, at the foot of the slope, squatted low in a clump of rag-weed.

So close to the house was he now that he could hear the dew rattling on the veranda roof. He saw shadowy figures appear, one after another, and take stations at the four corners of the house. The fifth man was somewhere near the out-buildings, very silent about whatever he had on hand.

The stillness was absolute save for the drumming dew and a faint ripple from the water's edge.

Smith crouched, listened, searched the starlight with intent eyes, and waited.

Until something happened he could not solve the problem before him. He could be of no use to Eve Strayer and to Stormont until he found out what Quintana was going to do.

He could be of little use anyway unless he got into the house, where two rifles might hold out against five.

There was no use in trying to get to Ghost Lake for assistance. He felt that whatever was about to happen would come with a rush. It would be all over before he had gone five minutes. No; the only thing to do was to stay where he was.

As for his pledge to the little Grand Duchess, that was always in his mind. Sooner or later, somehow, he was going to make good his pledge.

He knew that Quintana and his gang were here to find the Flaming Jewel.

Had he not encountered Quintana, his own errand had been the same. For Smith had started for Clinch's prepared to reveal himself to Stormont, and then, masked to the eyes—and to save Eve from a broken heart, and Clinch from States Prison—he had meant to rob the girl at pistol-point.

It was the only way to save Clinch; the only way to save the pride of this blindly loyal girl. For the arrest of Clinch meant ruin to both, and Smith realised it thoroughly.

A slight sound from one of the out-houses—a sort of wagon-shed—attracted his attention. Through the frost-blighted rag-weeds he peered intently, listening.

After a few moments a faint glow appeared in the shed. There was a crackling noise. The glow grew pinker.

III

Inside Clinch's house Eve awoke with a start. Her ears were filled with a strange, rushing, crackling noise. A rosy glare danced and shook outside her windows.

As she sprang to the floor on bandaged feet, a shrill scream burst out in the ruddy darkness—unearthly, horrible; and there came a thunderous battering from the barn.

The girl tore open her bedroom door. "Jack!" she cried in a terrified voice. "The barn's on fire!"

"Good God!" he said, "—my horse!"

He had already sprung from his chair outside her door. Now he ran downstairs, and she heard bolt and chain clash at the kitchen door and his spurred boots land on the porch.

"Oh," she whimpered, snatching a blanket wrapper from a peg and struggling into it. "Oh, the poor horse! Jack! Jack! I'm coming to help! Don't risk your life! I'm coming—I'm coming—"

Terror clutched her as she stumbled downstairs on bandaged feet.

As she reached the door a great flare of light almost blinded her.

"Jack!"

And at the same instant she saw him struggling with three masked men in the glare of the wagon-shed afire.

His rifle stood in the corridor outside her door. With one bound she was on the stairs again. There came the crash and splinter of wood and glass from the kitchen, and a man with a handkerchief over his face caught her on the landing.

Twice she wrenched herself loose and her fingers almost touched Stormont's rifle; she fought like a cornered lynx, tore the handkerchief from her assailant's face, recognised Quintana, hurled her very body at him, eyes flaming, small teeth bared.

Two other men laid hold. In another moment she had tripped Quintana, and all four fell, rolling over and over down the short flight of stairs, landing in the kitchen, still fighting.

Here, in darkness, she wriggled out, somehow, leaving her blanket wrapped in their clutches. In another instant she was up the stairs again, only to discover that the rifle was gone.

The red glare from the wagon-house lighted her bedroom; she sprang inside and bolted the door.

Her chamois jacket with its loops full of cartridges hung on a peg. She got into it, seized her rifle and ran to the window just as two masked men, pushing Stormont before them, entered the house by the kitchen way.

Her own door was resounding with kicks and blows, shaking, shivering under the furious impact of boot and rifle-butt.

She ran to the bed, thrust her hand under the pillow, pulled out the case containing the Flaming Jewel, and placed it in the breast pocket of her shooting jacket.

Again she crept to the window. Only the wagon-house was burning. Somebody, however, had led Stormont's horse from the barn, and had tied it to a tree at a safe distance. It stood there, trembling, its beautiful, nervous head turned toward the burning building.

The blows upon her bedroom door had ceased; there came a loud trampling, the sound of excited voices; Quintana's sarcastic tones, clear, dominant:

"Dios! The police! Why you bring me this gendarme? What am I to do with a gentleman of the Constabulary, eh? Do you think I am fool enough to cut his throat? Well, Señor Gendarme, what are you doing here in the Dump of Clinch?"

Then Stormont's voice, clear and quiet: "What are *you* doing here? If you've a quarrel with Clinch, he's not here. There's only a young girl in this house."

"So?" said Quintana. "Well, that is what I expec', my frien'. It is thees lady upon whom I do myse'f the honour to call!"

Eve, listening, heard Stormont's rejoinder, still, calm, and very grave:

"The man who lays a finger on that young girl had better be dead. He's as good as dead the moment he touches her. There won't be a chance for him.... Nor for any of you, if you harm her."

"Calm youse'f, my frien'," said Quintana. "I demand of thees young lady only that she return to me the property of which I have been rob by Monsieur Clinch."

"I knew nothing of any theft. Nor does she—"

"Pardon; Señor Clinch knows; and I know." His tone changed, offensively: "Señor Gendarme, am I permit to understan' that you are a frien' of thees young lady?—a heart-frien', per'aps—"

"I am her friend," said Stormont bluntly.

"Ah," said Quintana, "then you shall persuade her to return to me thees packet of which Monsieur Clinch has rob me."

There was a short silence, then Quintana's voice again:

"I know thees packet is concel in thees house. Peaceably, if possible, I would recover my property.... If she refuse—"

Another pause.

"Well?" inquired Stormont, coolly.

"Ah! It is ver' painful to say. Alas, Señor Gendarme, I mus' have my property.... If she refuse, then I mus' sever one of her pretty fingers.... An' if she still refuse—I sever her pretty fingers, one by one, until—"

"You know what would happen to *you?*" interrupted Stormont, in a voice that quivered in spite of himself.

"I take my chance. Señor Gendarme, she is within that room. If you are her frien', you shall advise her to return to me my property."

After another silence:

"Eve!" he called sharply.

She placed her lips to the door: "Yes, Jack."

He said: "There are five masked men out here who say that Clinch robbed them and they are here to recover their property.... Do you know anything about this?"

"I know they lie. My father is not a thief.... I have my rifle and plenty of ammunition. I shall kill every man who enters this room."

For a moment nobody stirred or spoke. Then Quintana strode to the bolted door and struck it with the butt of his rifle.

"You, in there," he said in a menacing voice, "—you listen once to *me!* You open your door and come out. I give you one minute!" He struck the door again: "*One* minute, señorita!—or I cut from your frien', here, the hand from his right arm!"

There was a deathly silence. Then the sound of bolts. The door opened. Slowly the girl limped forward, still wearing the hunting jacket over her night-dress.

Quintana made her an elaborate and ironical bow, slouch hat in hand; another masked man took her rifle.

"Señorita," said Quintana with another sweep of his hat, "I ask pardon that I trouble you for my packet of which your father has rob me for ver' long time."

Slowly the girl lifted her blue eyes to Stormont. He was standing between two masked men. Their pistols were pressed slightly against his stomach.

Stormont reddened painfully:

"It was not for myself that I let you open your door," he said. "They would not have ventured to lay hands on *me*."

"Ah," said Quintana with a terrifying smile, "you would not have been the first gendarme who had—*accorded me his hand!*"

Two of the masked men laughed loudly.

Outside in the rag-weed patch, Smith rose, stole across the grass to the kitchen door and slipped inside.

"Now, señorita," said Quintana gaily, "my packet, if you please—and we leave you to the caresses of your faithful gendarme—who should thank God that he still possesses two good hands to fondle you! Alons! Come then! My packet!"

One of the masked men said: "Take her downstairs and lock her up somewhere or she'll shoot us from her window."

"Lead out that gendarme, too!" added Quintana, grasping Eve by the arm.

Down the stairs tramped the men, forcing their prisoners with them.

In the big kitchen the glare from the burning out-house fell dimly; the place was full of shadows.

"Now," said Quintana, "I take my property and my leave. Where is the packet hidden?"

She stood for a moment with drooping head, amid the sombre shadows, then, slowly, she drew the emblazoned morocco case from her breast pocket.

What followed occurred in the twinkling of an eye: for, as Quintana extended his arm to grasp the case, a hand snatched it, a masked figure sprang through the doorway, and ran toward the barn.

Somebody recognised the hat and red bandanna:

"Salzar!" he yelled. "Nick Salzar!"

"A traitor, by God!" shouted Quintana. Even before he had reached the door, his pistol flashed twice, deafening all in the semi-darkness, choking them with stifling fumes.

A masked man turned on Stormont, forcing him back into the pantry at pistol-point. Another man pushed Eve after him, slammed the pantry door and bolted it.

Through the iron bars of the pantry window, Stormont saw a man, wearing a red bandanna tied under his eyes, run up and untie his horse and fling himself astride under a shower of bullets.

As he wheeled the horse and swung him into the clearing toward the foot of Star Pond, his seat and horsemanship were not to be mistaken.

He was gone, now, the gallop stretching into a dead run; and Quintana's men still following, shooting, hallooing in the starlight like a pack of leaping shapes from hell.

But Quintana had not followed far. When he had emptied his automatic he halted.

Something about the transaction suddenly checked his fury, stilled it, summoned his brain into action.

For a full minute he stood unstirring, every atom of intelligence in terrible concentration.

Presently he put his left hand into his pocket, fitted another clip to his pistol, turned on his heel and walked straight back to the house.

Between the two locked in the pantry not a word had passed. Stormont still peered out between the iron bars, striving to catch a glimpse of what was going on. Eve crouched at the pantry doors, her face in her hands, listening.

Suddenly she heard Quintana's step in the kitchen. Cautiously she turned the pantry key from inside.

Stormont heard her, and instantly came to her. At the same moment Quintana unbolted the door from the outside and tried to open it.

"Come out," he said coldly, "or it will not go well with you when my men return."

"You've got what you say is your property," replied. Stormont. "What do you want now?"

"I tell you what I want ver' damn quick. Who was he, thees man who rides with my property on your horse away? Eh? Because it was not Nick Salzar! No! Salzar can not ride thees way. No! Alors?"

"I can't tell you who he was," replied Stormont. "That's your affair, not ours."

"No? Ah! Ver' well, then. I shall tell you, Señor Flic! He was one of *yours*. I understan'. It is a trap, a cheat—what you call a *plant!* Thees man who rode your horse he is disguise! Yes! He also is a gendarme! Yes! You think I let a gendarme rob me? I got you where I want you now. You shall write your gendarme frien' that he return to me my property, *one day's time* , or I send him by parcel post two nice, fresh-out righthands—your sweetheart's and your own!"

Stormont drew Eve's head close to his:

"This man is blood mad or out of his mind! I'd better go out and take a chance at him before the others come back."

But the girl shook her head violently, caught him by the arm and drew him toward the mouth of the tile down which Clinch always emptied his hootch when the Dump was raided.

But now, it appeared that the tile which protruded from the cement floor was removable.

In silence she began to unscrew it, and he, seeing what she was trying to do, helped her.

Together they lifted the heavy tile and laid it on the floor.

"You open thees door!" shouted Quintana in a paroxysm of fury. "I give you one minute! Then, by God, I kill you both!"

Eve lifted a screen of wood through which the tile had been set. Under it a black hole yawned. It was a tunnel made of three-foot aqueduct tiles; and it led straight into Star Pond, two hundred feet away.

Now, as she straightened up and looked silently at Stormont, they heard the trample of boots in the kitchen, voices, the bang of gun-stocks.

"Does that drain lead into the lake?" whispered Stormont.

She nodded.

"Will you follow me, Eve?"

She pushed him aside, indicating that he was to follow her.

As she stripped the hunting jacket from her, a hot colour swept her face. But she dropped on both knees, crept straight into the tile and slipped out of sight.

As she disappeared, Quintana shouted something in Portuguese, and fired at the lock.

With the smash of splintering wood in his ears, Stormont slid into the smooth tunnel.

In an instant he was shooting down a polished toboggan slide, and in another moment was under the icy water of Star Pond.

Shocked, blinded, fighting his way to the surface, he felt his spurred boots dragging at him like a ton of iron. Then to him came her helping hand.

"I can make it," he gasped.

But his clothing and his boots and the icy water began to tell on him in mid-lake.

Swimming without effort beside him, watching his every stroke, presently she sank a little and glided under him and a little ahead, so that his hands fell upon her shoulders.

He let them rest, so, aware now that it was no burden to such a swimmer. Supple and silent as a swimming otter, the girl slipped lithely through the chilled water, which washed his body to the nostrils and numbed his legs till he could scarcely move them.

And now, of a sudden, his feet touched gravel. He stumbled forward in the shadow of overhanging trees and saw her wading shoreward, a dripping, silvery shape on the shoal.

Then, as he staggered up to her, breathless, where she was standing on the pebbled shore, he saw her join both hands, cup-shape, and lift them to her lips.

And out of her mouth poured diamond, sapphire, and emerald in a dazzling stream—and, among them, one great, flashing gem blazing in the starlight—the Flaming Jewel!

Like a naiad of the lake she stood, white, slim, silent, the heaped gems glittering in her snowy hands, her face framed by the curling masses of her wet hair.

Then, slowly she turned her head to Stormont.

"These are what Quintana came for," she said. "Could you put them into your pocket?"

Episode Eight
CUP AND LIP

I

Two miles beyond Clinch's Dump, Hal Smith pulled Stormont's horse to a walk. He was tremendously excited.

With naïve sincerity he believed that what he had done on the spur of the moment had been the only thing to do.

By snatching the Flaming Jewel from Quintana's very fingers he had diverted that vindictive bandit's fury from Eve, from Clinch, from Stormont, and had centred it upon himself.

More than that, he had sown the seeds of suspicion among Quintana's own people. They never could discover Salzar's body. Always they must believe that it was Nicolas Salzar and no other who so treacherously robbed them, and who rode away in a rain of bullets, shaking the emblazoned morocco case above his masked head in triumph, derision and defiance.

At the recollection of what had happened, Hal Smith drew bridle, and, sitting his saddle there in the false dawn, threw back his handsome head and laughed until the fading stars overhead swam in his eyes through tears of sheerest mirth.

For he was still young enough to have had the time of his life. Nothing in the Great War had so thrilled him. For, in what had just happened, there was humour. There had been none in the Great Grim Drama.

Still, Smith began to realise that he had taken the long, long chance of the opportunist who rolls the bones with Death. He had kept his pledge to the little Grand Duchess. It was a clean job. It was even good drama—

The picturesque angle of the affair shook Hal Smith with renewed laughter. As a moving picture hero he thought himself the funniest thing on earth.

From the time he had poked a pistol against Sard's fat paunch, to this bullet-pelted ride for life, life had become one ridiculously exciting episode after another.

He had come through like the hero in a best-seller.... Lacking only a heroine.... If there had been any heroine it was Eve Strayer. Drama had gone wrong in that detail.... So perhaps, after all, it was real life he had been living and not drama. Drama, for the masses, must have a definite beginning and ending. Real life lacks the latter. In life nothing is finished. It is always a premature curtain which is yanked by that doddering old stage-hand, Johnny Death.

Smith sat his saddle, thinking, beginning to be sobered now by the inevitable reaction which follows excitement and mirth as relentlessly as care dogs the horseman.

He had had a fine time—save for the horror of the Rocktrail.... He shuddered.... Anyway, at worst he had not shirked a clean deal in that ghastly game.... It was God's mercy that he was not lying where Salzar lay, ten feet—twenty—a hundred deep, perhaps—in immemorial slime—

He shook himself in his saddle as though to be rid of the creeping horror, and wiped his clammy face.

Now, in the false dawn, a blue-jay awoke somewhere among the oaks and filled the misty silence with harsh grace-notes.

Then reaction, setting in like a tide, stirred more sombre depths in the heart of this young man.

He thought of Riga; and of the Red Terror; of murder at noon-day, and outrage by night. He remembered his only encounter with a lovely child—once Grand Duchess of Esthonia—then a destitute refugee in silken rags.

What a day that had been.... Only one day and one evening.... And never had he been so near in love in all his life....

That one day and evening had been enough for her to confide to an American officer her entire life's history.... Enough for him to pledge himself to her service while life endured.... And if emotion had swept every atom of reason out of his youthful head, there in the turmoil and alarm—there in the terrified, riotous city jammed with refugees, reeking with disease, half frantic from famine and the filthy, rising flood of war—if really it all had been merely romantic impulse, ardour born of overwrought sentimentalism, nevertheless, what he had pledged that day to a little Grand Duchess in rags, he had fulfilled to the letter within the hour.

As the false dawn began to fade, he loosened hunting coat and cartridge sling, drew from his shirt-bosom the morocco case.

It bore the arms and crest of the Grand Duchess Theodorica of Esthonia.

His fingers trembled slightly as he pressed the jewelled spring. It opened on an empty casket.

In the sudden shock of horror and astonishment, his convulsive clutch on the spring started a tiny bell ringing. Then, under his very nose, the empty tray slid aside revealing another tray underneath, set solidly with brilliants. A rainbow glitter streamed from the unset gems in the silken tray. Like an incredulous child he touched them. They were magnificently real.

In the centre lay blazing the great Erosite gem—the Flaming Jewel itself. Priceless diamonds, sapphires, emeralds ringed it. In his hands he held nearly four millions of dollars.

Gingerly he balanced the emblazoned case, fascinated. Then he replaced the empty tray, closed the box, thrust it into the bosom of his flannel shirt and buttoned it in.

Now there was little more for this excited young man to do. He was through with Clinch. Hal Smith, hold-up man and dish-washer at Clinch's Dump, had ended his career. The time had now arrived for him to vanish and make room for James Darragh.

Because there still remained a very agreeable rôle for Darragh to play. And he meant to eat it up—as Broadway has it.

For by this time the Grand Duchess of Esthonia—Ricca, as she was called by her companion, Valentine, the pretty Countess Orloff-Strelwitz—must have arrived in New York.

At the big hunting lodge of the late Henry Harrod—now inherited by Darragh—there might be a letter—perhaps a telegram—the cue for Hal Smith to vanish and for James Darragh to enter, play his brief but glittering part, and—

Darragh's sequence of pleasing meditations halted abruptly.... To walk out of the life of the little Grand Duchess did not seem to suit his ideas—indefinite and hazy as they were, so far.

He lifted the bridle from the horse's neck, divided curb and snaffle thoughtfully, touched the splendid animal with heel and knee.

As he cantered on into the wide forest road that led to his late uncle's abode, curiosity led him to wheel into a narrower trail running east along Star Pond, and from whence he could take a farewell view of Clinch's Dump.

He smiled to think of Eve and Stormont there together, and now in safety behind bolted doors and shutters.

He grinned to think of Quintana and his precious crew, blood-crazy, baffled, probably already distrusting one another, yet running wild through the night like starving wolves galloping at hazard across a famine-stricken waste.

"Only wait till Stormont makes his report," he thought, grinning more broadly still. "Every State Trooper north of Albany will be after Señor Quintana. Some hunting! And, if he could understand, Mike Clinch might thank his stars that what I've done this night has saved him his skin and Eve a broken heart!"

He drew his horse to a walk, now, for the path began to run closer to Star Pond, skirting the pebbled shallows in the open just ahead.

Alders still concealed the house across the lake, but the trail was already coming out into the starlight.

Suddenly his horse stopped short, trembling, its ears pricked forward.

Darragh sat listening intently for a moment. Then with infinite caution, he leaned over the cantle and gently parted the alders.

On the pebbled beach, full in the starlight, stood two figures, one white and slim, the other dark.

The arm of the dark figure clasped the waist of the white and slender one.

Evidently they had heard his horse, for they stood motionless, looking directly at the alders behind which his horse had halted.

To turn might mean a shot in the back as far as Darragh knew. He was still masked with Salzar's red bandanna. He raised his rifle, slid a cartridge into the breech, pressed his horse forward with a slight touch of heel and knee, and rode slowly out into the star-dusk.

What Stormont saw was a masked man, riding his own horse, with menacing rifle half lifted for a shot! What Eve Strayer thought she saw was too terrible for words. And before Stormont could prevent her she sprang in front of him, covering his body with her own.

At that the horseman tore off his red mask:

"Eve! Jack Stormont! What the devil are you doing over *here?*"

Stormont walked slowly up to his own horse, laid one unsteady hand on its silky nose, kept it there while dusty, velvet lips mumbled and caressed his fingers.

"I knew it was a cavalryman," he said quietly. "I suspected you, Jim. It was the sort of crazy thing you were likely to do.... I don't ask you what you're up to, where you've been, what your plans may be. If you needed me you'd have told me.

"But I've got to have my horse for Eve. Her feet are wounded. She's in her night-dress and wringing wet. I've got to set her on my horse and try to take her through to Ghost Lake."

Darragh stared at Stormont, at the ghostly figure of the girl who had sunk down on the sand at the lake's edge. Then he scrambled out of the saddle and handed over the bridle.

"Quintana came back," said Stormont. "I hope to reckon with him some day.... I believe he came back to harm Eve.... We got out of the house.... We swam the lake.... I'd have gone under except for her—"

In his distress and overwhelming mortification, Darragh stood miserable, mute, irresolute.

Stormont seemed to understand: "What you did, Jim, was well meant," he said. "I understand. Eve will understand when I tell her. But that fellow Quintana is a devil. You can't draw a herring across any trail he follows. I tell you, Jim, this fellow Quintana is either blood-mad or just plain crazy. Somebody will have to put him out of the way. I'll do it if I ever find him."

"Yes.... Your people ought to do that.... Or, if you like, I'll volunteer.... I've a little business to transact in New York, first.... Jack, your tunic and breeches are soaked; I'll be glad to chip in something for Eve.... Wait a moment—"

He stepped into cover, drew the morocco box from his grey shirt, shoved it into his hip pocket.

Then he threw off his cartridge belt and hunting coat, pulled the grey shirt over his head and came out in his undershirt and breeches, with the other garments hanging over his arm.

"Give her these," he said. "She can button the coat around her waist for a skirt. She'd better go somewhere and get out of that soaking-wet night-dress—"

Eve, crouched on the sand, trying to wring out and twist up her drenched hair, looked up at Stormont as he came toward her holding out Darragh's dry clothing.

"You'd better do what you can with these," he said, trying to speak carelessly.... "*He* says you'd better chuck—what you're wearing—"

She nodded in flushed comprehension. Stormont walked back to his horse, his boots slopping water at every stride.

"I don't know any place nearer than Ghost Lake Inn," he said ... "except Harrod's."

"That's where we're going, Jack," said Darragh cheerfully.

"That's *your* place, isn't it?"

"It is. But I don't want Eve to know it.... I think it better she should not know me except as Hal Smith—for the present, anyway. You'll see to that, won't you?"

"As you wish, Jim.... Only, if we go to your own house—"

"We're not going to the main house. She wouldn't, anyway. Clinch has taught that girl to hate the very name of Harrod—hate every foot of forest that the Harrod game keepers patrol. She wouldn't cross my threshold to save her life."

"I don't understand, but—it's all right—whatever *you* say, Jim."

"I'll tell you the whole business some day. But where I'm going to take you now is into a brand new camp which I ordered built last spring. It's within a mile of the State Forest border. Eve won't know that it's Harrod property. I've a hatchery there and the State lets me have a man in exchange for free fry. When I get there I'll post my man.... It will be a roof for to-night, anyway, and breakfast in the morning, whenever you're ready."

"How far is it?"

"Only about three miles east of here."

"That's the thing to do, then," said Stormont bluntly.

He dropped one sopping-wet sleeve over his horse's neck, taking care not to touch the saddle. He was thinking of the handful of gems in his pocket; and he wondered why Darragh had said nothing about the empty case for which he had so recklessly risked his life.

What this whole business was about Stormont had no notion. But he knew Darragh. That was sufficient to leave him tranquil, and perfectly certain that whatever Darragh was doing must be the right thing to do.

Yet—Eve had swum Star Pond with her mouth filled with jewels.

When she had handed the morocco box to Quintana, Stormont now realised that she must have played her last card on the utterly desperate chance that Quintana might go away without examining the case.

Evidently she had emptied the case before she left her room. He recollected that, during all that followed, Eve had not uttered a single word. He knew why, now. How could she speak with her mouth full of diamonds?

A slight sound from the shore caused him to turn. Eve was coming toward him in the dusk, moving painfully on her wounded feet. Darragh's flannel shirt and his hunting coat buttoned around her slender waist clothed her.

The next instant he was beside her, lifting her in both arms.

As he placed her in the saddle and adjusted one stirrup to her bandaged foot, she turned and quietly thanked Darragh for the clothing.

"And that was a brave thing you did," she added, "—to risk your life for my father's property. Because the morocco case which you saved proved to be empty does not make what you did any the less loyal and gallant."

Darragh gazed at her, astounded; took the hand she stretched out to him; held it with a silly expression on his features.

"Hal Smith," she said with perceptible emotion, "I take back what I once said to you on Owl Marsh. No man is a real crook by nature who did what you have done. That is 'faithfulness unto death'—the supreme offer—loyalty—"

Her voice broke; she pressed Darragh's hand convulsively and her lip quivered.

Darragh, with the morocco case full of jewels buttoned into his hip pocket, stood motionless, mutely swallowing his amazement.

What in the world did this girl mean, talking about an *empty* case?

But this was no time to unravel that sort of puzzle. He turned to Stormont who, as perplexed as he, had been listening in silence.

"Lead your horse forward," he said. "I know the trail. All you need do is to follow me." And, shouldering his rifle, he walked leisurely into the woods, the cartridge belt sagging *en bandouliere* across his woollen undershirt.

II

When Stormont gently halted his horse it was dawn, and Eve, sagging against him with one arm around his neck, sat huddled up on her saddle fast asleep.

In a birch woods, on the eastern slope of the divide, stood the log camp, dimly visible in the silvery light of early morning.

Darragh, cautioning Stormont with a slight gesture, went forward, mounted the rustic veranda, and knocked at a lighted window.

A man, already dressed, came and peered out at him, then hurried to open the door.

"I didn't know you, Captain Darragh—" he began, but fell silent under the warning gesture that checked him.

"I've a guest outside. She's Clinch's step-daughter, Eve Strayer. She knows me by the name of Hal Smith. Do you understand?"

"Yes, sir—"

"Cut *that* out, too. I'm Hal Smith to you, also. State Trooper Stormont is out there with Eve Strayer. He was a comrade of mine in Russia. I'm Hal Smith to him, by mutual agreement. *Now* do you get me, Ralph?"

"Sure, Hal. Go on; spit it out!"

They both grinned.

"You're a hootch runner," said Darragh. "This is your shack. The hatchery is only a blind. That's all you have to know, Ralph. So put that girl into my room and let her sleep till she wakes of her own accord.

"Stormont and I will take two of the guest-bunks in the *L*. And for heaven's sake make us some coffee when you make your own. But first come out and take the horse."

They went out together. Stormont lifted Eve out of the saddle. She did not wake. Darragh led the way into the log house and along a corridor to his own room.

"Turn down the sheets," whispered Stormont. And, when the bed was ready: "Can you get a bath towel, Jim?"

Darragh fetched one from the connecting bath-room.

"Wrap it around her wet hair," whispered Stormont. "Good heavens, I wish there were a woman here."

"I wish so too," said Darragh; "she's chilled to the bone. You'll have to wake her. She can't sleep in what she's wearing; it's almost as damp as her hair—"

He went to the closet and returned with a man's morning robe, as soft as fleece.

"Somehow or other she's got to get into that," he said.

There was a silence.

"Very well," said Stormont, reddening.... "If you'll step out I'll—manage...." He looked Darragh straight in the eyes: "I have asked her to marry me," he said.

When Stormont came out a great fire of birch-logs was blazing in the living-room, and Darragh stood there, his elbow on the rough stone mantel-shelf.

Stormont came straight to the fire and set one spurred boot on the fender.

"She's warm and dry and sound asleep," he said. "I'll wake her again if you think she ought to swallow something hot."

At that moment the fish-culturist came in with a pot of steaming coffee.

"This is my friend, Ralph Wier," said Darragh. "I think you'd better give Eve a cup of coffee." And, to Wier, "Fill a couple of hot water bags, old chap. We don't want any pneumonia in this house."

When breakfast was ready Eve once more lay asleep with a slight dew of perspiration on her brow.

Darragh was half starved: Stormont ate little. Neither spoke at all until, satisfied, they rose, ready for sleep.

At the door of his room Stormont took Darragh's offered hand, understanding what it implied:

"Thanks, Jim.... Hers is the loveliest character I have ever known.... If I weren't as poor as a homeless dog I'd marry her to-morrow.... I'll do it anyway, I think.... I *can't* let her go back to Clinch's Dump!"

"After all," said Darragh, smiling, "if it's only money that worries you, why not talk about a job to *me!*"

Stormont flushed heavily: "That's rather wonderful of you, Jim—"

"Why? You're the best officer I had. Why the devil did you go into the Constabulary without talking to me?"

Stormont's upper lip seemed inclined to twitch but he controlled it and scowled at space.

"Go to bed, you darned fool," said Darragh, carelessly. "You'll find dry things ready. Ralph will take care of your uniform and boots."

Then he went into his own quarters to read two letters which, conforming to arrangements made with Mrs. Ray the day he had robbed Emanuel Sard, were to be sent to Trout Lodge to await his arrival.

Both, written from the Ritz, bore the date of the day before: the first he opened was from the Countess Orloff-Strelwitz:

> "Dear Captain Darragh,
>
> "—You are so wonderful! Your messenger, with the *ten* thousand dollars which you say you already have recovered from those miscreants who robbed Ricca, came aboard our ship before we landed. It was a godsend; we were nearly penniless—and oh, *so* shabby!
>
> "Instantly, my friend, we shopped, Ricca and I. Fifth Avenue enchanted us. All misery was forgotten in the magic of that paradise for women.
>
> "Yet, spendthrifts that we naturally are, we were not silly enough to be extravagant. Ricca was wild for American sport-clothes. I, also. Yet—only *two* gowns apiece, excepting our sport clothes. And other necessaries. Don't you think we were economical?"
>
> "Furthermore, dear Captain Darragh, we are hastening to follow your instructions. We are leaving to-day for your château in the wonderful forest, of which you told us that never-to-be-forgotten day in Riga.
>
> "Your agent is politeness, consideration and kindness itself. We have our accommodations. We leave New York at midnight.
>
> "Ricca is so excited that it is difficult for her to restrain her happiness. God knows the child has seen enough unhappiness to quench the gaiety of anybody!
>
> "Well, all things end. Even tears. Even the Red Terror shall pass from our beloved Russia. For, after all, Monsieur, God still lives.
>
> "Valentine."
>
> "P. S. Ricca has written to you. I have read the letter. I have let it go uncensored."

Darragh went to the door of his room:
"Ralph! Ralph!" he called. And, when Wier hurriedly appeared:
"What time does the midnight train from New York get into Five Lakes?"
"A little before nine—"
"You can make it in the flivver, can't you?"

"Yes, if I start *now*."

"All right. Two ladies. You're to bring them to the *house*, not *here*. Mrs. Ray knows about them. And—get back here as soon as you can."

He closed his door again, sat down on the bed and opened the other letter. His hand shook as he unfolded it. He was so scared and excited that he could scarcely decipher the angular, girlish penmanship:

"To dear Captain Darragh, our champion and friend—

"It is difficult for me, Monsieur, to express my happiness and my deep gratitude in the so cold formality of the written page.

"Alas, sir, it will be still more difficult to find words for it when again I have the happiness of greeting you in proper person.

"Valentine has told you everything, she warns me, and I am, therefore, somewhat at a loss to know what I should write to you.

"Yet, I know very well what I would write if I dare. It is this: that I wish you to know—although it may not pass the censor—that I am most impatient to see you, Monsieur. *Not* because of kindness past, nor with an unworthy expectation of benefits to come. But because of friendship—*the deepest, sincerest of my* WHOLE LIFE.

"Is it not modest of a young girl to say this? Yes, surely all the world which was once *en régle*, formal, artificial, has been burnt out of our hearts by this so frightful calamity which has overwhelmed the world with fire and blood.

"If ever on earth there was a time when we might venture to express with candour what is hidden within our minds and hearts, it would seem, Monsieur, that the time is now.

"True, I have known you only for one day and one evening. Yet, what happened to the world in that brief space of time—and to us, Monsieur—brought *us* together as though our meeting were but a blessed reunion after the happy intimacy of many years.... I speak, Monsieur, for myself. May I hope that I speak, also, for you?

"With a heart too full to thank you, and with expectations indescribable—but with courage, always, for any event—I take my leave of you at the foot of this page. Like death—I trust—my adieu is not the end, but the beginning. It is not farewell; it is a greeting to him whom I most honour in all the world.... And would willingly obey if he shall command. And otherwise—*all* else that in his mind—and heart—he might desire.

"THEODORICA."

It was the most beautiful love-letter any man ever received in all the history of love.

And it had passed the censor.

III

It was afternoon when Darragh awoke in his bunk, stiff, sore, confused in mind and battered in body.

However, when he recollected where he was he got out of bed in a hurry and jerked aside the window curtains.

The day was magnificent; a sky of royal azure overhead, and everywhere the silver pillars of the birches supporting their splendid canopy of ochre, orange, and burnt-gold.

Wier, hearing him astir, came in.

"How long have you been back! Did you meet the ladies with your flivver?" demanded Darragh, impatiently.

"I got to Five Lakes station just as the train came in. The young ladies were the only passengers who got out. I waited to get their two steamer trunks and then I drove them to Harrod Place—"

"How did they seem, Ralph—worn-out—worried—ill?"

Wier laughed: "No, sir, they looked very pretty and lively to me. They seemed delighted to get here. They talked to each other in some foreign tongue—Russian, I should say—at least, it sounded like what we heard over in Siberia, Captain—"

"It *was* Russian.... You go on and tell me while I take another hot bath!—"

Wier followed him into the bath-room and vaulted to a seat on the deep set window-sill:

"—When they weren't talking Russian and laughing they talked to me and admired the woods and mountains. I had to tell them everything—they wanted to see buffalo and Indians. And when I told them there weren't any, enquired for bears and panthers.

"We saw two deer on the Scaur, and a woodchuck near the house; I thought they'd jump out of the flivver—"

He began to laugh at the recollection: "No, sir, they didn't act tired and sad; they said they were crazy to get into their knickerbockers and go to look for you—"

"Where did you say I was?" asked Darragh, drying himself vigorously.

"Out in the woods, somewhere. The last I saw of them, Mrs. Ray had their hand-bags and Jerry and Tom were shouldering their trunks."

"I'm going up there right away," interrupted Darragh excitedly. "—Good heavens, Ralph, I haven't any clothes here, have I?"

"No, sir. But those you wore last night are dry—"

"Confound it! I meant to send some decent clothes here— All right; get me those duds I wore yesterday—and a bite to eat! I'm in a hurry, Ralph—"

He ate while dressing, disgustedly arraying himself in the grey shirt, breeches, and laced boots which weather, water, rock, and brier had not improved.

In a pathetic attempt to spruce up, he knotted the red bandanna around his neck and pinched Salzar's slouch hat into a peak.

"I look like a hootch-running Wop," he said. "Maybe I can get into the house before I meet the ladies—"

"You look like one of Clinch's bums," remarked Wier with native honesty.

Darragh, chagrined, went to his bunk, pulled the morocco case from under the pillow, and shoved it into the bosom of his flannel shirt.

"That's the main thing anyway," he thought. Then, turning to Wier, he asked whether Eve and Stormont had awakened.

It appeared that Trooper Stormont had saddled up and cantered away shortly after sunrise, leaving word that he must hunt up his comrade, Trooper Lannis, at Ghost Lake.

"They're coming back this evening," added Wier. "He asked you to look out for Clinch's step-daughter."

"She's all right here. Can't you keep an eye on her, Ralph?"

"I'm stripping trout, sir. I'll be around here to cook dinner for her when she wakes up."

Darragh glanced across the brook at the hatchery. It was only a few yards away. He nodded and started for the veranda:

"That'll be all right," he said. "Nobody is coming here to bother her.... And don't let her leave, Ralph, till I get back—"

"Very well, sir. But suppose she takes it into her head to leave—"

Darragh called back, gaily: "She can't: she hasn't any clothes!" And away he strode in the gorgeous sunshine of a magnificent autumn day, all the clean and vigorous youth of him afire in anticipation of a reunion which the letter from his lady-love had transfigured into a tryst.

For, in that amazing courtship of a single day, he never dreamed that he had won the heart of that sad, white-faced, hungry child in rags— silken tatters still stained with the blood of massacre—the very soles of her shoes still charred by the embers of her own home.

Yet, that is what must have happened in a single day and evening. Life passes swiftly during such periods. Minutes lengthen into days; hours into years. The soul finds itself.

Then mind and heart become twin prophets—clairvoyant concerning what hides behind the veil; comprehending with divine clair-audience what the Three Sisters whisper there—hearing even the whirr of the spindle—the very snipping of the Eternal Shears!

The soul finds itself; the mind knows itself; the heart perfectly understands.

He had not spoken to this young girl of love. The blood of friends and servants was still rusty on her skirt's ragged hem.

Yet, that night, when at last in safety she had said good-bye to the man who had secured it for her, he knew that he was in love with her. And, at such crises, the veil that hides hearts becomes transparent.

At that instant he had seen and known. Afterward he had dared not believe that he had known.

But hers had been a purer courage.

As he strode on, the comprehension of her candour, her honesty, the sweet bravery that had conceived, created, and sent that letter, thrilled this young man until his heavy boots sprouted wings, and the trail he followed was but a path of rosy clouds over which he floated heavenward.

About half an hour later he came to his senses with a distinct shock.

Straight ahead of him on the trail, and coming directly toward him, moved a figure in knickers and belted tweed.

Flecked sunlight slanted on the stranger's cheek and burnished hair, dappling face and figure with moving, golden spots.

Instantly Darragh knew and trembled.

But Theodorica of Esthonia had known him only in his uniform.

As she came toward him, lovely in her lithe and rounded grace, only friendly curiosity gazed at him from her blue eyes.

Suddenly she knew him, went scarlet to her yellow hair, then white: and tried to speak—but had no control of the short, rosy upper lip which only quivered as he took her hands.

The forest was dead still around them save for the whisper of painted leaves sifting down from a sunlit vault above.

Finally she said in a ghost of a voice: "My—friend...."

"If you accept his friendship...."

"Friendship is to be shared.... Ours mingled—on that day.... Your share is—as much as pleases you."

"All you have to give me, then."

"Take it ... all I have...." Her blue eyes met his with a little effort. All courage is an effort.

Then that young man dropped on both knees at her feet and laid his lips to her soft hands.

In trembling silence she stood for a moment, then slowly sank on both knees to face him across their clasped hands.

So, in the gilded cathedral of the woods, pillared with silver, and azure-domed, the betrothal of these two was sealed with clasp and lip.

Awed, a little fearful, she looked into her lover's eyes with a gaze so chaste, so oblivious to all things earthly, that the still purity of her face seemed a sacrament, and he scarcely dared touch the childish lips she offered.

But when the sacrament of the kiss had been accomplished, she rested one hand on his shoulder and rose, and drew him with her.

Then *his* moment came: he drew the emblazoned case from his breast, opened it, and, in silence, laid it in her hands. The blaze of the jewels in the sunshine almost blinded them.

That was *his* moment.

The next moment was Quintana's.

Darragh hadn't a chance. Out of the bushes two pistols were thrust hard against his stomach. Quintana's face was behind them. He wore no mask, but the three men with him watched him over the edges of handkerchiefs—over the sights of levelled rifles, too.

The youthful Grand Duchess had turned deadly white. One of Quintana's men took the morocco case from her hands and shoved her aside without ceremony.

Quintana leered at Darragh over his levelled weapons:

"My frien' Smith!" he exclaimed softly. "So it is you, then, who have twice try to rob me of my property!

"Ah! You recollec'? Yes? How you have rob me of a pacquet which contain only some chocolate?"

Darragh's face was burning with helpless rage.

"My frien', Smith," repeated Quintana, "do you recollec' what it was you say to me? Yes?... How often it is the onexpected which so usually happen? You are quite correc', l'ami Smith. It has happen."

He glanced at the open jewel box which one of the masked men held, then, like lightning, his sinister eyes focussed on Darragh.

"So," he said, "it was also you who rob me las' night of my property.... What you do to Nick Salzar, eh?"

"Killed him," said Darragh, dry lipped, nerved for death. "I ought to have killed you, too, when I had the chance. But—*I'm* white, you see."

At the insult flung into his face over the muzzles of his own pistols, Quintana burst into laughter.

"Ah! You *should* have shot me! You are quite right, my frien'. I mus' say you have behave ver' foolish."

He laughed again so hard that Darragh felt his pistols shaking against his body.

"So you have kill Nick Salzar, eh?" continued Quintana with perfect good humour. "My frien', I am oblige to you for what you do. You are surprise? Eh? It is ver' simple, my frien' Smith. What I want of a man who can be kill? Eh? Of what use is he to me? Voilà!"

He laughed, patted Darragh on the shoulder with one of his pistols.

"You, now—*you* could be of use. Why? Because you are a better man than was Nick Salzar. He who kills is better than the dead."

Then, swiftly his dark features altered:

"My frien' Smith," he said, "I have come here for my property, not to kill. I have recover my property. Why shall I kill you? To say that I am a better man? Yes, perhaps. But also I should be oblige to say that also I am a fool. Yaas! A poor damfool."

Without shifting his eyes he made a motion with one pistol to his men. As they turned and entered the thicket, Quintana's intent gaze became murderous.

"If I mus' kill you I shall do so. Otherwise I have sufficient trouble to keep me from ennui. My frien', I am going home to enjoy my property. If you live or die it signifies nothing to me. No! Why, for the pleasure of killing you, should I bring your dirty gendarmes on my heels?"

He backed away to the edge of the thicket, venturing one swift and evil glance at the girl who stood as though dazed.

"Listen attentively," he said to Darragh. "One of my men remains hidden very near. He is a dead shot. His aim is at your—sweetheart's—body. You understan'?"

"Yes."

"Ver' well. You shall not go away for one hour time. After that—" he took off his slouch hat with a sweeping bow—"you may go to hell!"

Behind him the bushes parted, closed.

José Quintana had made his adieux.

Episode Nine
THE FOREST AND MR. SARD

I

When at last José Quintana had secured what he had been after for years, his troubles really began.

In his pocket he had two million dollars worth of gems, including the Flaming Jewel.

But he was in the middle of a wilderness ringed in by hostile men, and obliged to rely for aid on a handful of the most desperate criminals in Europe.

Those openly hostile to him had a wide net spread around him—wide of mesh too, perhaps; and it was through a mesh he meant to wriggle, but the net was intact from Canada to New York.

Canadian police and secret agents held it on the north: this he had learned from Jake Kloon long since.

East, west and south he knew he had the troopers of the New York State Constabulary to deal with, and in addition every game warden and fire warden in the State Forests, a swarm of plain clothes men from the Metropolis, and the rural constabulary of every town along the edges of the vast reservation.

Just who was responsible for this enormous conspiracy to rob him of what he considered his own legitimate loot Quintana did not know.

Sard's attorney, Eddie Abrams, believed that the French police instigated it through agents of the United States Secret Service.

Of one thing Quintana was satisfied, Mike Clinch had nothing to do with stirring up the authorities. Law-breakers of his sort don't shout for the police or invoke State or Government aid.

As for the status of Darragh—or Hal Smith, as he supposed him to be—Quintana took him for what he seemed to be, a well-born young man gone wrong. Europe was full of that kind. To Quintana there was nothing suspicious about Hal Smith. On the contrary, his clever recklessness confirmed that polished bandit's opinion that Smith was a gentleman degenerated into a crook. It takes an educated imagination for a man to do what Smith had done to him. If the common crook has any imagination at all it never is educated.

Another matter worried José Quintana: he was not only short on provisions, but what remained was cached in Drowned Valley; and Mike Clinch and his men were guarding every outlet to that sinister region, excepting only the rocky and submerged trail by which he had made his exit.

That was annoying; it cut off provisions and liquor from Canada, for which he had arranged with Jake Kloon. For Kloon's hootch-runners now would be stopped by Clinch; and not one among them knew about the rocky trail in.

All these matters were disquieting enough: but what really and most deeply troubled Quintana was his knowledge of his own men.

He did not trust one among them. Of international crookdom they were the cream. Not one of them but would have murdered his fellow if the loot were worth it and the chances of escape sufficient.

There was no loyalty to him, none to one another, no "honour among thieves"—and it was José Quintana who knew that only in romance such a thing existed.

No, he could not trust a single man. Only hope of plunder attached these marauders to him, and merely because he had education and imagination enough to provide what they wanted.

Anyone among them would murder and rob him if opportunity presented.

Now, how to keep his loot; how to get back to Europe with it, was the problem that confronted Quintana after robbing Darragh. And he determined to settle part of that question at once.

About five miles from Harrod Place, within a hundred rods of which he had held up Hal Smith, Quintana halted, seated himself on a rotting log, and waited until his men came up and gathered around him.

For a little while, in utter silence, his keen eyes travelled from one visage to the next, from Henri Picquet to Victor Georgiades, to Sanchez, to Sard. His intent scrutiny focussed on Sard; lingered.

If there were anybody he might trust, a little way, it would be Sard.

Then a polite, untroubled smile smoothed the pale, dark features of José Quintana:

"Bien, messieurs, the coup has been success. Yes? Ver' well; in turn, then, en accord with our custom, I shall dispose myse'f to listen to your good advice."

He looked at Henri Picquet, smiled and nodded invitation to speak.

Picquet shrugged: "For me, mon capitaine, eet ees ver' simple. We are five. Therefore, divide into five ze gems. After zat, each one for himself to make his way out—"

"Nick Salzar and Harry Beck are in the Drowned Valley," interrupted Quintana.

Picquet shrugged again; Sanchez laughed, saying: "If they are there it is their misfortune. Also, we others are in a hurry."

Picquet added: "Also five shares are sufficient division."

"It is propose, then, that we abandon our comrades Beck and Salzar to the rifle of Mike Clinch?"

"Why not?" demanded Georgiades sullenly;—"we shall have worse to face before we see the Place de l'Opéra."

"There remains, also, Eddie Abrams," remarked Quintana.

Crooks never betray their attorney. Everybody expressed a willingness to have the five shares of plunder properly assessed to satisfy the fee due to Mr. Abrams.

"Ver' well," nodded Quintana, "are you satisfy, messieurs, to divide an' disperse?"

Sard said, heavily, that they ought to stick together until they arrived in New York.

Sanchez sneered, accusing Sard of wanting a bodyguard to escort him to his own home. "In this accursed forest," he insisted, "five of us would attract attention where one alone, with sufficient stealth, can slip through into the open country."

"Two by two is better," said Picquet. "You, Sanchez, shall travel alone if you desire—"

"Divide the gems first," growled Georgiades, "and then let each do what pleases him."

"That," nodded Quintana, "is also my opinion. It is so settle. Attention!" Two pistols were in his hands as by magic. With a slight smile he laid them on the moss beside him.

He then spread a large white handkerchief flat on the ground; and, from his pockets, he poured out the glittering cascade. Yet, like a feeding panther, every sense remained alert to the slightest sound or movement elsewhere; and when Georgiades grunted from excess emotion, Quintana's right hand held a pistol before the grunt had ceased.

It was a serious business, this division of loot; every reckless visage reflected the strain of the situation.

Quintana, both pistols in his hands, looked down at the scintillating heap of jewels.

"I estimate two and one quartaire million of dollaires," he said simply. "It has been agree that I accep' for me the erosite gem known as The Flaming Jewel. In addition, messieurs, it has been agree that I accep' for myse'f one part in five of the remainder."

A fierce silence reigned. Every wolfish eye was on the leader. He smiled, rested his pair of pistols on either knee.

"Is there," he asked softly, "any gentleman who shall objec'?"

"Who," demanded Georgiades hoarsely, "is to divide for us?"

"It is for such purpose," explained Quintana suavely, "that my frien',

Emanuel Sard, has arrive. Monsieur Sard is a brokaire of diamon's, as all know ver' well. Therefore, it shall be our frien' Sard who will divide for us what we have gain to-day by our—industry."

The savage tension broke with a laugh at the word chosen by Quintana to express their efforts of the morning.

Sard had been standing with one fat hand flat against the trunk of a tree. Now, at a nod from Quintana, he squatted down, and, with the same hand that had been resting against the tree, he spread out the pile of jewels into a flat layer.

As he began to divide this into five parts, still using the flat of his pudgy hand, something poked him lightly in the ribs. It was the muzzle of one of Quintana's pistols.

Sard, ghastly pale, looked up. His palm, sticky with balsam gum, quivered in Quintana's grasp.

"I was going to scrape it off," he gasped. "The tree was sticky—"

Quintana, with the muzzle of his pistol, detached half a dozen diamonds and rubies that clung to the gum on Mr. Sard's palm.

"Wash!" he said drily.

Sard, sweating with fear, washed his right hand with whiskey from his pocket-flask, and dried it for general inspection.

"My God," he protested tremulously, "it was accidental, gentlemen. Do you think I'd try to get away with anything like that—"

Quintana coolly shoved him aside and with the barrel of his pistol he pushed the flat pile of gems into five separate heaps. Only he and Georgiades knew that a magnificent diamond had been lodged in the muzzle of his pistol. The eyes of the Greek flamed with rage at the trick, but he awaited the division before he should come to any conclusion.

Quintana coolly picked out The Flaming Jewel and pocketed it. Then, to each man he indicated the heap which was to be his portion.

A snarling wrangle instantly began, Sanchez objecting to rubies and demanding more emeralds, and Picquet complaining violently concerning the smallness of the diamonds allotted him.

Sard's trained eyes appraised every allotment. Without weighing, and, lacking time and paraphernalia for expert examination, he was inclined to think the division fair enough.

Quintana got to his feet lithely.

"For me," he said, "it is finish. With my frien' Sard I shall now depart. Messieurs, I embrace and salute you. A bientôt in Paris—if it be God's will! Donc—au revoir, les amis, et à la bonheur! Allons! Each for himself and gar' aux flics!"

Sard, seized with a sort of still terror, regarded Quintana with enormous eyes. Torn between dismay of being left alone in the wilderness, and a very natural fear of any single companion, he did not know what to say or do.

En masse, the gang were too distrustful of one another to unite on robbing any individual. But any individual might easily rob a companion when alone with him.

"Why—why can't we all go together," he stammered. "It is safer, surer—"

"I go with Quintana and you," interrupted Georgiades, smilingly; his mind on the diamond in the muzzle of Quintana's pistol.

"I do not invite you," said Quintana. "But come if it pleases you."

"I also prefer to come with you others," growled Sanchez. "To roam alone in this filthy forest does not suit me."

Picquet shrugged his shoulders, turned on his heel in silence. They watched him moving away all alone, eastward. When he had disappeared among the trees, Quintana looked inquiringly at the others.

"Eh, bien, non alors!" snarled Georgiades suddenly. "There are too many in your trupeau, mon capitaine. Bonne chance!"

He turned and started noisily in the direction taken by Picquet.

They watched him out of sight; listened to his careless trample after he was lost to view. When at length the last distant sound of his retreat had died away in the stillness, Quintana touched Sard with the point of his pistol.

"Go first," he said suavely.

"For God's sake, be a little careful of your gun—"

"I am, my dear frien'. It is of *you* I may become careless. You will mos' kin'ly face south, and you will be kin' sufficient to start immediate. Tha's what I mean.... I thank you.... Now, my frien', Sanchez! Tha's correc'! You shall follow my frien' Sard ver' close. Me, I march in the rear. So we shall pass to the eas' of thees Star Pon', then between the cross-road an' Ghos' Lake; an' then we shall repose; an' one of us, en vidette, shall discover if the Constabulary have patrol beyon'.... Allons! March!"

II

Guided by Quintana's directions, the three had made a wide detour to the east, steering by compass for the cross-roads beyond Star Pond.

In a dense growth of cedars, on a little ridge traversing wet land, Quintana halted to listen.

Sard and Sanchez, supposing him to be at their heels, continued on, pushing their way blindly through the cedars, clinging to the hard ridge in terror of sink-holes. But their progress was very slow; and they were still in sight, fighting a painful path amid the evergreens, when Quintana suddenly squatted close to the moist earth behind a juniper bush.

At first, except for the threshing of Sard and Sanchez through the massed obstructions ahead, there was not a sound in the woods.

After a little while there *was* a sound—very, very slight. No dry stick cracked; no dry leaves rustled; no swish of foliage; no whipping sound of branches disturbed the intense silence.

But, presently, came a soft, swift rhythm like the pace of a forest creature in haste—a discreetly hurrying tread which was more a series of light earth-shocks than sound.

Quintana, kneeling on one knee, lifted his pistol. He already felt the slight vibration of the ground on the hard ridge. The cedars were moving just beyond him now. He waited until, through the parted foliage, a face appeared.

The loud report of his pistol struck Sard with the horror of paralysis. Sanchez faced about with one spring, snarling, a weapon in either hand.

In the terrible silence they could hear something heavy floundering in the bushes, choking, moaning, thudding on the ground.

Sanchez began to creep back; Sard, more dead than alive, crawled at his heels. Presently they saw Quintana, waist deep in juniper, looking down at something.

And when they drew closer they saw Georgiades lying on his back under a cedar, the whole front of his shirt from chest to belly a sopping mess of blood.

There seemed no need of explanation. The dead Greek lay there where he had not been expected, and his two pistols lay beside him where they had fallen.

Sanchez looked stealthily at Quintana, who said softly:

"Bien sure.... In his left side pocket, I believe."

Sanchez laid a cool hand on the dead man's heart; then, satisfied, rummaged until he found Georgiades' share of the loot.

Sard, hurriedly displaying a pair of clean but shaky hands, made the division.

When the three men had silently pocketed what was allotted to each, Quintana pushed curiously at the dead man with the toe of his shoe.

"Peste!" he remarked. "I had place, for security, a ver' large diamon' in my pistol barrel. Now it is within the interior of this gentleman...." He turned to Sanchez: "I sell him to you. One sapphire. Yes?"

Sanchez shook his head with a slight sneer: "We wait—if you want your diamond, mon capitaine."

Quintana hesitated, then made a grimace and shook his head.

"No," he said, "he has swallow. Let him digest. Allons! March!"

But after they had gone on—two hundred yards, perhaps—Sanchez stopped.

"Well?" inquired Quintana. Then, with a sneer: "I now recollec' that once you have been a butcher in Madrid.... Suit your tas'e, l'ami Sanchez."

Sard gazed at Sanchez out of sickened eyes.

"You keep away from me until you've washed yourself," he burst out, revolted. "Don't you come near me till you're clean!"

Quintana laughed and seated himself. Sanchez, with a hang-dog glance at him, turned and sneaked back on the trail they had traversed. Before he was out of sight Sard saw him fish out a Spanish knife from his hip pocket and unclasp it.

Almost nauseated, he turned on Quintana in a sort of frightened fury:

"Come on!" he said hoarsely. "I don't want to travel with that man! I won't associate with a ghoul! My God, I'm a respectable business man—"

"Yaas," drawled Quintana, "tha's what I saw always myse'f; my frien' Sard he is ver' respec'able, an' I trus' him like I trus' myse'f."

However, after a moment, Quintana got up from the fallen tree where he had been seated.

As he passed Sard he looked curiously into the man's frightened eyes. There was not the slightest doubt that Sard was a coward.

"You shall walk behin' me," remarked Quintana carelessly. "If Sanchez fin' us, it is well; if he shall not, that also is ver' well.... We go, now."

Sanchez made no effort to find them. They had been gone half an hour before he had finished the business that had turned him back.

After that he wandered about hunting for water—a rivulet, a puddle, anything. But the wet ground proved wet only on the surface moss. Sanchez needed more than damp moss for his toilet. Casting about him, hither and thither, for some depression that might indicate a stream, he came to a heavily wooded slope, and descended it.

There was a bog at the foot. With his fouled hands he dug out a basin which filled up full of reddish water, discoloured by alders.

But the water was redder still when his toilet ended.

As he stood there, examining his clothing, and washing what he could of the ominous stains from sleeve and shoe, very far away to the north he heard a curious noise—a far, faint sound such as he never before had heard.

If it were a voice of any sort there was nothing human about it....

Probably some sort of unknown bird.... Perhaps a bird of prey.... That was natural, considering the attraction that Georgiades would have for such creatures.... If it were a bird it must be a large one, he thought.... Because there was a certain volume to the cry.... Perhaps it was a beast, after all.... Some unknown beast of the forest....

Sanchez was suddenly afraid. Scarcely knowing what he was doing he began to run along the edge of the bog.

First growth timber skirted it; running was unobstructed by underbrush.

With his startled ears full of the alarming and unknown sound, he ran through the woods under gigantic pines which spread a soft green twilight around him.

He was tired, or thought he was, but the alarming sounds were filling his ears now; the entire forest seemed full of them, echoing in all directions, coming in upon him from everywhere, so that he knew not in which direction to run.

But he could not stop. Demoralised, he darted this way and that; terror winged his feet; the air vibrated above and around him with the dreadful, unearthly sounds.

The next instant he fell headlong over a ledge, struck water, felt himself whirled around in the icy, rushing current, rolled over, tumbled through rapids, blinded, deafened, choked, swept helplessly in a vast green wall of water toward something that thundered in his brain an instant, then dashed it into roaring chaos.

Half a mile down the turbulent outlet of Star Pond—where a great sheet of green water pours thirty feet into the tossing foam below—and spinning, dipping, diving, bobbing up like a lost log after the drive, the body of Señor Sanchez danced all alone in the wilderness, spilling from soggy pockets diamonds, sapphires, rubies, emeralds, into crystal caves where only the shadows of slim trout stirred.

Very far away to the eastward Quintana stood listening, clutching Sard by one sleeve to silence him.

Presently he said: "My frien', somebody is hunting with houn's in this fores'.

"Maybe they are not hunting *us*.... *Maybe*.... But, for me, I shall seek running water. Go you your own way! Houp! Vamose!"

He turned westward; but he had taken scarcely a dozen strides when Sard came panting after him:

"Don't leave me!" gasped the terrified diamond broker. "I don't know where to go—"

Quintana faced him abruptly—with a terrifying smile and glimmer of white teeth—and shoved a pistol into the fold of fat beneath Sard's double chin.

"You hear those dogs? Yes? Ver' well; I also. Run, now. I say to you run ver' damn quick. Hé! Houp! Allez vous en! Beat eet!"

He struck Sard a stinging blow on his fleshy ear with the pistol barrel, and Sard gave a muffled shriek which was more like the squeak of a frightened animal.

"My God, Quintana—" he sobbed. Then Quintana's eyes blazed murder: and Sard turned and ran lumbering through the thicket like a stampeded ox, crashing on amid withered brake, white birch scrub and brier, not knowing whither he was headed, crazed with terror.

Quintana watched his flight for a moment, then, pistol swinging, he ran in the opposite direction, eastward, speeding lithely as a cat down a long, wooded slope which promised running water at the foot.

Sard could not run very far. He could scarcely stand when he pulled up and clung to the trunk of a tree.

More dead than alive he embraced the tree, gulping horribly for air, every fat-incrusted organ labouring, his senses swimming.

As he sagged there, gripping his support on shaking knees, by degrees his senses began to return.

He could hear the dogs, now, vaguely as in a nightmare. But after a little while he began to believe that their hysterical yelping was really growing more distant.

Then this man whose every breath was an outrage on God, prayed.

He prayed that the hounds would follow Quintana, come up with him, drag him down, worry him, tear him to shreds of flesh and clothing.

He listened and prayed alternately. After a while he no longer prayed but concentrated on his ears.

Surely, surely, the diabolical sound was growing less distinct.... It was changing direction too. But whether in Quintana's direction or not Sard could not tell. He was no woodsman. He was completely turned around.

He looked upward through a dense yellow foliage, but all was grey in the sky—very grey and still;—and there seemed to be no traces of the sun that had been shining.

He looked fearfully around: trees, trees, and more trees. No break, no glimmer, nothing to guide him, teach him. He could see, perhaps, fifty feet; no further.

In panic he started to move on. That is what fright invariably does to those ignorant of the forest. Terror starts them moving.

Sobbing, frightened almost witless, he had been floundering forward for over an hour, and had made circle after circle without knowing, when, by chance, he set foot in a perfectly plain trail.

Emotion overpowered him. He was too overcome to stir for a while. At length, however, he tottered off down the trail, oblivious as to what direction he was taking, animated only by a sort of madness—horror of trees—an insane necessity to see open ground, get into it, and lie down on it.

And now, directly ahead, he saw clear grey sky low through the trees. The wood's edge!

He began to run.

As he emerged from the edge of the woods, waist-deep in brush and weeds, wide before his blood-shot eyes spread Star Pond.

Even in his half-stupefied brain there was memory enough left for recognition.

He remembered the lake. His gaze travelled to the westward; and he saw Clinch's Dump standing below, stark, silent, the doors swinging open in the wind.

When terror had subsided in a measure and some of his trembling strength returned, he got up out of the clump of rag-weeds where he had lain down, and earnestly nosed the unpainted house, listening with all his ears.

There was not a sound save the soughing of autumn winds and the delicate rattle of falling leaves in the woods behind him.

He needed food and rest. He gazed earnestly at the house. Nothing stirred there save the open doors swinging idly in every vagrant wind.

He ventured down a little way—near enough to see the black cinders of the burned barn, and close enough to hear the lake waters slapping the sandy shore.

If he dared—

And after a long while he ventured to waddle nearer, slinking through brush and frosted weed, creeping behind boulders, edging always closer and closer to that silent house where nothing moved except the wind-blown door.

And now, at last, he set a furtive foot upon the threshold, stood listening, tip-toed in, peered here and there, sidled to the dining-room, peered in.

When, at length, Emanuel Sard discovered that Clinch's Dump was tenantless, he made straight for the pantry. Here was cheese, crackers, an apple pie, half a dozen bottles of home-brewed beer.

He loaded his arms with all they could carry, stole through the dance-hall out to the veranda, which overlooked the lake.

Here, hidden in the doorway, he could watch the road from Ghost Lake and survey the hillside down which an intruder must come from the forest.

And here Sard slaked his raging thirst and satiated the gnawing appetite of the obese, than which there is no crueller torment to an inert liver and distended paunch.

Munching, guzzling, watching, Sard squatted just within the veranda doorway, anxiously considering his chances.

He knew where he was. At the foot of the lake, and eastward, he had been robbed by a highwayman on the forest road branching from the main highway. Southwest lay Ghost Lake and the Inn.

Somewhere between these two points he must try to cross the State Road.... After that, comparative safety. For the miles that still would lie between him and distant civilisation seemed as nothing to the horror of that hell of trees.

He looked up now at the shaggy fringing woods, shuddered, opened another bottle of beer.

In all that panorama of forest, swale, and water the only thing that had alarmed him at all by moving was something in the water. When first he noticed it he almost swooned, for he took it to be a swimming dog.

In his agitation he had risen to his feet; and then the swimming creature almost frightened Sard out of his senses, for it tilted suddenly and went down with a report like the crack of a pistol.

However, when Sard regained control of his wits he realised that a swimming dog doesn't dive and doesn't whack the water with its tail.

He dimly remembered hearing that beavers behaved that way.

Watching the water he saw the thing out there in the lake again, swimming in erratic circles, its big, dog-like head well out of the water.

It certainly was no dog. A beaver, maybe. Whatever it was, Sard didn't care any longer.

Idly he watched it. Sometimes, when it swam very near, he made a sudden motion with his fat arm; and crack!—with a pistol-shot report down it dived. But always it reappeared.

What had a creature like that to do with him? Sard watched it with failing interest, thinking of other things—of Quintana and the chances that the dogs had caught him—of Sanchez, the Ghoul, hoping that dire misfortune might overtake him, too;—of the dead man sprawling under the cedar-tree, all sopping crimson— Faugh!

Shivering, Sard filled his mouth with apple-pie and cheese and pulled the cork from another bottle of home-brewed beer.

III

About that time, a mile and a half to the southward, James Darragh came out on the rocky and rushing outlet to Star Pond.

Over his shoulder was a rifle, and all around him ran dogs—big, powerful dogs, built like foxhounds but with the rough, wiry coats of Airedales, even rougher of ear and features.

The dogs—half a dozen or so in number—seemed very tired. All ran down eagerly to the water and drank and slobbered and panted, lolling their tongues, and slaking their thirst again and again along the swirling edge of a deep trout pool.

Darragh's rifle lay in the hollow of his left arm; his khaki waistcoat was set with loops full of cartridges. From his left wrist hung a raw-hide whip.

Now he laid aside his rifle and whip, took from the pocket of his shooting coat three or four leather dog-leashes, went down among the dogs and coupled them up.

They followed him back to the bank above. Here he sat down on a rock and inspected his watch.

He had been seated there for ten minutes, possibly, with his tired dogs lying around him, when just above him he saw a State Trooper emerge from the woods on foot, carrying a rifle over one shoulder.

"Jack!" he called in a guarded voice.

Trooper Stormont turned, caught sight of Darragh, made a signal of recognition, and came toward him.

Darragh said: "Your mate, Trooper Lannis, is down stream. I've two of my own game wardens at the cross-roads, two more on the Ghost Lake Road, and two foresters and an inspector out toward Owl Marsh."

Stormont nodded, looked down at the dogs.

"This isn't the State Forest," said Darragh, smiling. Then his face grew grave: "How is Eve?" he asked.

"She's feeling better," replied Stormont. "I telephoned to Ghost Lake Inn for the hotel physician.... I was afraid of pneumonia, Jim. Eve had chills last night.... But Dr. Claybourn thinks she's all right.... So I left her in care of your housekeeper."

"Mrs. Ray will look out for her.... You haven't told Eve who I am, have you?"

"No."

"I'll tell her myself to-night. I don't know how she'll take it when she learns I'm the heir to the mortal enemy of Mike Clinch."

"I don't know either," said Stormont.

There was a silence; the State Trooper looked down at the dogs: "What are they, Jim?"

"Otter-hounds," said Darragh, "—a breed of my own.... But that's *all* they are capable of hunting, I guess," he added grimly.

Stormont's gaze questioned him.

Darragh said: "After I telephoned you this morning that a guest of mine at Harrod Place, and I, had been stuck up and robbed by Quintana's outfit, what did you do, Jack?"

"I called up Bill Lannis first," said Stormont, "—then the doctor. After he came, Mrs. Ray arrived with a maid. Then I went in and spoke to Eve. Then I did what you suggested—I crossed the forest diagonally toward The Scaur, zig-zagged north, turned by the rock hog-back south of Drowned Valley, came southeast, circled west, and came out here as you asked me to."

"Almost on the minute," nodded Darragh.... "You saw no signs of Quintana's gang?"

"None."

"Well," said Darragh, "I left my two guests at Harrod Place to amuse each other, got out three couple of my otter-hounds and started them—as I hoped and supposed—on Quintana's trail."

"What happened?" inquired Stormont curiously.

"Well—I don't know. I think they were following some of Quintana's gang—for a while, anyway. After that, God knows—deer, hare, cottontail—*I* don't know. They yelled their bally heads off—I on the run—they're slow dogs, you know—and whatever they were after either fooled them or there were too many trails.... I made a mistake, that's all. These poor beasts don't know anything except an otter. I just *hoped* they might take Quintana's trail if I put them on it."

"Well," said Stormont, "it can't be helped now.... I told Bill Lannis that we'd rendezvous at Clinch's Dump."

"All right," nodded Darragh. "Let's keep to the open; my dogs are leashed couples."

They had been walking for twenty minutes, possibly, exchanging scarcely a word, and they were now nearing the hilly basin where Star Pond lay, when Darragh said abruptly:

"I'm going to tell you about things, Jack. You've taken my word so far that it's all right—"

"Naturally," said Stormont simply.

The two men, who had been brother officers in the Great War, glanced at each other, slightly smiling.

"Here it is then," said Darragh. "When I was on duty in Riga for the Intelligence Department, I met two ladies in dire distress, whose mansion had been burned and looted, supposedly by the Bolsheviki.

"They were actually hungry and penniless; the only clothing they possessed they were wearing. These ladies were the Countess Orloff-Strelwitz, and a young girl, Theodorica, Grand Duchess of Esthonia.... I did what I could for them. After a while, in the course of other duty, I found out that the Bolsheviki had had nothing to do with the arson and robbery, but that the crime had been perpetrated by José Quintana's gang of international crooks masquerading as Bolsheviki."

Stormont nodded: "I also came across similar cases," he remarked.

"Well, this was a flagrant example. Quintana had burnt the château and had made off with over two million dollars worth of the little Grand Duchess's jewels—among them the famous Erosite gem known as The Flaming Jewel."

"I've heard of it."

"There are only two others known.... Well, I did what I could with the Esthonian police, who didn't believe me.

"But a short time ago the Countess Orloff sent me word that Quintana really was the guilty one, and that he had started for America.

"I've been after him ever since.... But, Jack, until this morning Quintana did not possess these stolen jewels. *Clinch did!* "

"What!"

"Clinch served over-seas in a Forestry Regiment. In Paris he robbed Quintana of these jewels. That's why I've been hanging around Clinch."

Stormont's face was flushed and incredulous. Then it lost colour as he thought of the jewels that Eve had concealed—the gems for which she had risked her life.

He said: "But you tell me Quintana robbed you this morning."

"He did. The little Grand Duchess and the Countess Orloff-Strelwitz are my guests at Harrod Place.

"Last night I snatched the case containing these gems from Quintana's fingers. This morning, as I offered them to the Grand Duchess, Quintana coolly stepped between us—"

His voice became bitter and his features reddened with rage poorly controlled:

"By God, Jack, I should have shot Quintana when the opportunity offered. Twice I've had the chance. The next time I shall kill him any way I can.... Legitimately."

"Of course," said Stormont gravely. But his mind was full of the jewels which Eve had. What and whose were they—if Quintana again had the Esthonian gems in his possession?

"Had you recovered all the jewels for the Grand Duchess?" he asked Darragh.

"Every one, Jack.... Quintana has done me a terrible injury. I shan't let it go. I mean to hunt that man to the end."

Stormont, terribly perplexed, nodded.

A few minutes later, as they came out among the willows and alders on the northeast side of Star Pond, Stormont touched his comrade's arm.

"Look at that enormous dog-otter out there in the lake!"

"Grab those dogs! They'll strangle each other," cried Darragh quickly. "That's it—unleash them, Jack, and let them go!"—he was struggling with the other two couples while speaking.

And now the hounds, unleashed, lifted frantic voices. The very sky seemed full of the discordant tumult; wood and shore reverberated with the volume of convulsive and dissonant baying.

"Damn it," said Darragh, disgusted, "—that's what they've been trailing all the while across-woods—that devilish dog-otter yonder.... And I had hoped they were on Quintana's trail—"

A mass rush and scurry of crazed dogs nearly swept him off his feet, and both men caught a glimpse of a large bitch-otter taking to the lake from a ledge of rock just beyond.

Now the sky vibrated with the deafening outcry of the dogs, some taking to water, others racing madly along shore.

Crack! The echo of the dog-otter's blow on the water came across to them as the beast dived.

"Well, I'm in for it now," muttered Darragh, starting along the bank toward Clinch's Dump, to keep an eye on his dogs.

Stormont followed more leisurely.

IV

A few minutes before Darragh and Stormont had come out on the farther edge of Star Pond, Sard, who had heard from Quintana about the big drain pipe which led from Clinch's pantry into the lake, decided to go in and take a look at it.

He had been told all about its uses—how Clinch—in the event of a raid by State Troopers or Government enforcement agents—could empty his contraband hootch into the lake if necessary—and even could slide a barrel of ale or a keg of rum, intact, into the great tile tunnel and recover the liquor at his leisure.

Also, and grimly, Quintana had admitted that through this drain Eve Strayer and the State Trooper, Stormont, had escaped from Clinch's Dump.

So now Sard, full of curiosity, went back into the pantry to look at it for himself.

Almost instantly the idea occurred to him to make use of the drain for his own safety and comfort.

Why shouldn't he sleep in the pantry, lock the door, and, in case of intrusion—other exits being unavailable—why shouldn't he feel entirely safe with such an avenue of escape open?

For swimming was Sard's single accomplishment. He wasn't afraid of the water; he simply couldn't sink. Swimming was the only sport he ever had indulged in. He adored it.

Also, the mere idea of sleeping alone amid that hell of trees terrified Sard. Never had he known such horror as when Quintana abandoned him in the woods. Never again could he gaze upon a tree without malignant hatred. Never again did he desire to lay eyes upon even a bush. The very sight, now, of the dusky forest filled him with loathing. Why should he not risk one night in this deserted house—sleep well and warmly, feed well, drink his bellyfull of Clinch's beer, before attempting the dead-line southward, where he was only too sure that patrols were riding and hiding on the lookout for the fancy gentlemen of José Quintana's selected company of malefactors?

Well, here in the snug pantry were pies, crullers, bread, cheeses, various dried meats, tinned vegetables, ham, bacon, fuel and range to prepare what he desired.

Here was beer, too; and doubtless ardent spirits if he could nose out the hidden demijohns and bottles.

He peered out of the pantry window at the forest, shuddered, cursed it and every separate tree in it; cursed Quintana, too, wishing him black mischance. No; it was settled. He'd take his chance here in the pantry.... And there must be a mattress somewhere upstairs.

He climbed the staircase, cautiously, discovered Clinch's bedroom, took the mattress and blankets from the bed, dragged them to the pantry.

Could any honest man be more tight and snug in this perilous world of the desperate and undeserving? Sard thought not. But one matter troubled him: the lock of the pantry door had been shattered. To remedy this he moused around until he discovered some long nails and a clawhammer. When he was ready to go to sleep he'd nail himself in. And in the morning he'd pry the door loose. That was simple. Sard chuckled for the first time since he had set eyes upon the accursed region.

And now the sun came out from behind a low bank of solid grey cloud, and fell upon the countenance of Emanuel Sard. It warmed his parrotnose agreeably; it cheered and enlivened him.

Not for him a night of terrors in that horrible forest which he could see through the pantry window.

A sense of security and of well-being pervaded Sard to his muddy shoes. He even curled his fat toes in them with animal contentment.

A little snack before cooking a heavily satisfactory dinner? Certainly.

So he tucked a couple of bottles of beer under one arm, a loaf of bread and a chunk of cheese under the other, and waddled out to the veranda door.

And at that instant the very heavens echoed with that awful tumult which had first paralysed, then crazed him in the woods.

Bottles, bread, cheese fell from his grasp and his knees nearly collapsed under him. In the bushes on the lake shore he saw animals leaping and racing, but, in his terror, he did not recognise them for dogs.

Then, suddenly, he saw a man, close to the house, running: and another man not far behind. *That* he understood, and it electrified him into action.

It was too late to escape from the house now. He understood that instantly.

He ran back through the dance-hall and dining-room to the pantry; but he dared not let these intruders hear the noise of hammering.

In an agony of indecision he stood trembling, listening to the infernal racket of the dogs, and waiting for the first footstep within the house.

No step came. But, chancing to look over his shoulder, he saw a man peering through the pantry window at him.

Ungovernable terror seized Sard. Scarcely aware what he was about, he seized the edges of the big drain-pipe and crowded his obese body into it head first. He was so fat and heavy that he filled the tile. To start himself down he pulled with both hands and kicked himself forward, tortoise-like, down the slanting tunnel, sticking now and then, dragging himself on and downward.

Now he began to gain momentum; he felt himself sliding, not fast but steadily.

There came a hitch somewhere; his heavy body stuck on the steep incline.

Then, as he lifted his bewildered head and strove to peer into the blackness in front, he saw four balls of green fire close to him in darkness.

He began to slide at the same instant, and flung out both hands to check himself. But his palms slid in the slime and his body slid after.

He shrieked once as his face struck a furry obstruction where four balls of green fire flamed horribly and a fury of murderous teeth tore his face and throat to bloody tatters as he slid lower, lower, settling through crimson-dyed waters into the icy depths of Star Pond.

Stormont, down by the lake, called to Darragh, who appeared on the veranda:

"Oh, Jim! Both otters crawled into the drain! I think your dogs must have killed one of them under water. There's a big patch of blood spreading off shore."

"Yes," said Darragh, "something has just been killed, somewhere ... Jack!"

"Yes?"

"Pull both your guns and come up here, quick!"

Episode Ten
THE TWILIGHT OF MIKE

I

When Quintana turned like an enraged snake on Sard and drove him to his destruction, he would have killed and robbed the frightened diamond broker had he dared risk the shot. He had intended to do this anyway, sooner or later. But with the noise of the hunting dogs filling the forest, Quintana was afraid to fire. Yet, even then he followed Sard stealthily for a few minutes, afraid yet murderously desirous of the gems, confused by the tumult of the hounds, timid and ferocious at the same time, and loath to leave his fat, perspiring, and demoralised victim.

But the racket of the dogs proved too much for Quintana. He sheered away toward the South, leaving Sard floundering on ahead, unconscious of the treachery that had followed furtively in his panic-stricken tracks.

About an hour later Quintana was seen, challenged, chased and shot at by State Trooper Lannis.

Quintana ran. And what with the dense growth of seedling beech and oak and the heavily falling birch and poplar leaves, Lannis first lost Quintana and then his trail.

The State Trooper had left his horse at the cross-roads near the scene of Darragh's masked exploit, where he had stopped and robbed Sard—and now Lannis hastened back to find and mount his horse, and gallop straight into the first growth timber.

Through dim aisles of giant pine he spurred to a dead run on the chance of cutting Quintana from the eastward edge of the forest and forcing him back toward the north or west, where patrols were more than likely to hold him.

The State Trooper rode with all the reckless indifference and grace of the Western cavalryman, and he seemed to be part of the superb animal he rode—part of its bone and muscle, its litheness, its supple power—part of its vertebræ and ribs and limbs, so perfect was their bodily co-ordination.

Rifle and eyes intently alert, the rider scarce noticed his rushing mount; and if he guided with wrist and knee it was instinctive and as though the horse were guiding them both.

And now, far ahead through this primeval stand of pine, sunshine glimmered, warning of a clearing. And here Trooper Lannis pulled in his horse at the edge of what seemed to be a broad, flat meadow, vividly green.

But it was the intense, arsenical green of hair-fine grass that covers with its false velvet those quaking bogs where only a thin, crust-like skin of root-fibre and vegetation cover infinite depths of silt.

The silt had no more substance than a drop of ink colouring the water in a tumbler.

Sitting his fast-breathing mount, Lannis searched this wide, flat expanse of brilliant green. Nothing moved on it save a great heron picking its deliberate way on stilt-like legs. It was well for Quintana that he had not attempted it.

Very cautiously Lannis walked his horse along the hard ground which edged this marsh on the west. Nowhere was there any sign that Quintana had come down to the edge among the shrubs and swale grasses.

Beyond the marsh another trooper patrolled; and when at length he and Lannis perceived each other and exchanged signals, the latter wheeled his horse and retraced his route at an easy canter, satisfied that Quintana had not yet broken cover.

Back through the first growth he cantered, his rifle at a ready, carefully scanning the more open woodlands, and so came again to the cross-roads.

And here stood a State Game Inspector, with a report that some sort of beagle-pack was hunting in the forest to the northwest; and very curious to investigate.

So it was arranged that the Inspector should turn road-patrol and the Trooper become the rover.

There was no sound of dogs when Lannis rode in on the narrow, spotted trail whence he had flushed Quintana into the dense growth of saplings that bordered it.

His horse made little noise on the moist layer of leaves and forest mould; he listened hard for the sound of hounds as he rode; heard nothing save the chirr of red squirrels, the shriek of a watching jay, or the startling noise of falling acorns rapping and knocking on great limbs in their descent to the forest floor.

Once, very, very far away westward in the direction of Star Pond he fancied he heard a faint vibration in the air that might have been hounds baying.

He was right. And at that very moment Sard was dying, horribly, among two trapped otters as big and fierce as the dogs that had driven them into the drain.

But Lannis knew nothing of that as he moved on, mounted, along the spotted trail, now all a yellow glory of birch and poplar which made the woodland brilliant as though lighted by yellow lanterns.

Somewhere among the birches, between him and Star Pond, was Harrod Place. And the idea occurred to him that Quintana might have ventured to ask food and shelter there. Yet, that was not likely because Trooper Stormont had called him that morning on the telephone from the Hatchery Lodge.

No; the only logical retreat for Quintana was northward to the mountains, where patrols were plenty and fire-wardens on duty in every watch-tower. Or, the fugitive could make for Drowned Valley by a blind trail which, Stormont informed him, existed but which Lannis never had heard of.

However, to reassure himself, Lannis rode as far as Harrod Place, and found game wardens on duty along the line.

Then he turned west and trotted his mount down to the hatchery, where he saw Ralph Wier, the Superintendent, standing outside the lodge talking to his assistant, George Fry.

When Lannis rode up on the opposite side of the brook, he called across to Wier:

"You haven't seen anything of any crooked outfit around here, have you, Ralph? I'm looking for that kind."

"See here," said the Superintendent, "I don't know but George Fry may have seen one of your guys. Come over and he'll tell you what happened an hour ago."

Trooper Lannis pivotted his horse and put him to the brook with scarcely any take-off; and the splendid animal cleared the water like a deer and came cantering up to the door of the lodge.

Fry's boyish face seemed agitated; he looked up at the State Trooper with the flush of tears in his gaze and pointed at the rifle Lannis carried:

"If I'd had *that*," he said excitedly, "I'd have brought in a crook, you bet!"

"Where did you see him?" inquired Lannis.

"Jest west of the Scaur, about an hour and a half ago. Wier and me was stockin' the head of Scaur Brook with fingerlings. There's more good water—two miles of it—to the east, and all it needed was a fish-ladder around Scaur Falls.

"So I toted in cement and sand and grub last week, and I built me a shanty on the Scaur, and I been laying up a fish-way around the falls. So that's how I come there—" He clicked his teeth and darted a furious glance at the woods. "By God," he said, "I was such a fool I didn't take no rifle. All I had was an axe and a few traps.... I wasn't going to let the mink get our trout whatever you fellows say," he added defiantly, "—and law or no law—"

"Get along with your story, young man," interrupted Lannis; "—you can spill the rest out to the Commissioner."

"All right, then. This is the way it happened down to the Scaur. I was eating lunch by the fish-stairs, looking up at 'em and kind of planning how to save cement, and not thinking about anybody being near me, when *something* made me turn my head.... You know how it is in the woods.... I kinda *felt* somebody near. And, by cracky!—there stood a man with a big, black automatic pistol, and he had a bead on my belly.

"'Well,' said I, 'what's troubling *you* and your gun, my friend?'—I was that astonished.

"He was a slim-built, powerful guy with a foreign face and voice and way. He wanted to know if he had the honour—as he put it—to introduce himself to a detective or game constable, or a friend of Mike Clinch.

"I told him I wasn't any of these, and that I worked in a private hatchery; and he called me a liar."

Young Fry's face flushed and his voice began to quiver:

"That's the way he misused me: and he backed me into the shanty and I had to sit down with both hands up. Then he filled my pack-basket with grub, and took my axe, and strapped my kit onto his back.... And talking all the time in his mean, sneery, foreign way—and I guess he thought he was funny, for he laughed at his own jokes.

"He told me his name was Quintana, and that he ought to shoot me for a rat, but wouldn't because of the stink. Then he said he was going to do a quick job that the police were too cowardly to do;—that he was a-going to find Mike Clinch down to Drowned Valley and kill him; and if he could catch Mike's daughter, too, he'd spoil her face for life—"

The boy was breathing so hard and his rage made him so incoherent that Lannis took him by the shoulder and shook him:

"What next?" demanded the Trooper impatiently. "Tell your story and quit thinking how you were misused!"

"He told me to stay in the shanty for an hour or he'd do for me good," cried Fry.... "Once I got up and went to the door; and there he stood by the brook, wolfing my lunch with both hands. I tell you he cursed and drove me, like a dog, inside with his big pistol—my God—like a dog....

"Then, the next time I took a chance he was gone.... And I beat it here to get me a rifle—" The boy broke down and sobbed: "He drove me around—like a dog—he did—"

"You leave that to me," interrupted Lannis sharply. And, to Wier: "You and George had better get a gun apiece. That fellow *might* come back here or go to Harrod Place if we starve him out."

Wier said to Fry: "Go up to Harrod Place and tell Jansen your story and bring back two 45-70's.... And quit snivelling.... You may get a shot at him yet."

Lannis had already ridden down to the brook. Now he jumped his horse across, pulled up, called back to Wier:

"I think our man is making for Drowned Valley, all right. My mate, Stormont, telephoned me that some of his gang are there, and that Mike Clinch and his gang have them stopped on the other side! Keep your eye on Harrod Place!"

And away he cantered into the North.

Behind the curtains of her open window Eve Strayer, lying on her bed, had heard every word.

Crouched there beside her pillow she peered out and saw Trooper Lannis ride away; saw the Fry boy start toward Harrod Place on a run; saw Ralph Wier watch them out of sight and then turn and re-enter the lodge.

Wrapped in Darragh's big blanket robe she got off the bed and opened her chamber door as Wier was passing through the living-room.

"Please—I'd like to speak to you a moment," she called.

Wier turned instantly and came to the partly open door.

"I want to know," she said, "where I am."

"Ma'am?"

"What is this place?"

"It's a hatchery—"

"Whose?"

"Ma'am?"

"Whose lodge is this? Does it belong to Harrod Place?"

"We're h-hootch runners, Miss—" stammered Wier, mindful of instructions, but making a poor business of deception; "—I and Hal Smith, we run a 'Easy One,' and we strip trout for a blind and sell to Harrod Place—Hal and I—"

"*Who* is Hal Smith?" she asked.

"Ma'am?"

The girl's flower-blue eyes turned icy: "Who is the man who calls himself Hal Smith?" she repeated.

Wier looked at her, red and dumb.

"Is he a Trooper in plain clothes?" she demanded in a bitter voice. "Is he one of the Commissioner's spies? Are *you* one, too?"

Wier gazed miserably at her, unable to formulate a convincing lie.

She flushed swiftly as a terrible suspicion seized her:

"Is this Harrod property? Is Hal Smith old Harrod's heir? *Is* he?"

"My God, Miss—"

"He *is!*"

"Listen, Miss—"

She flung open the door and came out into the living-room.

"Hal Smith is that nephew of old Harrod," she said calmly. "His name is Darragh. And you are one of his wardens.... And I can't stay here. Do you understand?"

Wier wiped his hot face and waited. The cat was out; there was a hole in the bag; and he knew there was no use in such lies as he could tell.

He said: "All I know, Miss, is that I was to look after you and get you whatever you want—"

"I want my clothes!"

"Ma'am?"

"My *clothes!*" she repeated impatiently. "I've *got* to have them!"

"Where are they, ma'am?" asked the bewildered man.

At the same moment the girl's eyes fell on a pile of men's sporting clothing—garments sent down from Harrod Place to the Lodge—lying on a leather lounge near a gun-rack.

Without a glance at Wier, Eve went to the heap of clothing, tossed it about, selected cords, two pairs of woollen socks, grey shirt, puttees, shoes, flung the garments through the door into her own room, followed them, and locked herself in.

When she was dressed—the two heavy pairs of socks helping to fit her feet to the shoes—she emptied her handful of diamonds, sapphires and emeralds, including the Flaming Jewel, into the pockets of her breeches.

Now she was ready. She unlocked her door and went out, scarcely limping at all, now.

Wier gazed at her helplessly as she coolly chose a rifle and cartridge-belt at the gun-rack.

Then she turned on him as still and dangerous as a young puma:

"Tell Darragh he'd better keep clear of Clinch's," she said. "Tell him I always thought he was a rat. Now I know he's one."

She plunged one slim hand into her pocket and drew out a diamond.

"Here," she said insolently. "This will pay your *gentleman* for his gun and clothing."

She tossed the gem onto a table, where it rolled, glittering.

"For heaven's sake, Miss—" burst out Wier, horrified, but she cut him short:

"—He may keep the change," she said. "We're no swindlers at Clinch's Dump!"

Wier started forward as though to intercept her. Eve's eyes flamed. And he stood still. She wrenched open the door and walked out among the silver birches.

At the edge of the brook she stood a moment, coolly loading the magazine of her rifle. Then, with one swift glance of hatred, flung at the place that Harrod's money had built, she sprang across the brook, tossed her rifle to her shoulder, and passed lithely into the golden wilderness of poplar and silver birch.

II

Quintana, on a fox-trot along the rock-trail into Drowned Valley, now thoroughly understood that it was the only sanctuary left him for the moment. Egress to the southward was closed; to the eastward, also; and he was too wary to venture westward toward Ghost Lake.

No, the only temporary safety lay in the swamps of Drowned Valley.

And there, he decided as he jogged along, if worse came to worst and starvation drove him out, he'd settle matters with Mike Clinch and break through to the north.

He meant to settle matters with Mike Clinch anyway. He was not afraid of Clinch; not really afraid of anybody. It had been the dogs that demoralised Quintana. He'd had no experience with hunting hounds— did not know what to expect—how to manœuvre. If only he could have *seen* these beasts that filled the forest with their hob-goblin outcries— if he could have had a good look at the creatures who gave forth that weird, crazed, melancholy volume of sound!—

"Bon!" he said coolly to himself. "It was a crisis of nerves which I experience. Yes.... I should have shot him, that fat Sard. Yes.... Only those damn dog— And now he shall die an' rot—that fat Sard—all by himse'f, parbleu!—like one big dead thing all alone in the wood.... A puddle of guts full of diamonds! Ah!—mon dieu!—a million francs in gems that shine like festering stars in this damn wood till the world end. Ah, bah— nome de dieu de—"

"Halte là!" came a sharp voice from the cedar fringe in front. A pause, then recognition; and Henri Picquet walked out on the hard ridge beyond and stood leaning on his rifle and looking sullenly at his leader.

Quintana came forward, carelessly, a disagreeable expression in his eyes and on his narrow lips, and continued on past Picquet.

The latter slouched after his leader, who had walked over to the lean-to before which a pile of charred logs lay in cold ashes.

As Picquet came up, Quintana turned on him, with a gesture toward the extinguished fire: "It is cold like hell," he said. "Why do you not have some fire?"

"Not for me, non," growled Picquet, and jerked a dirty thumb in the direction of the lean-to.

And there Quintana saw a pair of muddy boots protruding from a blanket.

"It is Harry Beck, yes?" he inquired. Then *something* about the boots and the blanket silenced him. He kept his eyes on them for a full minute, then walked into the lean-to. The blanket also covered Harry Beck's features and there was a stain on it where it outlined the prostrate man's features, making a ridge over the bony nose.

After a moment Quintana looked around at Picquet:

"So. He is dead. Yes?"

Picquet shrugged: "Since noon, mon capitaine."

"Comment?"

"How shall I know? It was the fire, perhaps—green wood or wet—it is no matter now.... I said to him, 'Pay attention, Henri; your wood makes too much smoke.' To me he reply I shall go to hell.... Well, there was too much smoke for me. I arise to search for wood more dry, when, crack!—they begin to shoot out there—" He waved a dirty hand toward the forest.

"'Bon,' said I, 'Clinch, he have seen your damn smoke!'

"'What shall I care?' he make reply, Henri Beck, to me. 'Clinch he shall shoot and be damn to him. I cook me my déjeûner all the same.'

"I make representations to that Johnbull; he say to me that I am a frog, and other injuries, while he lay yet more wood on his sacré fire.

"Then crack! crack! crack! and zing-gg!—whee-ee! come the big bullets of Clinch and his voyous yonder.

"'Bon,' I say, 'me, I make my excuse to retire.'

"Then Henri Beck he laugh and say, 'Hop it, frog!' And that is all he has find time to say, when crack! spat! Bien droit he has it—tenez, mon capitaine—here, over the left eye!... Like a beef surprise he go over, crash! thump! And like a beef that dies, the air bellows out from his big lungs—"

Picquet looked down at the dead comrade in a sort of weary compassion for such stupidity.

"—So he pass, this ros-biff goddam Johnbull.... Me, I roll him in there.... Je ne sais pas pourquoi.... Then I put out the fire and leave."

Quintana let his sneering glance rest on the dead a moment, and his thin lip curled immemorial contempt for the Anglo-Saxon.

Then he divested himself of the basket-pack which he had stolen from the Fry boy.

"Alors," he said calmly, "it has been Mike Clinch who shoot my frien' Beck. Bien."

He threw a cartridge into the breech of his rifle, adjusted his ammunition belt *en bandoulière*, carelessly.

Then, in a quiet voice: "My frien' Picquet, the time has now arrive when it become ver' necessary that we go from here away. Donc—I shall now go kill me my frien' Mike Clinch."

Picquet, unastonished, gave him a heavy, bovine look of inquiry.

Quintana said softly: "Me, I have enough already of this damn woods. Why shall we starve here when there lies our path?" He pointed north; his arm remained outstretched for a while.

"Clinch, he is there," growled Picquet.

"Also our path, l'ami Henri.... And, behind us, they hunt us now with *dogs*."

Picquet bared his big white teeth in fierce surprise. "Dogs?" he repeated with a sort of snarl.

"That is how they now hunt us, my frien'—like they hunt the hare in the Côte d'Or.... Me, I shall now reconnoitre—*that* way!" And he looked where he was pointing, into the north—with smouldering eyes. Then he turned calmly to Picquet: "An' you, l'ami?"

"At orders, mon capitaine."

"C'est bien. Venez."

They walked leisurely forward with rifles shouldered, following the hard ridge out across a vast and flooded land where the bark of trees glimmered with wet mosses.

After a quarter of a mile the ridge broadened and split into two, one hog-back branching northeast! They, however, continued north.

About twenty minutes later Picquet, creeping along on Quintana's left, and some sixty yards distant, discovered something moving in the woods beyond, and fired at it. Instantly two unseen rifles spoke from the woods ahead. Picquet was jerked clear around, lost his balance and nearly fell. Blood was spurting from his right arm, between elbow and shoulder.

He tried to lift and level his rifle; his arm collapsed and dangled broken and powerless; his rifle clattered to the forest floor.

For a moment he stood there in plain view, dumb, deathly white; then he began screaming with fury while the big, soft-nosed bullets came streaming in all around him. His broken arm was hit again. His screaming ceased; he dragged out his big clasp-knife with his left hand and started running toward the shooting.

As he ran, his mangled arm flopping like a broken wing, Byron Hastings stepped out from behind a tree and coolly shot him down at close quarters.

Then Quintana's rifle exploded twice very quickly, and the Hastings boy stumbled sideways and fell sprawling. He managed to rise to his knees again; he even was trying to stand up when Quintana, taking his time, deliberately began to empty his magazine into the boy, riddling him limb and body and head.

Down once more, he still moved his arms. Sid Hone reached out from behind a fallen log to grasp the dying lad's ankle and draw him into shelter, but Quintana reloaded swiftly and smashed Hone's left hand with the first shot.

Then Jim Hastings, kneeling behind a bunch of juniper, fired a high-velocity bullet into the tree behind which Quintana stood; but before he could fire again Quintana's shot in reply came ripping through the juniper and tore a ghastly hole in the calf of his left leg, striking a blow that knocked young Hastings flat and paralysed as a dead flounder.

A mile to the north, blocking the other exit from Drowned Valley, Mike Clinch, Harvey Chase, Cornelius Blommers, and Dick Berry stood listening to the shooting.

"B'gosh," blurted out Chase, "it sounds like they was goin' through, Mike. B'gosh, it does!"

Clinch's little pale eyes blazed, but he said in his soft, agreeable voice:

"Stay right here, boys. Like as not some of 'em will come this way."

The shooting below ceased. Clinch's nostrils expanded and flattened with every breath, as he stood glaring into the woods.

"Harve," he said presently, "you an' Corny go down there an' kinda look around. And you signal if I'm wanted. G'wan, both o' you. Git!"

They started, running heavily, but their feet made little noise on the moss.

Berry came over and stood near Clinch. For ten minutes neither man moved. Clinch stared at the woods in front of him. The younger man's nervous glance flickered like a snake's tongue in every direction, and he kept moistening his lips with his tongue.

Presently two shots came from the south. A pause; a rattle of shots from hastily emptied magazines.

"G'wan down there, Dick!" said Clinch.

"You'll be alone, Mike—"

"Au' right. You do like I say; git along quick!"

Berry walked southward a little way. He had turned very white under his tan.

"Gol ding ye!" shouted Clinch, "take it on a lope or I'll kick the pants off'n ye!"

Berry began to run, carrying his rifle at a trail.

For half an hour there was not a sound in the forests of Drowned Valley except in the dead timber where unseen woodpeckers hammered fitfully at the ghosts of ancient trees.

Always Clinch's little pale eyes searched the forest twilight in front of him; not a falling leaf escaped him; not a chipmunk.

And all the while Clinch talked to himself; his lips moved a little now and then, but uttered no sound:

"All I want God should do," he repeated again and again, "is to just let Quintana come *my* way. 'Tain't for because he robbed my girlie. 'Tain't for the stuff he carries onto him.... No, God, 'tain't them things. But it's what that there skunk done to my Evie.... O God, be you listenin'? He *hurt* her, Quintana did. That's it. He misused her.... God, if you had seen my girlie's little bleeding feet!— *That's* the reason.... 'Tain't the stuff. I can work. I can save for to make my Evie a lady same's them high-steppers on Fifth Avenoo. I can moil and toil and slave an' run hootch—hootch— They wuz wine 'n' fixin's into the Bible. It ain't you, God, it's them fanatics.... Nobody in my Dump wanted I should sell 'em more'n a bottle o' beer before this here prohybishun set us all crazy. 'Tain't right.... O God, don't hold a little hootch agin me when all I want of you is to let Quintana—"

The slightest noise behind him. He waited, turned slowly. Eve stood there.

Hell died in his pale eyes as she came to him, rested silently in his gentle embrace, returned his kiss, laid her flushed, sweet cheek against his unshaven face.

"Dad, darling?"

"Yes, my baby—"

"You're watching to kill Quintana. But there's no use watching any longer."

"Have the boys below got him?" he demanded.

"They got one of his gang. Byron Hastings is dead. Jim is badly hurt; Sid Hone, too—not so badly—"

"Where's Quintana?"

"Dad, he's gone.... But it don't matter. See here!—" She dug her slender hand into her breeches' pocket and pulled out a little fistful of gems.

Clinch, his powerful arm closing her shoulders, looked dully at the jewels.

"You see, dad, there's no use killing Quintana. These are the things he robbed you of."

"'Tain't them that matter.... I'm glad you got 'em. I allus wanted you should be a great lady, girlie. Them's the tickets of admission. You put 'em in your pants. I gotta stay here a spell—"

"Dad! Take them!"

He took them, smiled, shoved them into his pocket.

"What is it, girlie?" he asked absently, his pale eyes searching the woods ahead.

"I've just told you," she said, "that the boys went in as far as Quintana's shanty. There was a dead man there, too; but Quintana has gone."

Clinch said—not removing his eyes from the forest: "If any o' them boys has let Quintana crawl through I'll kill *him*, too.... G'wan home, girlie. I gotta mosey—I gotta kinda loaf around f'r a spell—"

"Dad, I want you to come back with me—"

"You go home; you hear me, Eve? Tell Corny and Dick Berry to hook it for Owl Marsh and stop the Star Peak trails—both on 'em.... Can Sid and Jimmy walk?"

"Jim can't—"

"Well, let Harve take him on his back. You go too. You help fix Jimmy up at the house. He's a little fella, Jimmy Hastings is. Harve can tote him. And you go along—"

"Dad, Quintana says he means to kill you! What is the use of hurting him? You have what he took—"

"I gotta have more'n he took. But even that ain't enough. He couldn't pay for all he ever done to me, girlie.... I'm aimin' to draw on him on sight—"

Clinch's set visage relaxed into an alarming smile which flickered, faded, died in the wintry ferocity of his eyes.

"Dad—"

"G'wan home!" he interrupted harshly. "You want that Hastings boy to bleed to death?"

She came up to him, not uttering a word, yet asking him with all the tenderness and eloquence of her eyes to leave this blood-trail where it lay and hunt no more.

He kissed her mouth, infinitely tender, smiled; then, again prim and scowling:

"G'wan home, you little scut, an' do what I told ye, or, by God, I'll cut a switch that'll learn ye good! Never a word, now! On yer way! G'wan!"

Twice she turned to look back. The second time, Clinch was slowly walking into the woods straight ahead of him. She waited; saw him go in; waited. After a while she continued on her way.

When she sighted the men below she called to Blommers and Dick Berry:

"Dad says you're to stop Star Peak trail by Owl Marsh."

Jimmy Hastings sat on a log, crying and looking down at his dead brother, over whose head somebody had spread a coat.

Blommers had made a tourniquet for Jimmy out of a bandanna and a peeled stick.

The girl examined it, loosened it for a moment, twisted it again, and bade Harvey Chase take him on his back and start for Clinch's.

The boy began to sob that he didn't want his brother to be left out there all alone; but Chase promised to come back and bring him in before night.

Sid Hone came up, haggard from pain and loss of blood, resting his mangled hand in the sling of his cartridge-belt.

Berry and Blommers were already starting across toward Owl Marsh; and the latter, passing by, asked Eve where Mike was.

"He went into Drowned Valley by the upper outlet," she said.

"He'll never find no one in them logans an' sinks," muttered Chase, squatting to hoist Jimmy Hastings to his broad back.

"I guess he'll be over Star Peak side by sundown," nodded Blommers.

Eve watched him slouching off into the woods, followed sullenly by Berry. Then she looked down at the dead man in silence.

"Be you ready, Eve?" grunted Chase.

She turned with a heavy heart to the home trail; but her mind was passionately with Clinch in the spectral forests of Drowned Valley.

III

And Clinch's mind was on her. All else—his watchfulness, his stealthy advance—all the alertness of eye and ear, all the subtlety, the cunning, the infinite caution—were purely instinctive mechanics.

Somewhere in this flooded twilight of gigantic trees was José Quintana. Knowing that, he dismissed that fact from his mind and turned his thoughts to Eve.

Sometimes his lips moved. They usually did when he was arguing with God or calling his Creator's attention to the justice of his case. His *two* cases—each, to him, a cause célèbre; the matter of Harrod; the affair of Quintana.

Many a time he had pleaded these two causes before the Most High.

But now his thoughts were chiefly concerned with Eve—with the problem of her future—his master passion—this daughter of the dead wife he had loved.

He sighed unconsciously; halted.

"Well, Lord," he concluded, in his wordless way, "my girlie has gotta have a chance if I gotta go to hell for it. That's sure as shootin'.... Amen."

At that instant he saw Quintana.

Recognition was instant and mutual. Neither man stirred. Quintana was standing beside a giant hemlock. His pack lay at his feet.

Clinch had halted—always the mechanics!—close to a great ironwood tree.

Probably both men knew that they could cover themselves before the other moved a muscle. Clinch's small, light eyes were blazing; Quintana's black eyes had become two slits.

Finally: "You—dirty—skunk," drawled Clinch in his agreeably misleading voice, "by Jesus Christ I got you now."

"Ah—h," said Quintana, "thees has happen ver' nice like I expec'.... Always I say myse'f, yet a little patience, José, an' one day you shall meet thees fellow Clinch, who has rob you.... I am ver' thankful to the good God—"

He had made the slightest of movements: instantly both men were behind their trees. Clinch, in the ferocious pride of woodcraft, laughed exultingly—filled the dim and spectral forest with his roar of laughter.

"Quintana," he called out, "you're a-going to cash in. Savvy? You're a-going to hop off. An' first you gotta hear why. 'Tain't for the stuff. Naw! I hooked it off'n you; you hooked it off'n me; now I got it again. *That's* all square.... No, 'tain't *that* grudge, you green-livered whelp of a cross-bred, still-born slut! No! It's becuz you laid the heft o' your dirty little finger onto my girlie. 'N' now you gotta hop!"

Quintana's sinister laughter was his retort. Then: "You damfool Clinch," he said, "I got in my pocket what you rob of me. Now I kill you, and then I feel ver' well. I go home, live like some kings; yes. But you," he sneered, "you shall not go home never no more. No. You shall remain in thees damn wood like ver' dead old rat that is all wormy.... Hé! I got a million dollare—five million franc in my pocket. You shall learn what it cost to rob José Quintana! Unnerstan'?"

"You liar," said Clinch contemptuously, "I got them jools in my pants pocket—"

Quintana's derisive laugh cut him short: "I give you thee Flaming Jewel if you show me you got my gems in you pants pocket!"

"I'll show you. Lay down your rifle so's I see the stock."

"First you, my frien' Mike," said Quintana cautiously.

Clinch took his rifle by the muzzle and shoved the stock into view so that Quintana could see it without moving.

To his surprise, Quintana did the same, then coolly stepped a pace outside the shelter of his hemlock stump.

"You show me now!" he called across the swamp.

Clinch stepped into view, dug into his pocket, and, cupping both hands, displayed a glittering heap of gems.

"I wanted you should know who's gottem," he said, "before you hop. It'll give you something to think over in hell."

Quintana's eyes had become slits again. Neither man stirred. Then: "So you are buzzard, eh, Clinch? You feed on dead man's pockets, eh? You find Sard somewhere an' you feed." He held up the morocco case, emblazoned with the arms of the Grand Duchess of Esthonia, and shook it at Clinch.

"In there is my share.... Not all. Ver' quick, now, I take yours, too—"

Clinch vanished and so did his rifle; and Quintana's first bullet struck the moss where the stock had rested.

"You black crow!" jeered Clinch, laughing, "—I need that empty case of yours. And I'm going after it.... But it's because your filthy claw touched my girlie that you gotta hop!"

Twilight lay over the phantom wood, touching with pallid tints the flooded forest.

So far only that one shot had been fired. Both men were still manœuvring, always creeping in circles and always lining some great tree for shelter.

Now, the gathering dusk was making them bolder and swifter; and twice, already, Clinch caught the shadow of a fading edge of something that vanished against the shadows too swiftly for a shot.

Now Quintana, keeping a tree in line, brushed with his lithe back a leafless moose-bush that stood swaying as he avoided it.

Instantly a stealthy hope seized him: he slipped out of his coat, spread it on the bush, set the naked branches swaying, and darted to his tree.

Waiting, he saw that the grey blot his coat made in the dusk was still moving a little—just vibrating a little bit in the twilight. He touched the bush with his rifle barrel, then crouched almost flat.

Suddenly the red crash of a rifle lit up Clinch's visage for a fraction of a second. And Quintana's bullet smashed Clinch between the eyes.

After a long while Quintana ventured to rise and creep forward.

Night, too, came creeping like an assassin amid the ghostly trees.

So twilight died in the stillness of Drowned Valley and the pall of night lay over all things—living and dead alike.

Episode Eleven
THE PLACE OF PINES

I

The last sound that Mike Clinch heard on earth was the detonation of his own rifle. Probably it was an agreeable sound to him. He lay there with a pleasant expression on his massive features. His watch had fallen out of his pocket.

Quintana shined him with an electric torch; picked up the watch. Then, holding the torch in one hand, he went through the dead man's pockets very thoroughly.

When Quintana had finished, both trays of the flat morocco case were full of jewels. And Quintana was full of wonder and suspicion.

Unquietly he looked upon the dead—upon the glittering contents of the jewel-box—but always his gaze reverted to the dead. The faintest shadow of a smile edged Clinch's lips. Quintana's lips grew graver. He said slowly, like one who does his thinking aloud:

"What is it you have done to me, l'ami Clinch?... Are there truly then two sets of precious stones?—*two* Flaming Jewels?—two gems of Erosite like there never has been in all thees worl' excep' only two more?... Or is one set false?... Have I here one set of paste facsimiles?... My frien' Clinch, why do you lie there an' smile at me so ver' funny ... like you are amuse?... I am wondering what you may have done to me, my frien' Clinch...."

For a while he remained kneeling beside the dead. Then: "Ah, bah," he said, pocketing the morocco case and getting to his feet.

He moved a little way toward the open trail, stopped, came back, stood his rifle against a tree.

For a while he was busy with his sharp Spanish clasp knife, whittling and fitting together two peeled twigs. A cross was the ultimate result. Then he placed Clinch's hands palm to palm upon his chest, laid the cross on his breast, and shined the result with complacency.

Then Quintana took off his hat.

"L'ami Mike," he said, "you were a *man!*... Adios!"

Quintana put on his hat. The path was free. The world lay open before José Quintana once more;—the world, his hunting ground.

"But," he thought uneasily, "what is it that I bring home this time? How much is paste? My God, how droll that smile of Clinch.... Which is the false—his jewels or mine? Dieu que j'étais bête!— Me who have not suspec' that there are *two* trays within my jewel-box!... I unnerstan'. It is ver' simple. In the top tray the false gems. Ah! Paste on top to deceive a thief!... Alors.... Then what I have recover of Clinch is the *real*!... Nom de Dieu!... How should I know? His smile is so ver' funny.... I think thees dead man make mock of me—all inside himse'f—"

So, in darkness, prowling south by west, shining the trail furtively, and loaded rifle ready, Quintana moved with stealthy, unhurried tread out of the wilderness that had trapped him and toward the tangled border of that outer world which led to safe, obscure, uncharted labyrinths— old-world mazes, immemorial hunting grounds—haunted by men who prey.

The night had turned frosty. Quintana, wet to the knees and very tired, moved slowly, not daring to leave the trail because of sink-holes.

However, the trail led to Clinch's Dump, and sooner or later he must leave it.

What he had to have was a fire; he realised that. Somewhere off the trail, in big timber if possible, he must build a fire and master this deadly chill that was slowly paralysing all power of movement.

He knew that a fire in the forest, particularly in big timber, could be seen only a little way. He must take his chances with sink-holes and find some spot in the forest to build that fire.

Who could discover him except by accident?

Who would prowl the midnight wilderness? At thirty yards the fire would not be visible. And, as for the odour—well, he'd be gone before dawn.... Meanwhile, he must have that fire. He could wait no longer.

He cut a pole first. Then he left the trail where a little spring flowed west, and turned to the right, shining the forest floor as he moved and sounding with his pole every wet stretch of moss, every strip of mud, every tiniest glimmer of water.

At last he came to a place of pines, first growth giants towering into night, and, looking up, saw stars, infinitely distant, ... where perhaps those things called souls drifted like wisps of vapour.

When the fire took, Quintana's thin dark hands had become nearly useless from cold. He could not have crooked finger to trigger.

For a long time he sat close to the blaze, slowly massaging his torpid limbs, but did not dare strip off his foot-gear.

Steam rose from puttee and heavy shoe and from the sodden woollen breeches. Warmth slowly penetrated. There was little smoke; the big dry branches were dead and bleached and he let the fire eat into them without using his axe.

Once or twice he sighed, "Oh, my God," in a weary demi-voice, as though the content of well-being were permeating him.

Later he ate and drank languidly, looking up at the stars, speculating as to the possible presence of Mike Clinch up there.

"Ah, the dirty thief," he murmured; "—nevertheless a man. Quel homme! Mais bête à faire pleurer! Je l'ai bien triché, moi! Ha!"

Quintana smiled palely as he thought of the coat and the gently-swaying bush—of the red glare of Clinch's shot, of the death-echo of his own shot.

Then, uneasy, he drew out the morocco case and gazed at the two trays full of gems.

The jewels blazed in the firelight. He touched them, moved them about, picked up several and examined them, testing the unset edges against his under lip as an expert tests jade.

But he couldn't tell; there was no knowing. He replaced them, closed the case, pocketed it. When he had a chance he could try boiling water for one sort of trick. He could scratch one or two.... Sard would know. He wondered whether Sard had got away, not concerned except selfishly. However, there were others in Paris whom he could trust—at a price....

Quintana rested both elbows on his knees and framed his dark face between both bony hands.

What a chase Clinch had led him after the Flaming Jewel. And now Clinch lay dead in the forest—faintly smiling. At *what?*

In a very low, passionless voice, Quintana cursed monotonously as he gazed into the fire. In Spanish, French, Portuguese, Italian, he cursed Clinch. After a little while he remembered Clinch's daughter, and he cursed her, elaborately, thoroughly, wishing her black mischance awake and asleep, living or dead.

Darragh, too, he remembered in his curses, and did not slight him. And the trooper, Stormont—ah, he should have killed all of them when he had the chance.... And those two Baltic Russians, also, the girl duchess and her friend. Why on earth hadn't he made a clean job of it? Over-caution. A wary disinclination to stir up civilization by needless murder. But after all, old maxims, old beliefs, old truths are the best, God knows. The dead don't talk! And that's the wisest wisdom of all.

"If," murmured Quintana fervently, "God gives me further opportunity to acquire a little property to comfort me in my old age, I shall leave no gossiping fool to do me harm with his tongue. No! I kill.

"And though they raise a hue and cry, dead tongues can not wag and

I save myse'f much annoyance in the end."

He leaned his back against the trunk of a massive pine.

Presently Quintana slept after his own fashion—that is to say, looking closely at him one could discover a glimmer under his lowered eyelids. And he listened always in that kind of sleep. As though a shadowy part of him were detached from his body, and mounted guard over it.

The inaudible movement of a wood-mouse venturing into the firelit circle awoke Quintana. Again a dropping leaf amid distant birches awoke him. Such things. And so he slept with wet feet to the fire and his rifle across his knees; and dreamed of Eve and of murder, and that the Flaming Jewel was but a mass of glass.

At that moment the girl of whose white throat Quintana was dreaming, and whining faintly in his dreams, stood alone outside Clinch's Dump, rifle in hand, listening, fighting the creeping dread that touched her slender body at times—seemed to touch her very heart with frost.

Clinch's men had gone on to Ghost Lake with their wounded and dead, where there was fitter shelter for both. All had gone on; nobody remained to await Clinch's home-coming except Eve Strayer.

Black Care, that tireless squire of dames, had followed her from the time she had left Clinch, facing the spectral forests of Drowned Valley.

An odd, unusual dread weighted her heart—something in emotions that she never before had experienced in time of danger. In it there was the deathly unease of premonition. But of what it was born she did not understand—perhaps of the strain of dangers passed—of the shock of discovery concerning Smith's identity with Darragh—Darragh!—the hated kinsman of Harrod the abhorred.

Fiercely she wondered how much her lover knew about this miserable masquerade. Was Stormont involved in this deception—Stormont, the object of her first girl's passion—Stormont, for whom she would have died?

Wretched, perplexed, fiercely enraged at Darragh, deadly anxious concerning Clinch, she had gone about cooking supper.

The supper, kept warm on the range, still awaited the man who had no more need of meat and drink.

Of the tragedy of Sard Eve knew nothing. There were no traces save in the disorder in the pantry and the bottles and chair on the veranda.

Who had visited the place excepting those from whom she and Stormont had fled, did not appear. She had no idea why her stepfather's mattress and bed-quilt lay in the pantry.

Her heart heavy with ceaseless anxiety, Eve carried mattress and bed-clothes to Clinch's chamber, re-made his bed, wandered through the house setting it in order; then, in the kitchen, seated herself and waited until the strange dread that possessed her drove her out into the starlight to stand and listen and stare at the dark forest where all her dread seemed concentrated.

It was not yet dawn, but the girl could endure the strain no longer.

With electric torch and rifle she started for the forest, almost running at first; then, among the first trees, moving with caution and in silence along the trail over which Clinch should long since have journeyed homeward.

In soft places, when she ventured to flash her torch, foot-prints cast curious shadows, and it was hard to make out tracks so oddly distorted by the light. Prints mingled and partly obliterated other prints. She identified her own tracks leading south, and guessed at the others, pointing north and south, where they had carried in the wounded and had gone back to bring in the dead.

But nowhere could she discover any impression resembling her stepfather's—that great, firm stride and solid imprint which so often she had tracked through moss and swale and which she knew so well.

Once when she got up from her knees after close examination of the muddy trail, she became aware of the slightest taint in the night air— stood with delicate nostrils quivering—advanced, still conscious of the taint, listening, wary, every stealthy instinct alert.

She had not been mistaken: somewhere in the forest there was smoke. Somewhere a fire was burning. It might not be very far away; it might be distant. *Whose fire?* Her father's? Would a hunter of men build a fire?

The girl stood shivering in the darkness. There was not a sound.

Now, keeping her cautious feet in the trail by sense of touch alone, she moved on. Gradually, as she advanced, the odour of smoke became more distinct. She heard nothing, saw nothing; but there was a near reek of smoke in her nostrils and she stopped short.

After a little while in the intense silence of the forest she ventured to touch the switch of her torch, very cautiously.

In the faint, pale lustre she saw a tiny rivulet flowing westward from a spring, and, beside it, in the mud, imprints of a man's feet.

The tracks were small, narrow, slimmer than imprints made by any man she could think of. Under the glimmer of her torch they seemed quite fresh; contours were still sharp, some ready to crumble, and water stood in the heels.

A little way she traced them, saw where their maker had cut a pole, peeled it; saw, farther on, where this unknown man had probed in moss and mud—peppered some particularly suspicious swale with a series of holes as though a giant woodcock had been "boring" there.

Who was this man wandering all alone at night off the Drowned Valley trail and probing the darkness with a pole?

She knew it was not her father. She knew that no native—none of her father's men—would behave in such a manner. Nor could any of these have left such narrow, almost delicate tracks.

As she stole along, dimly shining the tracks, lifting her head incessantly to listen and peer into the darkness, her quick eye caught something ahead—something very slightly different from the wall of black obscurity—a vague hint of colour—the very vaguest tint scarcely perceptible at all.

But she knew it was firelight touching the trunk of an unseen tree.

Now, soundlessly over damp pine needles she crept. The scent of smoke grew strong in nostril and throat; the pale tint became palely reddish. All about her the blackness seemed palpable—seemed to touch her body with its weight; but, ahead, a ruddy glow stained two huge pines. And presently she saw the fire, burning low, but redly alive. And, after a long, long while, she saw a man.

He had left the fire circle. His pack and belted mackinaw still lay there at the foot of a great tree. But when, finally, she discovered him, he was scarcely visible where he crouched in the shadow of a tree-trunk, with his rifle half lowered at a ready.

Had he heard her? It did not seem possible. Had he been crouching there since he made his fire? Why had he made it then—for its warmth could not reach him there. And why was he so stealthily watching— silent, unstirring, crouched in the shadows?

She strained her eyes; but distance and obscurity made recognition impossible. And yet, somehow, every quivering instinct within her was telling her that the crouched and shadowy watcher beyond the fire was Quintana.

And every concentrated instinct was telling her that he'd kill her if he caught sight of her; her heart clamoured it; her pulses thumped it in her ears.

Had the girl been capable of it she could have killed him where he crouched. She thought of it, but knew it was not in her to do it. And yet Quintana had boasted that he meant to kill her father. That was what terribly concerned her. And there must be a way to stop that danger— some way to stop it short of murder—a way to render this man harmless to her and hers.

No, she could not kill him this way. Except in extremes she could not bring herself to fire upon any human creature. And yet this man must be rendered harmless—somehow—somehow—ah!—

As the problem presented itself its solution flashed into her mind. Men of the wilderness knew how to take dangerous creatures alive. To take a dangerous and reasoning human was even less difficult, because reason makes more mistakes than does instinct.

Stealthily, without a sound, the girl crept back through the shadows over the damp pine needles, until, peering fearfully over her shoulder, she saw the last ghost-tint of Quintana's fire die out in the terrific dark behind.

Slowly, still, she moved until her sensitive feet felt the trodden path from Drowned Valley.

Now, with torch flaring, she ran, carrying her rifle at a trail. Before her, here and there, little night creatures fled—a humped-up raccoon, dazzled by the glare, a barred owl still struggling with its wood-rat kill.

She ran easily—an agile, tireless young thing, part of the swiftness and silence of the woods—part of the darkness, the sinuous celerity, the ominous hush of wide, still places—part of its very blood and pulse and hot, sweet breath.

Even when she came out among the birches by Clinch's Dump she was breathing evenly and without distress. She ran to the kitchen door but did not enter. On pegs under the porch a score or more of rusty traps hung. She unhooked the largest, wound the chain around it, tucked it under her left arm and started back.

When at last she arrived at the place of pines again, and saw the far, spectral glimmer of Quintana's fire, the girl was almost breathless. But dawn was not very far away and there remained little time for the taking alive of a dangerous man.

Where two enormous pines grew close together near a sapling, she knelt down, and, with both hands, scooped out a big hollow in the immemorial layers of pine needles. Here she placed her trap. It took all her strength and skill to set it; to fasten the chain around the base of the sapling pine.

And now, working with only the faintest glimmer of her torch, she covered everything with pine needles.

It was not possible to restore the forest floor; the place remained visible—a darker, rougher patch on the bronzed carpet of needles beaten smooth by decades of rain and snow. No animal would have trodden that suspicious space. But it was with man she had to deal—a dangerous but reasoning man with few and atrophied instincts—and with no experience in traps; and, therefore, in no dread of them.

Before she started she had thrown a cartridge into the breech of her rifle.

Now she pocketed her torch and seated herself between the two big pines and about three feet behind the hidden trap.

Dawn was not far away. She looked upward through high pine-tops where stars shone; and saw no sign of dawn. But the watcher by the fire beyond was astir, now, in the imminence of dawn, and evidently meant to warm himself before leaving.

Eve could hear him piling dry wood on the fire; the light on the tree trunks grew redder; a pungent reek of smoke was drawn through the forest aisles. She sniffed it, listened, and watched, her rifle across her knees.

Eve never had been afraid of anything. She was not afraid of this man. If it came to combat she would have to kill. It never entered her mind to fear Quintana's rifle. Even Clinch was not as swift with a rifle as she.... Only Stormont had been swifter—thank God!—

She thought of Stormont—sat there in the terrific darkness loving him, her heart of a child tremulous with adoration.

Then the memory of Darragh pushed in and hot hatred possessed her. Always, in her heart, she had distrusted the man.

Instinct had warned her. A spy! What evil had he worked already? Where was her father? Evidently Quintana had escaped him at Drowned Valley.... Quintana was yonder by his fire, preparing to flee the wilderness where men hunted him.... But where was Clinch? Had this sneak, Darragh, betrayed him? Was Clinch already in the clutch of the State Troopers? Was he in *jail*?

At the thought the girl felt slightly faint, then a rush of angry blood stung her face in the darkness. Except for game and excise violations the stories they told about Clinch were lies.

He had nothing to fear, nothing to be ashamed of. Harrod had driven him to lawlessness; the Government took away what was left him to make a living. He had to live. What if he did break laws made by millionaire and fanatic! What of it? He had her love and her respect—and her deep, deep pity. And these were enough for any girl to fight for.

Dawn spread a silvery light above the pines, but Quintana's fire still reddened the tree trunks; and she could hear him feeding it at intervals.

Finally she saw him. He came out on the edge of the ruddy ring of light and stood peering around at the woods where already a vague greyness was revealing nearer trees.

When, finally, he turned his back and looked at his fire, Eve rose and stood between the two big pines. Behind one of them she placed her rifle.

It was growing lighter in the woods. She could see Quintana in the fire ring and outside—saw him go to the spring rivulet, lie flat, drink, then, on his knees, wash face and hands in the icy water.

It became plain to her that he was nearly ready to depart. She watched him preparing. And now she could see him plainly, and knew him to be Quintana and no other.

He had a light basket pack. He put some articles into it, stretched himself and yawned, pulled on his hat, hoisted the pack and fastened it to his back, stood staring at the fire for a long time; then, with a sudden upward look at the zenith where a slight flush stained a cloud, he picked up his rifle.

At that moment Eve called to him in a clear and steady voice.

The effect on Quintana was instant; he was behind a tree before her voice ceased.

"Hallo! Hi! You over there!" she called again. "This is Eve Strayer. I'm looking for Clinch! He hasn't been home all night. Have you seen him?"

After a moment she saw Quintana's head watching her—not at the shoulder-height of a man but close to the ground and just above the tree roots.

"Hey!" she cried. "What's the matter with you over there? I'm asking you who you are and if you've seen my father?"

After a while she saw Quintana coming toward her, circling, creeping swiftly from tree to tree.

As he flitted through the shadows the trees between which she was standing hid her from him a moment. Instantly she placed her rifle on the ground and kicked the pine needles over it.

As Quintana continued his encircling manœuvres Eve, apparently perplexed, walked out into the clear space, putting the concealed trap between her and Quintana, who now came stealthily toward her from the rear.

It was evident that he had reconnoitred sufficiently to satisfy himself that the girl was alone and that no trick, no ambuscade, threatened him.

And now, from behind a pine, and startlingly near her, came Quintana, moving with confident grace yet holding his rifle ready for any emergency.

Eve's horrified stare was natural; she had not realised that any man could wear so evil a smile.

Quintana stopped short a dozen paces away. The dramatic in him demanded of the moment its full value. He swept off his hat with a flourish, bowed deeply where he stood.

"Ah!" he cried gaily, "the happy encounter, Señorita. God is too good to us. And it was but a moment since my thoughts were of you! I swear it!—"

It was not fear; it was a sort of slow horror of this man that began to creep over the girl. She stared at his brilliant eyes, at his thick mouth, too red—shuddered slightly. But the toe of her right foot touched the stock of her rifle under the pine needles.

She held herself under control.

"So it's you," she said unsteadily. "I thought our people had caught you."

Quintana laughed: "Charming child," he said, "it is *I* who have caught your people. And now, my God!—I catch *you!*... It is ver' funny. Is it not?"

She looked straight into Quintana's black eyes, but the look he returned sent the shamed blood surging into her face.

"By God," he said between his white, even teeth—"by God!"

Staring at her he slowly disengaged his pack, let it fall behind him on the pine needles; rested his rifle on it; slipped out of his mackinaw and laid that across his rifle—always keeping his brilliant eyes on her.

His lips tightened, the muscles in his dark face grew tense; his eyes became a blazing insult.

For an instant he stood there, unencumbered, a wiry, graceful shape in his woollen breeches, leggings, and grey shirt open at the throat. Then he took a step toward her. And the girl watched him, fascinated.

One pace, two, a third, a fourth—the girl's involuntary cry echoed the stumbling crash of the man thrashing, clawing, scrambling in the clenched jaws of the bear-trap amid a whirl of flying pine needles.

He screamed once, tried to rise, turned blindly to seize the jaws that clutched him; and suddenly crouched, loose-jointed, cringing like a trapped wolf—the true fatalist among our lesser brothers.

Eve picked up her rifle. She was trembling violently. Then, mastering her emotion, she walked over to the pack, placed Quintana's rifle and mackinaw in it, coolly hoisted it to her shoulders and buckled it there.

Over her shoulder she kept an eye on Quintana who crouched where he had fallen, unstirring, his deadly eyes watching her.

She placed the muzzle of her rifle against his stomach, rested it so, holding it with one hand, and her finger at the trigger.

At her brief order he turned out both breeches pockets. She herself stooped and drew the Spanish clasp-knife from its sheath at his belt, took a pistol from the holster, another out of his hip pocket. Reaching up and behind her, she dropped these into the pack.

"Maybe," she said slowly, "your ankle is broken. I'll send somebody from Ghost Lake to find you. But whether you've a broken bone or not you'll not go very far, Quintana.... After I'm gone you'll be able to free yourself. But you can't get away. You'll be followed and caught.... So if you can walk at all you'd better go in to Ghost Lake and give yourself up.... It's that or starvation.... You've got a watch.... Don't stir or touch that trap for half an hour.... And that's all."

As she moved away toward the Drowned Valley trail she looked back at him. His face was bloodless but his black eyes blazed.

"If ever you come into this forest again," she said, "my father will surely kill you."

To her horror Quintana slowly grinned at her. Then, still grinning, he placed the forefinger of his left hand between his teeth and bit it.

Whatever he meant by the gesture it seemed unclean, horrible; and the girl hurried on, seized with an overwhelming loathing through which a sort of terror pulsated like evil premonition in a heavy and tortured heart.

Straight into the fire of dawn she sped. A pale primrose light glimmered through the woods; trees, bushes, undergrowth turned a dusky purple. Already the few small clouds overhead were edged with fiery rose.

Then, of a sudden, a shaft of flame played over the forest. The sun had risen.

Hastening, she searched the soft path for any imprint of her father's foot. And even in the vain search she hoped to find him at home—hurried on burdened with two rifles and a pack, still all nervous and aquiver from her encounter with Quintana.

Surely, surely, she thought, if he had missed Quintana in Drowned Valley he would not linger in that ghastly place; he'd come home, call in his men, take counsel perhaps—

Mist over Star Pond was dissolving to a golden powder in the blinding glory of the sun. The eastern window-panes in Clinch's Dump glittered as though the rooms inside were all on fire.

Down through withered weeds and scrub she hurried, ran across the grass to the kitchen door which swung ajar under its porch.

"Dad!" she called, "Dad!"

Only her own frightened voice echoed in the empty house. She climbed the stairs to his room. The bed lay undisturbed as she had made it. He was not in any of the rooms; there were no signs of him.

Slowly she descended to the kitchen. He was not there. The food she had prepared for him had become cold on a chilled range.

For a long while she stood staring through the window at the sunlight outside. Probably, since Quintana had eluded him, he'd come home for something to eat.... Surely, now that Quintana had escaped, Clinch would come back for some breakfast.

Eve slipped the pack from her back and laid it on the kitchen table. There was kindling in the wood-box. She shook down the cinders, laid a fire, soaked it with kerosene, lighted it, filled the kettle with fresh water.

In the pantry she cut some ham, and found eggs, condensed milk, butter, bread, and an apple pie. After she had ground the coffee she placed all these on a tray and carried them into the kitchen.

Now there was nothing more to do until her father came, and she sat down by the kitchen table to wait.

Outside the sunlight was becoming warm and vivid. There had been no frost after all—or, at most, merely a white trace in the shadow—on a fallen plank here and there—but not enough to freeze the ground. And, in the sunshine, it all quickly turned to dew, and glittered and sparkled in a million hues and tints like gems—like that handful of jewels she had poured into her father's joined palms—yesterday—there at the ghostly edge of Drowned Valley.

At the memory, and quite mechanically, she turned in her chair and drew Quintana's basket pack toward her.

First she lifted out his rifle, examined it, set it against the window sill. Then, one by one, she drew out two pistols, loaded; the murderous Spanish clasp-knife; an axe; a fry-pan and a tin pail, and the rolled-up mackinaw.

Under these the pack seemed to contain nothing except food and ammunition; staples in sacks and a few cans—lard, salt, tea—such things.

The cartridge boxes she piled up on the table; the food she tossed into a tin swill bucket.

About the effects of this man it seemed to her as though something unclean lingered. She could scarcely bear to handle them—threw them from her with disgust.

The garment, also—the heavy brown and green mackinaw—she disliked to touch. To throw it out doors was her intention; but, as she lifted the coat, it unrolled and some things fell from the pockets to the kitchen table—money, keys, a watch, a flat leather case—

She looked stupidly at the case. It had a coat of arms emblazoned on it.

Still, stupidly and as though dazed, she laid one hand on it, drew it to her, opened it.

The Flaming Jewel blazed in her face amid a heap of glittering gems.

Still she seemed slow to comprehend—as though understanding were paralysed.

It was when her eyes fell upon the watch that her heart seemed to stop. Suddenly her stunned senses were lighted as by an infernal flare.... Under the awful blow she swayed upright to her feet, sick with fright, her eyes fixed on her father's watch.

It was still ticking.

She did not know whether she cried out in anguish or was dumb under it. The house seemed to reel around her; under foot too.

When she came to her senses she found herself outside the house, running with her rifle, already entering the woods. But, inside the barrier of trees, something blocked her way, stopped her—a man—*her* man!

"Eve! In God's name!—" he said as she struggled in his arms; but she fought him and strove to tear her body from his embrace:

"They've killed Dad!" she panted— "Quintana killed him. I didn't know—oh, I didn't know!—and I let Quintana go! Oh, Jack, Jack, he's at the Place of Pines! I'm going there to shoot him! Let me go!—he's killed Dad, I tell you! He had Dad's watch—and the case of jewels—they were in his pack on the kitchen table—"

"Eve!"

"Let me go!—"

"*Eve!*" He held her rigid a moment in his powerful grip, compelled her dazed, half-crazed eyes to meet his own:

"You must come to your senses," he said. "Listen to what I say: they are *bringing in your father*."

Her dilated blue eyes never moved from his.

"We found him in Drowned Valley at sunrise," said Stormont quietly. "The men are only a few rods behind me. They are carrying him out."

Her lips made a word without sound.

"Yes," said Stormont in a low voice.

There was a sound in the woods behind them. Stormont turned. Far away down the trail the men came into sight.

Then the State Trooper turned the girl very gently and placed one arm around her shoulders.

Very slowly they descended the hill together. His equipment was shining in the morning sun: and the sun fell on Eve's drooping head, turning her chestnut hair to fiery gold.

An hour later Trooper Stormont was at the Place of Pines.

There was nothing there except an empty trap and the ashes of the dying fire beyond.

Episode Twelve
HER HIGHNESS INTERVENES

I

Toward noon the wind changed, and about one o'clock it began to snow.

Eve, exhausted, lay on the sofa in her bedroom. Her step-father lay on a table in the dance hall below, covered by a sheet from his own bed. And beside him sat Trooper Stormont, waiting.

It was snowing heavily when Mr. Lyken, the little undertaker from Ghost Lake, arrived with several assistants, a casket, and what he called "swell trimmings."

Long ago Mike Clinch had selected his own mortuary site and had driven a section of iron pipe into the ground on a ferny knoll overlooking Star Pond. In explanation he grimly remarked to Eve that after death he preferred to be planted where he could see that Old Harrod's ghost didn't trespass.

Here two of Mr. Lyken's able assistants dug a grave while the digging was still good; for if Mike Clinch was to lie underground that season there might be need of haste—no weather prophet ever having successfully forecast Adirondack weather.

Eve, exhausted by shock and a sleepless night, was spared the more harrowing details of the coroner's visit and the subsequent jaunty activities of Mr. Lyken and his efficient assistants.

She had managed to dress herself in a black wool gown, intending to watch by Mike, but Stormont's blunt authority prevailed and she lay down for an hour's rest.

The hour lengthened into many hours; the girl slept heavily on her sofa under blankets laid over her by Stormont.

All that dark, snowy day she slept, mercifully unconscious of the proceedings below.

In its own mysterious way the news penetrated the wilderness; and out of the desolation of forest and swamp and mountain drifted the people who somehow existed there—a few shy, half wild young girls, a dozen silent, lank men, two or three of Clinch's own people, who stood silently about in the falling snow and lent a hand whenever requested.

One long shanked youth cut hemlock to line the grave; others erected a little fence of silver birch around it, making of the enclosure a "plot."

A gaunt old woman from God knows where aided Mr. Lyken at

intervals: a pretty, sulky-eyed girl with her slovenly, red-headed sister cooked for anybody who desired nourishment.

When Mike was ready to hold the inevitable reception everybody filed into the dance hall. Mr. Lyken was master of ceremonies; Trooper Stormont stood very tall and straight by the head of the casket.

Clinch wore a vague, indefinable smile and his best clothes—that same smile which had so troubled José Quintana.

Light was fading fast in the room when the last visitor took silent leave of Clinch and rejoined the groups in the kitchen, where were the funeral baked meats.

Eve still slept. Descending again from his reconnaissance, Trooper Stormont encountered Trooper Lannis below.

"Has anybody picked up Quintana's tracks?" inquired the former.

"Not so far. An Inspector and two State Game Protectors are out beyond Owl Marsh. The Troopers from Five Lakes are on the job, and we have enforcement men along Drowned Valley from The Scaur to Harrod Place."

"Does Darragh know?"

"Yes. He's in there with Mike. He brought a lot of flowers from Harrod Place."

The two troopers went into the dance hall where Darragh was arranging the flowers from his greenhouses.

Stormont said quietly: "All right, Jim, but Eve must not know that they came from Harrod's."

Darragh nodded: "How is she, Jack?"

"All in."

"Do you know the story?"

"Yes. Mike went into Drowned Valley early last evening after Quintana. He didn't come back. Before dawn this morning Eve located Quintana, set a bear-trap for him, and caught him with the goods—"

"What goods?" demanded Darragh sharply.

"Well, she got his pack and found Mike's watch and jewelry in it—"

"What jewelry?"

"The jewels Quintana was after. But that was after she'd arrived at the Dump, here, leaving Quintana to get free of the trap and beat it.

"That's how I met her—half crazed, going to find Quintana again. We'd found Mike in Drowned Valley and were bringing him out when I ran into Eve.... I brought her back here and called Ghost Lake.... They haven't picked up Quintana's tracks so far."

After a silence: "Too bad this snow came so late," remarked Trooper Lannis. "But we ought to get Quintana anyway."

Darragh went over and looked silently at Mike Clinch.

"I liked you," he said under his breath. "It wasn't your fault. And it wasn't mine, Mike.... I'll try to square things. Don't worry."

He came back slowly to where Stormont was standing near the door: "Jack," he said, "you can't marry Eve on a Trooper's pay. Why not quit and take over the Harrod estate?... You and I can go into business together later if you like."

After a pause: "That's rather wonderful of you, Jim," said Stormont, "but you don't know what sort of business man I'd make—"

"I know what sort of officer you made.... I'm taking no chance.... And I'll make my peace with Eve—or somebody will do it for me.... Is it settled then?"

"Thanks," said Trooper Stormont, reddening. They clasped hands. Then Stormont went about and lighted the candles in the room. Clinch's face, again revealed, was still faintly amused at something or other. The dead have much to be amused at.

As Darragh was about to go, Stormont said: "We're burying Clinch at eleven to-morrow morning. The Ghost Lake Pilot officiates."

"I'll come if it won't upset Eve," said Darragh.

"She won't notice anybody, I fancy," remarked Stormont.

He stood by the veranda and watched Darragh take the Lake Trail through the snow. Finally the glimmer of his swinging lantern was lost in the woods and Stormont mounted the stairs once more, stood silently by Eve's open door, realised she was still heavily asleep, and seated himself on a chair outside her door to watch and wait.

All night long it snowed hard over the Star Pond country, and the late grey light of morning revealed a blinding storm pelting a white robed world.

Toward ten o'clock, Stormont, on guard, noticed that Eve was growing restless.

Downstairs the flotsam of the forest had gathered again: Mr. Lyken was there in black gloves; the Reverend Laomi Smatter had arrived in a sleigh from Ghost Lake. Both were breakfasting heavily.

The pretty, sulky-faced girl fetched a tray and placed Eve's breakfast on it; and Trooper Stormont carried it to her room.

She was awake when he entered. He set the tray on the table. She put both arms around his neck.

"Jack," she murmured, her eyes tremulous with tears.

"Everything has been done," he said. "Will you be ready by eleven? I'll come for you."

She clung to him in silence for a while.

At eleven he knocked on her door. She opened it. She wore her black wool gown and a black fur turban. Some of her pallor remained—traces of tears and bluish smears under both eyes. But her voice was steady.

"Could I see Dad a moment alone?"

"Of course."

She took his arm: they descended the stairs. There seemed to be many people about but she did not lift her eyes until her lover led her into the dance hall where Clinch lay smiling his mysterious smile.

Then Stormont left her alone there and closed the door.

In a terrific snow-storm they buried Mike Clinch on the spot he had selected, in order that he might keep a watchful eye upon the trespassing ghost of old man Harrod.

It blew and stormed and stormed, and the thin, nasal voice of "Rev. Smatter" was utterly lost in the wind. The slanting lances of snow drove down on the casket, building a white mound over the flowers, blotting the hemlock boughs from sight.

There was no time to be lost now; the ground was freezing under a veering and bitter wind out of the west. Mr. Lyken's talented assistants had some difficulty in shaping the mound which snow began to make into a white and flawless monument.

The last slap of the spade rang with a metallic jar across the lake, where snow already blotted the newly forming film of ice; the human denizens of the wilderness filtered back into it one by one; "Rev. Smatter" got into his sleigh, plainly concerned about the road; Mr. Lyken betrayed unprofessional haste in loading his wagon with his talented assistants and starting for Ghost Lake.

A Game Protector or two put on snow-shoes when they departed. Trooper Lannis led out his horse and Stormont's, and got into the saddle.

"I'd better get these beasts into Ghost Lake while I can," he said. "You'll follow on snow-shoes, won't you, Jack?"

"I don't know. I may need a sleigh for Eve. She can't remain here all alone. I'll telephone the Inn."

Darragh, in blanket outfit, a pair of snow-shoes on his back, a rifle in his mittened hand, came trudging up from the lake. He and Stormont watched Lannis riding away with the two horses.

"He'll make it all right, but it's time he started," said the latter.

Darragh nodded: "Some storm. Where is Eve?"

"In her room."

"What is she going to do, Jack?"

"Marry me as soon as possible. She wants to stay here for a few days but I can't leave her here alone. I think I'll telephone to Ghost Lake for a sleigh."

"Let me talk to her," said Darragh in a low voice.

"Do you think you'd better—at such a time?"

"I think it's a good time. It will divert her mind, anyway. I want her to come to Harrod Place."

"She won't," said Stormont grimly.

"She might. Let me talk to her."

"Do you realise how she feels toward you, Jim?"

"I do, indeed. And I don't blame her. But let me tell you; Eve Strayer is the most honest and fair-minded girl I ever knew.... Except one.... I'll take a chance that she'll listen to me.... Sooner or later she will be obliged to hear what I have to tell her.... But it will be easier for her—for everybody—if I speak to her now. Let me try, Jack."

Stormont hesitated, looked at him, nodded. Darragh stood his rifle against the bench on the kitchen porch. They entered the house slowly. And met Eve descending the stairs.

The girl looked at Darragh, astonished, then her pale face flushed with anger.

"What are you doing in this house?" she demanded unsteadily. "Have you no decency, no shame?"

"Yes," he said, "I am ashamed of what my kinsman has done to you and yours. That is partly why I am here."

"You came here as a spy," she said with hot contempt. "You lied about your name; you lied about your purpose. You came here to betray Dad! If he'd known it he would have killed you!"

"Yes, he would have. But—do you know why I came here, Eve?"

"I've told you!"

"And you are wrong. I didn't come here to betray Mike Clinch: I came to save him."

"Do you suppose I believe a man who has lied to Dad?" she cried.

"I don't ask you to, Eve. I shall let somebody else prove what I say. I don't blame you for your attitude. God knows I don't blame Mike Clinch. He stood up like a man to Henry Harrod.... All I ask is to undo some of the rotten things that my uncle did to you and yours. And that is partly why I came here."

The girl said passionately: "Neither Dad nor I want anything from Harrod Place or from you! Do you suppose you can come here after Dad is dead and pretend you want to make amends for what your uncle did to us?"

"Eve," said Darragh gravely, "I've made some amends already. You don't know it, but I have.... You may not believe it, but I liked your father. He was a real man. Had anybody done to me what Henry Harrod did to your father I'd have behaved as your father behaved; I'd never have budged from this spot; I'd have hunted where I chose; I'd have borne an implacable hatred against Henry Harrod and Harrod Place, and every soul in it!"

The girl, silenced, looked at him without belief.

He said: "I am not surprised that you distrust what I say. But the man you are going to marry was a junior officer in my command. I have no closer friend than Jack Stormont. Ask him whether I am to be believed."

Astounded, the girl turned a flushed, incredulous face to Stormont.

He said: "You may trust Darragh as you trust me. I don't know what he has to say to you, dear. But whatever he says will be the truth."

Darragh said, gravely: "Through a misunderstanding your father came into possession of stolen property, Eve. He did not know it had been stolen. I did. But Mike Clinch would not have believed me if I had told him that the case of jewels in his possession had been stolen from a woman.... Quintana stole them. By accident they came into your father's possession. I learned of this. I had promised this woman to recover her jewels.

"I came here for that purpose, Eve. And for two reasons: first, because I learned that Quintana also was coming here to rob your father of these gems; second, because, when I knew your father, and knew *you*, I concluded that it would be an outrage to call on the police. It would mean prison for Clinch, misery and ruin for you, Eve. So—I tried to steal the jewels ... to save you both."

He looked at Stormont, who seemed astonished.

"To whom do these jewels belong, Jim?" demanded the trooper.

"To the young Grand Duchess of Esthonia.... Do you remember that I befriended her over there?"

"Yes."

"Do you remember that the Reds were accused of burning her château and looting it?"

"Yes, I remember."

"Well, it was Quintana and his gang of international criminals who did that," said Darragh drily.

And, to Eve: "By accident this case of jewels, emblazoned with the coat of arms of the Grand Duchess of Esthonia, came into your father's possession. That is the story, Eve."

There was a silence. The girl looked at Stormont, flushed painfully, looked at Darragh.

Then, without a word, she turned, ascended the stairs, and reappeared immediately carrying the leather case.

"Thank you, Mr. Darragh," she said simply; and laid the case in his hand.

"But," said Darragh, "I want you to do a little more, Eve. The owner of these gems is my guest at Harrod Place. I want you to give them to her yourself."

"I—I can't go to Harrod Place," stammered the girl.

"Please don't visit the sins of Henry Harrod on me, Eve."

"I—don't. But—but that place—"

After a silence: "If Eve feels that way," began Stormont awkwardly, "I couldn't become associated with you in business, Jim—"

"I'd rather sell Harrod Place than lose you!" retorted Darragh almost sharply. "I want to go into business with you, Jack—if Eve will permit me—"

She stood looking at Stormont, the heightened colour playing in her cheeks as she began to comprehend the comradeship between these two men.

Slowly she turned to Darragh, offered her hand:

"I'll go to Harrod Place," she said in a low voice.

Darragh's quick smile brightened the sombre gravity of his face.

"Eve," he said, "when I came over here this morning from Harrod Place I was afraid you would refuse to listen to me; I was afraid you would not even see me. And so I brought with me—somebody—to whom I felt certain you would listen.... I brought with me a young girl—a poor refugee from Russia, once wealthy, to-day almost penniless.... Her name is Theodorica.... Once she was Grand Duchess of Esthonia.... But this morning a clergyman from Five Lakes changed her name.... To such friends as you and Jack she is Ricca Darragh now ... and she's having a wonderful time on her new snow-shoes—"

He took Eve by one hand and Stormont by the other, and drew them to the kitchen door and kicked it open.

Through the swirling snow, over on the lake-slope at the timber edge, a graceful, boyish figure in scarlet and white wool moved swiftly over the drifts with all the naïve delight of a child with a brand new toy.

As Darragh strode out into the open the distant figure flung up one arm in salutation and came racing over the drifts, her brilliant scarf flying.

All aglow and a trifle breathless, she met Darragh just beyond the veranda, rested one mittened hand on his shoulder while he knelt and unbuckled her snow-shoes, stepped lightly from them and came forward to Eve with out-stretched hand and a sudden winning gravity in her lovely face.

"We shall be friends, surely," she said in her quick, winning voice;—"because my husband has told me—and I am so grieved for you—and I need a girl friend—"

Holding both Eve's hands, her mittens dangling from her wrist, she looked into her eyes very steadily.

Slowly Eve's eyes filled; more slowly still Ricca kissed her on both cheeks, framed her face in both hands, kissed her lightly on the lips.

Then, still holding Eve's hands, she turned and looked at Stormont.

"I remember you now," she said. "You were with my husband in Riga."

She freed her right hand and held it out to Stormont. He had the grace to kiss it and did it very well for a Yankee.

Together they entered the kitchen door and turned into the dining room on the left, where were chairs around the plain pine table.

Darragh said: "The new mistress of Harrod Place has selected your quarters, Eve. They adjoin the quarters of her friend, the Countess Orloff-Strelwitz."

"Valentine begged me," said Ricca, smiling. "She is going to be lonely without me. All hours of day and night we were trotting into one another's rooms—" She looked gravely at Eve: "You will like Valentine; and she will like you very much.... As for me—I already love you."

She put one arm around Eve's shoulders: "How could you even think of remaining here all alone? Why, I should never close my eyes for thinking of you, dear."

Eve's head drooped; she said in a stifled voice: "I'll go with you.... I want to.... I'm very—tired."

"We had better go now," said Darragh. "Your things can be brought over later. If you'll dress for snow-shoeing, Jack can pack what clothes you need.... Are there snow-shoes for him, too?"

Eve turned tragically to her lover: "In Dad's closet—" she said, choking; then turned and went up the stairs, still clinging to Ricca's hand and drawing her with her.

Stormont followed, entered Clinch's quarters, and presently came downstairs again, carrying Clinch's snow-shoes and a basket pack.

He seated himself near Darragh. After a silence: "Your wife is beautiful, Jim.... Her character seems to be even more beautiful.... She's like God's own messenger to Eve.... And—you're rather wonderful yourself—"

"Nonsense," said Darragh, "I've given my wife her first American friend and I've done a shrewd stroke of business in nabbing the best business associate I ever heard of—"

"You're crazy but kind.... I hope I'll be some good.... One thing; I'll never get over what you've done for Eve in this crisis—"

"There'll be no crisis, Jack. Marry, and hook up with me in business. That solves everything.... Lord!—what a life Eve has had! But you'll make it all up to her ... all this loneliness and shame and misery of Clinch's Dump—"

Stormont touched his arm in caution: Eve and Ricca came down the stairs—the former now in the grey wool snow-shoe dress, and carrying her snow-shoes, black gown, and toilet articles.

Stormont began to stow away her effects in the basket pack; Darragh went over to her and took her hand.

"I'm so glad we are to be friends," he said. "It hurt a lot to know you held me in contempt. But I had to go about it that way."

Eve nodded. Then, suddenly recollecting: "Oh," she exclaimed, reddening, "I forgot the jewel case! It's under my pillow—"

She turned and sped upstairs and reappeared almost instantly, carrying the jewel-case.

Breathless, flushed, thankful and happy in the excitement of restitution, she placed the leather case in Ricca's hands.

"My jewels!" cried the girl, astounded. Then, with a little cry of delight, she placed the case upon the table, stripped open the emblazoned cover, and emptied the two trays. All over the table rolled the jewels, flashing, scintillating, ablaze with blinding light.

And at the same instant the outer door crashed open and Quintana covered them with Darragh's rifle.

"Now, by Christ!" he shouted, "who stirs a finger shall go to God in one jump! You, my gendarme frien'—*you*, my frien' Smith—turn your damn backs—han's up high!—tha's the way!—now, ladies!—back away there—get back or I kill!—sure, by Jesus, I kill you like I would some white little mice!—"

With incredible quickness he stepped forward and swept the jewels into one hand—filled the pocket of his trousers, caught up every stray stone and pocketed them.

"You gendarme," he cried in a menacing voice, "you think you shall follow in my track. Yes? I blow your damn head off if you stir before the hour.... After that—well, follow and be damn!"

Even as he spoke he stepped outside and slammed the door; and Darragh and Stormont leaped for it. Then the loud detonation of Quintana's rifle was echoed by the splintering rip of bullets tearing through the closed door; and both men halted in the face of the leaden hail.

Eve ran to the pantry window and saw Quintana in somebody's stolen lumber-sledge, lash a big pair of horses to a gallop and go floundering past into the Ghost Lake road.

As he sped by in a whirl of snow he fired five times at the house, then, rising and swinging his whip, he flogged the frantic horses into the woods.

In the dining room, Stormont, red with rage and shame, and having found his rifle in the corridor outside Eve's bedroom, was trying to open the shutters for a shot; and Darragh, empty-handed, searched the house frantically for a weapon.

Eve, terribly excited, came from the pantry:

"He's gone!" she cried furiously. "He's in somebody's lumber-sledge with a pair of horses and he's driving west like the devil!"

Stormont ran to the tap-room telephone, cranked it, and warned the constabulary at Five Lakes.

"Good God!" he exclaimed, turning to Darragh, scarlet with mortification, "what a ghastly business! I never dreamed he was within miles of Clinch's! It's the most shameful thing that ever happened to me—"

"What could anybody do under that rifle?" said Eve hotly. "That beast would have murdered the first person who stirred!"

Darragh, exasperated and dreadfully humiliated, looked miserably at his brand-new wife.

Eve and Stormont also looked at her. She had come forward from the rear of the stairway where Quintana had brutally driven her. Now she stood with one hand on the empty leather jewel case, looking at everybody out of pretty, bewildered eyes.

To Darragh, in a perplexed, unsteady voice: "Is it the same bandit who robbed us before?"

"Yes; Quintana," he said wretchedly. Rage began to redden his features. "Ricca," he said, "I promised I'd find your jewels.... I promise you again that I'll never drop this business until your gems—and the Flaming Jewel—are in your possession—"

"But, Jim—"

"I swear it!" he exclaimed violently. "I'm not such a stupid fool as I seem—"

"Dear!" she protested excitedly, "you *have* done what you promised. My gems *are* in my possession—I believe—"

She caught up the emblazoned case, stripped out the first tray, then the second, and flung them aside. Then, searching with the delicate tip of her forefinger in the empty case, she suddenly pressed the bottom hard—thumb, middle finger and little finger forming the three apexes of an equilateral triangle.

There came a clear, tiny sound like the ringing of the alarm in a repeating watch. Very gently the false bottom of the case detached itself and came away in the palm of her hand.

And there, each embedded in its own shaped compartment of chamois, lay the Esthonian jewels—the true ones—deep hidden, always doubly guarded by two sets of perfect imitations lining the two visible trays above.

And, in the centre, blazed the Erosite gem—the magnificent Flaming Jewel, a glory of living, blinding fire.

Nobody stirred or spoke. Darragh blinked at the crystalline blaze as though stunned.

Then the young girl who had once been Her Serene Highness Theodorica, Grand Duchess of Esthonia, looked up at her brand-new husband and laughed.

"Did you really suppose it was these that brought me across the ocean? Did you suppose it was a passion for these that filled my heart? Did you think it was for these that I followed you?"

She laughed again, turned to Eve:

"*You* understand. Tell him that if he had been in rags I would have followed him like a gypsy.... They say there is gypsy blood in us.... God knows.... I think perhaps there is a little of it in all real women—" Still laughing she placed her hand lightly upon her heart—"In all women—perhaps—a Flaming Jewel imbedded here—"

Her eyes, tender, and mocking, met his; she lifted the jewel-case, closed it, and placed it in his hands.

"Now," she said, "you have everything in your possession; and we are safe—we are quite safe, now, my jewels and I."

Then she went to Eve and rested both hands on her shoulders.

"Shall we put on our snow-shoes and go—home?"

Stormont flung open the bullet-splintered door. Outside in the snow he dropped on both knees to buckle on Eve's snow-shoes.

Darragh was performing a like office for his wife, and the State Trooper, being unobserved, took Eve's slim hands and kissed them, looking up at her where he was kneeling.

Her pale face blushed as it had that day in the woods on Owl Marsh, so long, so long ago, when this man's lips first touched her hands.

As their eyes met both remembered. Then she smiled at her lover with the shy girl's soul of her gazing out at him through eyes as blue as the wild blind-gentians that grow among the ferns and mosses of Star Pond.

Far away in the northwestern forests Quintana still lashed his horses through the primeval pines.

Triumphant, reckless, resourceful, dangerous, he felt that now nothing could stop him, nothing bar his way to freedom.

Out of the wilderness lay his road and his destiny; out of it he must win his way, by strategy, by cunning, by violence—creep out, lie his way out, shoot his way out—it scarcely mattered. He was going out! He was going back to life once more. Who could forbid him? Who stop him? Who deny him, now, when, in his pockets, he held all that was worth living for—the keys to power, to pleasure—the key to everything on earth!

In fierce exultation he slapped the glass jewels in his pocket and laughed aloud.

"The keys to the world!" he cried. "Let him stop me and take them who is a better man than I!" Then his long whip whistled and he cursed his horses.

Then, of a sudden, close by in the snowy road ahead, he saw a State Trooper on snow-shoes—saw the upflung arm warning him—screamed curses at his horses, flogged them forward to crush this thing to death that dared menace him—this object that suddenly rose up out of nowhere to snatch from him the keys of the world—

For a moment the State Trooper looked after the runaway horses. There was no use following; they'd have to run till they dropped.

Then he lowered the levelled rifle from his shoulder, looked grimly at the limp thing which had tumbled from the sledge into the snowy road and which sprawled there crimsoning the spotless flakes that fell upon it.

THE END

THE TALKERS

ROBERT W. CHAMBERS

To My Friend
ROBERT H. DAVIS

CHAPTER I

Sadoul's only experiences in love had been gross. The cynic in him admitted nothing better. Saturnine, without delusions, he went about his business in life, doing no particular good, and with a capacity for harm limited only by his talents.

He had been a little of everything, and always clever—art student, medical student, reporter, critic, writer—intelligent, adroit.

His was a mordant pen and brilliant; and it was for sale.

The query, "Have you read Sadoul's article in the *Wasp?*" or in the *View Point*, or in some one of many irregular publications, was not an uncommon question in the metropolis.

Sadoul on this or that had become fairly familiar to a talkative public. He had something to say about everything and anything. His personal convictions made no difference. And he always was interesting.

The second year after the war ended he went to France again. At the University of Paris he took courses in psychology and philology: in the Ecole de Médecine he attended lectures. Clinics where hypnosis induced supplanted anesthesia in minor operations fascinated him.

But life, there, taught him nothing nobler to expect of a world already proven sordid by personal experience.

He entertained no delusions concerning mankind, its friendship, or its love; he neither expected nor desired anything of it except the saturnine amusement which he extracted from it, and which was his principal form of pleasure.

Then Chance tripped him up. Needing an English stenographer one day, the American firm on the Rue Colchas sent him a girl equipped to take dictation.

It appeared that she was equipped for more than that. Sadoul silently went mad about her.

A sort of still terror also took possession of the girl—the hopeless immobility of a doomed thing, conscious of menace, apparently unable to escape.

Resistance seemed to hold only along certain lines.

Otherwise there was no defence. She had stepped from reality into a dream.

At his inquiry she told him her story. She did not wish to do so.

There was a ball in the Latin Quarter given by Julian's that evening. Sadoul took her. She wore pale, lunar green; which went with her red hair and deep green eyes.

She had little to say to Sadoul's friends. So reticent, so dazed she seemed that some, troubled and perplexed by her youth and beauty, suspected her of an addiction to drugs.

As for Sadoul, he had gone completely mad over her. He became her shadow everywhere. And, save only for certain lines of resistance, he seemed to have utterly mastered her.

But those occult lines held. The conflict almost crazed him—so pliant, so yielding she seemed, so obedient had he made her in all excepting certain lines. His dark face greyed at times under the strain. He abased himself and begged; he grinned and told her what to expect if she ever tricked him. The lines held.

His impression upon her had already been made; he could stamp it no deeper; the girl was not in love with him. She never would be. And he knew it.

She seemed to be a passionless little thing, her beauty a golden chrysalis containing nothing—the Psyche within aborted.

In the Latin Quarter, lack of animation is unpopular. There was about her that innocent detachment one notices in the preoccupation of a nun. Invited, at first she went everywhere with Sadoul.

After a while they were seldom invited where pleasure was noisy and untrammelled.

Early in spring a cabled offer from New York brought Sadoul's affairs to a climax.

For three days Sadoul beat at her very soul to club it into submission. Then he crawled and wept. The lines held.

Again he battered her with his implacable will till her bruised, stupefied mind gave up. But the lines held.

She was in a daze when the civil ceremony was performed. He cabled to New York, giving up his quarters at the Fireside Club, and requesting his friend Pockman to secure for him a furnished housekeeping apartment on Riverside Drive.

He was having his way with her—or tried to believe he was having it.

And then Destiny pulled an ugly face at him. For the girl utterly refused to submit to the religious ceremony. And the old lines still held.

Early summer in Paris is paradise. But it had become a hell to Sadoul. He walked the earth like a damned soul chained to its victim.

In July he secured passage for them both.

CHAPTER II

George Derring, Julian Fairless, and Harry Stayr organized the Fireside Club in New York to gratify the instincts of the slovenly well-to-do. Limited membership and a long waiting-list told its successful story.

Derring also had financed the big new building on 57th Street, where the Fireside occupied the entire second floor.

The remainder of the building harboured members in apartments of one to three rooms. Some apartments had studios attached.

The Fireside Club was the common meeting-ground. Members could sprawl there in evening dress or bath-robe and slippers, all day and all night if they liked.

Men with an inclination to conversation and a disinclination for work seemed to compose the bulk of membership. Which gave to the Fireside that intellectual allure so impressive among the mindless millions.

The glamour of genius played about the Fireside like St. Anthony's fire; its Thinkers and its Talkers found its exclusive luxury a paradise.

But a few common and irreverent folk characterised it as an intellectual doldrums where talent lay becalmed; or a maelstrom of talk where creative energy was sucked under and ultimately engulfed.

In midsummer a majority of the Fireside wandered far and wide in that restless quest for satisfaction characteristic of those who talk much and do little.

But always a sprinkling remained to loaf about the club. From which retreat, having dined well, the dusky tropic brilliancy of Manhattan's streets lured them into endless wanderings through a thousand and one Metropolitan Nights.

Early in spring Sadoul had cabled from Paris that he was giving up his apartment there on May first. So somebody else moved in on that date.

Derring returned in June from a gastronomic tour of European Ritz's. He mentioned meeting Julian Fairless in Paris, but had not seen Sadoul.

Before Sadoul returned, Julian Fairless brought back a budget of gossip, including news of him. Only a small percentage of Talkers are doers. Fairless was industriously both.

To a question from Stayr he replied that Paris, the Latin Quarter, and Julian's were about the same as ever. A similar and dingy crowd infested the schools; similar masters gave similar instruction. All the unkempt ruck and reek of the atelier was there; massiers, models, blague, noise—nothing had changed except the individuals composing the mess.

Fairless, an incessant Talker, gossiped on without encouragement. Which is the instinct of the true Talker.

So-and-so was dead—killed at Verdun; so-and-so goes on crutches; old Clifford has a studio in the Court of the Dragon; Rowden died at Mons; Creed, now wealthy, lives in the Parc Monceau and paints no more; the Beaux Arts is below par this year, and "our men" appear to be the pick; etc., etc. So Fairless chattered on and on, talking the talk of the Talkers.

He was still at breakfast, eating a soft-boiled egg out of its own shell, in the rather dirty English fashion.

"I sold several pictures to profiteers," he continued; "Paris is lousy with nouveau riche. Derring bought two from me—"

Stayr remonstrated: "Derring isn't nouveau riche."

"Oh, no, but he played about with them. He wanted to see Julian's. I took him over. He was disgusted with the models. Besides, he kept his hat on and they bawled him out."

Fairless wallowed in a finger-bowl, dried his celebrated scarab ring: "I saw quite a lot of Casimir Sadoul. He was doing philology at the University, but he associated mostly with Julian men…. He had a girl; went about everywhere with her. That's a new idea for him, eh?"

"I suppose Sadoul did not wish to be conspicuous in the Quarter," suggested Mortimer Lyken.

"This affair was conspicuous. Fancy the contrast!—that big, blackish, beetle-browed ruffian hooked up to a red-headed slip of a thing, so bashful that you got no more out of her than yes and no."

"Did she really belong to Sadoul?" asked Stayr.

"Apparently. He behaved savagely if you looked at her. Somebody told me he got her by hypnotising her."

"He knows how," remarked Pockman. "He's done it for me."

"Bunk," murmured Stayr, "—wasn't it?"

"Well," returned Pockman with his pallid smirk and hunching up his wide, bony shoulders, "I've performed minor operations on patients with Sadoul's aid, inducing hypnosis instead of anesthesia."

"The devil!" exclaimed Lyken. "That was Charcot's graft."

Fairless chattered on: "All the fellows concluded that Sadoul had some sort of hold on her. She seemed too pretty and refined to fall for a big, swarthy brute like Sadoul. She really was an exquisite little thing, Harry—such features, such skin, such hands and hair—and the fellows all wild to paint her—and old Sadoul foxy and sardonic…. They say the souls of the damned cast no shadows. I fancy Sadoul's girl still has a chance: he certainly was her shadow—always at her heels, always on the job.... Somebody said he had threatened to kill her if she ever fooled him. But I think Sadoul's more likely to beat up the man in the case."

Fairless got up from the table.

"Now, if you fellows care to see what I brought back—"

A few of the other men rose and followed Fairless upstairs to his studio where Angelo, his factotum, had already placed the first picture upon an easel.

As usual, all the elements of popularity were apparent in the picture—a typical Julian Fairless canvas, full of that obvious charm so attractive to an obvious public, so acceptable to the professional critic.

Fairless lit a cigarette and sat down to chat with Sidney Pockman, who didn't care for pictures.

"Where did Sadoul get that girl you mentioned?" he inquired; the smirk still stamped on his flat, colourless face.

"In Paris."

"How did she happen to be there?"

"Oh, a story of sorts. She and mama were living in London when the Huns dropped bombs. Mama was blown into unpleasant gobs all over the house. Then it was canteen work in Paris. Then no job. Then Sadoul ran into her. That's the story."

"She's English?"

"American, I believe. I couldn't tell by her speech. She's a dumb youngster."

"What's he going to do with her? Marry her?"

"Well, I don't know, Pockman. I fancy it's high time—if he means to do it at all."

"Oh, that sort?"

"She doesn't look it. She's so dumb she seems almost drugged. Maybe it's true he's obtained some sort of hold on her. I don't know."

"I had a letter from Sadoul last week," said Pockman. "He must be on his way back here by this time."

Fairless nodded inattentively, motioning Angelo to take away the picture and replace it by another.

Pockman seemed to grin at the new picture—or perhaps his pallid smirk was habitual.

"What do you get for that kind of painting?" he inquired.

"Five thousand."

"Did it take you very long?"

"Two mornings."

Pockman laughed: "Yours is a soft graft, Julian."

"So is yours, you pill-rolling fakir!"

"Not very soft, so far. But it ought to be when I succeed in grafting the nymphalic gland to a corpse and break fifty-fifty with the New Testament."

"Isn't Voronoff grafting glands and things?"

"Some glands; not the nymphalic. And that's the whole problem, because it governs—" Pockman hesitated, shrugged: "—Well, adios, Julian! Much obliged for a view of your new pictures. Hope you sting the profiteers."

"You bet," nodded Fairless complacently.

But July is too late for an "exhibition." Besides, the great American profiteer had been rolling in art since the war ended, and, now satiated after an orgy of antique-buying during the past winter and spring, had begun to build bungalows. October or the middle of November would see the town crawling again with newly rich. There was plenty of time to prepare pasture for absent cattle—ample time for Julian Fairless to plan his show. Besides, he desired a vacation at Greenwich, in the vicinity of Veronica Weld.

It was there, early in August, that Fairless again ran across Pockman entering the railroad station.

Among other items of gossip he learned that Sadoul had returned to New York, bringing with him his red-headed companion, and, furthermore, that the red-headed one had suddenly disappeared within the first week.

"Sadoul's a bad actor if you do things to him," added Pockman. "He's as vindictive as hell. I'm wondering what will happen if he ever finds a man with her.... Or finds her again, even alone."

"What's Sadoul doing?" inquired Fairless, pleasantly entertained with the account of another man's misfortune.

"Oh, he's writing his free-lance stuff, as usual, and hanging around my laboratory."

"Grouching?"

"No; he's rather quiet. I wouldn't care to be the Johnny in the case.... Or the girl, either."

Fairless shrugged; then, inattentive: "Where are you bound for? Town?"

"I came up here to get a gland."

"A what?"

"That young fellow who was killed here yesterday in the motor accident.... You heard? Well, he proved a healthy subject, and his nymphalic gland was of no further use to him. So I came up to get it."

"What good is a dead man's gland?" demanded Fairless.

"The gland isn't dead."

"What!"

"Not at all. I've got it in this grip packed in ice. I can keep it alive for weeks in a refrigerator."

"What for?"

"Graft it on some senile subject and add twenty years to his life."

"It's rather a loathsome business, yours," said Fairless frankly.

"Not at all. You'll need a new gland yourself some day. When you do, give me a ring."

Pockman smirked at the disgusted painter, picked up his satchel, and stalked off at a stiff, crazy gait characteristic of him. Stayr always said it reminded him of Holbein's Dance of Death.

When Pockman reached New York he telephoned Sadoul from his laboratory:

"Come on over; I've got a lively nymphalic on ice. Some gland, believe me, Sadoul."

But Sadoul seemed incurious and morose, and Pockman could not persuade him.

So the latter continued to examine and caress his rather ghastly acquisition, and Sadoul's powerful, bony fingers drove his pen through a mordant article destined to stimulate a moribund periodical in the senile stage, kept alive only by Derring's money.

Sadoul's and Pockman's remedies for inanition were, after all, similar: gall and gland to stimulate the decrepit and delay ultimate dissolution.

Derring, financing *The Revolt* to please a rather handsome woman with bobbed hair, had found himself let in for a deal of trouble.

She of the bobbed hair suggested that Sadoul "put a kick into the damn thing." Derring, at Newport, wired assent.

Sadoul, in seething silence, gave himself to the job with a fierce persistence which made *The Revolt* smoke enough to attract attention.

But it was all smoke: the fire itself smouldered in Sadoul, not in the magazine. All that long summer and autumn Sadoul watched and waited and burned. His olive skin and black eyes grew more shadowy; one noticed his teeth under the crisp beard when he smiled.

He was usually at the Fireside Club in the evenings, but he lived elsewhere—in a big, handsome housekeeping apartment, according to Julian Fairless, taken, probably, on account of the red-headed one, now vanished.

Twice, already, since her disappearance, Sadoul mistook others with auburn tresses for the slender runaway for whom his smouldering gaze was always searching amid the multitudes by night and day.

The third time there was no mistake. They met face to face on Fifth Avenue, the red-headed one and Casimir Sadoul.

"Where have you been?" said Sadoul, smiling and offering his hand. But his dark skin had turned greyish.

After the first startled glance, reassured by his smile and offered hand, the girl seemed inclined to meet the issue with laughing and youthful defiance.

She told him frankly that she had been bored; that she desired to enjoy herself like a modern girl, and meant to do so.

"The modern girl," said Sadoul, laughing, "is one who is determined to have a good time in the world, no matter at what cost."

"Yes, I suppose so," she conceded. "The trouble is that I don't know how to begin."

"Haven't you begun in all these months?" he inquired, fixing his black eyes on her.

She laughed, made a childish face at him, mocked him in friendly fashion.

"I'm not going to let you resume your way with me," she said.

"Will you let me lunch with you, Gilda?"

"Why, yes. It's nearly one, now. It's quite agreeable to see you again. I've sometimes wondered how it would seem …"

The Ritz was only a block away.

She was a piquant figure in her furs; and the touch of turquoise to her hat made her red hair redder and her white skin whiter as she faced the November east-wind beside Sadoul.

The raw air smelled of snow, but no flakes fell.

"So—you're having a good time," said Sadoul, showing his teeth in a sudden smile.

"I told you I haven't learned how, yet."

"Will you let me try again?"

"Not—that way," she said, colouring.

"No; that was a mistake, Gilda."

She laughed in surprise and relief: "So you admit it?" she cried.

"I've got to, haven't I? You left me flat."

"I had to."

She was animated and friendly at luncheon—perfectly frank as always heretofore, not untruthful, not evasive, but gaily declining information concerning her recent career and her present domicile.

"It's none of your business," she said decisively. "I can always find you if I care to."

This attitude seemed to amuse him. He appeared to her to be very much changed, and decidedly for the better.

He said: "George Derring is giving a dance at his studio apartment tonight. If you care to come you'll have one of those 'good times' you're always wishing for."

"Who is George Derring?"

"An intellectual panhandler."

"What?"

"A beggar begs food from door to door; Derring, brainless and resourceless, begs his daily modicum of amusement from friend to friend.... He's very rich. He has to be."

"That sounds more like you," she said with an uneasy smile.

"Oh, no; I'm off that stuff. Gilda, you'd better come to Derring's dance. It will be gay—a masked affair. All the men dress as kings; all the women as queens. You have that wonderful green costume you wore at the Julian ball, haven't you?"

She nodded. Her eyes, which were emerald green, widened.

"I'd like to go," she said.

"Very well. But where am I to call for you?"

At that she laughed outright. "I'll take a taxi and drive to your apartment. But I shall not go in."

He made no attempt to persuade her. They fixed the hour amicably; she told him in her frank way that if he followed her and attempted to spy on her, she'd move elsewhere.

So, when luncheon ended, he lifted his hat and turned away, leaving her to find her own taxi. Which she did, and drove to the matinée for which she had a ticket, but where, alas! nobody awaited her.

For, even after all these months alone, and free to seek pleasure where she wished, the acme, so far, of the "good time" so ardently desired by her was a matinée; and the most delirious dissipation a drive on Fifth Avenue all alone in a small limousine car hired and steered entirely by herself.

Sadoul's face was ghastly when he entered Pockman's laboratory, and the latter noticed it and commented.

"Gilda Greenway is coming to Derring's party with me," he said.

"Oh, is she back?"

"No. I met her on the street."

Pockman cast a stealthy glance at Sadoul, then continued to filter the contents of one test-tube into another. "You were—er—glad to see her?"

he inquired.

"Yes."

"Well," said Pockman, "you have a funny way of showing it. I'd run if I met you in a dark alley.... Hand me that smeared slide, will you—and that bowl of Reakirt's solution—"

CHAPTER III

A masked figure followed them noiselessly upstairs and slipped behind the portières to observe them.

Sutton, face to face with his first real adventure, was fascinated by the little Queen in Green—not prepared, perhaps, to encounter such youthful shyness at Derring's. And now he attempted to discover her identity, rather roughly, but she evaded his curiosity and ardent advances, and coaxed him to show her Derring's quarters.

The masked man watched them out of narrow eye-slits. They visited the further rooms; then, having satisfied her curiosity, the Queen in Green turned on her dainty heel.

As the two retraced their steps, she prettily avoided Sutton's love-making. It was only after he unmasked, and they had stopped by the portières—so close that the man behind them could have stabbed them—that the girl turned impulsively to Sutton, put her arms around his neck, and took his kiss as passionately as he gave it.

It lasted but a second. She stepped back against the portières. Both seemed hotly embarrassed.

A second later the Queen in Green was readjusting her gilt crown and laughing at some light jest he had made—he could not recall what it was afterward.

Below, the orchestra had begun again. He looked at her; she nodded. They waited to catch the beat of the music. She was still laughing when she placed her smooth little hand in his. But as he encircled her waist she drew a swift, agonised breath and lurched forward against him.

He reeled under the sudden impact; her silk-clad body sagged, her masked head fell backward, and then, as he caught her, the Queen in Green collapsed in his arms.

He half dragged her to an armchair. One of her slippers dropped off.

For a moment he stood helpless, looking down at her; then, anxious, and having had no experience with people who faint, he hurried downstairs, perplexed, to find Sadoul, who had brought the girl to the party.

After-supper-dancing was beginning again in the studio, and the music seemed unusually noisy. He tried to discover Sadoul, shouted his name, but everybody was still masked and Sutton hunted for him in vain.

Finally he continued on through the studio into the supper room to get a glass of ice-water, and saw Harry Stayr still browsing there.

As Sutton left the table, carrying the water, he said to Stayr in a worried voice:

"That Queen in Green—the one Sadoul brought—has fainted in Derring's quarters."

"Is she soused?" inquired Stayr, busy with food.

"No."

"Who is she?"

"I don't know. She wears a green mask. Casimir Sadoul brought her. If you see him tell him she's ill upstairs."

"Put some ice down her back," advised Stayr, reaching for the salad.

Sutton hastened on upstairs, hoping to find the lady better.

The Queen in Green lay face upward on the floor—a crumpled heap of pale green silks. Her ruddy hair was dishevelled; her gilt crown had rolled across the rug.

There was a day-bed beside the rose-shaded lamp. Sutton carried her to it, laid her there and smoothed her clothing.

Under the mask her lips and skin were livid, but through the eye-slits she seemed to be watching him.

He flushed, spoke to her, waited, then stripped off the green silk mask. It shocked him to discover that her eyes were open.

"That's a funny way to faint," he thought. And he lifted the glass and tipped it, spilling ice-water over the upturned face.

The water washed off some cosmetic but produced no other effect.

Scared, Sutton tried to find her pulse, and failed; tried to locate her heart and couldn't. There was nothing to loosen. He opened a window and came back to her. Then he went out to the gallery and shouted down through the clatter and music:

"Sadoul! Sadoul! Come up here!"

A masked figure in crown and crimson robes detached itself and came forward under the gallery, looking up. "Is that you, Sadoul?"

"Yes. What's the trouble?"

"Your girl—the girl you brought with you—has fainted. She's up here. Bring Pockman, too."

"What do you mean, my girl?" inquired Sadoul.

"The Queen in Green. You brought her, didn't you?"

"Oh! *That* girl? What's the matter with her?"

"I don't know. You'd better find Pockman and come up. *I* don't know what ails her."

Sutton went back to the day-bed and gazed nervously at the Queen in Green. Robes, stockings, slippers, jewels, all were green. Even her strangely open eyes seemed golden green as a cat's.

Sadoul and Pockman, in gorgeous costumes but unmasked, entered together in a few moments.

"She doesn't seem to be breathing, and I can't find any pulse," explained Sutton. "What on earth is the matter with her?"

Pockman bent over; Sadoul and Sutton watched him. She wore no stays—there was not much to her bodice, anyway—only a trifle more of her body visible when Pockman stripped off her waist than the waist had already revealed.

The two men watched him; the leisurely certainty of everything he was doing preoccupied Sutton.

"Why, she's dead," said Pockman coolly.

Sutton stared aghast.

Sadoul said: "Well, of all rotten luck!—What the devil was the matter with her?"

"I'm not sure."

"You mean—mean to say that this girl is dead!" faltered Sutton.

"She's been dead for more than twenty minutes.... *I* don't know what killed her—"

Sadoul glanced up at Pockman, who was staring intently at him.

Sutton said miserably: "Is there anything possible to do—any other and surer test to be made?"

"This girl is *dead*," repeated Pockman, still looking significantly at Sadoul. Then he shrugged his bony shoulders, went over to the telephone and called his laboratory. While waiting, he said to Sadoul: "Here's my chance, by God! It will take about three hours," he added, "—and half an hour more—" His connection interrupted; he asked for somebody named Stent, got him immediately, talked to him unhurriedly.

When he came back he asked Sutton to go into Derring's bedroom and get a sheet from the bed.

Sutton brought it; Pockman covered the recumbent figure decently, concealing the face also.

He said to Sutton: "Sadoul and I realise that this is a good opportunity for me to try something I am interested in.... It can't harm her, anyway—"

"Do you mean that there is any chance of reviving her?" asked Sutton, his voice still hoarse from shock.

"Well—she's dead.... Figure it out for yourself, Sutton." And to Sadoul: "This is a damned unpleasant episode for old Derring and his party—"

... "Who was that girl?" interrupted Sutton, harshly.

"Her name was Gilda Greenway," replied Sadoul, with composure; but his long fingers were working at the gilt fringe on his robe.

"Has she any family?" inquired Pockman.

"No, I believe not—"

"Well—what the devil!—She had a home somewhere, I suppose!"

Sadoul shook his head: "Possibly. I don't know where she lived."

Sutton opened the telephone directory. There were only two Greenways in the book. He called them up. Neither knew anything of Gilda Greenway.

Pockman turned to Sutton: "What were *you* doing with her up here?" he enquired with one of his pallid smirks.

"We were dancing—or going to. She wanted to look down at the floor from the gallery when they began throwing confetti."

"Oh, sure," said Pockman, but his pasty, flat features bore no trace of the sneer in his voice.

"We came up to the gallery," continued Sutton, "and watched the battle of confetti and flowers. Then she peeped into Derring's quarters and desired to inspect them.

"It was harmless curiosity—no matter what you're thinking, Pockman. She looked the place over; we were standing over there by the portières. She was laughing; and then the music began downstairs—and we were starting to dance up here.... And then—good God!—"

"Just like that," nodded Pockman, softly.

There was something subtly horrible about the vernacular as he used it in the dim room where death was. But death had become an old story to Pockman, and there were for him neither thrills nor shocks in the spectacle of human dissolution—nothing to awe or subdue or arouse emotion—only a fact of routine interest to a student preoccupied by original research.

He had a pale, flat, fat face, smoothly shaven; washed-out eyes; a tall, ill-made figure with very wide, square shoulders, and scanty, untidy hair of a faded hue.

He looked almost stealthily at Sutton, now, who, quite overcome by the tragedy, sat staring at the sheeted figure of the girl he had been laughing with half an hour ago.

"If you don't feel like dancing," said Pockman pleasantly, "stay here until my man Stent arrives. Sadoul and I are going down."

"You don't mean you are going to dance?"

"Sure," replied Pockman, adjusting his mask. "Why not?"

Sadoul said nothing. After a moment he slowly put on his mask.

"Aren't you going to tell Derring?" demanded Sutton.

"I'm no crape-hanger," replied Pockman. "Why spoil Derring's party?

If you insist on staying here until Stent comes, you'd better lock the door or some of those fair young things downstairs will get the shock of their variegated lives."

He started downstairs in his crown and fluttering yellow robes. Sadoul, in flamboyant crimson, followed him. After a moment Sutton got up and locked the door behind them, stood by it, looking back over his shoulder at the form on the day-bed, then he slowly returned to his chair.

The decency that kept him beside a dead stranger was purely emotional.

He gazed miserably at the shrouded figure. After a long while he rose, picked up her gilded crown and the little green slipper. The silken crescent which had masked her still lay beside her bed. This also he recovered, and then reseated himself, holding her toys in his lap, his boyish eyes full of tears.

It was all very well for a graduate physician like Pockman to exhibit callousness—and for the saturnine Sadoul—he of the long, horse face and black eyes and Vandyke—he of the murderous, mocking pen—the literary vivisectionist and jester at all lovable human frailties—it was well enough for him to remain obtuse.

But a plain young man, like Sutton, continues to be emotional, whatever garments of experience still clothe him. He was horribly, profoundly upset.

Several times an unseen clock in a farther room struck a treble note in the stillness.

Faintly, too, came music and tumult from the gaiety below. Even the odour of roses penetrated the locked room.

Sutton, staring at the covered form, was thinking it rotten hard luck to be dead so young. He wondered who she could have been; who were her people, her friends; what hearts were going to break for such an ending as this.

He wondered whether she had been respectable—was fiercely inclined to believe so—wondered why she had consented to come to Derring's party with Sadoul.

When again the silvery treble of the unseen clock sounded twice, Sutton glanced at his own timepiece. It lacked a few minutes of two o'clock. Gilda Greenway had been dead three hours and a half.

He rose and lifted a corner of the sheet. Her lower jaw had dropped. Horrified, he covered the dead face and went back to his chair, trembling.

CHAPTER IV

Somebody knocked at the door; Sutton rose nervously, unlocked and opened it, dazzled by the outer lights.

Figures in brilliant silks entered—Pockman, Sadoul, a man and a young woman in street clothes, carrying valises, and George Derring wearing violet royal robes and tinsel crown, his vizard pushed up over his bald forehead, a monocle shining in his pallid face.

"What the devil is all this?" he demanded. "If the girl is actually dead she can't remain in my place. The thing to do is to call up the proper authorities—"

"Keep your shirt on," interrupted Pockman calmly. "Come on in, Miss Cross. You can change your dress in the next bedroom. Come over here, Stent. Unpack your things on that table—"

"Is—this girl—dead?" faltered Derring, peering at the sheeted shape through his monocle.

Pockman consulted his watch: "She's been dead for three hours and forty minutes, George."

"Why didn't you t-tell me?" stammered Derring. "What are you going to do to her? This isn't a morgue. It isn't a place for autopsies—"

Sadoul drew the stammering man aside: "If you'll keep your mouth shut, Pockman will see to it that this affair is kept out of the newspapers. Go downstairs, George, and when your party breaks up, come back here and we'll fix it up for you so there'll be no notoriety or scandal."

Derring, white and inclined to tremble, suffered himself to be led to the door and thrust out. Sadoul turned the key with a grimace and came back to where Pockman stood aiding his assistant, Stent, to unpack the valises.

A case of surgical instruments was laid on the table. Beside this Stent placed a miniature porcelain refrigerator, several basins, packets of sterilized gauze, other objects unfamiliar to Sutton.

The young woman whom Pockman had addressed as Miss Cross came back from the further bedroom clad in the white garb of a hospital nurse. She seemed to know what was to be done with the several packages from the valises and became exceedingly busy.

Pockman and Sadoul, carrying other packets, went away together toward the bathroom, leaving Sutton standing alone by the table.

The efficient Miss Cross paid him no attention. She first unrolled a rubber sheet and then began to undress the dead girl.

Sutton pivoted in his tracks and went slowly toward the bathroom, where Pockman and Sadoul, their masquerade finery discarded, were dressing in the white robes of operating surgeons. A smell of disinfectants pervaded the place.

"What are you preparing to do?" asked Sutton.

"Stick around and see," replied Pockman flippantly. His white robes and flat, fat face made a most unpleasant impression upon Sutton.

Sadoul, also, was ready now; they returned to the room of death.

"If you're squeamish," remarked Sadoul, with his odd, shadowy smile, "you'd better leave the room, Sutton."

"What are you going to do?"

"I? Nothing. Pockman, however, is going to try something."

"If she's already dead, what more is there to try?" asked the other huskily.

"Stand over here and watch. We shan't be long."

"Is—is this sort of thing legal, Sadoul?"

"Certainly. At least there's no law forbidding it. Pockman is a graduate physician. There are no laws forbidding a qualified physician, who has been called in to do his best, from doing his best. And this is Pockman's one best bet."

"But—after death—what *is* there a physician can do?"

"What *is* death?" asked Sadoul, with his dark and shadowy smile.

There ensued a silence while the washing of the unclothed body was accomplished and the corpse laid face downward. One by one Pockman took certain sterilized instruments from Miss Cross, employed each with incredible deftness. Sutton had averted his head as Pockman made a tiny, deep incision at the nape of the girl's neck. The hemorrhage was slight; Sadoul opened the drawer of the miniature refrigerator, Miss Cross took from it something that she carefully placed in a vessel filled with liquid. Twice she tested the temperature of the liquid.

"Ready," she said in her low, pleasant voice.

With his forceps Pockman picked out from the liquid in the vessel something that seemed to resemble a small oviform body—like a lump of animal tissue, and inserted it in the incision which he had made at the nape of the dead girl's neck.

Deftly the wound was closed, sterilized, covered with a film of transparent liquid which instantly hardened. A few drops of blood had flowed freely.

"All right," murmured Pockman, "turn her over."

He cast another brief glance at the dead girl, then walked back to the bathroom to wash.

Sadoul followed him, wiping his dark, bony hands on a bit of gauze. Sutton, feeling slightly nauseated, turned away from the body which

Miss Cross was now swathing in a sterilized sheet.

He stood at one of the darkened and dripping windows, staring out. It was raining, but a few large snowflakes slanted through the downpour.

The odours in the room—the taint of death—were becoming insufferable; he went to the door, drew the bolt, and stepped outside onto the balcony.

The ball was over, the music gone. The last of the maskers were leaving the studio—a loud-voiced group lingering in the supper room, another near the entrance hall.

Old Derring, in his rumpled royal robes, his crown on the back of his ruddy, bald head, stood nervously receiving the adieux and noisy gratitude of his guests. The air reeked with perfume of roses and scent of wine; the floor was littered with debris of finery and confetti.

When at length Sutton returned to the room, the day-bed was empty; Stent had already repacked both valises and was putting his hat on and buttoning his overcoat. Pockman, Sadoul, and Miss Cross had gone into the farther bedroom, where a light burned. Sutton could see them through the vista of the connecting rooms, moving quietly about, dressed now in their street clothing—excepting Miss Cross, who still wore her nurse's garb.

When he went in to the chamber where they were gathered he discovered that the dead girl had been laid in Derring's guest-room bed.

She seemed asleep there on the pillow; her eyes were decently closed, the bed sheets drawn to her throat. Only her wax-like skin betrayed her condition.

As Sutton entered the room, Pockman turned toward him:

"Your views concerning the dignity and tragedy of death," he said, with that ever present undertone of irony, "are the popular and accepted views. So if you don't think it very charitable to leave this lady all alone here during the night, why not sit up with her until I return in the morning?"

Sutton flushed. "Somebody ought to remain here out of mere decency," he said slowly.

"All right. It's up to you. Miss Cross is to stay for another hour; and I'd really be obliged to you if you'd stand guard here tonight and keep old Derring from making a fuss. Will you?"

After a silence: "What was it you did to her?" enquired Sutton in a constrained voice, not yet under full control.

"Nothing illegal. I am within my rights. Ask Miss Cross. If nothing happens it won't make any difference, anyway. If anything should happen, why, I don't care how much it's talked about. Do you, Sadoul?"

"Rather not," said Sadoul, with that almost imperceptible smile on his dark face, that waned and waxed like a shadow.

"What *could* happen?" demanded Sutton. "Death is death—isn't it?"

Pockman shrugged, gathered up his discarded carnival robes, went over and gazed at the dead girl with a sort of mockery in his washed-out eyes—yet his silent scrutiny was sufficiently intent to reveal some graver motive—something deeper seated than sardonic indifference. Presently he turned away, with a characteristic hunching of his shoulders.

Sadoul followed him; Miss Cross went to the door with them and there they remained in low-voiced consultation until interrupted by the nervous entrance of Derring, still tremulous from shock but beginning to choke with indignation.

And his anger knew no bounds when he learned what disposition had been made of the dead girl; only a threat of newspaper notoriety hinted by Pockman checked his rush to the telephone.

"If she's dead," he kept repeating, "what the hell do you fellows mean by keeping her here in my apartment? It isn't done, dammit all—"

"You go to the Ritz tonight," counselled Sadoul. "She'll be taken away tomorrow morning without any fuss or scandal. Tell your man to pack a bag—there's a good fellow. Be a sport, Derring. Pockman is trying something he never had a chance to try—"

"Confound him, are there no hospitals and morgues? What does he mean by using my place to try his ghastly experiments—"

"Oh, shut up," said Sadoul, and shoved the master of the house through the door.

A fat man-servant arrived at his shrill summons, went into his master's bedroom, packed a suitcase, and carried it out again, breathing laboriously. Sadoul and Pockman also put on their hats and went out. Presently the front grille clanged distantly. Miss Cross dosed and locked the apartment door and came back to the chamber of death, where Sutton was standing, fumbling with a rose-bud which he had found in a silver vase.

"Yes," said Miss Cross encouragingly, "lay it on her chest if you choose."

He dried the stem with his handkerchief and laid the blossom on the white coverlet close to her snowy chin.

Miss Cross hovered over the dead girl, touched the bright hair here and there, deftly curled and brought a saucy, wandering tendril under graver discipline, more suitable to the circumstances.

"She was very pretty, wasn't she?" remarked Miss Cross in her low, pleasant voice, "—a very lovely young thing, physically—really quite perfect, I should say."

"What—what was it Pockman did to her in the other room?" enquired Sutton in a strained voice.

Miss Cross had taken a chair. She was a healthy, vigourous young woman, with black eyes and hair, a rosy and cheerful mouth, and a tip-tilted nose.

Replying to Sutton's question, she said: "If I answer you, I don't believe you'll entirely understand."

"Was it a precautionary test?"

"Oh, no. We all knew she was quite dead. Dr. Pockman desired to try something never before attempted—" She looked up at Sutton, hesitated. "—Why don't you smoke?" she suggested. "You are dreadfully nervous. It's no disrespect to her. Seat yourself, Mr. Sutton, and light a cigarette. I'm sure if she could speak she'd tell you to do so too, poor lamb."

CHAPTER V

Sutton sat in an armchair, a cigarette between his fingers, but he could not bring himself to light it. Miss Cross was seated rather nearer the bed. Behind them a small Chinese lamp burned, casting a topaz tinted light over the dead girl's folded hands.

"Poor baby," repeated Miss Cross, leaning forward and stroking the clasped fingers with a caressing touch. "Rigour has not yet set in," she added, "nor is there any discolouration of the skin…. Aren't you going to light your cigarette, Mr. Sutton?"

"I'd rather not, I think."

Miss Cross bent lower and looked wistfully into the girl's face. "You pathetic little thing," she murmured. "I wish you could open your eyes."

She resumed her position in her chair presently, and sat silently smoothing out her white clothing.

"Haven't you any idea what it was that Dr. Pockman attempted to do?" she asked.

He shook his head.

"Would you care to have me explain it as well as I am able? I'm not very clear at explanations, but it will help pass away the time."

She settled herself back for her narrative.

"First of all—I am not a graduate nurse, Mr. Sutton. I was merely a probationer at St. Stephen's. Dr. Pockman suggested that I assist in his research work. Microscope mostly. That's what I've been doing. Dr. Pockman is a most remarkable man."

Sutton's acquiescent nod was a very slight one. He did not care for

Pockman personally.

The nurse continued.

"What Metchnikoff began, what Claude Bernard continued, what Martens, Beyer, and Voronoff did, and are doing, Sidney Pockman is continuing. But all this means very little to a layman, I suppose?" she added amiably.

"I've heard of Metchnikoff," he said.

"Let us go farther back than Metchnikoff—farther back than any man, living or dead—farther back, even, than mankind itself—millions of years back," said Miss Cross, smiling.

"I'll tell you nothing about the origin of life—the first glimmer of life on this planet. Nobody can do more than speculate concerning the birth of life.

"But the *living thing* which most closely approaches that form of life which first appeared on earth is a tiny, microscopic being composed of a soft mass and a nucleus; and is in the shape of a cell.

"It is called an amoeba; it divides itself—reproduces swarms of its fellows by means of perpetual division. And it *never dies*."

Sutton seemed dully astonished.

"It's true," she said. "The amoeba never dies. Voronoff himself says decisively: 'The breath of life which for the first time gave animation to matter, held *nothing but life*. Nature, at that time, knew nothing of death.'"

Miss Cross leaned over toward Sutton, resting her elbows on her knees, and laid one forefinger across the palm of the other hand.

"It's this way," she explained; "the human body is not an individual entity; it is an ensemble composed of billions of cells of different sorts, each cell alive, each cell invested with its own special but limited functions and duties, and each cell busy night and day.

"The human body is a society, a state, a republic of living cells, ruled by the delicate cells that compose the brain.

"The primitive type of cell is the protozoan. Our body's various and highly organized cells are all derived from the elements of the initial cell.

"The initial cell is deathless. But its highly sensitive and more complicated descendants which compose our tissues have been greatly modified, and their life depends upon the assent and good will of all of the cells of our body.... I wonder if I am making it clear to you, Mr. Sutton?"

"Perfectly."

"Well, then, among all these billions of living and highly specialized workers called cells, which compose that beehive, or anthill community we call the human body, are many primitive cells without business or profession, and they reproduce themselves continually. These are the white blood corpuscles and the conjunctive cells; and they are always at war with the more highly developed cells.

"When they win that war, as they always do in the end, we *die*."

"What use are these conjunctive cells, then?" asked Sutton, mildly interested.

"They are the regular army of the body-republic, and they fight and slay foreign microbes which invade us. When they become unruly, insurgent, and a powerful majority, they attack their own fellow citizens. Then the body-republic falls. *That* is death, Mr. Sutton."

He said nothing, but the nurse saw he was more or less interested. She said:

"What controls and keeps in order these billions of citizen-cells in our body-republic are fluids from certain vital glands. If these glands are removed, the cells go crazy and murder one another, and we die."

"What are these vital glands?" he enquired.

"The thyroid in the throat; four small para-thyroid glands no bigger than a needle's eye near it; the two small supra-renal glands; the little pituitary gland under the brain; the pineal gland in the middle brain, which, a million years ago, was perhaps a third eye; and the gland called the metathoracic or nymphalic gland, which lies deep in the nape of the neck and which means instant death if injured or removed.... And that, Mr. Sutton, was what caused this poor child's death."

"What?"

"You were not watching closely, were you, when Dr. Pockman operated?"

"Not—closely, no."

"You did not see him draw a long, gold-headed steel pin from where it was imbedded in the back of her neck?"

"Good God! I didn't see that!"

"It had been, probably, in her hair—to hold on her crown, perhaps, and had become dislodged. If she threw back her head suddenly it might have driven the pin deep into her neck.... Well, there it was, under the soft, bright hair at the nape of her neck. Death must have been instantaneous."

"Did Pockman tell you I was dancing with her at the time—or about to—I already had placed my arm around her. She was laughing at something I said.... I remember, now, that she threw back her head and laughed.... And crumpled up in my arms.... It is horrible—horrible beyond words!—"

Miss Cross nodded. "Yes, Dr. Pockman told me. No wonder you are upset.... I really wish you'd light your cigarette." But he shook his head.

After a moment he looked up at the nurse in pallid inquiry.

She nodded. "Now I'll try to explain what Dr. Pockman did," she said in her cheerful voice. "He telephoned for Mr. Stent and me. You saw that miniature refrigerator?"

"Yes."

"Listen, Mr. Sutton. Death stops the heart and produces functional discord of the organs. The individual is dead then. Very well. But the several tissues composing that individual's body are not dead yet. Not at all. Hair continues to grow; the skin is alive; the bones retain vitality; the brain, the glands, almost all the organs still remain alive as long as eighteen hours.

"And if these organs are removed from the body before their own individual death, they may be kept alive for weeks if preserved in a zero temperature. Did you know that?"

"No."

"Yes, they retain all their vital energy for weeks."

There was a silence.

"Shall I tell you what Dr. Pockman accomplished?"

"Please."

"Dr. Pockman's original research is in the direction of gland grafting. Today a girl died at St. Stephen's, of a fractured skull. Dr. Pockman is externe there. He operated but could not save her. However, finding the nymphalic gland uninjured and alive, he removed it in a jar of Ringer's liquid maintained at a temperature of some forty degrees.

"I preserved this living gland in the refrigerator you saw. When he telephoned, Mr. Stent and I brought it here. You saw us place it in Ringer's liquid again, didn't you?"

"Yes—I suppose so."

"You saw Dr. Pockman make the incision, remove the injured gland, and graft this living gland in its place."

"Was that what he did?"

"That was what he did, Mr. Sutton."

After a tense silence: "Why did Pockman do it?" demanded Sutton hoarsely. "Had he any hope—any idea that—that death is not finality?"

She replied frankly: "He desired to know what effect on the cells the secretions of this living gland might produce under these conditions. Nobody knows. It never has been tried before. Theoretically it ought to restrain the conjunctive cells in their onslaught against the nobler cells, and invigorate and stiffen the resistance of these latter in the increasing anarchy now running riot."

"How long before any conclusion can be reached?"

"By morning, perhaps. If there is anything to be noticed, four to five hours will show it.... Meanwhile, I must get some sleep." She rose. "If you think—if you feel that somebody ought to watch here tonight," she added, "why, you may remain, of course. But really it is not necessary, I assure you."

"I think I'll remain until Pockman arrives."

"That is nice of you, Mr. Sutton."

She left the room. After a while she returned wearing hat and street costume and carrying her satchel.

For a few moments she bent silently over the bed, then, pausing to offer a firm, cool hand to Sutton, went away with a nod and a slight smile. The outer grille clanged. Sutton and the dead were alone.

CHAPTER VI

Sutton was too much wrought up to fall asleep, although reaction from shock now weighted him with physical weariness. Still dazed and depressed by the swift tragedy of his first romance, the memory of it both confused and accused him. In his anguished mind he reviewed it; their chance encounter in the throng; a dance together; other dances; the engaging shyness of the girl; her evident inexperience; something vaguely disturbing in the girlish fragrance of her. Then the lovely revelation of a youthful heart caught off its guard—and, suddenly, the swift blaze of impulse flaming to a kiss!—and the silent confusion of two disordered minds—to remember it overwhelmed him anew; even now a dull glow kindled through his veins.

He lifted his heavy head from the armchair and gazed at her folded hands, so still—so terribly still—

He was at that psychological period of general revolt when youth is most pitifully at the mercy of The Talkers—the period when faith becomes clouded and old beliefs grow obscure. He had heard The Talkers prove that there is no future existence. But now, gazing at the dead, he felt that there ought to be some compensation.

After a while he got up heavily, went to the bed and dropped on his knees.

Prayer, which The Talkers had proven to be a survival of gross superstition, and to which he had been, lately, unaccustomed, now proved difficult. He was ashamed to pray only in emergency. Confused, weary, he strove to think and to behave unemotionally; tried to ask in her behalf merely an equity in abstract justice.

In his boy's heart, as in all hearts, there still remained fragments of that temple builded to "the unknown God," which men call Hope.

His prayer was primitive enough—to the "Power responsible for the source of life"—asking decent compensation for this young death. It took long to formulate; left him on his knees with his head resting against the bed, very tired.

And, after a time, and still on his knees, he fell into a troubled doze.

Only when the clock again was striking did he become conscious. Stiff, benumbed, he stumbled to his feet. Recollection returned in horror; realisation frightened him.

He dragged himself to the curtained window. It was still dark outside, but the rain had ceased and snow covered the sill. He looked at his watch. It was nearly six o'clock in the morning.

For a little while he stood gazing into darkness, dreading to move. Then, very slowly he turned and went to the silent bedside.

And noticed that her clasped hands had fallen apart.

Lethargy still fettered mind and body; dully he noticed; dully attempted to account. Then the shock came. For her right hand clutched his rose-bud. And her fingers were stirring now—the hand almost imperceptibly creeping across the counterpane.

At that instant the girl opened her eyes.

There was no recognition in her gaze, no consciousness of environment. But consciousness was dawning. It came with a spasm of pain.

Suddenly she sat up.

"I want to get out of bed!" she said in a frightened voice, struggling to free her body of the sheets. Already she was touching the floor with one foot, when, half senseless himself, he restrained her, forcing her back to her pillow with shaking hands.

And now recognition dawned in her terrified eyes.

"Help me," she said faintly. "Such—such a pain!—in my neck—deep inside. Could I have a drink of water?"

He brought it, trembling. She propped herself on one elbow, set her burning lips to the glass, draining it.

She asked for more; he brought it.

"Where is Casimir Sadoul?" she asked. "How long have I been here?"

"All night." But she seemed not to comprehend him.

"My neck burns me so!" she whimpered. "Where are my clothes? I must have been very ill."

"Yes, very ill," he said thickly.

"I can't see—clearly—" she murmured. "I can't hear the music, either. Where is my green gown and my crown? Where are my clothes? I can't stay here. I want to go!"

"Wait a little while—"

"Oh, goodness—goodness!" she whimpered, resting on one arm and gazing piteously around the room. "I must have been very, very ill. But I am well now. I want to get up—"

Her nervously moving hands encountered the rose-bud again. She looked at it stupidly, already half-blinded by a rush of tears.

"I—I want to go," she sobbed, bowing her ruddy head and covering her face with desperate white hands.

His stupefaction was vanishing in the overwhelming surge of rising excitement. He brought her clothing to the bedside, drew her hands from her convulsed face:

"I want you to be careful," he said. "You've been unconscious for six hours. There is a wound at the back of your neck. Do you understand?"

"Is that what burns me?" she asked tremulously, touching her neck with one finger.

"For God's sake be careful!"

"It isn't bleeding," she said, looking at her finger.

Then she drew the sheets closer about her shoulders and bowed her head on her knees.

"Please let me dress," she whispered.

"Are you strong enough?"

"I'll call if I need you."

He went out, drugged with excitement, incapable of reasoning—unable to realise—not daring to think—knowing only that the horror of that night was over, the frightful nightmare ended.

It was very dark outside; no hint of dawn above the chimneys opposite. Snow lay everywhere, dim but unsullied. Familiar sounds of the living world, however, now broke the wintry morning stillness. Once, to the westward, an elevated train roared past; two trams clanged and clattered south along Sixth Avenue; toward Broadway a taxi became audible.

When she called to him the sound of her voice almost stopped his heart. She had contrived to dress herself in her ball gown, and was twisting up her hair with her back to the mirror as he entered the room. Her features were painfully flushed; traces of tears marred her features.

"Could you find my masquerade costume for me?" she asked. "—And one of my green slippers is missing—"

He brought the golden-green robes of royalty and the missing slipper.

"Are you in much pain?" he ventured.

"I deserve it. What did they do to my neck?"

"That long, steel pin you wore wounded it. A physician cared for you."

"What pin do you mean? These?" She displayed a bronze hairpin for his inspection and then passed it through a thick, ruddy strand that clustered over one ear.

"I think it had a gold hilt. You wore it to hold on your crown, didn't you?"

"Oh. That was a 'misericorde.' My father gave it to me.... You don't know how deathly strange I feel," she murmured. "I had horrible dreams.... We fought."

"Who fought?"

"Another woman and I. Ugh! It was too ghastly! ... What time is it?"

"Half past six in the morning. You had better put on your costume, too. It's cold outdoors."

"I have a fur coat in the cloak room downstairs.... I am ready if you are."

He made a bundle of his own costume and they went out of Derring's living quarters, leaving the lamps burning; and so, slowly, down the studio stairs to the littered ball-room, where the stale air stank of rotting flowers.

He discovered her fur coat. When she was well wrapped in it, they went through the hall to the grille and let themselves out. Dawn already grayed the street. A battered taxi, returning to headquarters, stopped for them. She gave Sutton her address; he directed the driver and they drove away over the snow, as yet unsoiled by traffic.

Lamp posts still remained lighted as they turned east into Thirty-fifth Street and drew up along the curb. Looking out, Sutton saw a line of darkened shops. Over them, the row of old-time brick houses evidently had been converted into apartments.

In silence he aided her to descend.

"Are you still in pain?" he asked.

"Not in pain.... No."

"I think I'd better help you up the stairs."

"If you will, please."

He told the driver to wait, supported the girl to the swinging street door which was open, and aided her to mount a dark, uncarpeted stairway.

At the top of this was a narrow landing, a shop on the second floor, to the left, and another swinging door to the right, also open, revealing a shorter flight of carpeted stairs. She was slow in mounting, rested on the landing of the third floor, supporting herself against the old-fashioned banisters. From the pocket of her fur coat she drew a gold-mesh bag and handed it to him. Among its varied contents he discovered keys. She indicated the right one; he fitted it and opened the door.

In a narrow hallway an electric bulb burned. To the right was a dim dining-room, to the left a living-room, where a lighted lamp stood on a piano.

He turned and closed the hallway door and led the girl into the large, square, lamp-lit room. Her bedroom opened out of it.

"Have you a maid?" he asked.

"She doesn't sleep here."

He drew off her fur coat, disembarrassed her of her masquerade robes, seated her in an upholstered armchair, and turned on the ceiling chandelier, which flooded everything with brilliant light. The room seemed very cold.

"Let me look at your injury," he said. And she bent her head and remained so, resting her face between both hands.

The tiny vertical scar was purple, the area indurated but only slightly swelled.

"Does it pain very much?"

She shook her head.

"Shall I try to get a physician?"

"No, please."

"What time does your maid arrive?"

"After ten. But I need nobody."

After a silence: "Have you a telephone? ... I should like to call you later to inquire how you are."

She gave him her private number and he tore the margin from an evening paper and wrote it.

That seemed to be all there was to say. He picked up his hat; she extended her hand. He retained it for a moment, but neither spoke until he turned and opened the hallway door.

"I think you're all right," he said. "I'll call up to be sure."

"Yes, call me."

And that was all.

CHAPTER VII

Sutton slept late. The telephone beside his bed rang repeatedly but did not awaken him. He was still stupid with sleep when he opened his eyes. From habit he rang for coffee and a newspaper. And he was preparing for further sleep when he remembered what had happened the night before.

Instantly his startled brain cleared; he snatched his coat from the chair, discovered the slip bearing the telephone number, seized the receiver, and called her.

Only when he recognised her voice did he realise what a panic possessed him. Intense relief rendered him inarticulate for the moment.

"Yes?" she repeated; but her voice was almost a whisper.

"This is Stuart Sutton speaking," he managed to say.

After a pause "Yes, Mr. Sutton?"

"I am very anxious to know how you are today?"

"I am—well."

"Do you feel any ill effects?"

"None."

"No pain?"

"None."

"Have you heard from Sadoul?"

"No," she replied in a ghost of a voice.

"Do you expect to?"

"No."

Her brevity disconcerted him. He said: "I should like to see you again. Would you be at home at five?"

There was a pause. Then her voice again almost inaudible: "I did not imagine you would wish to see me again."

"Why not?"

"The inconvenience—annoyance I put you to—"

"Good heavens! Could you help being ill? Let me come down—"

"I'm ashamed—I could not face you—I haven't the—the assurance—Mr. Sutton—"

"I'm coming to see you at five," he interrupted confidently.

Waiting for a reply, after a little while he heard it very faintly: "Good-bye, then."

A servant brought his breakfast and usual Sunday newspaper, a swollen bundle of coloured print. He got back into bed and took the tray on his knees. Coffee, clear, was all he could tolerate. Nor did the bloated Sunday paper appeal to any need in him.

For now, all the confused emotions of the night before were astir again. Vivid recollections, both poignant and charming, flared in succession—his encounter with Gilda Greenway; his gay, irresponsible courtship, her shyness; then her sudden response and swift embrace; and then the swifter tragedy—all the horror of it—every circumstance—the warm scent of roses in the room, the distant laughter, music, the girl's dead eyes fixed on him through her slitted mask, death stamped on the pallid, upturned face, his fear and horror!

And suddenly he remembered his demand for justice—saw himself again, scared, half stunned, down beside her bed—heard again his own plea to the Source of Life—to "The Unknown God."

And now remembered that God and gods were easily proven to be myths where The Talkers gather to explain all things to all men, and play at God one with another.

Had the Unknown God answered his demand? Was this a resurrection? A miracle? A reply? Had the girl really died who now was alive?

He wished to believe so. His recent fright had left him receptive, humble—grateful, too, to somebody.

He lay back on his pillow, willing, anxious to be reassured, inviting memories long dormant—recollections of quieter years—safe years—the years when problems were simple—when the Source of Life was God—a God who protected, who took the heavy responsibility of the world from a boy's shoulders.

Lying there with his arms crossed behind his crisp, blond head, he tried to remember whose daughter it was who had been raised from the dead.

A sinister and forbidding legend of the Old Testament kept intruding among his thoughts; but it was not of Jephthah's daughter he had been thinking—not of pagan sacrifice and bloody altars, but of the still brightness shining from Christ.... And of a little dead girl whom he made alive again....

The Talkers had explained it, offering several solutions so that a wistful world, reproved and disillusioned, might take its choice:

The episode was a myth; or, whosesoever daughter it was had not been dead at all but in a coma; or, the account was not to be taken literally because it was merely metaphor, Oriental imagery—all Orientals being fond of extravagant analogy—etc., etc.

Sutton was becoming perplexed and troubled, wavering between a boyish need and a boy's respect for The Talkers—"The Talkers who talk of the Beginning and the End."

He got up heavily, looked at his watch. By half past four he had completed his toilet, and was already leaving the room when the telephone rang.

It was Sadoul's voice, strained, scarcely controlled: "Sutton? Are you crazy? I've been trying to find you all day—"

"What's on your mind, Sadoul?" he interrupted.

"Where did you send that body?" demanded Sadoul harshly. "I've called the morgue and the hospitals—"

"Nonsense! The girl woke up and went home."

"Good God! You tell me she's—*alive!*"

"Rather. Your friend Pockman made a fool of himself. It looks like malpractice to me—"

"Do you mean—mean to tell me that she *got up* and—and *went away?*"

"I do. She was quite all right—except where that ass Pockman jabbed her in the neck."

"Where did she go?" demanded Sadoul in a strangled voice.

"Home, I believe."

Sadoul's voice had become almost a whisper: "Where does she live, Sutton?"

"You ought to know; you brought her to Derring's."

"I don't know. Tell me."

"Why do you ask *me?*"

"You know where she lives, don't you?"

"Possibly. Does that ass Pockman want to experiment further with her?"

Sadoul's voice became harsher: "Sutton, she was *dead!* Absolutely *dead!* She had been dead three hours when Pockman operated. He knows she was dead. So does Miss Cross. If she is actually alive now, it is Sidney Pockman who put life into a corpse! And it is Pockman's right to know where to find her. You understand that, don't you?"

"Not entirely."

"Well, understand this, then: Gilda Greenway is a friend of mine. I have known her for years. She is alone in New York—"

"You left her alone, too, when you thought her dead, Sadoul."

"Will you tell me where she is?" demanded Sadoul, violently.

"Why do you assume that I know?"

"Because everybody saw how you behaved with her last night. You're headed for trouble if you continue."

"Trouble with you?"

"Perhaps. Now, are you going to tell me where she lives, or not?"

"Probably—not," drawled Sutton.

"Will you tell Pockman where to find her?"

"I'll consider that matter."

"Are you trying to make an enemy of me, Sutton?"

"I'm not trying to, Sadoul."

"Then tell me where Gilda Greenway lives."

"I'll tell her that you inquired. Then it will be up to her."

"You promise to tell her?"

"Yes," said the other curtly.

"Will you ask her to communicate with me? And tell her it's vitally important—"

"I'll tell her that you say it is."

"When do you expect to see her?"

"At her convenience, Sadoul."

There was a pause; then: "Very well, Sutton." And Casimir Sadoul was off the wire, leaving a most disagreeable impression on Sutton.

Presently it occurred to him that he might even be spied upon and followed if he lingered. He took his hat, overcoat and stick, went out and down in the lift, stopped a taxi, and directed the chauffeur to drive toward the Park.

He was surprised at himself for his disinclination to reveal Gilda Greenway's whereabouts to Sadoul; more surprised, still, that Sadoul should be ignorant of her address.

It had begun to snow again; the air was hazy with fine particles but not very cold.

The Sunday traffic on Fifth Avenue was not heavy; but by the time his taxi reached the Plaza it was time to turn around.

He alighted before the row of basement shops on Thirty-fifth Street, exactly at five o'clock.

A moment later, on the second landing, Gilda Greenway herself opened her door to him.

"How d'you do?" she murmured, in flushed confusion. "My maid takes Sundays out, but I've made tea—if you care for it—"

She lingered shyly while he disposed of overcoat, hat and stick, then led the way into her living room, where a tea-tray stood beside a wood fire.

"It's amazing to me," he said, "that you seem to feel so perfectly well. You look wonderfully fit, too."

"Why, it was only a very little wound," she protested. "I'm disgusted with myself—"

"May I look at it?"

She bent her head obediently. Like many people with red hair, her skin was that dazzling, snowy white which flushes easily; and now a swift, shell-pink stain deepened and waned as he examined the closed wound.

"It's healing perfectly," he said. "This is absolutely astonishing."

She straightened herself, turned and poured tea, the colour still vivid in her cheeks.

"It was so absurd of me to faint," she said, "—so humiliating—"

"I'd scarcely call it that. It was tragic. Did you know that you were unconscious for six hours?"

"How ghastly!"

"Rather. We thought you dead, you know."

For an instant she failed to grasp the startling import of what he had said; then, looking quickly around at him:

"Are you serious, Mr. Sutton?"

He decided to enlighten her; and he told her as much as he himself understood of the affair, speaking gravely enough to impress without frightening her.

Gilda Greenway's gaze never left his face. There was no fear in her eyes, only growing astonishment.

When he had ended his narrative, her first comment startled him:

"How perfectly awful for *you*, Mr. Sutton!"

"For *me!*"

"Your horrid situation—if I had really died!"

There was a silence. Her face had become very grave and she shuddered slightly once.

Presently she said: "You were more than kind to me. I—hadn't realised—"

"I did nothing—"

"You sat there all night because you thought me dead. Is that nothing?"

"One doesn't leave the dead alone all night—" he muttered.

"The others did. Even Sadoul."

He was silent.

"So they all thought me dead," she murmured. "And they all went away—even Casimir Sadoul—"

Reminded suddenly of Sadoul's message, he gave it to her.

"I don't want Sadoul to know where I live," she said quickly. "Is he a friend of yours?"

"I've known him for some time. He's very clever and amusing, when he chooses."

"Yes, I know," she said in a low voice, "I know Sadoul."

There was a silence, then they spoke of other things. She had become diffident, almost unresponsive. Unless he spoke of the night before, conversation seemed difficult; for these two had no real knowledge of each other—no knowledge at all save for that brief flash of passion amid the mocking unreality of masquerade.

"I am wondering how you happened to go to Derring's party with Sadoul?" he ventured at last.

The girl blushed scarlet. "I—I met him quite by chance on the street two weeks ago. I hadn't seen him for—months. We talked. I lunched with him. He asked me to go with him to Mr. Derring's party, and he described the costumes to be worn. I wanted to go. I had to have a dinner gown anyway, this winter—or thought I had to have one.... Last night I put on my costume here and drove in a taxi to the St. Regis, where Sadoul was waiting under the porte cochère.... That is how it happened."

They were busied with their tea for a while before he ventured a lighter tone.

"I am considering the eccentric capers of Fate," he said. She looked up at him.

"When your mask slipped as we passed," he went on, "it was Fate that loosened it. Do you doubt it?"

Her lowered face was all surging with colour now; she bent over her cup, motionless.

That the girl dreaded further reminiscences was pathetically plain to him. And again her shyness puzzled him as it had the night before. Because one scarcely expected to meet a novice at one of Derring's parties.

Again he became conscious of the subtle charm of her—felt the faint, sweet warmth of her presence invading him.

"It would have been a jolly party if—" he stopped short, aware already of his mistake.

She sat with head averted, but he suspected tears. After a little while she crumpled her handkerchief, nervously, touched her eyes with it.

"You are still under the strain," he said in a low voice. "No wonder. But it came out all right, thank God—"

"I—I can't—bear—" She shrank back against the sofa and hid her face in her arms.

"There's nothing to feel that way about," he said, reassuringly. "Everything is all right now —"

"I—I can't bear it!—what happened. I can't endure the thought of— of what they m-must have done to me—"

He reddened but said coolly: "There was nothing unusual—when one is desperately ill—"

"They treated me as—as the dead are treated—"

"The physician and the nurse—"

"Sadoul was there.... Were *you?*"

"No," he said, lying.

After a while he ventured to unclasp the desperate fingers from their clutch on the sofa—ventured to raise her to a sitting posture.

"Come," he repeated confidently, "it's all over. You're behaving like a kid," he added, forcing her to turn her head.

The glimmering eyes opened on him, closed quickly, and the tears rolled down her cheeks.

"It's all over," he insisted; "isn't it?"

He held both her hands. She released them. "Yes," she whispered, "it is all over—all of it—all, all! ..." She slowly straightened her shoulders, slowly dried her cheeks, still sitting there with closed eyes. And speaking so:

"It's the end.... And a new beginning.... I think the girl you knew really did die last night.... I am not that girl."

"Oh, yes, you are, Gilda Greenway," he said cheerfully; "you are that very same and very delightful Queen in Green!"

"Do you think so?"

Her eyes unclosed. She considered him curiously, her gaze wandering over him almost absently.

The room had grown dusky. She reached behind her and lighted the lamp on the piano.

"That's jolly," he said. "I wonder if you feel like playing something."

"Would you like it?"

She stood up mechanically, moved to the piano and seated herself.

After a moment a deadened chord or two broke the stillness. Then the old and well-known melody of Schubert grew more softly ominous in the demi-light, lingered in deep, velvety pulsations, slowly expired. Silence absorbed the last muffled chord. The girl's hands drooped motionless; she lifted her deep green eyes and looked across the piano at Sutton. Her face was partly masked by the transverse shadow of the lampshade.

"What was it you played?" he asked.

"'The Young Girl and Death.'"

"That's a cheerful jazz," he remarked, getting up. He took an uncertain step or two, looked at her irresolutely, then went over to the piano and leaned on both elbows.

"We mustn't turn morbid," he said. "We've had the shock of our lives, but it won't do to brood on it.... I want you to be as you were last night."

She looked up at him, her hands still resting on the keys.

"You were so jolly—such a bashful, charming kid," he added.

Something suddenly glimmered in her shadowed eyes. "Are you smiling?" he asked.

"I think I—am."

"Well, it's about time! I'm trying to remember what it was I said that made you laugh, just before you—you were taken ill."

She could not seem to recall it; absently ran a scale or two; rested.

"We were beginning to have such a gay evening together—weren't we?" he insisted.

"Yes.... I enjoyed it."

"The fact is," he went on, "I kidnapped you, didn't I?"

"Kidnapped? Are you really so old?" In her shadowy eyes the glimmer appeared again.

"No, I'm not very aged, but Sadoul—I stole you from him, you know."

"Did you find it—difficult?"

She moved as she spoke, and the lamp-light fell full across her face.

Again he was conscious of warmth in his veins—of a heart quickening a little in the shy revelation of her smile.

And again he tried to account for her presence at Derring's party, where there was more pulchritude than bashfulness, and more experience than both.

About Gilda Greenway there seemed always a hint of wistful inexperience—a sort of unchastened innocence, which was not without its provocation, too.

In his rather brief career, Sutton had never encountered what is called "danger" among women within his own caste or outside of it. Only the male ass need dread the "vamp"; but he never does.

As for all the subtler species known as dangerous, from cradle-snatcher to the married-but-misunderstood, few had floated within his social ken where, on the Hudson, ancient respectability in substantial estates maintained colonial tradition in summer, and modest but grim town houses in winter.

Smiling at the girl, now—wondering a little concerning her—and curious, too—he asked her whether, like most of the others at Derring's, she was on the stage.

It seemed she was not.

"Nor in pictures?"

"No."

Her reserve was a smiling one, yet not encouraging him to further inquiry.

"You dance so delightfully," he said, "that I thought—perhaps—"

"No; I don't do anything, Mr. Sutton."

He dissented and tapped the piano as emphasis.

"Oh, I play a little."

The bench she was seated upon was long and narrow.

He stepped around the piano; she laughed and made room for him.

"Tell me about all your accomplishments," he insisted.

"They are too numerous to catalogue. I can cook if I have to; make a bed, wash windows, read, write, add and subtract—"

"Are you American, Gilda?"

"Yes."

"But you've lived elsewhere?"

"Abroad."

It was plain that she had little inclination to speak of herself.

He wondered why she was living alone in New York. Suddenly he desired to ask her other questions—from whom she inherited her delicate beauty and shy manners—her cultivated speech, her pretty green eyes.

"Don't you want to tell me anything about yourself?" he asked.

"It isn't necessary, is it?"

He laughed. "There is no necessity about the matter, you funny child!"

She seemed relieved for a moment, then a little troubled.

"What worries you, Gilda?" he demanded, still smiling.

"Nothing.... Would it be impertinent for me to ask your advice before we really know each other?"

"Nonsense! What is it?"

"There are several things I would like to ask you—if I might—"

"For example?" he inquired, much amused.

"Well, one thing is that I have some money. I'd like to ask you how to invest it."

"Good heavens!" he said. "You don't know anything about me! I might be the King of the Crooks, for all you—"

She did not seem to notice what he was saying, for she went on very seriously:

"—Also, I'd like to have you recommend to me a lawyer whom you believe trustworthy—"

"Enter crook number two! All right, Gilda. What else?"

"Quite a number of things—when we begin to know each other—a little—"

"Haven't we even begun to know each other?"

"Why, no," she said, surprised.

"Then isn't it rather rash of you to ask me about investments?"

She smiled at him. It was her charming answer—as pretty a compliment as ever was paid a man.

"Gilda Greenway," he said with youthful rashness, "ask me anything and I'll do my best! You seem to know I will, too; but how you guessed it, I don't know."

He got up, took a short turn or two, stood looking at nothing for a few moments.

"Don't tell Sadoul where I live," she said in a low voice.

He swung around: the girl's expression had changed and her face seemed shadowy and pale.

"No," he said, "I shall not tell Sadoul.... Are you feeling ill?"

"Not ill—"

She rose abruptly, and again her changed expression struck him. It seemed almost as though her features had altered subtly—as though something familiar was fading, something he had forgotten in her face was becoming vaguely visible.

"I want you to go, please," she said in a dazed way.

"If you are feeling ill—"

"No, not ill.... You must go."

"But, Gilda, don't you want me to come again?"

"Yes.... Telephone me.... But you must go!—oh, please!—please!—"

The strangeness of her face silenced him.

She followed to the little hall, waited for his departure, her face averted. To his perplexed and troubled adieux her response was inaudible.

The next moment the door closed behind him and he stood alone in the wintry dusk of the shabby corridor.

CHAPTER VIII

The intimacy between Sidney Pockman and Casimir Sadoul was a companionship rather than a friendship—a personal association based on similar tastes, similar inclinations, and a common lack of scruple.

This mutual accord seemed to be sincere; stood the usual strains to which real friendship is subject; and, so far, had remained unimpaired.

But when, that night at Derring's, Pockman raised his pale gaze from the dead girl and rested it on Sadoul, Sadoul realised instantly that he had never trusted Sidney Pockman. And for the first time in his life he knew what it was to be afraid.

The following afternoon, closeted in the private office of the laboratory with Pockman, and having recounted his telephone conversation with Sutton, he awaited Pockman's comment with a mind already darkly on its guard.

The first unhealthy colour of excitement had faded from Pockman's flat features; he was taking the astounding news coolly enough. Even a slight smirk returned as he looked up at Sadoul, who still wore his faded soft hat and brown overcoat.

"You'll have to find her for me," he said.

"I don't have to do anything for you," retorted Sadoul softly.

After a silence Pockman stole a stealthy glance at him, and learned nothing. However, he was already convinced.

"Don't you think it's up to you to find Gilda Greenway?"

"I'm not certain it's up to me, Pockman."

"Who is to do it, then?"

"There's Sutton. And if he refuses, then there are confidential agencies—"

"Hadn't we better *cover* this affair between ourselves?" inquired Pockman. "It's safer for—everybody—I imagine."

The slight menace was not lost on Sadoul, but he coolly chose to misinterpret it.

"You're a little worried about the irregularity of what you did, I suppose."

"Not the irregularity of what—*I* did," retorted Pockman, smirking.

"What's bothering you, then?"

Pockman opened a desk drawer, flicked a blue-print toward Sadoul.

"What's this?" asked the other.

"Finger-prints. They were on the gold-headed pin—or dirk—or stiletto—whatever *you* call it," he added with a slight snicker.

Sadoul studied the blue-print. Then he glanced up inquiringly.

"Whose?" he asked.

"*Yours*, Sadoul."

Sadoul continued to examine the whorls with detached interest.

"Well?" he inquired finally. "What's the idea?"

"Nothing," said Pockman; "you needn't worry—only—*lay off on that stuff*, Sadoul.... Because I happen to need your girl in my business. That's all there will be to it—as far as I'm concerned.... Let me have that blue-print."

Sadoul passed it back to him across the desk, thoughtfully:

"Do you really think I killed her?" he asked, with his shadowy smile. "Or are you facetious?"

"I'm not speculating.... She isn't dead, anyway.... And I mean to see that she remains alive and kicking. That's all.... So—" He smirked, dropped the blue-print into the drawer, locked it, and pocketed the key.

"In my safe-deposit box there's a duplicate print," he remarked. "Also a statement.... I want to observe this girl for a while. *I don't want anything to happen to her.* When I'm through with her—you can have the finger-prints back if you like.... And the—weapon. Is it understood?"

Sadoul, apparently preoccupied, and sitting motionless in his chair, made no reply. But his brain was a flaming hell.

Impulse after impulse flashed up and raged through him, tearing at self-control. For the first terrified instinct of self-preservation had instantly become a violent desire to end forever the danger threatening him. His powerful frame was tense with purpose. Yet, a trace of reason remained. And he seemed to realise that, even if he could bring himself to do it—and devise a way—it would not help matters to kill Pockman. It was too late. He understood that. But his burning brain raged on.

Sadoul had never before planned murder. He had never even thought of it as a solution for any problem until he saw Gilda Greenway in Sutton's arms. Then he went mad.

But, even then, had she not been so close—the warm fragrance of her very body in his nostrils—and a weapon at hand, dangling from her perfumed hair—

His swarthy face grayed a little: he got up from his chair, as though very tired, and put on his shabby hat.

"Whatever you think," he said in an altered voice, "you have no business to threaten me.... Gilda is perfectly safe—you have my word of honour, if you wish. But you must let me have those—blue-prints."

Pockman was looking at him with intense curiosity. In his gaze there was, also, a sort of half-fearful respect which the habitual smirk intensified.

"My God, Sadoul," he murmured, "I never even dreamed that sort of thing was in you."

Sadoul picked up his worn portfolio, slowly buttoned his overcoat, stood so with head lowered.

"I must have the prints," he repeated in a low voice. Then he raised his smouldering eyes.

After a silence: "Do you give me your solemn promise to let her alone?" demanded Pockman.

"I promise not to—harm her."

"I want you to keep away from her."

Sadoul thought for a few moments: "Pockman," he said calmly, "I shan't interfere with you if you desire to keep her under professional observation. But, *otherwise*—I tolerate no other man."

The unhealthy flush made Pockman's face a livid pink again.

"My interest in your damned girl is purely professional," he said.

"Let it remain so. Because my interest is slightly different."

"What's *your* interest in her? I thought you were through," sneered Pockman.

"I'm still—interested."

"That girl is turning you crazy!" burst out Pockman. "You'd better look out or you'll find yourself on the front page some morning—"

Sadoul turned on him, baring every tooth: "*Tomorrow* morning!—if you don't get those prints for me. And you'll be there, too."

"Get out of my office, you crazy bum!" shouted Pockman.

"Do you really mean that?"

There was a long and tense silence.

Presently Pockman found his voice, weakly: "What in Christ's name has got into you, anyway!" he demanded.

Sadoul shook his sombre head: "I don't know.... I don't know, Pockman.... I can't manage to forget her—and I can't go on this way—always—"

Pockman ventured to lay one hand, fearfully, on Sadoul's shoulder—he had to force himself to do it.

"I wasn't serious. Hell! I'll get those things for you. Then you'd better go away somewhere and rid yourself of this fool obsession before it kills you—or somebody—"

"All right.... Thanks."

After a moment he opened the door and went out, moving as though fatigued, his shabby portfolio hanging from one bony hand.

CHAPTER IX

Sadoul went home. His thoughts were not very clear. The interview at the laboratory seemed unreal; the day itself like one that had not dawned. He remembered little of what they said in the office—except that Pockman had called him a crazy bum.

The large apartment which he had furnished for two, but which he alone inhabited awaiting the expiration of the lease, appeared unusually dreary and unreal.

The two canaries he had bought, the black cat, the potted flowers, furniture, books—everything had taken on a misty, wavering aspect. He had a numb sensation in his head, and he seated himself in the living room, his hat and coat still on.

The only sound that broke the silence was the interminable seed-cracking of the canaries.

In the dull aftermath of fear, lethargy drugged his nerves and clouded thought.

He was tired to his very bones, tired, benumbed. And so, rested all alone there in the gray daylight.

The cat came in, and, passing his chair, paused to look up at him. Then went on, noiselessly, without further notice.

About one o'clock his Japanese servant announced luncheon.

Sadoul awoke, rid himself slowly of coat and hat, went to the dining room, and ate what was offered.

After that he sought his study, where some manuscripts lay in various untidy stages.

After all, he had to keep going—he had to eat and clothe himself and go on living—or—*did* he have to go on at all?

He seemed, finally, to come to that conclusion, pulled a pad toward him, inked his pen.

He had been writing for two hours or more when his servant came and announced a lady.

"Who?" demanded Sadoul.

"She no name, sir."

"All right—in a minute."

The Jap retired; Sadoul went on writing—was still writing when something moved at his doorway; and he raised his head. Gilda Greenway stood there.

Sadoul's visage turned a clay grey; Gilda's face, too, was very white, framed in her dark furs.

"Sadoul," she said in a low voice, "what have you done to me?"

He sat as though paralysed for a while. Finally the shock passed; he got up, rested against his desk, and after a moment found his voice:

"Are you coming back?" he asked, somewhat indistinctly.

"No. Answer me; what is it you have done to me?" she repeated.

He moistened his lips, staring at her:

"I don't know what you mean, Gilda."

"Yes, you do."

"Sit down and tell me what you—think I have done to you."

"Very well." She seated herself. He took his desk chair, his eyes never leaving her.

"Now," she said, "tell me what you have done to me."

"Nothing. You fainted at Derring's. Pockman brought you around—"

"You thought me dead!"

"Did Stuart Sutton say so?"

"Yes, he told me."

"Did he tell you what Pockman did to—revive you?"

"No."

"Well, I'll tell you. A gold-headed pin got loose from your hair and pierced a vital spot in the nape of your neck.... That was our theory. Sutton came to me; I got Pockman; he operated. That's all."

"You thought me dead. So did Dr. Pockman."

"We were mistaken. What of it?"

"But you *did* think I was dead!"

"What of it?" he repeated, now in full control of his voice and himself.

She leaned a little toward him: "Were you alone with me—after you thought me dead?"

"No."

"That is a lie, Sadoul."

"Why do you think so?"

"I know it's a lie. You were alone with me after you thought me dead. I *saw* you!"

He made no reply, waiting.

"That is all I remember," she said, "—lying dead on a chair and looking at you.... I was dead. I didn't know it until now—until this very instant. But I know it, absolutely, now."

His sombre eyes regarded her without expression and in silence.

She was watching them, too; and now she drew her white-gloved hand from her muff and rested it on her knee, clenched tightly.

"You once told me," she said, "that I never could escape you, even by dying.

"You told me that while Charcot was interested only in paralysing the body by inducing hypnosis, there was no reason why the indestructible life-principle itself could not be caught and controlled at the moment of death.... Did you tell me that?"

"Yes."

"What did you mean by the indestructible life-principle? The escaping soul?"

"You can call it that if you like."

She clenched her gloved hand tighter:

"You told me that, at death, the life-principle has been seen and even photographed. Is that true? Or is it one of your psychic lies?"

"It is faintly luminous and has been photographed in the dark," he said patiently, and now quite prepared for whatever else she had to say to him.

"What happened when *I* died?" she demanded, her childlike face whiter than ever.

"If you insist that you really died—I regret to say I was not present—"

"*I saw you!*"

His shadowy smile flickered a moment.

"Sadoul!"

"Well, Gilda?"

"Did you try to stop my soul from leaving me?"

"No; I wouldn't have been such a blithering fool. Where do you get that stuff?" he added with his sneering laugh. "I told you, once, that photographs had been made in a dark death-chamber, which did really show a nebulous something apparently freeing itself from the dead and assuming something like a human shape."

"Yes, you told me that."

"I certainly did. Also, I may have told you that psychic materialisations also have been photographed, exuding in rather unpleasant and luminous convolutions from the medium.

"All students of psychology are interested. I am. Psychic phenomena in their relation to hypnosis also interest me—"

"Yes. That is how you destroyed me."

After a silence: "There was no destruction," he said in a low voice.

"What do you call it then, Sadoul? You caught my soul—spirit—or whatever you call my tenant—outside my body. You hypnotised it, paralysed it, left my body for days without a tenant! ... And once, when you released me, and I returned, I found a new tenant in possession.... Since that time I have had to turn her out a thousand times! ... When I—died—she was there, waiting. We struggled for possession. And she is still waiting her opportunity to slip in—always watching—always near.... Last evening, suddenly, she got possession of me—I was tired—off my guard. She locked me out—"

Gilda's face began to flush and her gloved hands crisped and beat against her muff, crushing and scattering the bunch of violets:

"*That's* what you did to me!" she cried, "—you tried to catch my soul outside of me and kill it, or something—so you could let in that other one! You've always tried to—always, always! You wanted my body, not caring what tenant it had! And you've tried to drive me out and let the other in!—you tried it even when I was dead!"

She sat striking her muff hysterically with her little, gloved fists, her green eyes alight and the pretty mouth distorted with a rage she had never known until that instant.

"I've wanted to live rightly," she said; "but this *Other One* interferes! There was no other one until you let her in. She comes, now, before I know it.... When I am almost happy—thinking no wrong, God knows—"

She sprang up, trembling: "Can't you let me alone?" she said. "I never liked you; I never shall live with you."

Sadoul's eyes glowed, and he slowly got up from his chair:

"If you won't live with me, you'll live with no other man," he said.

"I don't want to! I couldn't, anyway—with the memory of that civil ceremony rising like a nightmare to frighten me—"

"You had better remember it ... when such men as Sutton are dangling around you," he said with his alarming smile.

Gilda's face flushed scarlet.

"*I* shall remember it," she said.... "It's the *Other One* who—who frightens me—"

She took up her muff, abruptly, walked swiftly to the door, turned, trembling, blinded with tears:

"*Now*, do you understand what you have done to me!" she said in a choking voice. "Even the *Other One* cares nothing for you! Even if she ever manages to destroy me, it gains you nothing! And that's what you've done to me and to yourself!"

He followed her to the hall and detained her on the landing.

"Remember," he said, "I tolerate no other man."

"There is no other man."

"There may be."

She pushed by him and pressed the elevator bell.

"My God!" he whispered—"My God! Can't you be even half human, Gilda?"

"That's the trouble. I'm not more than that, now, I suppose."

He kept on saying under his breath, "My God, my God! I can't go on this way! I can't go on without you—"

The ascending cage interrupted.

She nodded adieu.

"Let me know where you are," he said.

The cage dropped. She made no reply. He stood still for a moment, dragging at his lips with bony fingers, then he snatched his hat and ran down the spiral iron stairway.

But he was too late at the street door; and the porter had not noticed which way her taxi turned.

CHAPTER X

Gilda was in a hurry to get home, and this was the reason: A telephone call from Sutton had awakened her that morning; she had been glad to hear his voice again; the incident had made the beginning of a grey day very delightful.

Bathed, dressed, and having breakfasted, and still agreeably conscious of her waking pleasure, Gilda had gone lightly about her morning duties.

First there came a consultation with her maid-of-all-work concerning marketing. Then dish-washing. Then sweeping, dusting, airing, and bed-making, in which Gilda aided. Then accounts—Gilda crouched over her desk, very intent upon the few bills and advertisements which alone composed any morning's mail.

Mending was next in order. Then preparation for a walk, including shopping. After that, luncheon, the leisurely pleasure of a book, or a lazy needle embroidering towels—with contented glances at the comfortable and pretty things surrounding her.

Her bed-room, in blue, was an austere and rather dim place, with an etching or two on the wall, and a slim bed and chair patterned after some prim model of the 18th century.

But Gilda's living room was done in sunny hues which tinted it with a summery light, even on sour, grey days. And here amid upholstered furniture, a piano, old gilt mirror, a few mezzotints, hyacinths growing in a yellow bowl, a shelf of books, Gilda Greenway lived and had her highly complex being.

Earlier that afternoon she had been embroidering a doily with buttercups, sewing light-heartedly, with recollections of her pleasant waking to the sound of Sutton's voice.

She had ventured to ask him to tea; but he couldn't come until after six. But with this in agreeable prospect the winter day was passing tranquilly. Old, unhappy memories were being lulled by the soothing rhythm of her silken-threaded needle; old sorrows faded; her slowly moving hand at last ceased and lay idle on her knee.

After a while she no longer guided thought, but followed where it strayed.

Very stealthily Thought betrayed her.

It led her into a labyrinth and abandoned her there. Presently, into that magic labyrinth there glided the phantom of him she had followed thither; and, mentally, she went to him as she had that tragic night— yielded again to his swift embrace—to his lips—offering her own—

And awoke to find herself on her feet and every startled instinct striving to arouse her sleeping senses.

Still partly dazed, throbbing with fear and shame, her confused mind was offering no aid. With stiffened limbs and clenched hands she stood blindly facing what threatened her.

Desperately she strove to warn her mind against the warm, sweet impulse invading it—to free her excited heart of that which quickened it—to bar all ingress to that *Other One*—the invader—now gliding nearer.

As she struggled against the enchantment, she realised that the *Other One* had surprised her—that sensual thing which Sadoul had summoned, offering *her* as its abiding place—

Suddenly her anger blazed white. In raging silence she tore the shadowy intruder out of her, drove it forth, barred the citadel of her soul against it.

Flaming, breathless, still bewildered by the battle, she strove to think what must be done. Then fear came—the old dread began to creep upon her—old griefs stirred—the spectre of Sadoul took shape, menacing her with destruction.

Scarcely knowing what she was doing, she ran to her bed-room closet, pulled on her hat and fur coat, and took her muff to which the morning's violets were still pinned.

Then she went out into the city to seek Sadoul.

Thus it was that she had found him, had accused him, and demanded of him an answer. And, even as she demanded, a flash of clairvoyance answered her own question.

He had lied to her, but she already knew the truth.

So she had left him—hurrying because it was already late.

And now, driving east through the Park, where already electric lights sparkled amid naked trees, only one clear thought remained and persisted unconfused through all the tumult and bewilderment of mind—the calm recollection of her engagement with Sutton.

It was only five when she arrived—time enough to regain composure, change her gown, and make disposition of the few flowers which she had ordered that morning and which had been delivered while she was out.

Aglow from her bath, and a vigourous struggle with her thick, burnished hair, action already was driving from her mind the hateful shadow haunting it. Her maid came from the kitchen, wiped her efficient hands, and got Gilda into her gown.

Her mistress had never had a guest to dinner, so Freda made no inquiry concerning an improbable contingency; nor did Gilda even think of such a possibility.

She went into the sitting-room, examined herself approvingly at full length in the long gilt mirror, pirouetted, and immediately concerned herself with the flowers and the two glass vases destined for them. The carnations she placed on the piano, the roses on the tea-table. Then she lightly made the tour of the room, poked the fire, dusted the hearth, straightened pictures which the interminable jar of street traffic always left askew again.

She crossed to the piano, and, standing, ran scales nervously; then went over to her desk, seated herself, opened a drawer and consulted her bank-book.

She must ask Sutton to advise her. Something must be done with her money.

Delectable aromas from the kitchen reminded her agreeably that dinner was preparing—then, horrified, she rose and opened both windows, calling upon Freda to keep the kitchen door shut.

While the place was airing, she roamed about, casting frequent glances at the clock which had struck six some time ago, and was now preparing to announce the half hour.

An abrupt thought that Sutton might not come almost hurt. She gazed rather piteously around at her preparations—the prim sofa cushions in a row, the straightened pictures, the two vases full of flowers. She was realising how happily she had counted on his coming.

The half hour sounded. She felt she would have scarcely any time at all with him, dinner being so nearly ready.

She went slowly to the windows, closed them, drew the curtains. Her heart was becoming heavy.

Five minutes later she was giving him up.

At a quarter to seven she gave him up.

Confused, hurt, and innocently surprised at the hurt—and with an effort to believe that the disappointment was trivial—she heard seven o'clock strike and turned to nod to Freda, who came to announce her dinner.

"Those yoong yentleman do not come tonight?" inquired Freda.

"No, I think not."

Gilda walked slowly into her tiny dining room. Appetite had left her. As she seated herself, her door-bell rang.

CHAPTER XI

Sutton, always debonair, came in gaily:

"Awfully sorry to be so late," he said, gracefully saluting and retaining her hand. "I suppose you'll put me out bodily, as you did before—" He checked his breezy loquacity as the lighted dining room and table caught his eye.

"Oh, Lord! I didn't know I was that late!" he exclaimed. "Forgive me, Gilda, and let me come tomorrow—"

"No; stay, please."

"But this is rotten of me—"

"Please stay. I hadn't thought of your remaining to dinner, but I'd be happy if you would."

"You charitable girl!—you really don't want me—"

"I *do*."

He hesitated; he even had the grace to blush; then he disembarrassed himself of hat and overcoat, ashamed of himself for doing it.

Gilda ran into her bath-room, selected her best towels, combed out her silver brush, dusted the powder from the toilet table, and returned to Sutton.

"I'm a beastly bore," he said, "and you know it! Yet, now you propose to curry-comb me and feed me. Oh, Gilda!"

Her heart was blithe as she danced away to the kitchen door:

"Oh, Freda, Mr. Sutton will dine with me. There's enough, isn't there?"

Freda proved adequate to the emergency; a place was ready at table for Sutton when he reappeared.

There was a fragrant oyster stew, two chops and a baked potato apiece, half an artichoke with wonderful dressing, a cherry tart divided, camembert, coffee, cigarettes.

Sutton appeared to be enchanted. He had an easy way of seeming so, but he really was, this time.

Gilda was happy; her appetite had returned, and between them they ate everything.

She broke off a rose-bud and gave it to Sutton for his button-hole. Then they took their cigarettes and coffee into the living room, and sat down side by side on the wide sofa where Gilda had placed the row of prim cushions in pleasant anticipation of such an event.

Sutton was in high spirits, very sensible to the girl's beauty, very much the opportunist in any such situation.

"Why did you eject me so suddenly the other evening?" he asked in his gay, bantering way. "First you bowled me over, Gilda, then you threw me out!"

She turned shy at that, offering no reply, and addressed herself to her Minton coffee cup.

"Didn't I behave properly?" he insisted, laughing. But he could extract no comment from her, and her uncertain smile baffled him.

"Are you quite all right again?" he inquired. "You look so wonderfully fit that I didn't even ask you."

She said, diffidently, that she was perfectly recovered; and, at his request, suffered him to examine the nape of her neck.

"Amazing!" he exclaimed. "Have you heard from any of them—Pockman—Sadoul?—"

"I saw Sadoul."

"Really! When?"

"Today."

"Oh. What did he have to say about that rather ghastly affair?"

"He said I really died."

Sutton shrugged. He no longer believed it. "Death is death," he observed. "There is no remedy for death, and there never was—" Something seemed to check him; he hesitated—"Not since Christ, anyway," he added.

"I *did* die," she said in a low voice.

Her tranquil finality silenced him for a moment. He took her empty coffee cup and set it aside with his own.

"Gilda," he said, "I've a lot of very friendly curiosity about you—no use pretending I haven't. Am I impertinent?"

She remained mute, not looking at him, her slender and very white little hands clasped loosely in her lap.

He said: "The other evening you asked me to advise you in regard to investments, didn't you?"

She nodded.

"Well, then," he went on, "don't you think I'd better tell you something about myself?"

"If you care to."

"All right. I'm twenty-eight; I'm in the lumber business. That's what made me so late this evening—one of our men arrived unexpectedly from up-state. I had to talk to him. We're reforesting on a big scale—we're driven to do it. Everybody has got to come down to cases in our business, now, because the end of the standing timber is in sight, and there'll be no more lumber unless we lumbermen begin to grow some. But you're not interested in that—"

"I might be. I don't know anything about lumber."

"It's an interesting business, really—if you'll let me tell you sometime. But now, in regard to any advice from me—it being your money and not mine—all I could say to you would be on old-fashioned lines: buy for investment only; buy only what is absolutely safe."

"Is that what you would do if it were your money?"

"I'd probably speculate," he admitted with a grin.

"I'll do it if you advise it."

"I *don't!* Good heavens! I shouldn't want anything like that on my conscience.... Anyway, I know nothing about your circumstances—"

She told him very frankly and simply how much money she had. He pointed out that, even in spite of the income tax, safe investments in conservative securities would give her an income adequate to the needs and even the little luxuries required by any young girl living alone in New York.

She nodded: "I'll tell you a little more about myself. My father and mother did not live together. I grew up in boarding schools, here and in France. I never had seen my father. He wrote to me once a month. My mother sometimes visited me.... Then war came. My father suddenly sent for me and I went to London. That was the first time I ever saw him.... And the last."

"Troops were leaving; he was an officer.... I might have liked him.... But he went away.... Before he left, he made provision for me.... And that is the money I now have."

"What else happened?" asked Sutton gently.

"My father was killed in Asia."

"I see...."

"Mother arrived in London.... There was legal trouble.... I wanted her to have half, but my father's solicitors would not permit it. I was trying to devise a way to divide with her when the German airships came over.... Mother was killed ... in Regent Street.... They found her gold-mesh bag.... Nothing else."

Sutton waited gravely. Gilda sat with head lowered, her clasped hands lying loosely in her lap, her brooding gaze remote.

"What happened to you then?" he asked.

"I thought I ought to learn how to support myself in case the Germans overran the world and ruined everybody."

"It nearly came to that," he remarked.

"Yes.... So I hastened to learn shorthand and typing. When I was fairly efficient, there happened to be a demand in Paris for English stenographers who understood French.... So I took a position they offered with an English firm of stenographers in the Rue Colchas." ... She sat very still for a few moments, then, averting her head: "—That is all, Mr. Sutton."

Of course it was not all; she had not spoken of Sadoul nor of the period in her life wherein he had been a factor. However, it was, evidently, all she cared to tell him about herself.

He glanced sideways at her; she sat very still, gazing straight in front of her. The pretty, childish contours seemed altered, somehow—less youthful, sharper where shadow fell, accenting a profile almost nobly traced. He watched her furtively, curiously, interested in the detached sadness of a face so young, in its pale preoccupation with things beyond his ken.

The opportunist in him, too, had become subdued in the gravity of her altered mood.

The world always accepts you as you present yourself. So Sutton now found himself inclined to view Gilda Greenway more seriously than he had ever expected to. Usually he reserved for this sort of pretty girl those gay, casual, amiable, irresponsible qualities usually expected of a man by such girls.

She had not invited them, even at Derring's. Apparently she did not expect them.

Was she one of the impossible kind who supposed a man didn't know the difference? ... Or—was there, possibly, not as much difference as he naturally had supposed—meeting her sans façon at Derring's—and finding her so pliant in the end—

He had, of course, placed her, generally, but not at all definitely. There seemed to be nothing specific about her—with her freshness and youth and oddly winsome shyness.

Yet, there was Derring's anything but exclusive party; and there was Sadoul.... Certainly, he thought, there are all sorts in the world; and of new kinds there is no ending.

He was first to break the long silence with a banality: "Someday, Gilda, will you tell me more about yourself?"

She turned her head, faintly surprised: "No; I don't think so."

He took his snub with such unfeigned and flushed chagrin that she, also, blushed.

"I didn't mean it unkindly," she murmured. "It sounds so. I'm sorry."

Her concern was so candid, so unconsciously sweet, that he recovered much too quickly. Such young men do. That's the trouble with candour and inexperience.

He told her, impulsively, how deeply interested in her he was becoming. He took her passive little hands in his and told her again, with enough emotion in his voice to charm and trouble her.

The emotion was quite genuine. It always is in young men. The only trouble is that they have an unlimited capacity for it—if only the girl involved be fair to look upon.

But now, in hopeful recollection of an episode altogether charming, this young man was slightly surprised when Gilda's supple body stiffened, and her firm, cool hand removed his enterprising arm.

"Please," she said under her breath, "—I had rather not."

"You didn't say that at Derring's—"

Her lips tightened and she closed her eyes more tightly still, as though chagrined at the remembrance.

"Are you really sorry, Gilda?"

"Yes.... I mean I don't know whether I am.... I had rather you didn't kiss me—again—"

"I won't, if you don't wish it—"

"No."

He took it amiably enough—even a trifle anxiously, afraid of offending a girl who was beginning to pique his curiosity—that overwhelming symptom of masculine egotism ever latent in young men.

"Of course," he said gaily, "it was carnival time at Derring's... didn't mistake you for a moment.... I really like you tremendously, Gilda.... You are such a lovely thing, anyway—don't be too severe with me."

"Not severe—with you.... No. It isn't that." ... She drew a deep breath, smiled uneasily at him.

"I do like you.... I want to be friends.... Will you try always to remember that?"

"Yes, you charming girl!—"

"—Because—you may not think so, sometimes.... I may do things you will not understand.... It won't be because I don't—don't like you."

She rose; he stood up, too. She said slowly:

"I want you to go, now.... Will you still believe that I like you, very much, if I—I ask you to say good-night to me?"

"Of course! ... You're the most winsome girl, Gilda—the most delightful!—I *do* care a lot for you—"

"Telephone me—soon."

"Rather!" ... He had his coat on, now.... "I'll call you tomorrow, if I may."

She nodded and opened the door for him. He wanted her hand again and got it.

"You like me a little, don't you, Gilda?"

Her tightly held hand began to tremble in his, and she loosened it with a sudden nervous movement.

"I want you to go," she whispered.

There was a strange, uncontrolled note in her voice—and he looked at her green eyes in the demi-light.

"I'll tell you—sometime," she said breathlessly.... "I do care for you.... We must help each other—not destroy—"

"What frightens you?"

"Please go, if you care for me at all!"

He stepped back in silence; the door closed smartly, and he heard her bolt it. And, listening, he became aware of another sound in the stillness—a murmur, broken, incoherent, as though inside the door the girl were whispering to herself, and whimpering all alone.

CHAPTER XII

What was known concerning the extraordinary case of Gilda Greenway was being man-handled, daily, at the Fireside Club—old George Derring having gabbled widely to the fierce annoyance of Sadoul.

Pockman, also vastly annoyed, made the best of it—made no bones about it, in fact.

Badgered, disgusted, but at bay, he was perhaps too cynical, too indifferent, or possibly too confident of himself to lie or to evade newspaper publicity—the terror of all reputable physicians.

"Well, what astonishes you?" he retorted to the veiled gibes from his tormentors at the Fireside. "I've killed rats and done the same thing to them."

"Do you mean to tell us," demanded Harry Stayr, "that you've resurrected dead rats by grafting glands on their necks?"

"One gland—the nymphalic."

"Oh! Have rats got that gland, too?"

"All vertebrates have it."

"And those rats really were dead?"

"They were not only dead," said Pockman wearily, "but I'd had them in cold storage at zero for three months."

"And when you thawed 'em out and operated they came to and squealed their thanks," suggested Stayr, grinning.

"They became lively enough in a few hours."

"And squealed?"

"That's what they did, Harry."

"Did little Miss Greenway become gratefully demonstrative when you brought her back from the Pearly Gates," inquired Julian Fairless, "or did she cry for her harp and halo?"

"When she came to life she dressed and went home in taxi, I believe," replied Pockman drily.

"Where's Sadoul's girl to prove it?" demanded Sam Warne. "I'd like to ask her what she saw up aloft after she died."

"So you believe in the survival of the soul, do you, Sam?" said Fairless languidly.

"Well—Pockman says so "

"I did *not* say so," interrupted Pockman. "I said that I have proven survival of the life principle in certain glands; and that, after what we call death occurs, a state of anarchy prevails in the cadaver. All the organs are still alive; the cells which compose them are engaged in civil war."

"What is your theory, then?"

"A very simple one—that the secretions of the nymphalic gland control every one of the trillions of cells in the human body. I assume that ultimate dissolution begins with atrophy of this gland. I believe that, by grafting a new and young and living nymphalic gland upon a dead human body, the organs of that body can be revived, rejuvenated, and persuaded to resume their natural functions. And I am now absolutely satisfied that I have proven this theory to be a fact."

"Won't this make a considerable splash in the medical puddle?" asked Fairless.

"Not if the newspapers get hold of it," replied Pockman. "As Shakespeare says, 'Publicity doth make monkeys of us all'!" He glanced about him almost wistfully: "If you fellows would be reticent and decent and permit me to go on for a year or two, and then, when I'm ready, let me make my own announcement through proper channels—" He looked around again at The Talkers; then the habitual and glassy smirk disfigured him, and he shrugged his shoulders:

"What's the use?" he concluded. "You're born to talk and you'll do it. So I'll get the dirty end of the stick for awhile—I'll get what's coming to me from the newspapers. I'll get hell from my profession. You fellows couldn't hold your tongues if you wanted to."

"Matters discussed in a gentleman's club are sacred," observed somebody heavily.

"Sure," sneered Pockman; "—I've been a victim of gentlemen's agreements." His pale eyes rested mockingly on Derring, flickered, travelled on impartially.

"It's the dinner table that undoes you," he added, "—when it's not your best girl—in 'strictest confidence.' Yes—I know."

"That's a nasty thing to say about any member of this club," protested Julian Fairless. "I haven't the slightest desire to gossip, and your damned glands don't interest me."

"A nasty insinuation and a nasty subject," broke out Derring, in his high, shrill voice. "I'm sure I had enough of it when they put a corpse into my spare bed and performed autopsies all over my apartment—"

"Do you object to our talking to Sutton and Sadoul about it?" inquired Harry Stayr. "I promise you it won't get outside this club—"

But Pockman had no illusions: "Talk your damned heads off if you like," he said, getting out of his arm-chair and striding away in that ungainly, rickety gait which, Stayr insisted, always made him think of Holbein's "Dance of Death."

Death continued to be the topic of The Talkers gathered around the grate at the Fireside Club that snowy evening.

Sadoul, looking ill, wandered in later and joined the circle, but sullenly refused information regarding the episode in question, and stretched himself out on a lounge, his sombre eyes veiled in indifference. Only when Mortimer Lyken strolled in was the surgical aspect of the affair revived—Dr. Lyken's researches having associated him for years with the work of that shadowy personage generally known as The State Electrician.

But Sing Sing autopsies, not the grafting of glands, were Lyken's specialties, and he had nothing new to contribute to the talk of The Talkers.

So The Talkers, who loved to talk of The Beginning and of The End, fell, presently, to discussing the soul—the same old soul which so often they had proved non-existent, and merely a component part of the exploded God-myth.

Said Stayr, whose articles on "The God-myth and Its Origin" were known everywhere that Talkers talked:

"If some of you millionaires like George Derring will back me, I'll post a standing offer to perform any miracle mentioned in the New Testament or forfeit the stakes."

Somebody objected to treating such a matter as a sporting proposition.

"Why not?" insisted Stayr. "It's the way to exterminate the God-myth and Christ-superstition."

Sutton, who had come in unnoticed and seated himself by the fire, touched Stayr on the arm:

"Where does it get you, Harry, to prove there is no God?"

"Get me? What do you mean? Don't you want the truth?"

"Yes.... But are *you* authorised to dispense it?"

"Oh, well," said Stayr, "—if you want to take that tone you'd better stick to the God of your forefathers, Stuart."

"But where does it get you?" persisted Sutton, "if you convince people that there is no Divinity, no resurrection, no survival? The world is a wolf at heart. What's to control it if you destroy its belief in spiritual survival?"

"Self-interest. The good will continue to be good, not for any sordid reward hereafter, but because being good is good business. The bad will be canned for the same reason."

"You think the world could remain sane if it believed death meant spiritual annihilation?"

"Isn't the immortality of the cell enough?" inquired Lyken.

"He's an authority on cells," piped up old Derring:

> "Sing a song of Sing-Sing
> To see a poor guy die—"

His shrill doggerel ended in a cackle and he slapped his knee, convulsed. It was George Derring at his most brilliant. But he gave parties.

Lyken forced a smile: "You are composed of several billion cells that never can die, George. Ultimately these cells will reunite, form a new republic, and develop into another living being. Isn't that enough immortality for you?"

"That's all there is to this soul business, anyway," added Stayr. "There's no survival of individual personality after death."

"You seem to differ with Sir Oliver, Sir William, and Sir Conan," said Fairless, "—not to mention a few million other educated folk."

"I'll do that, too, if Derring will stake me," retorted Stayr. "I'll move tables, produce raps, report progress from celestial regions, and materialise spirits. I'll talk the jargon to you, too—all about psychic forces and planes and controls—the whole bunch of bunk!"

Sadoul sat up on his couch and peered through the firelight at Stayr.

"As long as the world can depend on your omnipotence, Harry," he sneered, "it won't miss God."

"What's worrying you?" retorted Stayr. "Do you believe in spiritual survival?"

Sadoul gazed about him. Half of his face was painted an infernal red by the firelight, half remained in shadow. His lambent gaze rested on Sutton, shifted from one man to the next, returned finally to Stayr.

"The life-principle survives after death," he said in a dull voice.

"Yes, several billions of 'em," rejoined Stayr, "—separately."

"No; there is *personal* survival—call it vital-principle life-origin"—he shrugged—"call it soul, spirit—anything you choose.... But it is indestructible; and it isn't one of a billion cells, or any of them, or all of them—the thing I speak of—it's *you* yourself; it's your individual, personal survival in form, feature, and intelligence."

"In other words, the same old orthodox soul we've canned so often," nodded Stayr. "But up it pops like jack-in-the-box, every time you psycho-hypnotic gentlemen wave your hands and murmur 'abracadabra.'"

Fairless said politely: "Perhaps Sadoul has proven his theory of individual spiritual survival."

"Pockman proved his theory of physical survival," added Warne, "—according to his own deposition."

"Do a hypnotic or psychic stunt for us," urged Derring shrilly. "Go ahead, Sadoul. Seeing is believing, you know," he added, cackling.

Sadoul glanced at him disdainfully.

Sutton said: "If seeing were believing, there had been no crucifixion."

"I'll believe what I see," piped Derring. "But you've got to show me, Sadoul."

Sadoul's sombre gaze returned to Derring. He looked at him intently for a moment; then, measuring his words:

"Very–well–Derring. I'll–show–you. But–you–can–never–see; never–understand. You–only–look–but–you–see–nothing. You–hear–but–you–understand–nothing.... Stand–up–you–old–ass."

Everybody had turned to stare at Derring. They saw him rise, obediently.

That he was under the control of Sadoul was evident to every man present. Nobody questioned that; nobody exclaimed.

"That's very clever of you, Sadoul," said Stayr, putting on his eye-glasses. "How did you pick him for a sure-fire subject?" He tried to speak easily.

"Can you make him turn a hand-spring?" asked Fairless.

"Don't make a monkey of him," said Sutton sharply.

Derring's faded, frivolous features remained fixed and rigid.

"Sit down," said Sadoul, contemptuously. Derring obediently resumed his chair.

Seated there, full in the firelight, there was something grotesquely revolting about this carefully preserved, empty-headed, garrulous bon-viveur, with all his shrill chatter shut off, all his fidgety initiative paralysed—nothing left except an inhabited suit of evening clothes and a foolish old face above a winged-collar—

"For heaven's sake," said Sutton, "wake him up, Sadoul."

"Wake up, Derring," said Sadoul carelessly.

Derring's eyes had been open. Now he moved in his chair, glanced about him, then looked at Sadoul.

"Well," he said shrilly, "seeing is believing. You've got to show me, Sadoul; I'm from—"

"Oh, for God's sake!" snarled Stayr, and spat into the fire. Then, looking at Sadoul: "Do you expect a thing like that to survive?"

"Expect what?" piped Derring. "What are you talking about? I missed something somebody said —"

Fairless interrupted, speaking across the fire to Sadoul: "Clean stuff," he said, "—very professional.... And can a surgeon operate under such conditions?"

"One first induces a more profound hypnosis.... After that—yes."

"Major operations?"

"Certainly."

"Treatment by suggestion, also, I suppose," ventured Sutton.

"Yes."

"Well," admitted Stayr, "you called a bluff very cleverly, Sadoul. I admit it. Now if you'll show us a soul or two—"

"I showed one to Derring," returned Sadoul with a slight sneer.

"Hey? Showed *me?* What do you mean?" cried Derring. "What did you show me? I didn't see anything—"

"I didn't say you did. I said you *looked* at something."

"God bless me, what the devil did I look at?" exclaimed Derring. "Come, now, Sadoul; that won't do, you know. That's all bunk, d'you see? I've been sitting here all the time and I didn't see anything unusual, nor did anybody else, I'll wager!"

Sam Warne laughed. Stayr, always bored and never amused by Derring's obvious antics, turned to Sadoul:

"Come on," he said impatiently. "Show me something I can't account for and I'll hand it to your orthodox God and go out of business."

"Why should I? I don't care what you believe," retorted Sadoul wearily.

"Don't you care if I believe you a fakir?"

"No."

"Well, then, as a sporting proposition?"

"No."

"Not even for the pleasure of making a monkey of me and putting me out of business?"

"If I showed you—something—you wouldn't believe you saw it."

Fairless asked Sadoul if it were necessary for him to go into a trance to materialise anything. Sadoul shook his head, but his sombre eyes remained fixed on Sutton.

"What a fakir you are, Sadoul," observed Stayr.

Sadoul, not noticing him, said to Sutton: "I can show *you* something."

"What?"

"Something you'll be up against unless you keep away from a certain person of whom I have already warned you.... Shall I show you?"

"I don't quite get you—"

"Very well. *Look!*"

Almost at the same moment Sutton saw something on the lounge beside Sadoul—a greyish figure that became more distinct as he stared at it—the figure of a girl—her face already assuming the contour and hue of life.

He realised it was Gilda he was staring at—yet a Gilda he had never seen in living shape—this sensuous young thing with softly rounded body, a trifle too heavy, with lips too full, too scarlet—this unknown Gilda with her languid eyes—her smiling lips scarce parted—

Swiftly the thing turned grey, faded—was no longer there.... Sutton got up; Sadoul rose, also.

"Did you see anything?" asked Sadoul grimly.

"Yes."

"Well—*that's* what the cat brought back! ... *You* wouldn't like it, Sutton.... But *I* do.... So keep away or there'll be trouble—"

Stayr, who had risen, took Sadoul by the elbow.

"Very clever," he said harshly, forcing his voice to steady it; "—very neat and professional, Sadoul. I saw a grey thing, resembling a human figure, seated on the lounge beside you.... You hypnotised me, of course—"

"I told you that you wouldn't believe what you saw," sneered Sadoul, shoving past him and striding toward the door.

"Did *you* see anything?" demanded Fairless, pulling Stayr's sleeve. "I didn't."

The latter glanced around at the others with an annoyed expression, yet slightly foolish, too.

Nobody else, it appeared, had noticed anything unusual, but everybody was curious to hear what Stayr had seen.

"That fellow, Sadoul," said Stayr, "is a fakir.... I thought I saw something.... I guess he got in some of his hypnotic bunk on me when I was off my guard.... Something like that.... Isn't that about how it hit you, Sutton?"

"Perhaps."

"You did see something, didn't you?"

"I don't know—I guess so," he said vaguely.

"Don't you want to talk about it?" asked Stayr uneasily.

Sutton shook his head and walked slowly toward the cloak-room.

CHAPTER XIII

Sutton's daily programme was characteristic of young men of his sort. He rose early enough in the morning to bolt a cup of coffee by nine o'clock, and be at his office by half-past nine.

In New York, workmen rise early; business men late—a custom that had better change before it is changed.

Sutton's business, in common with the business of most reputable people, had suffered under the eight years' blight of a mindless administration.

Even from the beginning, the grotesqueries of a comic-opera cabinet had alarmed the business world. Now, through eight incredible years, amid the ape-like leaps and capers of a contemptible Congress and the din of the demagogues in authority, a faint glimmer appeared in the grey obscurity.

Monstrous policies, infamous measures were nearing a climax; social unrest was approaching a boiling point; all the national and local scum from those eight miserable years was coming to the surface.

There it floated in its filth, stupidity, arrogance, incompetency—there seethed the dregs, too—national humiliation, sectional ruthlessness, class hatred, bitter consciousness of the world's amused contempt.

There were the poisonous precipitations, too, in this hell-broth wherein the nation was stewing—enmities sown recklessly abroad; at home, the most infamous tax laws ever imposed since the day of the German King of England, George III.

And then the grotesqueries—the fanatic, rampant and victorious, imposing his will as ruthlessly as the Holy Office had dealt with any who opposed its dogmas—an entire people indicted as drunkards, and laws made to discipline everybody—laws contemplated, advocated, to regulate a people's religious beliefs, devotional observances, spiritual requirements, minds—every inherent liberty which was theirs!

Everywhere the bigot, the despot, the mental pervert, were lifting hydra heads out of the accumulations of the last eight years. And, on this rotting culture, the crack-brain fed and battened—the parlour socialist; the ragged—and far more to be respected—anarchist; the miserable scribbler of seditious articles; the half-crazed intellectual, writing in praise of human equality—to which he must aspire in vain; the terrorist screaming in red print; the half-educated millionaire, with his mischievous efforts to start a religious pogrom; Congressmen of the "poor white" variety, appealing to sectionalism; and then the vast genus of Grafter—the contractor with his "code of practice"; the politician getting "his"; the walking delegate; the "leaders" who make the very name of "labour" a nauseating stink.

Now, in this grey, unhealthy obscurity befogging a nation, and gradually thickening during the last eight years, men's minds and thoughts became dull and greyish, too.

Dull minds ruled and dictated the "trend of modern thought," the cult of the commonplace made the average person duller, the stupid stupider, the intellectual morose.

It was an era of joyless dullness in literature and in art; creative work by the dull for the dull offered only what was negative and dreary. Solemnity reigned. The misty moroseness of Scandinavia and of Russia settled like a cloud over the country, clogging inspiration, tarnishing all brightness, reproving exuberance, so that in modern fiction there remained no buoyancy, no charm, no beauty, no tender frailty, nor any hint of sun and blue sky—nothing of human aspiration—no heart, no blood—only a monotony of all that is sordid, colourless, and passionless in human life.

In art, too, the plodding pedant spread the accentless cult of the commonplace, or of ugliness, physical and spiritual. That tour de force of degraded taste, *The Faun*, symbolised horribly the mental decadence of a sickened world.

The human-cow-school flourished: in every studio and art gallery cow-like human females suckled babies or dangled large bronze hands or marble feet over meaningless pedestals.

Architects beautified such squares as The Plaza with chunks of Indiana limestone and a series of superimposed cheeses for a fountain to face a gilded General, whose steed was led recklessly down town by a barefooted servant-girl wearing wings.

The ugliness that was New York's!—the ugliness that was the nation's!—physical, mental, spiritual, affronting a Creator who created nothing unlovely since the first nebulae floated incandescent on the ocean of the night.

CHAPTER XIV

The only sign to indicate the suite of offices was a bronze and marble tablet between elevators:

> SUTTON AND SON
> (INC. 1809)
> LUMBER

According to custom, the senior Sutton always retired upon arriving at the age of sixty, and turned over the business to his sons.

Stuart was the only son of the present generation.

So his father, Charles Edward Stuart Sutton, conforming to the custom of methodical forebears, strolled out of the flower-bedecked private office on his sixtieth birthday, wearing a white rose in his buttonhole, and a bland expression on his handsome features.

Which troubled mightily his son and heir.

"For heaven's sake, dad," he remonstrated, "you're not going to leave me flat like that, are you?"

"You bet," returned Sutton senior; "I've had enough. So hoist your own flag, Stuart, and lay your own course. Your mother and I propose to saunter through the remainder of our lives."

"But if I signal for a pilot—"

"Certainly. Set signals if you need me. But unless you're really in a pickle, be a good sport, Stuart."

They exchanged a handshake; Sutton senior strolled on; son, considerably sobered, stood motionless in the familiar private office, staring at the masses of flowers, feeling uncomfortably modest and slightly alarmed.

He had supposed that he had already discounted the inevitable retirement of his guide, prop, and mentor. He really had. This painful modesty was due to the sentimental shock that now stirred up his boyish emotions.

The normal boy experiences it at the moment his father leaves him at his first boarding school. All bumptiousness disappears. He needs his daddy.

The next day Sutton junior arrived alone at the office and was received respectfully as the head of the firm.

There were fresh flowers for him. The entire office force presented congratulations individually.

That ceremony over, Stuart closed the door, poked up the coal fire in the grate, went to his desk and laid violent hands on a formidable morning mail.

Until noon he dictated letters. He lunched at the Foresters Club—a luxurious place on top of the newest skyscraper.

All that rainy afternoon he remained busy with his secretary, Miss Tower, or with business callers, or with officers and clerks of his own entourage.

He left rather late, and was too late to dress for dinner, finding his father and mother already at table.

"Did you get along all right?" asked his father, carelessly.

"Well, yes, I think so. You know there's one thing you inaugurated, about which I don't know anything—"

"Our land reclamation policy?"

"That's it. I'd better go up and look over the new pineries."

"They're mostly under snow, now. But I think you better go in the spring."

His mother said: "It's all like a dream. I can't realize that your father has retired and that you are 'Sutton and Son.'"

"Well, *I* realise it," remarked the husband. "I've been trying to decide between California, the West Indies, and the Riviera. I can't. Can you, Helen?"

The mother smiled and looked at the son. She was loath to put such distances between them.

"If Stuart would only learn to take care of himself—"

"For heaven's sake, mother!"

"You won't go to a doctor when you take cold!" retorted his mother. "You smoke too much, you don't eat properly, you sit up too late. I shall worry if I go away."

Her son had passed the resentful age; some glimmer of understanding mitigated masculine impatience under maternal solicitude.

"I haven't had a cold this winter; or needed a pill, either. Go ahead and gallivant with dad."

Sutton senior and his wife were going to the opera, and the car had already arrived.

They lingered over coffee in the library, listening to Stuart's description of his first day down town as head of the firm.

Maternal pride struggled with eternal solicitude: "You'll stand by him at first, won't you, Charles? Stuart's shoulders must be gradually accustomed to such a burden. Before arriving at any vital decision he ought always to consult you; etc., etc."

Theirs was that solid respectability that maintains ancestral estates on the Hudson and a grim brownstone or brick foothold not too far from the Marble Arch.

That section of society known as the Zoo recognized them, mechanically; but there was no foregathering. Even the fat and formidable ring-mistress of the Zoo, now in her dotage, but still socially formidable—and whose only remaining pleasure was in making lists of people she did not want to know—had not cared to write off such folk as the Charles Edward Stuart Suttons.

The snob-sets were tolerantly aware of them; the intellectuals, the nomads, the scores of social whirlpools and puddles in which swam the contents of Blue Book and Register, all were politely conscious of that rather placid and dowdy circle born of the Hudson and rooted amid the rocks of old Manhattan since he of the wooden leg marched out and the red ensign shot up over old Fort George.

"They do anything they damn please, but ignore you if you do the same," was a complaint not unknown in New York regarding such folk as foregathered with the Suttons.

This was true. They made no bones about doing as they pleased within their circle or outside it. But in one respect they were beyond reproach; they seldom made an undignified marriage. Where other sets had been diluted by frequent mésalliances, they married and propagated their own sort. No obscure beauty born in outer barbarism, no frail and lovely meteor from the Follies, no charming daughter of the nouveau riche, had penetrated, matrimonially, those dull and dowdy mansions which gazed complacently upon the Hudson—frequently through dirty windows.

A rather frowsy maid in limp black came to announce the family bus—a limousine of pre-war excellence and dignity, and not to be discarded in deference to fashion.

For six years it had rolled majestically over New York asphalt and the Boston Post Road, and had borne the Suttons between the town house on Ninth Street and Heron Nest, the ancestral Hudson home.

Now it was solidly ready to bear them unto the temple of music, and thence homeward ere it was solemnly put to bed.

Going, his mother fulfilled the ceremony of the family kiss:

"Good night, Stuart. Don't sit up late; you won't feel well in the morning.... I forgot to say there was a girl called you on the telephone about six o'clock—I should say a well-bred person from her voice. Her name was Greenway. But I don't seem to remember any Greenways—"

"There were the Courtland Greenways—" remarked Sutton senior, giving his son the family handshake.

Descending the stairs, his wife reminded him that the Courtland Greenways were in London.

As the front door closed below, Stuart unhooked the telephone receiver and called Gilda Greenway's number.

He waited a long while. He could hear the operator ringing.

At last came the final nasal verdict: "The party doesn't answer."

He hung up, drew the evening paper toward him, hesitated.

Gilda's maid had gone home; Gilda had gone out.... He wondered where.... It was odd, but he hadn't thought of her as having friends—going about in the evenings.... Still, he had first seen her at Derring's.... Derring's.... Was that the sort of thing she had gone to? ... With whom? ... With Sadoul?

He spread his newspaper with decision, read the headlines successively—read on for a while ... sat thinking with the paper across his knees.

That saturnine mountebank, Sadoul! ... Clever, always; but always a charlatan.... Yet not entirely a fakir.... Derring had been clay in Sadoul's hands that evening at the Fireside Club.... And as for the—whatever it was —vision, or image—the shape he saw—thought he saw.... Of course that was some sort of mental suggestion—hypnotic suggestion—something of that sort—

An impertinent thing for Sadoul to do.... Clever, of course—a trick.... But outrageous to evoke—project—materialise—or rather, mentally suggest, to him such an aspect of Gilda.... That sensual, wanton-eyed, languid girl with her heavier limbs and her thick red lips—

He picked up his newspaper, tried hard to read it, flung it onto the sofa, and went to the telephone.

Her number did not answer.

CHAPTER XV

The firm of Sutton & Son, while solvent, had been hard hit. All honest business was in the same pickle or in a worse one.

Through a murk of business despair the miserable year approached its end. The national administrative body, too, like a dying rat, was now nearing dissolution—with kicks and jerks and spasms from the intellectual tatterdemalions who composed the vital parts of it.

Distant, still, loomed the incoming administration. It was too early to expect—perhaps even too early to hope—that the scandalous inequality of taxation might be remedied—that economical decency might prevail, founded upon a budget system—that universal service, military and civil, might unify the nation and make it secure and self-respecting—that an international tribunal, reserving national self-determination, and backed by proper means to enforce its verdicts, might be erected upon the ruins of the ridiculous league which the nation had repudiated.

Perhaps such a programme was too much to hope for, judging from the congressional scum still stagnating in what had become the national disposal plant.

And New York was depressed with the approach of a blue Christmas, a bluer New Year, and prospects of the very bluest blue.

And, among others, Sutton & Son paid the fourth quarter of its income tax and found that it had nothing left to lay aside.

So the Year of Graft was closing amid a mess of scandals—municipal, industrial—all the old symptoms of corruption, and a few new ones.

A good man is a good thing; and the American people, who love good things, gorge themselves, over-eat, spew it up, and blame the good thing.

So went the greatest modern American; so went the best modern mayor of Gotham; and the American people turned gratefully to their swill again.

Stuart had come uptown early, aghast at the future taxes to be faced, terribly depressed by a long consultation with his bankers and the utter impossibility of obtaining sufficient financial aid.

But he had no intention of carrying such a face home. He continued on uptown, trying to walk himself into a glow of cheerfulness.

But the crowds on Fifth Avenue lent him no countenance; it was a noticeably subdued throng, in spite of the late sunshine—not the bustling, cheery, complacent crowd that, in former years, stimulated already by the distant prospect of Christmas, surged gaily north and south along acres of gilded grilles and plate glass.

He thought he would go as far as The Province Club—that dull oasis of social respectability usually avoided by its members—but the sight of it annoyed him and he kept on.

Sunset still reddened the western wastes of Jersey as he entered the Park.

But there the sheer dreariness of everything halted him.

A first and sure symptom of hidden corruption is municipal neglect of the Park.

Dead trees stood everywhere. The long row of elms stretching up Fifth

Avenue, decimated, had been replaced by wretched little elms, instead of the only tree suitable—the sycamore.

Untidy scraps of paper fluttered over path and grass; untidy employees slouched and dawdled and puttered among eroded hillocks and crippled vegetation.

High in the sunset sky sea-gulls passed over toward the reservoirs and North River; and across dead grass starlings walked and chilly sparrows hopped and quarrelled.

Stuart turned back again into the shabbiest metropolis in the world—but a good enough city for its fool inhabitants—and, not knowing where to take such a solemn face as he wore, walked on at hazard, infinitely depressed by the dinginess of life.

With the crowd he waited while the glare in the traffic-towers died out and a crimson lens and a green one signalled cross-street vehicles to move. Then, as the white flare played out once more over the Avenue, he walked on mechanically, a prey to sinister reflections, noticing no passing face, no lighted window, nothing specific in the moving swarm or in the glass corridors through which it poured.

At Forty-second Street, traffic having halted, he turned to cross to the west side of the Avenue. Somebody, crossing eastward, nodded, passing him. As he took off his hat and turned to identify her, she also looked back.

"Gilda!" he exclaimed, retracing his steps to join her.

She was in black and white and wore silver-fox and violets—a slender, elegant figure of Gotham type indigenous nowhere else on earth.

"Are you shopping?" he asked, "or are you homeward bound—or elsewhere?"

"I'm homeward bound, Mr. Sutton. Will you walk with me?"

"If I may."

"Of course.... It's two weeks since I have heard a single word from you."

"Two weeks ago tonight I telephoned you," he retorted bluntly.

She frowned, considering, trying to recollect. "Two weeks ago *today?*" Suddenly she remembered, with a rush of vivid colour to her cheeks.

"I called you at eight-thirty, and again at ten," he went on; "but your house did not answer."

"I'm sorry.... My maid sleeps out.... "

"You also must have been out."

"Yes." She offered no further information. Her affairs were, obviously, none of his business; yet once more he felt that slight resentment, as though some explanation were due him.

At the corner of Thirty-fifth Street she stopped in the glare of the show windows.

After a moment's hesitation, she offered her white-gloved hand.

"Are you dismissing me?" he asked good-humouredly.

"Why, no," she said with a quick blush, "—if you care to—remain with me—"

"Shall we dine somewhere and go to a show, Gilda?"

"I'd love to; only, you see ... my maid already is preparing dinner." There was a pause: she looked away from him, hesitated, added shyly: "Would you care to dine with me?"

"Do you really want me again?" he laughed.

She looked up, smiling: "I'm dying to have you," she said. "You know it."

The winning candour of the girl enchanted him, quickening the dull mind and heart he had carried about with him all day long.

"You're charmingly generous," he said, walking on beside her; "it hasn't been a very gay day down town and I'm not in extravagantly high spirits."

"I'm so sorry. I'll try—try to—"

"—To put me in boisterous humour?" he inquired. They both laughed as they climbed the dusky stairway to her apartment.

"I'll try to be cheerful anyway," she said, unlocking her door.

They went in.

She left him to look after himself and continued on toward the kitchen. Her maid presently appeared, turned up the lights, smiled at Sutton, and offered conveniences to enable him to rid himself of the accumulated grime of Gotham.

Later, when he was seated on the sofa with the evening paper, the maid reappearad and closed Gilda's bedroom door.

He glanced at the financial columns; and gloom returned. There was more unpleasantness on the front page, with its scare-heads recording graft, violence, greed, at home and abroad.

Gilda took the usual three evening papers—the one popularly supposed to make vice attractive, the one notorious for making virtue odious, and the third unpopularly known as "pink and punk."

There was nothing of merit in any of them. The same clowns conducted special sections as vehicles for a sort of mother-wit; the same critics devoted the same space to exploitation of their own idiosyncrasies, offering the reader nothing of value concerning the books and plays which they pretended to discuss.

An incredible meanness seemed to characterise these modern papers; there was in them nothing generous, nothing just, nothing honest—nothing, in fact, except the dreary evidence of uneducated contributors and of vulgar intelligences furtively directing them.

Stuart's depression had now returned with a vengeance. He got up and began to walk about, nervously inspecting Gilda's household gods—the few inexpensive mezzotints, the orange-tinted curtains and upholstery; the silvery-green carpet, the desk of sycamore and tulip wood painted with tiny flowers, where lay writing materials, wax, seal, and a silver-gilt candlestick bearing a yellow taper.

Except for the Adam desk, the English mirror, and a couple of old Sceaux figures on the mantel, there was nothing either antique or valuable in the room. Yet taste and colour charm were everywhere evident—in the yellow Japanese bowl where flowers were growing, in the lamp shades, draperies, pictures.

He went to the shelf of books and looked at their titles. All were standard works in French or English—dramatists, essayists, poets, historians, haphazard memoirs—Saint-Simon, Fanny Burney, Lady Russell, Cardinal Retz, Evelyn, Pepys—a sprinkling of dictionaries and reference books—all of Tennyson, all of Shakespeare, volumes of Coleridge, Keats, Robert Browning, the Laus Veneris—all of Molière, some of Racine, Musset, Hugo—but nothing modern save Rostand and Maeterlinck.

And among all there was not one unused volume, nor one doubtful or unhealthy or degenerate book—no fiction later than Dickens, Scott, Thackeray, Hugo and Dumas, except the Belgian mystic and the great French poet.

The whole place, in fact, gave Stuart an odd sensation of having seen such a room somewhere else.

He said so when Gilda's door opened and she came forward in a black dinner gown, smiling inquiringly as though to ask him how he had spent the time awaiting her. "It's so comfortable—all this—" he indicated the ensemble.

"It's cheerful, isn't it?" she assented, pivoting to review the familiar place.... "There was a room in my father's house in London— ... I tried to make this look a little like it."

"That's probably what I feel," he nodded; "—it's like a room in an English home.... And as for you, Gilda, you are very beautiful in black; do you know it?"

"No," she said, laughing. "I don't."

All men like feminine youthfulness in black, but feminine youthfulness usually avoids black until it becomes inadvisable to wear it.

"You're lovely," he repeated. "I once thought you very fetching in green, but you're adorable in black."

She gave him a demure glance to see if he were in earnest, and, seeing that he was, turned happily to nod to Freda, then took his offered arm lightly, with exaggerated ceremony.

"We're to dine on last night's turkey, my poor friend; do you mind?" she explained gaily, as Freda set the better part of a fine roasted bird in front of Stuart.

"The wonder to me is that anybody can afford turkey," he remarked, preparing to carve.

"Oh, this bird was a present. It's a wild turkey. I have some mallard ducks, too, in the ice chest, and several quail."

Always it seemed to surprise him to discover that Gilda had other friends than himself. He wondered who had sent her the game—a man, of course, and, of course, a wealthy one. Always, too, the slightest sense of uneasiness accompanied such discovery—perhaps with the memory of Derring's party in mind—the memory of Sadoul, too, and of Pockman, and all that irresponsible, over-accented crew of irregulars from which, sooner or later, are recruited the frail battalions of Cytherea.

Yet why he should make it a personal matter at all was not clear to him: it was none of his concern what friends this young girl had—this girl whose status had seemed more or less obvious when he first met her, and afterward anything but obvious.

For since then he had come to realise that he knew absolutely nothing about her—that he never had encountered any prototype with which to compare her.

Only one thing seemed evident; she didn't belong to Sadoul; she didn't belong in the Cytherean element where he had found her. He simply couldn't determine what might be her proper habitat, or to what genus to assign her.

Gilda was gaily animated during dinner—having discovered that shooting interested her somewhat subdued guest. And presently Stuart warmed up, stimulated by her tactful questions; and he began to tell her all about the game club in Virginia of which he and his father were members, and about the upland and water shooting to be had there— the live decoys and how they were cared for, handled, and bred; the kennels, and how promising pups were trained—all the gossip and lore of masculine haunts whither man repairs to shoot and drink and gamble and sprawl and gossip with his brother man.

After dinner she was still the interested hostess whose light, swift response to the voluble mood she had evoked in him gave him no interval for gloomy reaction.

But reaction was inevitable; it was coming now. Aware of it, she went to the piano and started midway in one of those vivid, impetuous Hungarian fragments, wild as a Tzigane's frolic where the flashing skirts reveal a knife in every garter.

He leaned moodily on the piano, passing his fingers through his crisp, blond hair, his gaze absently following her flying hands hovering like white moths above the keys.

Stopping capriciously, she rose and reached over for a pile of tattered music; but his hand checked hers; held it.

"I want to talk to you, Gilda."

She nodded, came from behind the piano: "Please don't look so worried, Mr. Sutton. Can't I make you forget for a while?"

They had seated themselves on the lounge where her prim cushions stood in a tidy row.

"Anyway," she said, "your troubles can not be really vital."

He looked at her with sudden curiosity:

"No, they are not vital. Are yours?"

"Mine? ... I have no troubles."

After a silence she said lightly, but with an effort: "Anyway, we are not going to compare troubles this evening, I hope. Otherwise, I'm a miserable failure at amusing you."

"I'm not thinking of my own troubles, Gilda."

"I have not asked you to concern yourself with mine," she said coolly.

"Is that a snub?"

She flushed: "Do you think I could afford to snub my only friend in New York?"

"You have other friends, haven't you?"

She shrugged her shoulders and her head remained lowered.

"You never speak of your friends to me, Gilda," he added.

"Do you speak of yours to me, Mr. Sutton?"

Naturally he had not. There had been no reason to—no point of contact or of interest, of course, between the people he knew and a girl he had picked up at Derring's.

She lifted her head and looked at him gravely:

"I am not interested in your friends. As for the people I know, I do not believe they would interest you. They scarcely even interest *me*," she added with a ghost of a smile.

"Do *I* interest you, Gilda?"

"Do *I* interest *you*, Mr. Sutton?"

"More than—than I can find words to tell you," he blurted.

"Oh.... There's a dictionary in my bookcase—if you require words—" He turned very red.

"To aid your limited vocabulary," she explained, already uneasy at her own badinage. But the next second he was laughing, and she seemed much relieved.

Her unexpected and delicate impertinence, and now her confused smile, enchanted him.

"I don't need your dictionary," he said, "to say you're the most charming girl I ever knew—and that's how much you interest me!"

He took one of her hands. She suffered it to remain in his possession but gave him a sweet, confused look, utterly irresistible to sentimental youth.

Like the majority of young men under similar circumstances, he had no particular intentions when he drew her forward into his arms and kissed her. She shook her head, averted her face; but he tipped her head back against him; and she remained so, restless, unresponsive, silent.

A little flame flickered in the boy's heart and stole through his veins, hurrying the rhythm of every pulse. The faint, warm scent of her restless head—the softness of her body—were thrilling him; but he tried to speak lightly:

"—There was once a little Queen in Green who returned a kiss I gave her—"

"I can't—anymore."

"Why?"

She was silent.

"Why?" he urged.

"Because there is somebody else to consider!"

Chilled, he released her. She drew away slowly.

"You didn't understand me," she said, not looking at him.

"You meant that there is another man to consider, didn't you?"

"I meant that I must consider myself.... Indiscretion is a temptation when I'm with you."

He drew a swift breath of delight and relief: "But, Gilda dear, there is nothing to be afraid of with me!"

"How do you know!"

"Because there's nothing rotten about me—"

"How do you know there isn't about *me?*"

"What!" he cried incredulously; and caught her in his arms, laughing, drawing her closer.

"Now," he said gaily, holding her imprisoned, "are you afraid anymore?"

"Yes."

"You weren't afraid at Derring's."

"No.... But—that was before I—I died."

"What do you mean, Gilda?" he demanded.

She said almost fiercely: "Because I *do* care for you, I've got to tell you everything, I suppose! ... I wasn't afraid for myself that night at Derring's.... I was merely bashful and stupid about it. But *now*, afraid.... Because I—I am *not* that same girl you kissed at Derring's. That girl died."

"What! Do you actually believe you died that night?"

"I *know* I died.... And when my soul—or whatever it is called—tried to reenter my body she found another occupant there!"

"Another—soul?"

"Yes, a stranger. My own soul drove her out! I *saw* that other one. She was a sly, supple, beastly thing; and she struggled to stay.... I might as well tell you, too, that she often comes back, slinking around, lurking about to get possession.... I suppose you'll think me insane to tell you this. But—I like you—so much—that I had to tell you.... And that's why I'm afraid—to let you—touch me—"

"Good heavens, Gilda," he said, "this is a sort of waking nightmare—an obsession—"

"I knew you wouldn't understand.... Ask Sadoul, then—"

"Sadoul!" And all at once he remembered the shadow-shape he saw on the lounge beside Sadoul that night at the Fireside.

A sudden, raging curiosity seized him, overwhelmed him, to learn more—if there was more to learn—if, indeed, there was anything at all real and coherent in this wild absurdity he had listened to.

He said: "Sadoul is a clever fakir—I suppose he hypnotised me—for he once showed me something that vaguely resembled you—parodied you, Gilda, in a rather dreadful way—"

"When?" she whispered.

He told her everything briefly. "If that's the thing you're afraid of," he added, "make yourself easy, Gilda, for it's not real; it's not a spirit; it's nothing but a rather beastly brain-figment shaped by Sadoul's mind. By hypnotic suggestion he made me see it, too. That's all there was to that affair."

She sat white, drooping, silent—not resisting when he drew her to him.

"You mustn't be afraid," he said. "You didn't really die, of course. Nothing threatens your soul, or mine."

She looked up, still very white; he put one hand behind her head, but she turned her cheek to his kiss, shivering in his arms.

"I tell you," she said in a low, hurried voice, "that the *Other One* is watching us. I've got to be on my guard—"

"You darling. You need not be—"

"Stuart!—for God's sake—listen—"

"Are you afraid to let me kiss you, you adorable child?"

"Yes! And I'm afraid to tell you—tell you what I've got to tell you, now—that it was not I who called you on the telephone two weeks ago. It was the *Other One!* It was—it was *that thing you—you saw seated beside Sadoul!"*

"Are you mad?"

She said desperately: "I'm trying to tell you something terrible that has happened to me. I'm trying to tell you that my own soul had been driven out of me when I telephoned you, and that the *Other* was in possession!

"And—and not finding you, that *Other One* called Sadoul."

"Sadoul!"

"My God, yes! But only to mock and torment him—not for the reason that I—that it called you.... I want you to listen to me, Stuart.... Sadoul came here that evening. I was waiting and ready, burning, the very devil in me. We dined at the Palais Royal—danced. Then there were other places.... And later a party at Harry Stayr's.... I drank enough to terrify myself.... It was daylight before the dance ended. I don't know what I said to the men there or the women. Women still call me up every day. Men send flowers and ask me to dinner. One of them sent me that game from the South.... And that's what I did!—God knows why! ... *Now*, do you want to kiss me? Do you want to touch me? Do you care to chance what might happen if the *other* caught us off our guard?"

His face had become ghastly. He got up from the sofa, took an uncertain step toward the door; looked back at her in horror; and saw her eyes blinded with welling tears.

"I had to tell you," she said.... "You won't care to—to see me again, will you? ... Because I told you I was afraid—if you kiss me—you might find the—the *Other One* in your arms—"

He came back to her in a sudden passion:

"I'd better look after you, I think, if you're likely to make another night of it!"

"Stuart—do you care?"

"Of course, damn it! You don't belong on Broadway. You don't belong at Derring's or at Harry Stayr's! I don't know what this crazy obsession of yours amounts to.... It can't be true. There are no such things as malign spirits watching to possess and destroy anybody.... And God knows *I* shan't ever harm you—Gilda—Gilda!—"

CHAPTER XVI

When Stuart Sutton told Gilda Greenway that he intended to keep an eye on her, he meant it. Her own account of her behaviour surprised and disconcerted him. He hadn't supposed she was likely to do that sort of thing; yet, after all there was no reason for him to think otherwise.

Somehow, his boyish egotism persuaded him that he had become a factor in Gilda's career. He had airily taken it for granted that, since their encounter at Derring's, the girl had lost interest in other parties and other men.

Her description of her conduct had jarred, disappointed, even irritated him, although he realised it was none of his business.

However, all that was one thing; and her amazing belief in her spiritual peril was another.

Undoubtedly the girl's dread was genuine. There could be no question that she believed herself to be threatened by what she called the *Other One*.

Sutton had heard The Talkers talk about "possession"—the temporary but repeated seizure of the human body by mischievous disincarnate intelligences, when that human body was in a defenceless state due to physical insensibility, either healthy or morbid.

Science recognised the phenomenon, examples of which varied. The personalities of the subjects "possessed" were as far apart as Mr. Hyde and Sir William Crooke's pretty little helpmeet in her teens.

Hypnotic and psychic phenomena, in their sensational aspects, interest everybody.

Stuart Sutton had read a little—and superficially—concerning the latter subject. He had heard The Talkers arguing about it. It was the fashion to take it seriously. Stuart so took it.

Like the majority of people, he also concluded that individual survival after death, even if not scientifically proven, was safely to be assumed as a fact. He had really never doubted anything about it except its orthodoxy. The indestructibility of that living, individual intelligence we call the soul is a belief necessary to the world's moral health.

But to Stuart, as to the majority, the soul is a widely different thing from the physically living being which harbours it.

Modern scientific investigators, however, seem to think otherwise. Among these were Sidney Pockman and Casimir Sadoul.

Stuart came into the Fireside Club for dinner one wet, windy night, tired from a bad day down town, where the banks cared to lend little money and everybody wore long faces and stocks had tumbled from seven to ten points at closing.

The boy was nervous, depressed, needed a cheerful face and voice, and found neither. He had called Gilda on the telephone but her maid said she was dining out—another disconcerting item in the long day's list.

His father and mother had gone to California; he dreaded a solitary dinner alone; the dull, pompous atmosphere of the Province Club repelled him; it lay between the Harvard and the Fireside; and he chose the latter.

He noticed Sadoul and Pockman dining together at a small table, and it relieved him to know that Gilda was dining with neither.

He exchanged nods with them. Pockman looked as unhealthy as usual. Sadoul's long, dark visage seemed thinner and more shadowy, and his eyes smouldered like a man's sick with fever.

Derring was there in evening dress with Julian Fairless; Lyken wore a dressing gown and slippers, and was talking animatedly to Harry Stayr over a chafing-dish full of shrimps and whitebait.

"There's no doubt," he was saying, "that consciousness remains in the brain for an appreciable time after death. A swiftly severed head is perfectly conscious of its own ghastly predicament—the guillotine experiments have suggested that —and now it has been proven in our research laboratories."

"Well," said Stayr, busy with his food, as always, "what happens to the wretched boob in the chair at Sing Sing when the State Electrician pulls the lever? Does he know he's dead?"

"The mind knows."

"What? With all those volts tearing tissues to pulp and vapour?"

"You can't kill the indestructible," insisted Lyken. "You can kill the body, all right; but it takes time for the 'soul' to leave it.... Sometimes quite a long time even when bodily death is instantaneous."

Stuart, listening to the cheerless conversation, finished his dinner gloomily and went into the great main room to smoke.

Here, by the fire, The Talkers, as usual, had gathered to "tell the world."

There seemed to be nothing they did not know. And there was nothing anybody else knew. They were there to persuade, to explain, to controvert. They were The Talkers, and they were there to talk.

Yet, before these men joined the Ancient and Unmitigated Order of Talkers, many among them had promised brilliancy in their several professions—science, art, literature, medicine, the law.

But talk is a stealthy and subtle malady which, discounting initiative, infects talent and ability, gradually renders them sterile, paralyses action, and ultimately atrophies all functions except the vocal.

Stuart listened to The Talkers for a while; but action down town had already satiated him. He got up and went slowly into another room, where a cannel-coal fire burned in a smoke-blackened grate. Nobody else was there. He dropped into a deep leather armchair, as though very tired.

He may have fallen into a light sleep. Something caused him to open his eyes. A cake of fat coal had crumbled, blazing with a sort of frying-crackle as the flames set shadows dancing on the wall.

One of these shadows seemed to detach itself—a shape seated in sombre silhouette before the fire. And, as Sutton looked, he saw it was Sadoul's dark head resting against his hand, redly edged with firelight.

Stuart broke the silence: "I've been asleep, I think. When did you come in?"

"Not long ago."

Neither spoke for some minutes. Then Sadoul turned slightly in his armchair:

"Do you want to talk, Sutton?"

"All right."

"There's a person who seems to cause some little feeling between you and me. I suppose you guess who I mean."

"Little Miss Greenway?"

"Yes. I thought I'd speak of her—" Sadoul half rose from the depths of his chair and turned full on Stuart: "I thought I'd be circumspect—beat about the bush—convey, intimate—as well bred men handle such matters—that possibly you are seeing Gilda Greenway oftener than might be good for her."

Stuart bade him go to the devil in a low voice.

Sadoul slowly shook his head.

"No," he said, "that gets us nowhere. And I'm not going about the matter politely, either: I'm going to speak quite plainly if you'll listen. Will you?"

"I don't know."

"Try. It's better to understand each other. May I speak?"

"Go on."

"Then, there's no use in telling you that I've been in love with Gilda Greenway from the moment I laid eyes on her

"You left her lying alone in Derring's bed when you thought she was dead."

"I know what you think

"You went downstairs to dance!"

"I went downstairs to—kill myself."

Sutton sat up and shot an incredulous look at Sadoul.

"I went into the wash-room," said the latter quietly. "I had a gun—and there was a convenient mirror there.... Pockman stopped me and tried to take my gun. We discussed the chances of gland grafting. I'd seen him resurrect dead rats. So I thought I'd wait and see.... After the operation Pockman discovered my gun in my overcoat pocket, and he took it and drove to his laboratory.

"When I found the gun was missing, I suspected Pockman and I took a taxi after him. All I wanted was the gun. I was willing to go back to Gilda and wait the limit before killing myself. I didn't want to die if she was coming back. But Pockman tricked me into his dark room and turned the key on me.... That's the story. Ask Pockman if you care to."

Sutton listened sullenly, not doubting the explanation, and not much pleased with it, either.

"Well, what else?" he asked bluntly. "I'm not concerned with your morbid emotions, Sadoul."

"I suppose not. It was merely to make the case clearer. I want to clarify it still more. You speak of morbid emotions. My emotions are normal. I'm terribly in love."

"And I want to tell you a little about Gilda

"I don't want to hear anything that does not concern me

"It *does* concern you

"Or anything of a private nature in any way reflecting on her

"I don't lie about women. I don't even tell the truth if it's unsavory," said Sadoul coolly.

That was his reputation.

Sutton shrugged acquiescence, muttering something about lack of interest. But his boy's mind was flaming with interest if not with a curiosity more vulgar.

"Sadoul said: "The instant I set eyes on her I was in love. I couldn't help it. I wanted her or I didn't want to live.

"I couldn't help the nature of my passion. It suffocated me. I strove to involve her, to envelop her in it—not conscious, so help me God, that it was hypnosis, mostly, that caught and held her.

"Only by degrees did I realise it was mostly hypnosis that made her so exquisitely pliant, so docile. I tell you I had not consciously exercised any such power, in the beginning.

"The awakening was for me. It was not—pleasant.... It was less agreeable when I did use that force to awake the child to normal life.... My God, Sutton, when I discovered that the real Gilda cared nothing for me

He sat twisting his lank limbs and bony fingers like some living gargoyle in torment.

"My God," he said, "my God! ... Well—I used the hypnotic force that was in me. I sent her back into the negative state.... And she was pliant again—in a way... We were together.... I know she likes my mind. I'm intelligent. We went about together all the time.... She was amused.

"Then came a time when she had to go to England. A matter of property—attorneys to consult.... And I meant to tell you, every day or so there were terrible scenes if I let her slip back to normal even for a minute....

"After she returned from England I did everything desperation suggested to an unscrupulous man crazed with passion. I threw the hypnotic switch wide open. I gave her every volt I could control.... Because there is no other woman for me. Never will be. It's Gilda or none."

He sat in silence for a very long time. Then he rose stiffly, his shoulders sagging.

"Sometimes," he said, "it does not take long to die. But it always takes time for the indestructible life-principle to disengage itself from the body. If you think I speak at random, I can show you photographs of the process. It's a curious affair—not resembling the escape of the moth from its chrysalis—not a metamorphosis

"Are you trying to make me understand that the soul has been photographed while leaving the body?" demanded Sutton.

"Many times, recently; photographed, and also seen."

"You've seen it?"

"Several times."

"You talk very carelessly about seeing that which the world is longing to believe exists."

"If the world saw it the world would not believe it.... I showed you something, once. Today you do not believe you saw it."

Sutton flushed: "I don't understand such things."

"Nor does the world."

"Didn't you suggest to me what I saw?"

"No. But it became visible to you through both hypnosis and suggestion."

"Well, what I saw—thought I saw—was not Gilda Greenway."

"Not—yet." Sadoul seated himself. Suddenly he swung his long, dark head toward Sutton with a movement noticeable in powerful animals turning ugly. His eyes were wells of depthless shadow.

"The bond between a corpse and its leisurely escaping soul," he said, "is not more essential than the occult bond which knots my being to Gilda Greenway.

"Do you know that a faintly luminous umbilical cord unites the escaping soul to the body? When it is finally severed the body really dies—that is, the brain becomes empty of its deathless principle, though the various organs of the body continue living for a day or so....

"That is what will happen to me if Gilda goes out of my life completely. The tenuous bond will dissolve. I shall be dead—*here!*—" He covered his forehead with his hand.... "Sutton, is it worthwhile for a casual young man to interfere, wantonly?"

He sat with his hand still covering his forehead, gazing vacantly in front of him. After a moment the stare faded to a darker glimmer, and he looked directly at Sutton.

"I've told you as much as suits me—not all. I'll tell you one thing more: When Gilda's body was dead, I tried to hold back her escaping soul-principle long enough for Pockman to operate. But it got clear of her body except for the umbilical cord. And, no sooner was the new nymphalic gland in place, than another discarnate intelligence drew near and stood watching us.

"I recognised it, yet never before had seen it. Astronomers know that unseen stars exist. I knew this *Other One* existed. And now I encouraged it to seize Gilda's body for its habitation. *That* was the figure you saw seated on the lounge near me. That's what *I* wanted. And I aided it—tried to.... I wanted it to possess Gilda's body, and drive out the tenant that stood near her head, vaguely luminous, still attached by the umbilical cord to the corpse.... Do you think I have encouraged that *Other One* for the pleasure of any man except myself? ... Do you think I have started a spiritual conflict in Gilda Greenway for *your* ultimate gratification, damn you?"

Sadoul's voice had become a whisper; his hand fell from his forehead. He got to his feet again, a bent, grotesque phantom against the drifting glare of flame-tinged dusk.

"I—thought I'd say this," he muttered in an odd, querulous voice not like his own, but older, and with a sort of senile quaver.

Sutton got up, too:

"I don't quite see your object in telling me these things, Sadoul."

"I think you'll see it when you reflect.... There are other women, Sutton.... I mean for you. I hope you'll see it that way.... There are so many other women to play with. There are some even to fall in love with.... I hope you'll see it that way, Sutton.... So—good-night to you."

Sadoul went out through the ruddy shadows, passed without a sound across the velvet carpet, loomed for an instant, a wavering shape framed by the doorway, and was lost somewhere in the vista of uncertain light beyond.

CHAPTER XVII

At the office one afternoon Stuart discovered among his letters a note from Gilda Greenway: "Dear Mr. Sutton:

"Freda told me that you telephoned. I'm so sorry I was out. I haven't heard from you since. Are you discouraged? I thought you threatened to keep an eye on me. Empty threat!
"GILDA."

He really hadn't missed her, except when he chanced to remember her. Romance abhors a busy man.

But her note stirred him. He went to the inner office and called her.

"Is it really you?" she asked in the gayest of voices.

"Certainly. Are you all right?"

"Certainly," she mimicked him; "are you?"

"You sound very frivolous."

"I am—being no longer in dread of that threatened eye."

"Have you been going to parties?"

"Now and then."

"Have you seen Sadoul?"

"Oui, monsieur."

"I supposed you weren't going to."

"Why did you suppose that?"

"On account of his—influence—"

"Oh," she said carelessly, "that is of no use to him. Besides, it's worn out. I've grown up. On one of my minds he has no longer any influence; and he's afraid of my other mind."

"I suppose you know what you mean," he said curtly.

"Isn't that a trifle impertinent, Mr. Sutton?"

"Yes. I'm sorry."

"So am I.... But it's over now. What a wonderful day it is—the bluest sky and the air like champagne. I'm riding this afternoon. I wish you were."

"Have you a horse?" he asked, surprised.

"Oh, no, just an Academy nag. Could you ride with me?"

"I'm nailed down here at the office until six."

She waited. He said no more.

"Well," she said, "if you care to see me, sometime, you'll do it, I suppose."

"Do you care?"

"I do. But I've concluded that your Guardian Eye is otherwise occupied. There are so many girls in the world! To keep watch on all his friends, a modern young man ought to have more eyes than Argus—"

"Are you going home after your gallop?"

"Veronica Weld asked me to tea."

"I didn't know you knew her."

"I met her at Katherine Ashley's."

"The devil! Do you know her, too?"

"You speak as though you didn't consider me presentable."

"Nonsense. I didn't know you went about with those people; that's all."

"One must go where one is asked or remain a recluse."

"I suppose Derring and Warne and Fairless—all that crowd—will be there."

"Where?"

"At your confounded tea."

"Will you come and get me?—unless you are otherwise engaged—"

"I'll be there at six-thirty to keep an eye on you, as I threatened."

"Shall we dine—at—home?"

Her charming yet diffident acknowledgment of intimacy surprised and touched him. He began to realise how impatient he was becoming to see her again.

"That will be fine!" he exclaimed, with all his former enthusiasm. "I have missed you, Gilda."

"You're not obliged to say that merely because I have happened to miss you."

"Have you really? What an engaging child you can be—"

"Very full of engagements this afternoon. I've a taxi, now, spinning money down in the street. Will you really come to Veronica Weld's for me at six-thirty?"

"You bet—"

"Au revoir, donc—"

At six he left the office and departed for home in the family limousine. All the way uptown he thought of Gilda, sentimentally.

In high spirits, he took a red-hot bath and then an icy one; got into fresh linen and a dinner coat, and drove to Central Park, West, where dwelt Veronica Weld in a studio apartment overlooking the park.

Veronica, always fair, and now becoming plump, had stepped from the Winter Garden to the hymeneal altar with the button-headed scion of a wealthy New York family.

Scion lasted three months; then Family bought him back. And

Veronica maintained herself agreeably upon the net profit of the transaction.

She always had a penchant for intellectuals—which cast a raw light upon the scion episode—and she preferred mind to matter when she could afford it.

A tarnished residue of Talkers was apparent when Stuart entered the salon of Veronica Weld. Fashion, too, was represented in a few chicken-headed youths, a few rickety old sports of the Derring type, a woman or two who haunted the outer edges of things. As for Beauty, it was there, also—Katharine Ashley of the Filmy Films Studios; Eve Ferral (born O'Farrel), made famous overnight as *Godiva* in the great spectacle of that name at the Palisades Palace; and there were Gilda Greenway, and Frances Hazlet, the brown-eyed dancer, and other specimens of pulchritude, all enveloped in cigarette smoke, intellectual atmosphere, and pretty gowns.

Cups clattered, glasses tinkled accenting the tumult of The Talkers; Derring's falsetto titter added tintinnabulation to the general jingle, in the midst of which Stuart made his bow to Veronica and received her tapering hand heavy with rings.

"Toujours rondelette?" he murmured with debonaire impudence, saluting the most expensive ring.

"Old stuff, my dear," returned Veronica, unruffled; "the squelette is démodé."

"You're prettier than ever, Nika; the struggle with mighty intellects agrees with you."

She opened her fan and said confidentially: "Take it from me, Stuart, it's the baby-doll that's crazy for knowledge, not the girl born to Miss Spence's. No Johnny believes that, but it's true seven times in ten."

He smiled incredulously, declined the offered tea-cup, spoke to one or two people near him, stepped aside and gazed about him to discover Gilda.

There she was, cornered by Stayr with a plate of cake, and otherwise hemmed in by Pockman and Fairless, with Sadoul looming darkly in the background.

She wore black and white and her silver fox with somebody's orchids. She caught his eye, smiled and made a slight gesture of recognition.

When he came up and spoke to her, Stayr said: "You're as popular as a rattlesnake, Stuart. Aren't there any other girls in the room?"

Pockman said to Gilda: "Good-bye, then, and don't forget your promise. It means a lot to a poor devil of a doctor."

Frances Hazlet drifted by, shook hands vigorously with Stuart, and drifted on with Stayr and Julian Fairless in tow. As Pockman left,

Sadoul crossed over, nodded to Stuart and said to Gilda in a low voice: "I've a table at the Palais des Miroirs and theatre tickets—if you are free, Gilda."

"I'm sorry—"

"You're busy?"

"Yes."

He stood a moment, then turned on his heel without a glance at Stuart. The latter followed him with his eyes and saw him seat himself near the door, beside Katharine Ashley, where departing guests were within his range of vision.

Stuart shrugged and looked at Gilda, who understood his glance:

"Does it matter?" she said carelessly.

"Not to me."

They smiled.

"I'd forgotten how beautiful you are," he said, "—or do you really grow more lovely during my absence?"

This commonplace seemed to make her happy; she gave him one of those shy, disconcerted little laughs, but managed to sustain his gaze.

"Advanced thinkers," she ventured, "say that beauty is a necessity.... You don't seem to agree."

"Because I've remained away from you, and you are Beauty?"

"It was my deduction from your premises."

They laughed.

"Do you want more tea, more atmosphere, more talk," he inquired, "—or shall we go?"

"Don't you desire to converse with some of these interesting people?" She adjusted her furs as she spoke, seeming to expect no answer. There was a slight flush on her face as she went with Stuart to make adieux to Veronica.

"Don't forget you're dining with me Thursday," said the latter to Gilda, as they turned away.

Sadoul's sombre eyes avoided them as they passed him.

Stuart wondered whether he really might turn unpleasant some day, and the surmise aroused a vague anger in him.

His car was waiting.

"Oh, is it yours?" asked Gilda curiously.

"The family bus," he nodded; gave directions to the chauffeur, got in and pulled the fur robe over Gilda.

Probably the Sutton bus had never had so lovely an occupant since its ponderous wheels first turned on Gotham asphalt.

CHAPTER XVIII

By the middle of December there was some talk among The Talkers of Stuart Sutton and little Miss Greenway.

"She plays her game quietly," remarked Julian Fairless. "I haven't anything on her. She *looks* straight."

"Wasn't she Sadoul's girl?" asked Sam Warne.

"You never can tell whose girl any girl was."

Stayr said: "It's usually somebody you never heard of. Possibly she once made a monkey of Sadoul. Probably she's making another of Stuart Sutton. Certainly there has been, is, and will be a simian somewhere cherished by her."

"If it's true that there are two kinds of women," observed Fairless, "no man can guess which is which unless they tell you."

"There's only one kind," said Stayr.

"You mean potentially, I hope."

"Does it matter?" sneered Stayr. "If you marry you're stung; if you don't you're stung just the same. It's fifty-fifty however you play 'em or however they play you."

"Yours is not an amiable philosophy," said Warne, laughing.

"Listen, old sport, here's the true and only solution: take 'em easy when they come; give 'em three cheers when they go. The man who makes of woman anything more than an agreeable incident belongs to the era of the Dodo. Don't try to understand her. There's nothing to understand. You have only to observe her. She's utterly obvious. A protozoan is subtle compared to her.

"She has only one imperative function—so has a cat that fills a basket full of kittens. All her habits have their origin in that single necessity."

Thus talked The Talkers, whose necessity is to talk, and who can no more escape functional destiny than can the female cat.

Gilda was forming a habit of going about with Stuart more or less, traversing a lively but limited orbit the centre of which was a semi-intellectual coterie of unclassified modernists who knew no law except inclination.

All were opportunists, but lived up to that creed only lazily. For the inclination of the majority was to think idly, live idly, follow lines of least resistance, and balance the account with talk.

Gilda went with Stuart to various teas, dances, restaurants, theatres, exhibitions, lectures, conferences, and parties of sorts. He dined at her apartment now and then. Their preference for each other was discussed and the intimacy criticised with varying degrees of charity and cruelty.

What perplexed people was the absence of sentimental symptoms, none, so far, being apparent even to the most malicious scrutiny.

As though, in the banquet of youth, these two had begun at the wrong end with the dessert, and now were progressing tranquilly backward toward the hors d'oeuvres.

Even the smouldering gaze of Sadoul detected nothing to serve as fuel to feed inward fires. And Stayr, utterly gross, observed them uneasily, disturbed that any theory of his should be punctured with impunity.

"The trouble," snickered Pockman, "is with Sutton. He's one of those congenital celibates. The girl really is a little devil."

"What's the trouble then?" demanded Stayr. "Any girl ought to land any saint."

"The trouble," said Pockman, "is that she knows she's a devil, and watches herself."

"If she's a devil she'll behave like one someday. Otherwise, what's the fun in being one?"

"There you are, Harry. Sometimes a girl like that gets more pleasure out of martyrdom. And I think that's the case with Gilda Greenway."

"Isn't there any question of morals involved?" inquired Warne. "Some people have 'em, in spite of what you say."

"None. Chastity is an heirloom in some families—like the Hudson River Suttons. There are certain things such cattle *won't* do. As for the girl—well, maybe it's a moral kink—I guess she was born with the usual virginal instinct—but she's had a brand new fight on her hands ever since she died—"

He smirked and cast a stealthy glance at the men about him. Although a doer, in spite of professional fears Pockman was also a born Talker. He couldn't help it. But every indulgence in garrulous dissipation brought him remorse. Even now he knew he would regret what he was going to say. But he said it:

"I gave Gilda Greenway a new nymphalic gland and started her machinery again. Sadoul tried to give her a new ego. But the original ego came back, too; and now, I fancy, there's mental hell to pay at times."

"Do *you*, a reputable physician, believe that?" yawned Stayr in utter disgust.

"I'm telling you what Sadoul tried to do to her. I express no personal opinion concerning psycho-hypnosis. I entertain none concerning any psychic phenomena—not even when I see examples."

"*What* have you seen?"

"I saw Sadoul photograph the exuding ego from a cadaver in St. Stephen's Hospital."

"A soul?"

"Call it that."

"What did it look like?"

"It began to exude as a tenuous vapour, very faintly luminous. After forty-eight minutes and some fraction it commenced to assume human shape. An umbilical cord was visible.... The process continued for several hours."

"Sadoul photographed it?"

"He did. And when the cord dissolved and the formed ego was ready to depart, Sadoul actually halted it through what seemed to be hypnotic control.... My God," muttered Pockman, suddenly sweating at the recollection, "we had that damned thing in the death-chamber for hours, under Sadoul's control, and subject to his every suggestion.... I don't scare easily. But I got sick with—well—with superstitious fright, I suppose.... I believe I'd have gone crazy if Sadoul hadn't let the thing go."

Pockman's flat, livid features had become viscous with unhealthy sweat. He wiped his face, hunched his shoulders, and started to move away at his rickety "Holbein" gait.

"Go on and tell us more about those stunts!" called Sam Warne after him.

"Go to the devil," retorted Pockman. "I'm sorry I told you fellows anything. You're all mouth and ears and there's nothing else to you except intestines!"

There wasn't much else—merely a matter of degree. Stayr was a greater feeder than Derring; the latter had the larger ear area; Fairless more loquacity, etc., etc.

CHAPTER XIX

It was likely to be a dull evening at the Fireside. Frances Hazlet was giving a birthday party—or, rather, some kind gentleman was giving one for her, and had taken Fantozzi's drab, demure private mansion on Lexington Avenue.

Sutton had gone home from the office to dress. He was rather restless because he had not been able to get Gilda on the telephone. He dined alone at the Province Club, finally, but continued to haunt the telephone between courses.

Something in Freda's placid responses hatched suspicion in his mind.

He began to wonder if Gilda was really at home and wouldn't come to the telephone. He had vaguely suspected this on other occasions, but always concluded there could be no reason for such behaviour, and was ashamed to mention it to her.

However, the odd suspicion returned, now, to haunt him; and, the Province Club palling on him, he sent for a taxi and drove to the Fireside.

Seeing Sadoul reading in a corner relieved him, although Sadoul also was in evening dress and, moreover, wore a camelia. They exchanged nods but no words. Sadoul calmly turned a page in his book. Sutton sat down by the log fire to smoke a cigar.

Toward eleven Pockman came rocking in with his coattails flying, an opera hat crammed over his prominent ears. Sadoul laid aside his book, got up and went downstairs with him.

After that there was a gradual exodus from the club toward Fantozzi's. Warne went, Lyken, other men.

Sutton tried to read; couldn't; grew irritable; decided to go home; decided not to; tried Gilda's house again, but nobody answered, not even Freda.

His watch seemed to have gone wrong; he discredited what it reported. So he went downstairs and looked at the standard clock in the lobby; and discovered it was long after midnight.

Where could Gilda be? It was none of his business, which made him the madder. She had decided not to go to Frances Hazlet's party. She declined his guidance thither. Had she changed her mind?

Harry Stayr strolled into the cloak-room to reconstruct his white evening tie.

"Going to Fantozzi's?" he inquired, looking at Sutton in the mirror.

"No," said Stuart shortly.

Stayr turned, took him by the elbow; but Sutton demurred, saying he didn't feel like dancing.

"One can always eat and drink," observed Stayr. "Come on, like a sport. That Esthonian Prince and his suite are there, and it's likely to turn lively by this time. Besides, don't you want to pay homage to concentrated pulchritude?"

"I'm not in the humour—"

"You're going with *me*, old dick! Get into your bonnet!"

"It's one o'clock—nearly half past one, Harry—"

"Those night-blooming blossoms will be in the fuller bloom! Allons! Houp! Come into the garden, friend. There's many a nosegay to gather at Fantozzi's."

When they descended from their taxi there was not a gleam of light visible about the house; all shades were drawn; Fantozzi's had the aspect of a private mansion fast asleep.

They ascended the brownstone steps and rang. The door opened.

Into a dim vestibule they stepped; the outer door closed; then an inner grille clicked and they stepped into a glaring inferno of heat and noise.

Fantozzi's fairly seethed with colour and turmoil; the rooms to the right were swarming with dancers whirling through tobacco haze, amid a deafening outcrash from the energetic orchestra.

Upstairs, downstairs, *on* the stairs, everywhere were pretty faces—flushed, laughing, eager faces vis-a-vis masculine and ardent youth—lank youth, fat youth, chuckle-headed youth, handsome youth—and middle age, too, bearded and saturnine like Sadoul, with a half sneer on his features—dapper and bald like George Derring yonder, capering with Nikka Weld, whose bobbed hair bobbed as she danced.

And there was his Serene Highness of Esthonia footing it enthusiastically with Frances Hazlet. He and his suite looked like Ritz waiters—having no backs to their heads—but they were tenderly cherished by beauty, and seemed to be having a magnificent time.

Already the party had become a trifle rough. There was a girl there whose partner had lifted her off the floor, and was swinging her in circles, her body and legs nearly horizontal.

Sutton eluded collision with this pair of flying feet and backed into the hallway.

Here a girl he had never before beheld seized him and danced with him. Here, later, he encountered Frances Hazlet, who kissed him boisterously in return for birthday wishes.

About that time an Esthonian fell downstairs; and Freedom was preparing to shriek, but he landed uninjured on the back part of his skull which wasn't there.

The heat and noise were bewildering. Stayr beckoned Sutton to the punch bowl, where his Serene Highness, encouraged by Katharine Ashley, was bobbing for floating strawberries, amid shouts of laughter. He lifted a dripping muzzle in triumph and bolted a berry.

"Nasty beast," muttered Stayr, tucking several bottles of champagne under his arm and picking up a silver ice-bucket.

"Come on upstairs, Stuart, and we'll crack a quart like gentlemen."

There was tumult, too, above stairs; laughter and singing at the supper tables; a negro banjo trio hammering stridently; sporadic dancing and a riotous tendency to throw flowers and sweet-meats at all new arrivals.

Sutton received a heavy handful of flowers full in the face; then the girl in the white dinner gown, who had hurled them, rose straight up among the gay and disorderly group surrounding her, pushed her way violently through the throng, gained the hall, and already had started running downstairs, when Sutton caught her by the waist.

Both were breathing irregularly and fast when they confronted each other. Her cheeks burned crimson, and there was a scent of wine in her breath.

"I thought you weren't coming here," he said. "You told me so."

"*You* said *you* weren't coming!"

"Is that why *you* came?"

No answer.

"Tell me," he insisted.

"Yes, it is," she panted, "—if you've got to know! Please, may I pass you—"

"One moment, Gilda. Where are you going?"

"I'm going home."

"Then I'll take you—"

"I don't wish you to!"

"Is somebody else—"

"Yes, Sadoul!—if you've got to know."

The shock left him white and silent; the girl released herself, started to pass him, saw his ghastly face, stopped, stood motionless and mute with her green eyes fixed on him.

After a moment she shivered as though chilled. "I'm safe with Sadoul," she said. "Can't you understand that I'm safe with Sadoul when I'm this way?"

"Have you had too much wine?"

She shook her head, set one foot on the stair below, descended another step, laid her left hand on the banister, halted, looked back and upward.

"I'm better off with Sadoul," she said again.

He made no answer.

Suddenly she turned, sprang up the stairs and came close to him where he stood on the step above her:

"You are not to care what I do!" she cried. "Let me go home! You don't know what you're doing to me!"

"I'm not holding you," he said, astonished.

Her fingers tightened on the banisters. All at once her eyes were glittering with tears.

"Take me home," she whispered. "I can't stand this."

"Do you mean it?"

"Yes! Yes! Can't you see I do? ... Only—I was safer with Sadoul.... When this happens—when I'm this way—I'm safe with anybody except you."

She took his hands, strained them convulsively between her own. Cheeks, eyes, lips were burning; the column of her white throat was stretched up toward him. For the second time in their lives she threw both arms around his neck and returned his kiss as passionately as he gave it.

But now the hallway was invaded by a noisy company ascending the stairs. The girl clung tightly to his arm as he started downward with her through the increasing tumult and disorder.

She was tearful, excited, incoherent, when they entered the taxi; almost hysterical when they ran up the dark stairway, unlocked her door, and entered.

"I want you to go," she wailed. "I'm not myself tonight—not the girl you know—not even friendly—"

"Don't be frightened. Has Sadoul tried any of his beastly tricks—"

"Don't you understand what I mean!" she cried. "Can't you see it's not I who stand here? It's that damned *Other One!*

"It's the thing you saw! ... She'll tear my heart out for this! She'll tear my soul out! I'm trying to tell you that we're not safe with her.... I'm asking—you—to go—"

She turned with a tragic gesture and caught her quivering face in both hands. He stared. After a moment she dropped her snowy, naked arms, moved her lovely head until her eyes met his.

"I suppose you know I'm in love with you," she said.

When he could find his voice he said: "Do you know that I am in love with you, also?"

"I knew it tonight, on the stairs."

Neither stirred for the moment, but the boy was all a-quiver now; swept by his first overwhelming surge of passionate love.

She came to him and rested both white hands on his shoulders.

"What are we going to do about it?" she asked.

He gazed blindly into her altered face. All the flushed and sensuous stigmata were there. He felt the heavy sweetness of her body; the languour of her eyes invaded him.

Suddenly the clamour of the telephone filled his ears. She paid no heed to it; her gaze lost in his, searched deeper; her red lips, too full, trembled.

But the monotonous shrilling of the telephone had partly aroused him to some consciousness of the world about him—to *self*-consciousness, too. And, with this confused resurrection of submerged senses, came mental awakening—a glimmering recognition of facts.... Of indestructible facts which never change.... Old, old facts which never can be ignored, never altered....

There were two things which a man of his race did not do. One of these he was about to do now.

He took the girl into his arms and held her close, not kissing her.

"I'm in love with you, Gilda," he said unsteadily.

"I want you to be."

There was a brief and breathless silence, filled suddenly by the racket of the telephone bell. The metallic outburst cleared his brain, but it seemed to madden hers.

She flung wide her bare arms in a sort of childish rage, her lovely mouth distorted.

"Do you hear that telephone?" she cried. "That's Sadoul! And *this* is where his damned cleverness is urging me—not into *his* arms—into *yours!*—" And she clasped him fiercely, strained him to her with a little cry:

"It's *you*, not Sadoul! It's you! only you! Shall I prove I love you better than my soul?"

The boy turned scarlet: "I want—want you to marry me," he stammered.

"What!" she exclaimed in flushed astonishment.

"Didn't you understand?" he demanded.

"M-marry you?" she faltered. "*Darling!* What are you saying? Don't you know I can't *marry?*"

"Why not?"

"Because I *am* married."

He gazed at her aghast.

"Darling! I married Sadoul in Paris ten months ago. Didn't anybody ever tell you?"

He seemed stupefied.

"I thought you knew it," she repeated in a bewildered voice. "That's why I ask you what are we to do?"

"I don't know," he said vacantly; ... "I'd better leave you alone, I suppose—"

She caught his lips with hers to silence him; clung closer in a passion of fear until again he drew her to him.

She was trembling all over now, imprisoned in his arms. After a while the boy dropped his blond head beside hers, pressing his face against her hot cheek.

"I don't know what to do," he said, "—it isn't in me—it isn't in any of my race—to love—lawlessly...."

The girl was crying silently. But when he lifted his head she looked up at him through her tears:

"I didn't ever want you to see me when I am this way," she said tremulously. "That's why I always try to escape being with you when—when the *Other One* is in possession—and I seem to be what I am not—"

"Do you mean that this other—this intruder, this strange, depraved intelligence—is in possession of you *now!*" he demanded hoarsely.

"Can't you see? Look at me, Stuart. Can't you see that tonight I am the—the thing Sadoul showed you?"

But already he knew it was true; knew that he was in love with her even as he saw her now—even with this depraved intruder gazing out at him through Gilda's lovely eyes.

Exasperated, well nigh beside himself, he took the girl by her bare shoulders, violently:

"You've got to free yourself," he cried; "You've got to rid yourself of this obsession—this waking nightmare. You've got to divorce Sadoul—"

"He won't let me, Stuart. What can I expect from a man who trapped my soul when I lay dead and sent this *other* shameless thing into me, hoping it would prove a friend to him?"

"Can't your own soul drive it out?"

"It is fighting now.... By tomorrow, I hope—"

"But your mind is still your own, Gilda."

"My own soul controls that, always. It's the senses that the *Other* seizes."

He looked at her fearfully, unloosed his clasp from her waist, stepped backward, passing one hand heavily across his eyes.

"This is incredible," he muttered. "If it's true, it's too monstrous to be without remedy.... After all, God lives—somewhere—"

He pressed his hand, tight, over his eyes again.

"Stuart?"

"Yes," he said harshly.

"Shall I attempt to make it clearer to you? I think I can."

"How?"

She thought a moment: "Dearest, I am going to try to show you more than Sadoul once showed you. I want you to *know* exactly what happens to me. Come."

She took his hand, led him across the room, and opened her chamber door.

There was a bright ceiling lamp burning in her bedroom. She lighted the rose-shaded night lamp also, then pointed toward the lounge.

He seated himself. She said in a low voice: "I think God will let me show you.... I pray that He will.... Don't touch me—*afterward*. Don't even speak. Just turn out both lights and go home very quietly. Do you promise?"

He nodded.

The girl went over to the bed and lay down on the lace counterpane, extending her slender figure so that she rested on her left side. Her left arm lay extended; her eyes were covered by her right hand.

For a second or so she moved a little, adjusting herself; then she lay unstirring under the brilliant ceiling light.

Minutes passed. He scarcely stirred, watching her motionless form. But into his memory crowded poignant recollections of another night, when he had sat beside a dead girl until, unable to endure it, he had dropped on his knees beside her to ask an "Unknown God" for equity and justice.

Thinking of God now, and his eyes fixed upon the still form on the bed, he was suddenly aware of another person in the room—a girl, standing near the fireplace.

Over his neck and back and thighs slow chills crawled.

She was like Gilda; lovelier, possibly. The brilliancy of her complexion under the ceiling light—the exquisite, nameless grace of her somehow seemed to still the surging fear in him—quiet his pulse's panic.

In the flood of light where she stood there was absolutely nothing unreal about her. And had Gilda not been lying there on the bed he would have believed this girl was she.

Then, to his astonishment, she looked at him smilingly; came to him and rested a light hand on his shoulder. He could feel the warmth of it; he looked up into her face, and felt the fragrance of her breath.

This was no phantom. Scarcely knowing what he did, he started to rise, and was arrested by the pressure of her hand gently resisting.

"You promised," she said, smiling. The sweetness of the low voice was indescribable.

"Are you real?" he asked, under his breath.

She laughed silently. "Oh, very," she said. "Touch me." Her arms and body were warm and firm. She took his hand and placed it over her heart. Under it he felt the steady beating.

"Who are you?" he whispered.

"I am Gilda."

"Then—then *what* is that on the bed?"

"My home. There is an intruder in it.... Look! Do you see her lying there, watching us?"

And now, beside the motionless shape on the bed, he saw another figure lying, half hidden, peering stealthily at him over the naked shoulder of the unstirring form.

Slowly, furtively, its head lifted; and he recognised the sensual features of the thing that Sadoul had made him see—the languorous eyes, the scarlet lips, the neck too white and thick, the limbs, marble fair, heavy, marvelous—

The thing rose on the bed, supported by one naked arm to prop it. Suddenly it leaped lightly to the carpet—a living creature, breathing, palpable, utterly real.

The girl on the bed stirred slightly and a deep sigh escaped her.

The figure beside Stuart bent down and whispered to him to put out the lights and go.

He rose. The *Other One* laughed at him; touched his face with her soft pink fingers as he passed her to extinguish the rose-shaded night lamp.

Before he put out the ceiling light he paused, his hand on the electric button, and looked at the three he was leaving in the bed room—leaving in darkness there.

He looked at the motionless form on the lace counterpane; he looked at the *Other One* in all her flagrant beauty; he looked at his first and loveliest visitor, who returned his gaze sweetly, tranquilly, reassuringly.

Then he switched off the light.

CHAPTER XX

It being Saturday, and a half day down town, Stuart went to the Fireside on pretense of lunching, but particularly to find Casimir Sadoul.

From his office he had tried to get Gilda on the telephone, but she was still asleep. Then he called up Sadoul at his apartment and at the offices of one or two periodicals, without finding him.

Now, at the Fireside, he learned that Pockman and Sadoul, much the worse for wear, had breakfasted there about noon and had gone away together.

He had left word for Gilda to call him when she awoke. She had not done so. After lunch he telephoned again. Freda informed him that her mistress was still asleep.

Stuart had had no sleep, having arrived home only in time to bathe and change for the office.

But it was the nerve-shattering experience with Gilda which so disorganized him that he could scarcely hold a fork or lift a glass of water to his lips.

"Where do you suppose I could find Sadoul?" he asked Dr. Lyken, later, in the cloak-room.

"He's usually at Pockman's research laboratory in the afternoon. Have you ever been there, Sutton?"

"No."

"Some laboratory! You know what they're up to, don't you?"

"I know, vaguely, what Pockman is doing."

"Glands. And Sadoul has taken the other end, now. He writes his vitriolic stuff in the morning, and investigates psychic phenomena all the afternoon. Pockman staked him."

"Staked him?"

"Yes. Pockman has given Sadoul several rooms in the laboratory and has fitted them up. He must believe in such things, or he wouldn't have spent all that money on quarters and apparatus for that clever fakir, Sadoul. Why don't you go over and take a slant at the place?"

"Where is it?"

"Over toward Fifty-seventh Street and the East River. Of course, I can't bring myself to subscribe to such theories and procedure, although, like the majority of scientific men, I'm on the fence and ready to be convinced.... I couldn't tell you whether there is anything in it or not. I don't mean Pockman's work: that's sound; I mean Sadoul's psychophysical research.... If you're going over, I'm walking that way as far as Third Avenue."

They turned east at Fifty-seventh Street.

"It's quite a laboratory, Sadoul's," continued Lyken. "He's got one machine there invented, I understand, by Sir Oliver Lodge. It's an amazingly delicate affair. It keeps a record of all muscular effort on the part of a medium during tests. Any loss of weight, any addition, is accurately noted. It gives a continuous chart of temperature, pulse, breathing. It notes all mental activity; it even photographs visualisation when concentration is sufficient—"

"That's impossible!" ejaculated Stuart.

"No, it really isn't," said the other. "Sensitized plates wrapped in opaque coverings have been tried out. When the subject concentrates on any object there is a very good photograph of it on the plate. Which seems to prove that thought-waves are really projected—"

"Have *you* seen any?"

"Oh, yes."

"Made by Sadoul?"

"Yes."

After a silence, Lyken went on:

"Sadoul uses ultra-violet rays and quartz lenses when he takes a movie of any psychic proceedings.

"He's well equipped with x-ray apparatus, radium tubes—the latest and most delicate instruments.... You know you can't help respecting a man who is so patiently trying out evidence."

Sutton walked along in silence beside the garrulous Lyken, understanding little of what the latter was saying.

"I'm on the fence," repeated Lyken, "but I'm no bigot, and I'm quite in favour of research experiments along those lines—if anybody has the time and the courage."

"I suppose experimenters are ridiculed."

"Not so much, now. Too many great names are associated with the investigations—Lodge, Wallace, Crookes, Edison, Imoda, Van Zeist, Matla, Zaalberg—too many tremendous names to scoff at."

"What do they want to do?"

"Here's their programme: experiments in, and investigation of, clairvoyance, materialization, dual projection, levitation, soul photography, subconscious mind, human polarity—"

"I don't know what those are," interrupted Stuart bluntly.

"Nobody does. We don't even know what the electric fluid is; we know only that it's there."

"At least we can see it."

"We can see one phase of it. The vast, overwhelming forces—energy and its sources—are invisible. We know them only by their results. I don't see why these tremendous psychic forces should be visible, either. One thing is certain: they're there, and we know it because of their results. The thing to do is to find out what these forces really are—physical or psychical—manifestations of the psychical ego, the mental, or the spiritual."

They paused at Third Avenue.

"I'm taking the Elevated," remarked Lyken. "Are you going to swap yarns with Sadoul?"

"I don't know what I'm going to do with Sadoul," returned Stuart unsmilingly.

Pockman's laboratory consisted of several shabby old houses converted into a single rambling structure facing the river.

A young woman in nurse's uniform admitted him and showed him to a dingy waiting-room. Pockman presently appeared in white operating costume, which became him as cerements become a corpse.

"Glad to see you," he smirked. "What the hell put it into your blond head to come over here?"

"I'm looking for Sadoul," replied Stuart.

"He's in his own section. I'll send him in—"

"Pockman—just a second.... I want to ask you something—and I don't know how to put it.... Is there any actual—any scientific basis—anything to be taken seriously in these psycho-hypnotic tricks that

Sadoul does?"

Pockman hunched his bony shoulders and began to walk about the room in his jerky, cockroach way.

"I don't know how he does the things he does," he said. "Maybe he's faking; I can't tell.... But there seem to be phenomena along those lines worth investigating.... I've given him a place of his own in the next house.... If you want to talk to him—"

"Yes, I mean to talk to him.... But you're a graduate physician, Pockman—a specialist in certain lines of research—and your standing is high, according to all I hear about you.

"And so I desire to ask such a man as yourself about these disquieting and somewhat unpleasant performances of Sadoul's—"

"Which one in particular?"

"In particular I'm thinking of his meddling with little Miss Greenway."

"I supposed you had her in mind." Pockman cracked his knuckles, resumed his pacing, arms dangling and jerking: "She's a morbid subject," he said. "Otherwise he couldn't have snapped her up over there.... God knows what one human mind can do to another, Sutton. No use asking me; I can't tell you.... We don't know anything yet. You tell 'em! We don't know the alphabet of life. We don't know what life is, how, where, when it originated.... But we're going to know. You tell 'em that, too!"

He burst into a harsh twitter and went racking on around the room like some spavined thing, his arms jerking.

"I want to ask you," said Stuart in a low voice, "do you think Sadoul really has any psychic control over Miss Greenway?"

"Well, by God, I don't know!" almost shouted Pockman, coming to a stop in front of Sutton, his long arms flying about uncertainly:

"Here's a theory: we all have dual personalities—many of us have multiple. Personality is that indestructible identity which persists after bodily death. Call it a soul. It's a short word.

"Now, take little Miss Greenway's case. That girl's body died and remained physically dead for hours. No doubt about it, Sutton.

"But what happened to her soul I don't know of my own knowledge. That indestructible identity which was Gilda Greenway certainly returned as her body's tenant; but whether it found another lodger in possession and has had to put up a continual fight, as Miss Greenway says—"

"Did she tell *you* that?"

"Yes, she told me."

"When?"

"She speaks of it every time she comes here—"

"Here? Does Gilda come here?"

Pockman's flat face was all glistening with sweat; he wiped it, but the ghastly smirk remained.

"Say," he said, "you and Sadoul and Derring and Harry Stayr do nothing but camp on that kid's trail."

"I'm trying to keep tabs on her, and she's decent enough to see the scientific importance of submitting to daily observation. But you're all chasing her and keeping her excited and nervous, and where the hell do *I* come in?"

Sutton, astonished and troubled, said nothing; Pockman flourished his flail-like arms:

"I'm trying to keep a record of the only case on record. My God, can't you fellows show some decency and self-control—you, taking her about town at all hours and driving Sadoul insane with jealousy—Gilda claiming that Sadoul is having her shadowed by a disincarnate, homeless and malicious soul that has no morals and wants to drive out her own soul and get in—Sadoul, licking his chops as though it were true, and hopeful that there might be something for him with a new tenant in possession of Gilda's pretty body—and all those other johnnies chasing about, sending her flowers and fruit from Florida and ducks from—"

He went rocking and teetering around the room again, shaking his bony hands above his head:

"How am I going to observe the results of transplanting a nymphalic gland into a corpse with all this feverish hullabaloo going on in that child's life? What do you suppose it does to her?—all this excitement—"

"Wait a moment!" said Stuart, detaining him as he rambled past, and holding him by one flapping arm: "All I want you to tell me is whether, in your opinion, it is scientifically possible for Sadoul to meddle spiritually—or in any occult way—with what you call that indestructible identity which is Gilda Greenway's soul?"

"I'm telling you I don't know!" shouted Pockman. "He seems to be able to do things to identities. He materializes them, weighs them, takes their pulses, temperatures, blood-pressure—he photographs them, measures them, listens to their lung action— There seems to be no end to what we are learning about those disincarnate personalities vulgarly known as 'spirits' and so long exploited by psychic crooks and fake 'mejums.'"

He wiped his unhealthy skin with the sleeve of his operating robe.

"That's all very fine," he said. "Let others go to it. The nymphalic gland is my job—"

"You haven't answered my question, Pockman."

"Which one? Oh! Do I think it possible for Sadoul to encourage some homeless but more sensual spirit to enter little Miss Greenway and ultimately drive out her real identity?"

"That's what I asked you."

"Sutton, I don't know. I know he has always tried to arouse in the girl some response to his own morbid, lovesick importunities. Normally the girl always seems to have been fascinated by his brilliant intellectual equipment—seems, in a way, to have fallen a victim to it—probably aided by hypnosis.

"But for the rest—I guess not. No—I've studied her. She isn't that kind. The girl is, when let alone, perfectly normal in everything.

"The new nymphalic has put her in superb physical condition—a magnificent young animal!—that's what the girl is.... And as far as I can see she has, normally, a vigourous, healthy mind to control her every emotion.... And yet, she does break loose—like the other night at Fantozzi's.... But that's exuberance—letting off steam—"

"Do you call that normal, Pockman?"

"Well, no, I don't.... And she tells me—with some very wild and breathless tears—that it isn't natural for her to kick over the traces and raise the devil in that fashion."

"It would almost look, then, as though—" Stuart hesitated, his haunted eyes fixed on Pockman.

The latter said:

"Well, she claims it's what she calls the *Other One* that creeps in when she's asleep, or off her guard—at some psychological moment when her subconscious self is off duty.... *I* don't know. We've read 'Jekyll and Hyde,' and 'Peter Ibbetson,' and 'The Brushwood Boy'—and a score of other clever tales. This business of Gilda Greenway sounds like another volume of the same series.... And then, again"—he shrugged his bony shoulders—"the story of Gilda Greenway may be as true as anything in the world.... The world itself being only a big lie told to amuse a lot of gods—somewhere yonder—beyond the outer stars—and all laughing like hell—"

He stood rocking on heels and toes with the irresponsible movement of something inanimate swept by tempests.

"No," he muttered, wiping his clammy visage, "we don't know anything, so far.... My God, no.... Are you going in to talk to Sadoul?"

"Another time."

"Oh! From your face I thought you were looking for him to kill him."

"I'm not the killing sort, Pockman."

"Oh! Well, *he* is. It's a tip—if you ever mean to mix it with Casimir Sadoul."

Stuart looked neither interested nor surprised.

"I haven't yet decided what I want of Sadoul," he said without a trace of threat, yet with a simplicity that seemed to make no question of getting whatever he might wish for.

Pockman looked at him long out of fishy eyes. Then he snickered.

"Someday," he said, "if you and little Miss Greenway are good to me and let me observe her in peace, I'll tell you both something about Sadoul that will make it easier for you to put a crimp in him."

"No, thanks," said Stuart coldly.

"As you choose, Sutton.... Drop in again and look over my assortment of glands—all alive and guaranteed to start any corpse two-stepping...."

CHAPTER XXI

Often in those days, working with his secretary, or, in the little inner office, working alone, something approaching realisation of the problems in which he was being involved would suddenly confront Stuart, leaving him dismayed.

The simpler of the problems was less disturbing. Their solution, if they were to be solved, was obvious: he could ignore the traditions of his race and drift on with little Miss Greenway as his mistress; he could challenge those traditions and marry her—after her case had been pulled through some legal knot-hole or other.

He was now aware that he had only to choose. Either choice lay outside the customs and habits of his race. The Suttons had never condescended to irregular love affairs; the Suttons did not marry ineligible women.

The basic question, however, was yet to be solved—whether this impassioned preference for little Miss Greenway was actually love. It had several of love's ominous symptoms—all its impulse, restlessness and fever, all the familiar sieges, alarums, and excursions incident to the oldest story in the world—older even than death.

Not to see her for a day was endurable. And it was always during the first day's separation that he doubted the genuineness of his passion. A second day brought restlessness, and time lost in freeing his thoughts of her so that other matters might be pursued with a free mind.

Then, before the third day, his vague unease became a longing. The desire to see her set in like a tide—as passionless but as inevitable as some immemorial custom of nature obeying its law.

It was this phase that made him aware of depths within himself unstirred heretofore—blind, unplumbed depths, profoundly in motion.

Always their reunion quieted these deeps in him—even in that strange phase of her when her soul seemed helplessly entangled in obscurity and her over-flushed and altered beauty warned him of the dark transition.

For he found her, sometimes, during those unreal and shadowy moments when another intelligence possessed her.

In that lovely and tragic transfiguration she no longer attempted to avoid him. On the contrary, she now called him, her changed voice alone being sufficient warning.

For they had talked it over together, sadly, in fear, consulting each other what was safest for them while the shadow of the *Other One* possessed her.

The boy had laid down the law, furiously. She was to call on him; never again to face this obsession recklessly out of bounds.

No more parties where, unafraid and maliciously immune, she could watch Sadoul, undaunted, and taunt him with the very lips he had altered for his own desire. No more escapades. The fever must burn itself out behind doors that opened only to him.

He was to take the brunt of it—though, in tears, she bade him remember and beware of treachery within herself—warned him that she must prove a false ally in that occult crisis—in the burning obscurity of her obsessed mind; in the faithless intent of a subtle and uncaged heart.

"There is no other way, dearest," he said. "If there's ever a debacle then we crash down together."

"And when I awake, Stuart?"

"Had you rather awake in any other arms?"

"No.... But I don't want ever to awake that way.... Even in your arms.... What was it you told me about one of those Western states?"

"It's necessary to establish a residence."

"How?"

He went over it with her again—details that he spoke of with difficulty—the whole sordid legal procedure so utterly repugnant to them both, yet which held for them a miserable fascination. Also, there was Sadoul, and they did not know what he might do to fight divorce—she very certain that he would follow her—he aware that Sadoul could close her road to complete freedom and make it a drawn game.

One dark afternoon toward Christmas-tide, they had been speaking of it—an odd time to revert to so miserable a subject, for Gilda was going to have a tree for them both, and they had been dressing it.

Now she knelt beside the tree with yards of tinsel trailing from her hand, watching Stuart winding the electric wire, with its rows of tiny coloured bulbs, among the branches.

"I don't know," she murmured—"I think the only way is to go on as we are. Don't you, Stuart?"

He muttered something inaudible, twisted a strand of bulb-set wire through a fragrant green branch.

"We are anything but unhappy," she ventured. And, as he said nothing, busy with his wire among the branches: "I wonder why you care to marry me. It would not be agreeable to your family."

He turned around: "Why do you assume that?"

"I don't assume it, Stuart. Sadoul told me."

"What damned business is it of Sadoul's—"

"Please! The conversation had become general; Veronica was giving us tea; George Derring talked snobbishly about old families and social traditions. Somebody mentioned you. Sadoul etched one of his vivid portraits—a sort of composite portrait of a Sutton.... You know Sadoul is a master of trenchant English—a word is a phrase with him.... Your race lived for a hundred years when he spoke.... I was quite scared.... Then I realized that what he said was sneeringly meant for me.... That was all, Stuart."

After a silence he resumed his task among the branches: "A man marries to please himself," he said in a slightly sullen voice.

"Men of your race marry within their family's approbation."

"Good heavens, Gilda! That dreary, stilted era is as dead as Mrs. Grundy!"

"Sadoul says its traditions never die out among such families as yours."

That was true. He knew it. Even within himself, to his impatience and annoyance, the musty old precepts remained alive, surprising him at inopportune moments by their ridiculous virility.

"Well, Gilda," he said, "if there remain in us absurdities, narrowness, traces of the priggish Victorian, we're not utterly antediluvian. I do not believe for a moment that the attitude of my family would be anything but cordial to the girl I marry."

She drew the shining strands of tinsel slowly through her slender fingers, still kneeling, not looking up.

"I was not thinking of myself," she said.

"Of whom, then?"

"You, of course.... I would not have your pride suffer through me."

"How do you mean?"

The girl sighed lightly. "There are so many ways—situated as you are.... I know a little about the traditions of old and conservative families.... Their traditions are part of them. They are not to be suppressed or removed. They are as much part of them as heart and lungs: they last till death."

"You speak with familiar authority on such things," he said, smiling. She looked up.

"Yes," she said. "I am a victim of tradition."

He came over and knelt down on the floor, facing her.

"How do you mean, Gilda?" he asked curiously.

She was sorry she had spoken; that seemed evident. She said, reluctantly: "I am not yet twenty, Stuart.... I am living here in New York quite alone. Nobody related to me is visible. There seems to be nobody to vouch for me.... Do you imagine it always was so?"

"Dear, I don't suppose so. But you never have spoken to me of these things—"

She shook her head: "No; there's no reason to."

"But if we should ever marry—"

"Yes, there would be a reason then.... I would not wish you to think me less than I am."

The boy put both arms around her:

"I could not think more of you, dearest. I don't care what were your circumstances—"

"That's the darling thing about you, Stuart," she said, flushing and drawing his face to hers impulsively. "You know something about me. You know vaguely about Sadoul—that once he was part of my life— But what part you don't know, you never ask; you are just sweet and kind to me, Stuart, and I fell in love with you before I knew it—before I meant to—wanted to—"

Her fresh lips rested on his; she looked deep into his eyes.

"I didn't think there was any future for us when I fell in love," she said. "I didn't think of anything. If I had I'd have been frightened.... Because, if the world had not gone so wrong with me, I ought to have met you on your own level—if destiny intended us to meet."

"I've always thought that," he said.

"Have you? You're such a darling, Stuart. And you are not wrong.... I'd rather not talk about it—unless it ever should come true that we marry. Just believe that I am not—not less than you would wish me.... Not in *any* way, Stuart."

"Can't you tell me now?"

"I can't bring myself—please—you see there are—others to remember—shelter—unless I were married to you—when their honour becomes yours also—"

"I understand, Gilda."

"Do you? I am speaking of my father and mother. Unless I were married to you their tragedy could not be made a confidence between us to be guarded with our own honour by both of us."

He nodded gravely.

"It's as though," she explained wistfully, "there were such a tragedy in your own family. If I were less than your wife you could not permit me to take my share in it and help guard the common honour."

"Of course…. That I am in love with you is not enough."

"No, dear; not even if you were my lover."

"That's the only thing that would ever make me doubt your quality, Gilda—that you ever could consider such a thing possible—"

"Oh, Stuart, that *is* the peril to me when the *Other One* is in possession. Because you and I *are* of the same sort—and there is no condescension—only the common fault—to share between equals—"

"If Sadoul really gave that *Other* right of way into your heart, he's a devil incarnate," said Stuart, slowly.

"He did it because he wanted me at any cost. And it has cost *him* his last chance…. But *you*, Stuart!—*you* know that I'd be miserable, humiliated, heartbroken, if I were your mistress—no matter how much I was in love? It's only when the *Other One* is in possession—" She dropped her face on his breast, clung so, closely.

"I trust you so," she whispered, "—even when the dark transition comes—even when I am in your arms and the *Other One* looks at you out of my eyes—"

A quick little sob cut her short; she rested one hand on his shoulder, sprang to her feet, whisked away a tear, laughed uncertainly.

"Are we going to dress our tree? Or make each other unhappy—"

"We're going to dress this jolly little tree," he said, getting to his feet.

She brought a big pasteboard box full of brilliant, flimsy things—stars, globes, shining shapes of various patterns to dangle from the branches. He hung them subject to her approval, and they became very busy again.

"Tell me," he said, "what do you do over there at Pockman's laboratory when you go?"

"Oh, it's a nuisance, Stuart. Pockman fusses around. He has a lot of charts—I don't understand them. It seems that it's important, scientifically, for him to keep me under observation for a while. He takes measurements, pressures, all sorts of records—do you know I've grown a quarter of an inch since you first met me?"

"Good heavens, no!"

"I *have!* Also, I'm informed that I'm superbly healthy, and—if you please, monsieur—rather unusually symmetrical. Now, may I expect a more respectful attitude from you?"

"Am I lacking dear?"

"You never ask leave to kiss me."

He started toward her; she fled around the tree; taunted him; consented at last to kiss him through the branches; and came around to join him with her box of baubles.

"It's going to be charming!" she exclaimed, surveying the glistening boughs laden with glittering objects and striped canes of candy. "Stuart, there's only one thing I want you to give me for Christmas."

"What's that, darling?"

"A doll."

"All right. I'll give you a hum-dinger—"

"No! I want an old-fashioned French doll of wax. I want her eyes to open and shut. I should like to have her say *'Ma-ma!'* in a squeaky voice when her tummy is gently indented. Will you give me that kind?"

"You bet, sweetheart!"

"Thank you. What do you wish, Stuart?" she added. "If you say anything sentimental I'll throw this green globe at you!"

"Well, then"—he meditated for a moment—"give me a toy shovel and pail so I can transplant little pine trees this spring."

"Shovel and pail," she repeated, making a mental note. The dressing of the tree was resumed. Presently she said: "When do you expect to go North?"

"Not until the ground thaws."

"It must be very lovely up there where all your tiny new forests are growing."

"It's pretty except where it's been lumbered. We're planting that by degrees. And the standing timber, of course, is beautiful."

"It must be," she said, with an unconscious sigh.

"Would you like to come with me?" he said.

"Darling!" she protested with an enchanting smile.

"You mean the Grundy?"

"I do. You said she was dead, but I knew you were mistaken."

"Would you really like to come?"

"I'd adore it. But how?"

"There's Veronica—"

"Oh, Stuart, that wouldn't be wise. You know what they'd all think—Katharine Ashley, Frances Hazlet—and then the men—"

"Of course," he said, "we've got to care what is said about you.... If we could get into my car and just beat it someday, nobody would be the wiser; and you and I know we're all right—"

"That," she said quite seriously, "is the nuisance of not being married. And—oh, Stuart!—if ever you wanted to marry me afterward and your family found out!"

"Awkward," he admitted.

"What a perfectly beastly nuisance not to be married!" exclaimed the girl. "Think of the things we could do, Stuart. Have you any idea how my heart sinks when you have to go home, and I lock the door and come back here alone—thinking of a million things I forgot to tell you—"

"Do you, dear?"

"Yes. Don't you feel that way? Or are you pig enough not to?"

"Don't you suppose I miss you as much as you do me?"

"I don't know.... I want you desperately, sometimes. A woman's different, I suppose.... I don't think any woman in love is absolutely self-sufficient.... A man in love, I fancy, is not so dependent.... A girl admits a companion to her mind and heart for the first time in her life when she falls in love.... A man has other comradeships which stave off loneliness of mind—of heart, too, perhaps.... It's curious—and rather sad.... No woman ever completely filled her lover's mind. No lover but completely fills the mental and sentimental life of any girl who really loves."

The boy hung the last specimen of papier-maché fruit upon the tree, came around and took the girl's idle hands in his.

"Do you think I'm in love with you, Gilda?"

"I—think so."

"Are you in love with me?"

"Yes, I *know* it. You see, Stuart, it's merely the difference between knowledge and belief—the fundamental difference between our sexes. Belief satisfies us; knowledge alone satisfies you." She laughed, rested her lips lightly on his chin. "So—we both are satisfied."

They stood smiling at each other.

"I'll go home and dress and we'll dine at—"

"Dear! Freda has such a nice dinner!"

"Don't you want to see a show—"

"No!"

"Don't you want—"

"No. Are you tired of me?"

"You lovely little thing—"

"Let's stay with our tree. I adore it. I'll play for you, after dinner.... And we can read more of those vapid, egotistical memoirs—"

"That impossible woman!"

"Do you know," said Gilda, thoughtfully, "she really is not impossible. She's quite nice and human—even sweet to people she likes."

"You speak as if you knew her," he said.

"I do—" The girl flushed as though recollecting herself, gave him a confused look.

"You know the Countess of Wyvern, Gilda?"

"Yes," she said in a low voice. There was a silence. She lifted distressed eyes to his, looked elsewhere, stood nervously twisting her fingers.

"Lady Wyvern is—a relative," she murmured.

She had turned partly away. Now she went to the mantel and stood looking at the clock.

"If you have anything to do before dinner," she said over her shoulder—"I think I had better see what Freda is about—"

She turned on her boudoir and bathroom lights for him and continued on through the dining-room toward the kitchen.

CHAPTER XXII

The week had been a clear and joyous one for Gilda. Not a shadow disturbed it. Christmas Eve she was like a little girl, trotting about the apartment with ropes of evergreen, filling every vase with holly, hanging wreaths at every window, tying up dozens of little packages—inexpensive gifts all destined for Stuart.

That young man came in after dusk, his arms full of packages, and Gilda flew to him, on fire with curiosity, touching the brilliant Christmas ribbons with exploring forefinger.

"Everything is to be placed at the base of the tree," she explained breathlessly, "—yours are all there, Stuart—I *wonder* what is in this big box! Darling—shall I take one little look? Oh, no; it wouldn't do, would it?"

"Keep your lovely little hands off those packages," he warned her, laying aside his hat and overcoat.

They went into the living room and she stood watching him in youthful excitement as he squatted down and laid packet after packet around the base of the tree.

"It's the most real Christmas I ever had. It's a story-book Christmas. All mine were in schools and most uninteresting. Isn't our tree lovely? No, we must not light it until after dinner. Positively, dearest! And oh, Stuart, *did* you bring a stocking to hang up?"

He gravely unrolled and displayed the desired hosiery. Hers already hung from the mantel, daintily empty; and she hung his beside it, stepped back to view the effect, clasped her hands with a swift intake of breath.

"Don't they look perfectly darling together!" she said as he drew her head back against his shoulder. The next instant she wriggled free, pinned a twig of holly to each stocking.

"Poke the fire, Stuart. I want to see the sparks. There! Isn't it enchanting?"

Everything was "enchanting" or "adorable" or "darling" that Christmas Eve; the dinner, too, with its roast goose—reconnoitered with difficulty by an unskilled carver—its egg flip and mulled spiced wine, and its very British plum-pudding—that over-praised and soggy sham—which blazed gaily under its burning sauce, and exhaled the only appetising ingredient in it—its odour.

They stood up and drank to each other, almost unsmilingly, almost awkward in a seriousness unpremeditated.

That was in flip. He got up again later, and offered their "love everlasting" in a cup of mulled wine.

An odd shyness overcame her; she was able to reply only with a smile; but as she lifted her silver cup, a swift mist glimmered in her eyes.

She closed her eyes and kissed the rim of her goblet; they exchanged cups, drank to love in silence.

Very soon they were at their ease again with each other.

"A Christmas goose," he commented, "is very English."

"They always sent me one."

He looked up interrogatively.

"To school—wherever I happened to be—in Belgium, or France. There came always a Christmas box from my father—always."

He nodded gravely.

"Mother also sent me my Nöel," she added.

"That helped," he ventured.

"Yes.... Convent schools are not gay at Christmas-tide.... Isn't this a most enchanting Christmas?"

He thought: "You pathetic kid!" But he said it was truly an old fashioned and genuine Christmas Eve.

As they left the table she said a trifle bashfully to the boy:

"I don't know what Christmas bowl we should drink after dinner. I've looked all through Dickens and his stories are full of steaming bowls, but he doesn't say how they're made—"

Stuart shouted with laughter, and they went on gaily to the piano.

For a while she sang in her clear, childish voice the quaint French carols—the Nöel of the peasants, or its sweet and sophisticated modern equivalents—charming chorals of convent days.

She drifted to a familiar hymn. He leaned beside her, sang with her. Her white hands hung listlessly on the keys; her cheek touched his.

Hesitatingly she mentioned her own faith; waited for some response. In the wistful silence his boy's heart grew heavy. The Talkers had left in him little with which to meet her appeal.

"Have you no God?" she asked in a low voice.

"I would—would like to have one. Children are better off."

"You are only a boy, Stuart. You still need God."

He nodded. Presently he said: "I needed Him when you died that night. I asked Him to be fair to you."

"You prayed for me?"

"I asked justice. I was over-wrought, overwhelmed. I suppose I reached out instinctively for help—my mind confused with memories of Christ—of miracles—and the little dead girl He made alive again—"

"Jairus' daughter."

"I remember now.... You seemed such a little girl to be dead...."

She said, seriously: "Do you think it was Christ—or what Pockman did?"

"I want to think that what Pockman did was by grace of Christ.... I don't see why a modern mind may not believe that.... Except...."

"What, Stuart?"

"Oh, I don't know.... There is so much to think of ... so much science and logic—and the wisdom of modern thinkers to consider. The trend of thought is not toward Christ as the ultimate solution of the world's problems."

The girl sat very still, her cheek pressed against his shoulder.

She said: "How can modern science admit spiritual survival and deny Christ?"

"Spiritual survival is being proven."

After a pause: "I didn't think I was at liberty to tell," she said in a voice that was nearly a whisper, "but I saw Christ's shadow, once."

He turned slowly to look at her.

"When I lay dead in the chair.... You laid me there. Then you went away.... Shall I tell you?"

He scarcely nodded.

"I lay there, dead. Sadoul came from behind the portières. My soul was already leaving me. Sadoul saw it.

"God only knows what he meant to do—but suddenly the white shadow of Christ passed between Sadoul and me! ... I saw His shadow on the air, and knew it. And that is all I knew until I opened my eyes and saw you beside my bed—"

She pressed her face convulsively against him.

The boy caressed her passionately, in silence, trembling to remember.

What she had told him was the delirium of a dying brain. But he did not say so. All he did say was:

"Sadoul did not come from behind the portières. I was alone with you when you died."

"Sadoul was there."

"No, dear—"

"I tell you he was behind the curtains, Stuart!"

"But I went down stairs to find him—"

"You went down and did not find him. When you returned he was gone. But he *was* there. I saw him."

She sat upon the piano bench beside him and patted her bright hair into better order. He gave her a vague, incredulous look. Then an odd mental flash stilled his heart for an instant—a mere glimmer—a phantom thought scarce formed.

"Behind the curtains," he repeated, mechanically.

She nodded, still busy with her hair.

"Stuart," she said, "it is all passed and happily ended by the grace of God. I died: God heard your prayer and gave me my soul again. Pockman was only the instrument. He chose—"

She turned and took his hand impulsively:

"Darling, can't you believe that Christ made me alive again?"

"Yes, I can—in a way—"

"Believe it this Christmas Eve. That would be the most wonderful gift for us—your new faith. Because you saw. What more does anybody ask? What clearer proof had the publican, Jairus? He asked aid. Christ answered and raised his child from the dead. You asked God to help me—" She threw wide her arms—"here I am, alive!"

And she flung her arms around his neck.

She touched the keys again. He sat humbly beside her, silent, while she sang in her lovely, child's voice the nobler hymns, or, sometimes, only played them.

And very soon it was time to light the magic tree. But first she banished him to her bedroom, closed the door, then ran to her desk and took out the gaily beribboned little gifts for his stocking.

When it was filled and bulging, she called to him and, in turn, submitted to banishment, and he drew from his overcoat pocket the gifts destined for her slim stocking, filling it from toe to knee.

It lacked a few minutes to midnight when they lighted the tree. She cried out in delight and caught his hand. They stood so until the clock struck.

At the last stroke she turned and wished him an excited Christmas greeting, and:

"Oh, Stuart!" she cried, "I want to see what is in that large box!—"

It was her old-fashioned French doll of wax. It opened and shut its eyes. It bleated *"Ma-ma"* when its tummy was discreetly pressed.

She clung to it through all the heavenly excitement of that Christmas morn. A slim hoop of diamonds glittered on her wrist; there were some beautiful handkerchiefs, stockings, a garnished suitcase, boxes of gloves, books, bon-bons—and then the foolish little gifts, odd, pretty, dainty things without value. But amid all she clutched her doll to her breast in a passion of half laughing, half childish possession—the strange instinct that persists so often despite self-mockery, pretense, and denial—the little girl deathless in the adolescent—the heart's eternal youth till it beats its own requiem to the last faint throb—the Feminine, immutable, imperious, imperishable.

CHAPTER XXIII

They had expected to spend New Year's Eve together. She telephoned him at the office that morning, asking him to come uptown early. Something in her voice made him uneasy, and she admitted she was feeling a little restless, but did not seem apprehensive.

When he returned from lunching at the Forester's Club he learned that she had called him again but had left no message.

Vaguely disturbed, he hastened to conclude business affairs for the day and arrange for everything over the holidays.

He was longer than he expected; some final stock transactions calculated to mitigate taxes were not completed; the closing for a few days of such a business required precaution and careful attention to every detail in the machinery.

However, after five, he wished everybody a happy New Year and sped uptown in his car.

He did not find Gilda at home, but he found a vaguely worded note from her saying merely that she was too nervous to see him that evening, and had gone out with friends.

A hot flush of anger carried him to the Fireside Club; but anxiety chilled it. Few men were in the club; the stillness was unusual; the Talkers ceased because they were few; silence remained unbroken save when there came distantly out of the dark city a dull rumour of tumult from the "Roaring Forties."

Apprehension lay a dead weight on his heart; he made a pretense of eating; then, for an hour or two, he haunted the telephone booths below. But Freda had left by that time and there was no response.

Where Gilda had gone and with whom he dared not surmise. If her uneasiness of the morning had been caused by any occult apprehension—any premonition that the *Other One* threatened her with possession, she had not intimated as much. And it had been understood that, in such crises, she was to call him to bear the brunt of the dark obsession.

Stuart went home about eleven. His taxi skirted the Forties; far flashes from a river of fire revealed Broadway.

Before he fell asleep the vast droning of whistles penetrated his breezy bedroom. The miserable year was ending in folly amid the empty howling of a mindless people.

Freda answered his morning inquiry saying that her mistress was still sleeping.

He didn't bother to ring up again, and his resentment had not cooled any when he had dressed, breakfasted, and was on his way to call her to account.

Freda said that her mistress was not well—not even dressed. Stuart flung his coat and hat on the hall chair and went into the living room.

The curtains were still drawn. A chill demi-light revealed the shadowy Christmas tree still standing.

On the lounge lay Gilda's evening cloak and gloves, flung at random. It was cold in the grey obscurity of the place. As he turned he set his foot on something limp and slipper—a matted cluster of dead orchids—and he kicked them aside and went across to her bedroom.

The door hung ajar. The girl was sitting on her bed huddled in a grey wool wrapper, clasping her doll.

Her hair, loosened, fell in a coppery cascade; her little bare feet, slipperless, hung limp above the fur rug. She scarcely looked up when he opened the door.

"Where the devil have you been?" he asked harshly—suddenly reacting from the tension.

"Where—the devil—I don't know... I don't know ..." she said vaguely.

There was a silence; she drew the big wax doll closer, giving the boy a vacant look.

"Are you ill?" he asked bluntly.

"Ill? Yes—quite ill. The world slipped away—somewhere."

"Why didn't you call me?"

"I called you.... You were too far away.... Too far."

"With whom were you?"

"The night was squirming with faces... I am sick of faces. There was no shelter."

"Was Sadoul there?"

"Yes.... There was no shelter in that glare.... I am withered."

"So you spent the eve of the New Year with Sadoul in riot," he said fiercely.

"In hell," she repeated in a ghost of a voice. "The blaze has burned me out—burned out my mind—blackened me...."

She looked up out of the burnished disorder of her hair, and he saw in her eyes that the *Other One* was still in possession.

"Drive out that damned thing!" he cried in an ungovernable rage.

But the *Other* looked out of her eyes at him in dangerous beauty: "If we burn—together—our ashes will be clean.... Do you love me?"

"Get into that bed!" he said in a strangled voice; went to her, pushed her back among the pillows, and covered her to the face.

He stared at her for a moment—at her dangerous eyes looking at him, shadowed by her hair—at the vacant visage of the doll at her breast, its wax eyes closed.

He looked around him at the disorder—stockings, under-clothing trailing from the sofa or underfoot—a painted horn, a fancy paper cap on the mantel—

An indescribable anger seized him; he went to the bed again, leaned over:

"You poor little devil," he said in a strangled voice, "—you poor, miserable little devil—"

Always her eyes watched him, —depthless wells of peril.

"Don't get up. I want you to wait for me here. I'll be back this afternoon. Call Freda when you are able to eat. Do you promise, Gilda?"

She lifted both arms in the wool sleeves, rested them on his shoulders and lay looking at him, her red lips parted.

"Do you promise?" he repeated.

"Yes.... I am so in love—Stuart—"

"So am I. But not with the beastly thing in command of you now."

"If you are in love with me, don't go," she breathed.

"Because I am, I'm going—loosen your arms!—"

He used force; she lay on the pillows again, flushed, her eyes veiled with tears.

At the door he looked back. She had bowed her head against the blond head of the doll, burying both in the disordered glory of her hair.

CHAPTER XXIV

He went to the Fireside Club but neither Pockman nor Sadoul were there. He called a taxi and drove to the laboratory. It being New Year's Day, the place was closed; but a very dirty old man, who said he was the engineer, answered the bell. It seemed that, although the laboratory was closed and the employees absent, Dr. Pockman had come in. Probably he was in one of the research rooms.

Stuart climbed the iron stairs, knocked at the private office. Nobody answered; he went in. A flat, suspicious, morgue-like odour pervaded everything. Stuart opened the connecting door on a room full of jars and chemicals and unknown apparatus. A grey chill possessed the place and the sweetish odour hung heavily, horribly, as though it disguised a stench more foul.

The place was dusky and empty, but he heard a scuffling in the room beyond and went in.

In the dim, chilly light he saw Pockman running round and round after a crippled rat which had escaped. Along the wall hobbled and scrambled the hump-backed thing, trailing paralysed hind legs, dodging the bony grasp of Pockman in pursuit, who was capering about like Death gone crazy.

He caught the creature, which shrieked, and he held it up, twisting and trying to bite.

"Where the hell did you come from?" he demanded, seeing Stuart.

The latter was experiencing a slight sense of nausea.

"I'm looking for Sadoul," he managed to say.

Pockman held up the squirming rat. He had it by the back of the neck. Then he ambled over and thrust it into a wire-faced hutch.

"I gave it a shot of the nymphalic," he explained, wiping the sweat away. "It's an old rat on its last legs, and it's going crazy with a rush of youth. Look here; I want to show you a few creatures under observation—"

"I can't wait, now. Is Sadoul in the building?"

"I don't know. That was a rough night last night. You weren't along, were you, Sutton?"

"No."

"Your girl was. Didn't Eve Ferral ask you?"

"Yes. Was it her party?"

"Hers and Katharine Ashley's. The whole 'Godiva' company showed up. It was large, Sutton—very noisy and very large.... I haven't had any breakfast. You ought to have come; Gilda let go last night—"

Stuart's bloodless face checked him.

After a moment: "What part of the building does Sadoul occupy?" asked the boy.

"You can go through that door, follow the corridor.... He may not be there; I haven't seen him—"

Stuart had already passed through the door. A white-washed corridor, full of the evil odour, led him to an iron door. He opened without knocking; and saw a small room with a lounge in it. Sadoul lay on the lounge. His eyes were open. He looked at Sutton as he entered, but made no motion to rise.

Neither spoke for a few moments, but a sneer etched itself on Sadoul's dark features. Sutton came slowly toward him.

"Sadoul," he said, "will you tell me the truth?"

"I don't know. Perhaps."

"Have you really anything to do with these periodic outbreaks of Gilda Greenway?"

Sadoul disdained to evade the issue.

"I suppose so."

"How?"

"Well, if you want to know, I suppose I put some badly needed animation into her, widened her vision, stimulated a natural capacity for pleasure. She needed a liberal education. She got it."

"How did you do this?" asked Stuart curiously; but his clenched hand was quivering and he dropped it into his overcoat pocket.

"I used what skill I had," replied Sadoul, coolly.

"How? Psychically?"

"Possibly."

"Hypno-psychic suggestion?"

"A very interesting subject," sneered Sadoul.

"Yes.... You think, then, that Gilda's periodic outbreaks"—he moistened his lips—"these sudden alterations in her character—the total change—" He could not go on for a moment or two. Sadoul lay watching him out of smouldering, sardonic eyes.

"You believe you are responsible for these things?" he managed to say at last.

"Does Gilda think so?"

"Yes."

"I'm flattered."

"Sadoul," said the other slowly, "if it is true that you are responsible—that you have been able to call in another and sinister intelligence to combat her own self—break down in her all that instinct and education have made her—can you, who have done this to her, drive out this intruder—this enemy you called in?"

"Does it concern you, Sutton?"

"Yes."

"You are mistaken. It doesn't. But I'll tell you that I wouldn't undo anything I've done if I could."

"*Can* you?"

"I don't know. Possibly. Probably. I have not tried. I don't intend to try."

"But you could free her of this if you tried, couldn't you?"

"Yes."

"How? Through hypno-psychic suggestion?"

"Undoubtedly."

"Is there any other way?" asked Sutton, very white.

The two men looked hard at each other.

"If you died—for example," added Sutton in a scarcely audible voice. And he saw in Sadoul's burning eyes that Gilda's freedom lay that way.

"Sadoul," he said, "you had better free her of this obsession if you can. Because, if you do not, I'm going to do it for her."

Sadoul slowly raised himself to a sitting posture. There was murder in his eyes and his dark face sharpened.

Sutton nodded: "That's it, Sadoul. You understand. If you don't free her, I'm going to kill you. I'll give you time to do it. I'll give you reasonable time. I'll wait as long as I think proper. Then I'll set her free in my own way."

Sadoul got up, his eyes ablaze.

"So that's a threat, is it, Sutton?"

"Not all of it. What were you doing behind the curtain the night that Gilda Greenway died in my arms?"

Sadoul's whole figure froze; a pallour swept the blood out of every feature.

"I don't know how big a blackguard you were," said Stuart in a curiously still voice. "You may have killed her. You had a chance—with that misericordia. You look capable of it. I don't suppose we'll ever really know.

"But I know you've tried to kill her soul—you and that shadowy devil that you let into her.

"Now, take your shadow-devil and get out. Get out of her life; or I'll put you out of this life.

"That's all, Sadoul."

CHAPTER XXV

When Sutton came out on Fifty-seventh Street a raw wind was blowing from the river. Whether from this or from reaction the boy was shivering in his overcoat; and he turned up the collar around his pinched and bloodless face.

There was no vehicle to be seen; he walked westward along the wide, dreary street, bisected at intervals by filthy, rusting elevated structures and by desolate avenues through which dust whirled. Swarms of dingy people, shabby and purposeless as dirty, wind-driven leaves, eddied about the streets.

Half-frozen children, their faces masked or smeared with rouge and charcoal, drifted hither and thither, whining and begging for New Year's alms.

He hailed a taxi, at last, and drove to Thirty-fifth Street. Freda opened the door and went back to her kitchen. The place was still dusky, shades lowered, curtains drawn.

Again he passed by the ghostly Christmas tree, with its festoons of tinsel and its unlighted bulbs, and knocked at her bedroom door.

He heard her stir, heard a faint response, went in. She sat up sleepily, gave him a confused glance, stifled a yawn with the back of her hand.

But, in her clearing consciousness, now, he saw her own self looking at him out of sweetly disconcerted eyes.

"Stuart," she said, "this is rather casual of us, isn't it?—" But already she was remembering; the humourously uneasy expression faded from her features. She pushed aside her hair, gazed at him, then her face flushed to her throat, and her furtive gaze stole fearfully around the disordered room.

"Oh, my God!" she whispered to herself, and took her face between her snowy hands.

She remained so in the chill of the semi-dusk, her knees drawn up to her chin, her face dropped between her hands, unstirring, silent.

There was some wood by the hearth, kindling, last evening's paper still folded.

He built a fire, went into the bath-room and turned the hot water into the tub.

When he came out he stood looking at her for a moment.

"We'll talk it over when you are ready, Gilda. Don't worry; we'll fix it. You must never go through this again."

He went out, closing the bedroom door, rid himself of hat and overcoat, walked into the kitchen.

"Could we have breakfast in an hour?" he asked. "That's fine, Freda. We'll have it on a card-table in the living-room."

The living-room, evidently, had been swept and dusted, and Gilda's derelict evening garments removed.

He raised the shades and drew the curtains. A gleam of wintry sunshine struck the wall.

The fire being laid, he set a match to it, seated himself to collect his thoughts.

Reaction had brought that weariness for which rest seems to be no balm. His tired mind seemed like some infernal machine which went on running after all else had run down.

It continued hatching out thought—no use trying to stop it, quiet it, ignore the hellish monotony of its functioning. He had to follow the record of the machinery, endlessly committing the same words, the same scenes to the custody of his tired brain.

The mantel clock timed the wearying reiteration; the flames on the hearth asked the same questions and answered them softly, lightly, inexorably. To what had his chance encounter with this girl brought him? It had now brought him to the verge of murder.

Because he loved her? Yes, evidently. Because he loved her enough to lay down his own life for her happiness? Evidently. Then he really loved her? It seemed so. If there was no other way to help her he was going to kill a man for her sake. And pay the penalty.... And permit his father and mother to share the penalty?

Thought went on burrowing through his brain to find a way out of it. There was no way out, if he killed Sadoul.

There was no way out for Gilda, either, unless Sadoul held his hand—unless he should be able and willing to undo what he had done toward her spiritual destruction.

The boy stared, hot-eyed, at the flames.

Freda opened and placed a card table on wabbly legs. In a few minutes she brought breakfast. Gilda entered, fresh from the bath, her skin all roses and snow and her red-gold hair in two braids.

She stole a shamed look at Stuart as he set a chair for her by the hearth. They had little appetite, pretended to none. Freda took away table and tray and closed the door.

The girl sank back in her deep chair, rested her chin on one hand and looked steadily at the fire. The silk sleeve of her boudoir wrap fell to the elbow.

"Tell me, Gilda," said the boy in a low voice.

"Yes." Her gaze never left the fire. "I'll tell you, Stuart.... I hadn't slept well. I was a little restless; but I didn't think it was because of the *Other One*. Still, I wanted you—I wanted you to come early.... Because it didn't seem as though I—I could endure my love for you, alone.

"You were in my mind, in every breath I drew, in every heart-beat.... It seemed to become so overwhelming.... Then that strange buoyancy came over me; contact, touch of earth, consciousness of material ebbed.... That flame-like lightness was all there seemed to be of me.... Even then it all seemed too heavenly to fear.... I was lying on the couch.... I think my soul stood a little way from me. Over by the second window.... It's hard to remember. I can't remember, in fact.... Only my heart had been looking out of that second window from where it would be possible to see your taxi when you arrived...."

Her bright head dropped on her hand, and her eyes grew tragic.

"When I realised that the *Other* was in possession I got up in a dazed way. My heart was already in her control—I felt the fire stealing through my veins. But I thought my mind was still clear. I tried to pray.... And sat up laughing, reckless, blind, deaf to everything—"

She fell silent, dropped her hands in her lap and fell to turning a black pearl ring that she sometimes wore.

"Shall I tell you where I went?" she asked, intent on her ring.

"I have heard."

She gave him a startled glance.

"Pockman told me," he said in a dull voice.

The hot colour stained her to the forehead. Twisting her slim fingers, fighting to control her voice, she said:

"If a girl can become so depraved is—is it worth your while to try to hold her?"

"Are you depraved, Gilda?"

"Not utterly ... so far."

"Were you intoxicated?"

"Yes."

The boy's face had gone very white.

"What happened?"

"Nothing I dare not tell you."

He looked into her eyes.

"There are two ways out of this for you," he said. "Either Sadoul must undo what he has done to you, or—"

After a pause: "He will not help me. What is the other way?" she asked. And suddenly understood what he meant.

Presently she fell to shivering, placed her feet on the fender. His eyes rested on them. They were very white in the sandals.

"What good would it do me?" she asked, trembling. "Would it help if you destroyed yourself and your father and mother? There are other ways."

"What ways?"

"One, anyhow. Do you think I'd let you destroy yourself to save me? I'd rather give myself to you, innocence, evil, and all, and take the consequences!"

"Do you think it makes a difference *how* your spiritual destruction is wrought?" he demanded hotly.

"Yes! The difference is that it's you, not Sadoul. I'd rather kill myself.... I shall, if you talk that way—"

"Gilda—"

"I shall, I tell you. My physical virtue and bodily purity are not worth murder, if my mind is right. And my mind is right—my real mind. You cannot make it more upright by shooting Sadoul and ruining yourself and your family's honour."

"What do you expect me to do?" he said with an ugly light in his eyes, "—sit by complacently and see you go to hell?"

"Do you want to go, too, and leave your people to die under the disgrace?"

The boy gave her an agonized look, and she gave him a white and terrible look in return.

"There's another way," she said harshly. "You can step out of my life—or I can step out of yours."

His visage grew ghastly.

"Either that, or I become your mistress.... Or, if you're afraid I'd be too unhappy, I'll go away, or kill myself—"

She leaned forward, twisting her fingers convulsively, her voice scarcely controlled:

"If you think you are in love, I'll prove I love you better. If your conscience resents me, unmarried to you, send me away. I'll go. It'll hurt you. But you'll get well and marry somebody—"

"Don't!—Gilda—"

"Well, then, what? *What?* Tell me! It's *your* agony. You can't go on—can't continue. Killing Sadoul won't help. I'm trying to find something to help *you*. Don't you understand? I'm trying to think of something to take away pain from *you!*"

"It isn't that—"

"It is! *I* can stand anything. When a girl loves as I love she can stand anything. It's love that keeps one dauntless. If you were dead, it would keep my head up. If you were my lover—and my pride agonising within me—it would keep my head high, and my heart in my eyes for you to see where love dwells!—"

She got up, flushed, trembling, excited, took a step or two past the tree, turned and came back to confront him.

"I don't ask you to look out for me," she said. "I can do that. It is you who need aid, who need counsel, education in the courage of love. If you want me you shall have me. If it would help you to have me go, I'll go. It's for you to find out and tell me what to do for you."

He got up, dumb, crimson to his temples, confused and scorched by the girl's fiery outburst. Something in his face excited her compassion, and she went on recklessly, feeling the tears in her eyes and throat:

"You have said to me that men of your race are not accustomed to defy convention. You must not think that I would defy it, lightly. What do you suppose brought me here to New York, friendless, alone? Defiance of age-old law. But not by me.

"That is why I never had a home. All the misery of my childhood and youth arose from that. And do you think I would defy lightly the law that still revenges itself on a girl because the dead are beyond its punishment?"

The boy leaned heavily on the mantel, his face buried on his arm.

"There's no way out of it," he said.

"The way out of it is what you choose to have me do." She came nearer, almost blinded by tears:

"There remains the last hope of all—to ask the Christ, who gave me resurrection, to stand by us, now.... If you wouldn't mind praying beside my bed—with me—"

He looked up; she could scarcely see, holding out one hand toward him.

They went into her room together, settled to their knees beside each other. Her low, trembling voice drove all other thought out of his mind.

"O God," she whispered, "let Stuart be my husband, somehow—so that if I misbehave it will be with him—and let me marry him—unless it would make him unhappy and ashamed, or alienate him from his parents.... Amen."

CHAPTER XXVI

It was Life's first hurricane for Stuart Sutton. It had arisen in fury out of nothing; caught him unprepared. Where was it driving him? On what unknown shore would it wreck him; in what maelstrom engulf him?

In the first hour he had ever set eyes on Gilda Greenway the tempest began to gather. With incredible swiftness it had burst within that hour.

Then, for the first time in his life, he had seen Death in the midst of

Life. He had known its stupefaction, its horror; had struggled against it in anguished incredulity.

Bewildered, almost hysterical, he had demanded justice and equity of the Unknown God. Justice had been accorded—by somebody—something—somehow or other. The horror had dissolved overnight; daylight ended the dream of evil. But the tempest was still blowing, imperceptibly gathering force; storm clouds thickened, writhing around this woman and himself.

Suddenly out of the whirling, infernal light burst love, in flames, already full grown, fully armed, dangerous.

Beyond, a desolate vista opened through grey years, and endless, purposeless, hopeless as ages born of hell—

Out of nothing had been hatched this hurricane—born of a green disguise, a smile, a little mask half lifted—a kiss given; passionately forgiven.

All, instantly, became part of the boy's life. Death also entered, lingered, lightly withdrew.

But now the boy was learning that Death had left behind that which is stronger than Death—a lovely and defenceless tenement haunted of shadows—a young girl's body for a battle-ground—a sanctuary where victim and assassin lurked, watching each other behind the temple of the mind.

Where was the tempest driving him? Shallows of passion, deeps of love—over these he had been hurried, blindly, without choice; and suddenly, low on the horizon, leered the red smear of murder.

So far had the tempest hurled him.

There came an hour, late on a winter afternoon, when the last clerk had left his office, the last letter had been signed, and he remained alone at his desk, determined now to face the apparition of the future.

Into a life which had been so accentless, so methodical, so pre-ordered as his own, had stepped from outer bournes a girl in pale silks and a pale green mask.

What was he to do with her?

He was trying, now, to think what to do. Distant doors closing averted him of departing stenographers, clerks, heads of departments. Now and then he could hear the muffled stir in adjoining offices, the slam of roll-top desks, murmur of voices, a distant laugh.

Behind him the coal fire burned low. He rose, stirred the coals, stood irresolutely looking at his overcoat, then walked to the window.

Outside the pinnacles of Manhattan glittered like cliffs and peaks of solid jewels. There was a young moon in the southwest—a mere tracery in the sky—then the towered masses of light, huge standing shapes of shadow—bridges with necklaces of gems festooned above an unseen river—and the deep, interminable roaring rumour from below—New York aspiring to the stars, growling in its caverns—New York monstrously breathing, pulsing, gigantically, vulgarly vital, exhaling its false aura under the stars.

He looked up at that little immemorial virgin, the moon, thin-edged, sly, spinster-like, malicious—like all who endure aborted.

In that glimmering magic framed by his window there seemed nothing friendly. He turned, instinctively, to the fire.

What was he to do? Letters from his mother were in his pocket. California was warm, and sunny with ripe oranges.... And his father played golf.

There were other letters in his pocket—some stacked up on his desk—to be acknowledged, answered somehow.

A familiar, inherited social routine had been disrupted almost without explanation since he had met Gilda Greenway.

He had been, practically, nowhere in that limited world reserved as a matter of course for young men of his particular genus.

Dinners, dances, theatres, country parties—the usual succession of events in which youth of his race mechanically participated—he had avoided since he had known Gilda.

It was not a sudden distaste, not even inertia, not indifference. Except for the civilised routine required in avoiding them the boy had become oblivious to any social responsibility.

To be forgotten overnight in New York is inevitable unless one employs effort to avert personal annihilation.

Stuart made no effort. Possibly, in the back of his crisp, blond head, he realised that it is easy for such men as he to reappear.

But for some time, now, the clubs, the society, the amusements he chose were not those familiar to his parents or to people composing those interlinked circles wherein the Suttons were accustomed to consider themselves at home.

What should he do about it?

Here was a girl he couldn't marry. Her world was utterly alien to his own; her little circle peopled by garish imitations of the real—by painted shadows on the screen of Life—Veronica, Eve, Katharine, Frances—by monstrous mouths—The Talkers—those who think they do life's work with wagging jaws—and by darker phantoms—by Sadoul, and Pockman, with his spasm-like smirk, and Lyken, handler of lightning—blasted cadavers—Harry Stayr, sensualist, grossly feeding a swathe through life; Julian Fairless, nimble painter in thin colours, nimble-witted as a thimble-rigger whose public pays for the living he claims it owes him; Derring, empty as his own falsetto voice, fussing in the wake of noisy youth, sniffing its perfumed pleasures, a high-pitched titter amid its noisy gossip.

What was he to do? What was he becoming? Where was the end? Was there no end? By stepping out, the whole unreal pageant would pass like a dream. All this—all these tinted marionettes would go jerkily by him, on and on, dwindling into toy perspective—somewhere—wherever they came from.

All would pass on along a preordained path—all this grotesque Noah's Ark—men, women, beasts—Nika, Eve, Pockman, Stayr—the pickled things in jars, the crippled rats and shreds of human flesh—the Monstrous Mouths—all Talkers—and the phantoms, too—Sadoul, Gilda—

What was happening to him? What was happening to the safe, familiar world about him? Once, death had been death—irrevocable, definite, an end. Now it was no longer an end. There was no end to life; not even any orthodox conclusion.

The world was peopled with deathless shapes—it swarmed with shadows—some malignant, like the wanton thing that haunted Gilda—that sensuous, red-lipped shape that sometimes hid within her and looked at him out of her dear eyes—

"I don't know what to do," he said aloud, staring vacantly at the coals. "I thought we were protected from such things—that such things never had existed.... I supposed God was in absolute control over evil—"

He became silent as though somebody had spoken. Listening, he seemed to hear the words again: "Deliver us from Evil."

It was his own mind answering him.

"But deliver us from evil," he repeated. And sat thinking for a while.

Were, then, such wandering, disincarnate intelligences—such indestructible and sinister individual survivals—a form of evil hitherto unrecognised—or not recognised since the gross superstitions of former days peopled the earth with malignant phantoms?

"Deliver us from evil." Was prayer the remedy? Was it a weapon? Was it the whine of a coward for protection to a dull, monstrous, tyrannical God, or was it a call to arms to an ally against a common enemy?

The boy stared at the whitening ashes. He did not know what to think, what to do, whether he loved enough, or loved rightly. There seemed to be no outlook, no solution, no help.

As he got up and took his overcoat from the peg, his desk telephone rang.

"Is it you, Gilda?" he said, happily.

"What in the world are you thinking of, darling? It's after eight and poor Freda is frantic about the dinner."

"I'm sorry," he said, but his face had cleared and his voice was joyous, "—I'm so sorry, dear. Tell me, are you all right?"

"Of course I am. Are you?"

"Yes—now. I'll come uptown immediately—"

"Don't dare stop to dress, Stuart!"

"No. Are you particularly and enchantingly gowned?"

"I hope you'll think so."

"Had you rather I ate in the kitchen?"

"You silly thing!"

"Which are you hungriest for, dinner or me?"

"If I survive till you arrive I'll tell you. Hurry, dear, I'm starving!"

CHAPTER XXVII

Sadoul came into the laboratory where Pockman was taking a tray of frozen rats out of a refrigerator.

Sadoul looked thin and stooped; his clothes flapped on him. He glanced at the rows of frozen rats with a wizened sneer:

"I feel like one of those, sometimes."

"Sometimes you look like one," returned Pockman. He tittered and carried the tray to a porcelain table. First he sponged off the table with some pale yellow solution, then he placed three frozen rats on it. The vermin were rigidly congealed. They lay there stiff as bits of metal, discoloured teeth and naked feet exposed.

"Is Gilda Greenway here?" inquired Sadoul.

"Not yet. Why?"

"I wanted to see her after you had made your observations."

"She's late," said Pockman, absently. He counted out three more rats, laid them on top of a wire-screened box, then returned the tray with the remainder of the rats to the refrigerator.

Sadoul looked into the box. On a bed of sand lay several rat-snakes coiled together for warmth. Pockman took a frozen rat by the tail, opened the lid of the box, and dropped the rodent. A slow head stirred in the composite snaky mass. There was no other movement.

"They won't take it that way," said Pockman. "The trouble is that I've got to be careful they don't bite me."

"They're not poisonous snakes."

"All ophidians are more or less poisonous."

"You think so?" asked Sadoul.

"I've yet to find one from which I couldn't extract venom of one sort or another. It's not always poisonous to man."

Pockman took the frozen rat by the tail and began to draw it across the sand. Like lightning the stroke came from the snaky mass—a ratsnake had the rodent by the head. The next instant Pockman jerked away the rat by the tail and tossed it onto the porcelain table.

"That's all I wanted," he snickered. "Now we'll try to find out what a gland will do to that virus."

He immersed the rat in a dark solution which was warming in a porcelain basin over a low-turned lamp.

"They can eat the others," he said, taking the two remaining rats by the tails and dragging them across the sand.

Instantly a snake struck. After a few moments the snake's jaws widened spasmodically and a gush of saliva wet the frozen fur. Pockman went back to his simmering rodent; Sadoul watched the revolting process in the box.

The other snake took more time—less hungry perhaps—and held the rat crossways as a pickerel holds a minnow before bolting it by the head.

Pockman, busy with his four rats, and using a gland macerated to pulp for grafting, heard Sadoul cough now and then.

"If I had that bark I'd take it to Arizona," he said. "Why the hell don't you get your sputum analyzed?"

Sadoul dropped the wire lid and came over to the table.

"Pockman," he said, "did you ever tell anybody about those blueprints?"

"No. Why?"

"Sutton once said something to me."

"I've never uttered a word. What did Sutton say?"

"Nothing definite. He asked me why I was standing behind those curtains at Derring's that night."

After a moment Pockman leered at him sideways:

"*Were* you?"

"Whether I were or were not," returned Sadoul calmly, "he had no knowledge of it."

Pockman worked on, using a syringe. Presently:

"I'll tell you something, Sadoul. When little Miss Greenway lay dead on the chair where Sutton had propped her, with the misericordia imbedded in the nape of her neck, she—that is, her still living mind—saw you come out from behind those curtains."

"She told you that?"

"She did. Probably she has told Sutton. Is that an explanation?"

Sadoul slowly nodded.

"How long," he asked, "does consciousness persist in the brain after death?"

"For some appreciable time. It varies."

"If I had been there could she have been conscious of it?"

"Certainly," snickered Pockman.

"For how long?"

"I tell you the time varies. The process of death is, as you know, a slow and gradual detachment of the indestructible or etheric body from the corpse. There is resistance, sometimes. Some people die hard. There seems usually to be some difficulty."

"What is the average length of time it takes to detach the etheric body from the cadaver?"

"I couldn't tell you. I don't think we've struck any average, yet. You are as familiar as I am with the process.

"In a quick and easy death the cold creeps upward from the extremities to the brain. You and I have observed the procedure of the etheric body as it detaches itself from the physically dying body.

"Something—some occult energy—seems to shake the etheric body, or soul—loosen it, so to speak. When this lateral movement ceases, millions of gentle vibrations begin, from the soles of the feet, upward. The indestructible soul-principle begins to withdraw from the extremities, upward, toward the head. Life slowly fades at the knees, the thighs, the hips, the chest.... You and I have seen that faint brilliancy gathering around the head. That, I fancy, is where the delay usually occurs."

"I think the brain dies hard," said Sadoul.... "I wonder how long it takes."

Pockman shrugged and continued to wrap up his rats in sterilised cheese-cloth and deposit each one in a sort of incubator.

Sadoul roamed about the place; Pockman had finished washing and drying his hands when the door opened and Gilda Greenway came in.

The cold had made her pink; her furs accented the exquisite colour. Under her toque the gold-red hair edged her cheeks with burnished flame.

"How do you do, Dr. Pockman?" she said cheerfully.

"I'm sorry I am so late—" She caught sight of Sadoul. "Oh, I didn't know you were here!"

Her face altered, yet still remained smiling—an odd little smile, slightly humorous, slightly guarded, faintly sarcastic, and entirely devoid of fear.

He offered to shake hands with her, and she accepted with the hint of a shrug.

To Pockman she said: "Aren't you nearly finished investigating me? You must have volumes already on the history of my case."

Pockman tittered, smirked, hitched his shoulders, started jerkily for his private office. The girl turned, nodded to Sadoul, her gloved hand on the door.

"Could I see you when you've finished with Pockman?" asked Sadoul.

"If you like."

"I'll be in my end of the place."

"Very well."

She went out; Pockman teetered after her. Sadoul's shadowy visage still remained red from the encounter. He had joined his bony hands and was twisting them as though to subdue physical pain. His sunken eyes seemed filmy, unseeing, as he turned his head with the curious, nosing motion of a blind thing caged, striving to realise its limits.

After a patient examination, Miss Cross being present to record all observations, Gilda drew a quick breath of relief, smiled whimsically at Miss Cross, picked up her muff.

"You're destined to be a very celebrated young lady," said Miss Cross, smiling, "—if you permit Dr. Pockman to use your name in this report."

Gilda laughed. "He has agreed to mention me as Miss X. I don't wish to be celebrated as a pathological prodigy."

"You're a prodigy all right," snickered Pockman. "I am given to understand that you're even a more amazing girl than you appear to be to me."

"What do you mean, Dr. Pockman?"

"Psychically. I understand that you have an extraordinary potentiality. It's rather a pity you don't like Sadoul."

"I don't dislike him," she said quietly.

"I thought you did."

"I do not like some things about him. Otherwise, I have always been rather fascinated by his cleverness and intelligence. He can be an extraordinarily agreeable companion."

Pockman said in a low voice: "I never supposed you had any use for Sadoul except to torment him—even," he added, "when you let him take you to parties."

The girl flushed and glanced at Miss Cross. The latter, however, was beyond earshot; and left the room the next moment.

"That's what I hate about Sadoul," said Gilda, quickly, "—the material side of him. It angers me. It arouses cruelty. I have a contempt for that side of him, and he knows it!"

Pockman held no brief for Sadoul, but the girl's scorn seemed to pepper his sex generally.

"After all," he remarked, "he's only in love with you."

"Physically," she retorted, reddening.

"Well—my God—" began Pockman, thinking in terms of glands, but the girl interrupted:

"That's part of it, I suppose. In fact, I know it, now. And I don't wish to know any more about it—not from him—not from anybody.... What has he to say to me? Do you know, Dr. Pockman?"

"Well, I rather suspect it's something concerning your unusual psychic possibilities."

"Do you mean *his?*"

"I mean yours, Gilda."

"I didn't know I had any—independent of Sadoul's."

"His amount to little compared to yours," said Pockman.

She gazed at him incredulously; he smirked at her. "Te-hee," he tittered, "how do you suppose you've fought him off?"

"With mind and will."

"I mean in subconscious conditions—in successive periods of hypnosis—even in phases of obsession—how do you suppose you have held him off?"

"My soul is captain of my mind—whatever else invades my body to betray it!"

"How did you know that?"

"I don't know. My soul seems to know."

"And so you fight it out, between soul and body?"

"At times."

Pockman snickered, but his pale eyes were intent on her:

"Soul always comes out top dog, I suppose," he said. "There are no drawn battles, Gilda—"

"Yes, there are," she said, crimsoning at her own honesty.

"No drawn battles in which Sadoul figures? Hey?"

"No."

"Another man?"

"Yes."

"And the other man has only to chip in to turn the tide of war one way or the other?"

"Yes."

"Does he know this?"

"Yes. He stands as ally to my real self. Our minds are comrades."

"You're at his mercy then?"

"When the dark change comes, I am."

"Thin ice," tittered Pockman. "A man's a man. He's likely to change his battle-hymn to a Cytherean rag." Again judgment, conclusion were arrived at in terms of glands. Why not? The world's work is done through them. The world's Talk continues for lack of them.

"Cats and kittens," snickered Pockman. "It all filters out finally to these. You needn't fear Sadoul. You know it.... Of course, I don't see why you need fear anything. But folk-ways rule the world of folk. Taboo remains tyrant. Always will. However, there'll always be kittens."

Gilda turned aside and looked out of the window.

"Nice girl," said Pockman. "Morals are fashions. Always keep up with the latest creations. Smartness wins."

"Are you on Sadoul's side?" she asked, her face still averted.

"On the contrary. The biggest lie ever hatched is that all the world loves a lover. Half the world is masculine. The only lovers they love are themselves.... No; I'm not on Sadoul's side. I'm not on any *man's* side."

Gilda continued to gaze out of the window. What she looked at was rusty chimney pots against a heavenly blue sky. What the girl saw is another thing—for her eyes were as remote as the skies.

After a little while: "Is there anything abnormal about me, Dr. Pockman?" she asked, turning her head.

"No, Gilda.... No, not in a morbid sense, anyway."

At that she slowly faced around:

"You speak with reserve."

He hesitated; an unhealthy colour came into his flat face.

"It is possible," he said, "that, transplanting a brand new and very vigorous young nymphalic gland may have—have over-stimulated you a little—added powerfully, perhaps, to a naturally ardent physique."

Under his twitching smirk the girl lowered her eyes. She stood looking at her muff, pinching the fur with white-gloved fingers, smoothing it out.

"There is nothing to distress you in what I said," insisted Pockman. "You've doubled your natural vitality, that's all. You've doubled your years of youth, probably. You're to be envied, Gilda."

"I don't know. I may find life too long.... I was thinking that, the other day."

He looked at her keenly: "I suppose you can't get rid of Sadoul," he said in a lower voice. "He won't stand for it, will he?"

She shook her head.

"Can't have you himself and won't let any other man," commented Pockman with a subdued snigger. "Well, that's man—except in novels.... Or among the glandless. A Talker will talk himself into anything. Words are all he lives. If you'd been married to a Talker, now, he'd have done a lot of fine phrasing—talked himself into a thousand attitudes—but he'd have let you go.... Sadoul won't. He'll follow. He'll fight. I don't know what else he might do."

"Nor I," she said absently. "I think he is capable of killing me."

Pockman stole a look at the door.

"You obsessed him from the first. I think his mental balance isn't what it once was. I'm always noticing. He's suspicious—difficult to observe. I'd walk pussy-foot for the time being. After all, you've got time. You've more time coming to you than he has. He was handicapped anyway before I gave you a new gland. That man has no chance. Play the lady Fabian. That's where he loses. He can't wait. He can't stand the pace of Time. It's your make as the cards lie. Take your time."

She said in a low voice: "It's a ghastly game. It's cruel, revolting.... And he is so clever, so interesting—fascinating intellectually.... And has winning qualities. To subdue me, bend me to his will—dominate and direct my inclination—this is a tragic madness with him. All else is sane, likable, attractive. I ask no more amusing comrade, no more stimulating companion.... Only—underlying everything is the pitiable tragedy of a man sane on all subjects excepting one. And on that, ruthless, brutal, inexorable."

"Idée fixe," muttered Pockman. "You may expect anything from that egg.... Are you going in to see him?"

She nodded; he opened the door for her.

CHAPTER XXVIII

The room which Gilda peeped into resembled a chemical laboratory in a way. There was some equipment for physical research, also, an X-ray machine, a camera, electrical apparatus, dry batteries, arc lights, incandescent lights, Hewett-tubes, other paraphernalia less familiar. There was also a bare table and several uncomfortable chairs. A dark cabinet adjoined, hung with black velvet draperies.

Sadoul was seated on one of the small chairs, his thin elbows on his knees, his shadowy face framed in both hands. He got up as though fatigued when she came forward.

"Gilda," he said in a peculiarly agreeable voice, without any taint of the habitual sneer, "you are doing a lot of things to help Sidney Pockman. He's building future fame on your kindness. Submitting yourself to his observations means everything in the world to him."

"I'd be disgustingly selfish not to help him," she said, seating herself. "Whatever I am," she added lightly, "I'm not ungrateful." She rested her muff on the table and looked amiably, almost wistfully, at Sadoul.

He dropped both elbows on the same table, propping his chin on interlinked fingers—the pale, bony fingers of a sick man.

"I wondered," he said, "whether if I asked you'd be willing to help me a step or two toward fame and fortune." Irony in his voice was faint but it was there.

"Always," she said, "—reasonably."

"Would you lend yourself to an experiment or two?"

"Of what nature?"

"Psychic."

"Am I psychic, independently of you?"

"Unusually so."

"What do you wish me to do for you?"

"I want you to give me a chance to study your two selves at close range, with every paraphernalia, every equipment, every condition favourable to exhaustive observation."

A slight flush mounted to her cheeks: they looked intently at each other across the table.

"I have only one self—excepting the intruder you let in," she said curtly.

"There are always two selves, Gilda. What you call the *Other One* belonged to you. You say I called her in. She was already in attendance. She always has been. She's part of you—not the stranger you think—not an intruder from outer regions."

"She is *not* part of me!" cried the girl, blushing.

"She is and always has been," he repeated calmly; "—but she always had remained aloof—outside—during your waking hours. When you slept she crept in and slept, also. All I did was to awake her before it was time. And when you died, and your other self resisted her entrance, I gave her ingress. That is all I did; I aroused her before the—the conventional hour for her awakening had arrived. And when you fought to evict her, and bar yourself against her, I merely let her in."

He bent his cadaverous head; one hand shaded his eyes.

"I'm sorry I meddled," he said. "She has proved no friend to me."

Gilda fixed her eyes on her locked fingers.

She said slowly and without resentment: "It was a devilish thing to do to a girl."

She looked up, saw in his fixed gaze regret—not for what he had done, but because it had failed.

"You were willing to carry me to hell with you," she said.

"If there were no other way. Besides, there is no hell, except what I'm in now."

"Sadoul?"

"Yes, Gilda."

"How did you happen to be behind that curtain?"

He denied his presence, pleasantly.

"I was thinking," she said, "if you could do such a devilish thing as you did to me, perhaps you killed me."

"*Tu mihi solus eras.* I did not kill you, Gilda."

"With a misericordia?"

"Why?" he asked, patiently good humoured.

She dropped her head, thinking of Stuart and their first kiss. Then, vague eyed, she regarded Sadoul.

Strange scenes in her long resistance against this man took shape and faded in her mind. It seemed odd that she hated him so little—and only one phase of him. It seemed strange how much of sorrow, of pity, of wistfulness tempered her resentment—how much attraction remained, inclination to overlook, understand, forgive, this blazing, ruthless mind which had failed to subdue hers.

She looked sadly at his features, marred and worn and sunken by the sickness of aborted passion.

Undaunted, his deep set, smouldering eyes returned her gaze. Within that great, bony frame the dull fire burned on, stealthily devouring him. In his ravaged features she marked its devastation. And it would burn on, consuming all—even his mind in the end. She could not look at him unmoved.

Impulsively she placed a slim, gloved hand on his. She saw that her own cause was hopeless, appeal useless. But she was not thinking of herself.

"I am not your enemy," she said. "I'll help you if I can."

"You trust me?" he asked.

"No, Sadoul."

"You are afraid?"

She laughed miserably: "Oh, no, I'm not afraid. I never was. I'm so sorry you never understood that."

"I did understand. I knew it. The fear was mine alone. Fear! The most terrible thing in the world. Fear is the real Slayer; Death the gentle, grave physician who assists at the birth of souls. Death—the world's family doctor—wise, kind, faithful, always on time. He shuts the door against Fear and locks it. He delivers the soul, patiently, skillfully. He severs the natal cord. A new birth is tenderly accomplished."

"What have you feared, Sadoul?"

"To live without you."

Tears flooded her eyes: "I couldn't—under God—" she faltered. "I couldn't—I couldn't, Sadoul—"

She buried her face between her arms. Sadoul looked at her in silence: gazed, burned on.

After a little while she got up, found a handkerchief in her muff.

"I'm sorry," she said. She remained busy with her handkerchief for a few moments. Then:

"You'll have to show me what you wish me to do.... When shall I come?"

He suggested a day; asked her if she were free. She nodded. After a short silence she turned and walked toward the door.

He opened it for her. After she had gone he stood so, for a long while, peering down the empty corridor and nosing the silence like a great beast blinded, bereft, confused by its unutterable isolation.

CHAPTER XXIX

It being Saturday, Sutton came uptown early and found Gilda lying on the couch before the fire, still clad in a loose Chinese lounging robe and slippers.

"You're outrageously late," she said. "I've had no breakfast."

"Why didn't you wake up?"

"The bed was warm and I lazy. It doesn't excuse you for keeping breakfast waiting. You annoy me, Stuart."

He came over to her but she refused to kiss him, lay warm and spineless in his arms, half lifted from the couch.

"Darling, I'm sorry," he said. "I can feel that you've lost several pounds. You're wasting away!"

Her face remained averted but he could see she was smiling. Then, gradually her arms encircled his neck; she looked up at him, tenderly humorous, pretending defiance.

"You bully me," she said. "Kindly remove that blond head!"

"You're holding it."

"Am I? Well, it's mine. I don't know what to do with it either."

She considered him, searched him with hostile eyes, then with a swift sigh relented and gave him her lips.

Freda brought the card-table and spread it. Gilda, on the couch, one knee crossed over the other, glanced absently through the morning paper, pausing between pages to reach out her pretty hand to Stuart.

"Bosh," she said, "listen to this, Stuart: 'In response to cheers the President doffed his hat.' Did you ever hear anything as vulgarly expressed? A gentleman lifts his hat; an old gaffer 'doffs' it. Can you imagine the American newspaper as an educational influence? Or a schoolmaster using double negatives?"

Stuart laughed: "The Great American Boob doesn't know the difference. His native tongue, properly written, perplexes and annoys him. Like Mr. Lillyvick he doesn't 'like the langwidge.' Besides, it is he who is writing our newspapers and our novels for us; and he likes what he writes; he likes it fine, Gilda. *He* would doff *his* hat. What does he know about other people? Don't ever be afraid of anarchy. The terrifying part of the social revolution in America was accomplished long ago."

The girl swung her slippered foot and laughed, carelessly turning the pages of the great New York daily.

"I thought you were a good republican," she said. "Are you doomed to the guillotine, too?"

He smiled: "I love my country passionately," he said. "The people in it are its only defects."

"Oh, dear!" she exclaimed. "I can see where our heads are going to fall some day. Mine always did fall every time the blade dropped in the Place de la Revolution."

"I didn't know *you* felt that way."

"How should you know how a girl feels whom you picked up at Derring's? Dame Theroigne was a natural inference—"

"Good heavens," he protested, "—stop that baby chatter—"

"Didn't you pick me up?"

"Are you serious?"

"No, darling. You can't tell where you'll find a lost diamond, or why the setting wore out. They're even found in sewers, you know—"

"What the deuce," he exclaimed, irritated by her wayward humour.

"You sweet thing," she said, "I'm bad tempered because I'm hungry. You know I don't belong in a sewer. So do I. Where on earth is Freda?" She jerked the paper open again, swung her foot with the nervous grace of a kitten switching its tail.

"I'm cross," she remarked, "because I haven't a vocation."

"Do you want one, dear?"

"No, I don't."

They both laughed and she flung the paper at him.

"I don't want to do anything except be your wife," she said, swinging her slim foot to and fro and clasping her knee with both hands.

"I want children, too," she said with a rebellious little kick. Her slipper flew. He got up and replaced it, touching her instep with his lips.

"All that," he said, "is a vocation to which no other can compare."

"I don't believe you want me for your wife, Stuart."

"You believe it utterly."

She turned to him, searched his face. Slowly the smile dawned, deep-eyed, heavenly. She rested her cheek on her shoulder and watched him; abandoned her hand to him, her eyes, vaguely sweet, following his still caresses.

Freda came with breakfast, but they scarcely took the trouble to separate.

However, the grossly material perfume of hot muffins aroused Gilda from ethereal bowers, and she sat up hungrily surveying the tray.

During breakfast she told him about her promise to Sadoul, explained what was wanted of her.

He was hearing this for the first time, could not comprehend, was not at all edified.

"You darling," she said, vigorously occupied with bacon and coffee, "do you suppose I'd do anything I shouldn't?"

"I can't see how you can endure that man—"

"Nonsense! I always shall find him interesting. Whatever he did to me has wrecked him, not me.... And it may seem strange to you—to a man—but a woman is sorry.... If she really has been loved, she can't hate utterly. Sad indifference, regret for a man fiercely wasted, unhappy solicitude for mad perversity which brings only agony and disaster—these all generous women feel.... Once, on a lonely mountain, my collie dog went crazy and attacked me. Chasing me he fell into an abandoned well. I went back and saw the dog swimming around and 'round in the bottom of the well. There was no ladder, no rope, no way to save him. It tore my breast to look at him. I wanted to go away—but the creature had seen me, and kept up a horrible sort of screaming as it struggled.... I thought it did not want to die entirely alone.... It almost killed me to remain. But I—I talked to him—until the end."

"Where was this?"

"In Wales, when I was a child."

"It's like you, Gilda."

"It's like any woman—if a thing once loved her."

"You are willing to help Sadoul in his research work?"

"I am helping Dr. Pockman. I couldn't refuse Sadoul. He's not very successful. His books are partial failures. Outside of the free-lance press nobody reads him, nobody hears of Sadoul. Besides, I am not—untouched—by his unhappiness."

She lifted her lovely, honest eyes to Stuart:

"Out of your own abundance," she said, "give something to this man."

"You are giving."

"Not without permission."

"Dearest," he said, deeply stirred, "what you choose to do is my choice always."

"I knew it. Your will is mine, also." She smiled at him.

"What time are you due there?" he asked without enthusiasm.

"At three. But you are coming with me, of course."

"That may not please Sadoul."

"That," she remarked, "is of no consequence whatever. I never intended to go without you."

He drew a sharp breath of relief. "All right," he said.

CHAPTER XXX

At the laboratory they were shown into the small reception room. There was nothing there except a wired crate marked "Cobra. Do not handle."

"That's amusing," remarked Stuart. "What does Pockman want of a cobra?"

Miss Cross, in her neat uniform, came in. She remembered Sutton, gave him a quick look, clear, interested, but without conclusion concerning their appearance together for the second time within her personal experience.

She shook hands smilingly with Gilda, turned to Stuart, quizzical, amused:

"A more agreeable reunion than our first association, Mr. Sutton."

"Yes," he said. "I was pretty badly scared."

"You were the most tragic young man I ever beheld. You wouldn't smoke."

"You were very nice to me," he said, forcing a rather painful smile.

"I was sorry for you—" She looked at Gilda, "sorrier for you, dear. But it turned into a happy miracle." She smiled, looking from one to the other, the invisible and delicate antennae of feminine intuition exploring the situation without comprehension, until Gilda looked at Stuart, and the boy returned the fleeting glance.

Miss Cross knew, then. But that was all she knew.

Gilda inquired for a dressing room; Miss Cross took her away to hers. Stuart started to pace the narrow floor, but a door opened and Sadoul came in.

He was prepared to see Sutton; Gilda had averted him by telephone, tersely, hanging up as he began to demur.

"Come in, Sadoul," said Stuart coolly. "I'm rather relieved at the opportunity to tell you that I spoke thoughtlessly the other day."

"Oh, no," said Sadoul, "you'd thought it all out."

Sutton reddened. "Yes, I had. And I came here to say what I did say."

"Have you changed your mind?"

"Yes; I shan't ever kill you. It's one solution, but not a satisfactory one."

Sadoul laughed. "You mean not a respectable one. I'd die only once, but the Hudson River Suttons would die every day that they lived—" A fit of coughing interrupted him.

The colour in Stuart's face deepened.

"Undoubtedly. That's the only reason it's no solution for our problem."

"The problem's yours," remarked Sadoul, "not mine. As for Gilda, she belongs to me—whatever you and she choose to do about it. But I don't worry. The Gods of the Mountain—the Holy Catskills—will hold *you* to respectability. As for Gilda, her chastity is—more—admirable—"

Another fit of convulsive coughing shook his bony frame. He wiped his face, looked sneeringly at Stuart:

"What a gift of God is a truly good young man," he said. "But a respectable young man is a pearl without price—" Another access of coughing seized him. The crisis passed. He leered at Stuart, unable to speak.

The rushing, confused impulse to kill this man surged, ebbed, passed, leaving the boy dazed and pale.

"I thought you'd do it," panted Sadoul; "it would have been worth it to me to make a clean sweep of all Suttons. You got rather white. But respectability is a sheet-anchor and the Highlands of the Hudson a firm fortress—"

The words choked in his throat: a thin stream of bright blood squirted from his mouth—gushed over his chin.

Moments of silence, terribly significant: Sadoul, eyes closed, sopping his mouth with crimsoned handkerchief, the boy staring.

Sadoul opened his eyes, red with hell. His shoulders sagged, his gaunt chest heaved, he leaned trembling against the wall like a horse, sinking by the withers.

"Can I do anything, Sadoul?" ventured the boy in a ghostly voice.

Sadoul nodded: "Yes, mind your business."

"I don't care what you say to me."

"I don't either." Sadoul sat down, rested for a while, got up.

"Are you all right?" asked Stuart.

Their eyes met. Both knew now it was only a waiting game. And, with this astounding knowledge, the boy softened.

"You ought to go away," he said. "I'll play square."

"Arizona and a clean shirt?" sneered Sadoul. He looked at his wet handkerchief, at his stained hands.

"Play square, eh?" he repeated. "Well, that's a little more than being respectable. That's emotional. Respectability doesn't admit of any except prescribed and predigested emotions. Be prudent, Sutton, or your ancestors will squirm underground."

Stuart said: "Well, whatever you do I'll play square, Sadoul. I think I'd do it on my own account. But Gilda likes you—"

Sadoul, on his way out, paused at the door.

"You're never going to have her," he said. "So don't lie awake on my account."

He went out, leaving the door ajar. Sutton heard him in the washroom.

A little later Gilda returned alone, noticed his expression, came to him, questioningly.

"It's nothing. Sadoul was here. We always upset each other."

"I know it. I hated to ask you to come."

Pockman came in at his crazy gait, arms jerking and dangling and his face glistening with sweat.

"All ready," he said. "Lyken is in there with an electrician and camera man. I hope we'll get something. How do you feel, Miss Greenway?"

She smiled and said she felt very well indeed.

"Is Sutton expected to be present?" he asked with a smirk.

"Certainly," she said, "—if I am."

"Oh, sure!' He cast a stealthy glance at Stuart, then led the way out.

It was the same room in which she had last seen Sadoul. Except that the various machines were ready to go into action, and a lot of flowers about, the room was the same.

Dr. Lyken shook hands with her; the electrician and camera-man bowed.

Miss Cross came in with another young woman in uniform—a Miss Parry, who seated herself prepared to make stenographic records and fill in charts.

The electrician took up his station; to control and direct the delicate gradation of light was one of his jobs. The camera-man's assistant entered. A few minutes later Sadoul appeared, went immediately to Gilda. She removed her hat. Miss Cross took it. They consulted in quiet voices for a while, then she went with Sadoul into the dark cabinet.

Almost immediately Sadoul came out alone and nodded to Pockman. Lyken and Stuart also followed. The interior of the cabinet was very dark. Pockman flashed an electric torch.

Gilda lay on a fur rug on the floor, partly resting on her right side, her legs a little drawn up. Both hands covered her face. She did not stir. Her breathing was regular and quiet. Temperature, pulse, heart action, blood-pressure, all proved normal.

"Nothing morbid in that trance," said Pockman in a cautious tone.

They returned to their chairs near the table. Lights faded to a discreet twilight. Miss Parry withdrew to a corner where a shaded bulb hung low.

"Is that camera ready?" asked Sadoul.

Lyken whispered to Stuart: "He's using a quartz lens. They'll flood the room with violet rays when they shoot."

Pockman, on the other side of him, said: "The only thing to do is to settle the question definitely one way or another: whether these forces that 'sensitives' possess, and which induce psychical phenomena, are merely forces of nature at present unknown to us, or forces exerted by living identities which have survived physical death."

Sadoul, speaking in a natural voice, said to Lyken: "I've used a microscope on the body exudations from a highly sensitized medium. It disclosed living cells of a type not found in the human body."

"Was there a nucleus to each cell?"

"Positively."

Lyken seemed startled. "What are we to expect, now, from little Miss Greenway?" he inquired of Pockman.

"Dual projection, I believe."

"Materialization?"

"Yes," said Sadoul.

At that moment the vague dark draperies of the cabinet were flung aside and a young girl in white stepped out.

From somewhere a cool breeze stirred in the room, blowing the perfume of the cut flowers.

"Camera!" said Sadoul quietly. And, to the electrician: "Violet, please."

The figure in white came forward tranquilly, unembarrassed. As she neared the table a book lying there caught her eye, and she paused, turned the pages curiously, as though interested.

"It's Einstein's book," whispered Lyken. "If she can understand that she's better than I am."

The figure raised its head, smiling, as though she had overheard the remark.

She was a trifle shorter than Gilda, like her in a celestial way, with a more dazzling skin.

"Are you Gilda?" asked Sadoul.

"Yes," she said quietly. Her voice was like Gilda's, with another indefinable quality—something exquisitely lark-like, unsullied as pure song showered down from skies.

"Look at the *Other!*" exclaimed Lyken.

Sadoul called to the electrician: "Flood!" And to the camera-man, "Go on shooting. Get them both together!"

Stuart sat rigid in his chair, gripping it. He saw the *Other One* advancing, brilliant in white, exquisitely indolent, every movement gracefully sensuous, and her mouth a red flower in the demi-light.

She paused beside the table, leaned on it, bending her face to the flowers.

"Are you Gilda?" asked Sadoul unsteadily.

She looked up and laughed. Stuart saw her clearly for the first time, and trembled a little, so lovely she was. The other figure leaned there beside her, too, near-smiling, fresh, exquisite, unsullied.

"Sadoul," said the *Other One*, "why do you try to create dissension between us?" She encircled the other's waist. The latter looked seriously at Sadoul: "We are in harmony. Why do you try to separate us? Why try to distinguish between us? If you separate us you make us self-conscious. You offer us violence, Sadoul."

Sadoul got up from his chair. Both figures laid their hands on his. He drew them a little way aside.

"God," said Pockman, sweating, "that's going some! For Christ's sake keep on grinding that camera, you —"

Sadoul held the two white figures by their right hands resting between his own.

He said: "Is *that* why there is no hope for me? I didn't understand."

The *Other One* said: "You sow dissension between us who are twins. Didn't you understand that we really are one?"

"No.... That is the reason, then."

They nodded: "That is the reason, Sadoul."

He stood for a little while with dark head lowered, retaining their hands. The *Other One* seemed impatient; her companion drew a stem of freesia from the vase on the table and laid it in Sadoul's hand where her own had been lying.

Then she leisurely crossed the room, passing so close to Sutton that her white garment touched him, and he felt the breathing warmth of her body.

"Gilda," he whispered.

She paused, looked down at him.

"That's no ghost," said Lyken, nervously. "Ask her if she'll let you take her in your arms."

The figure looked uncertainly at Sutton as he rose.

"I won't hurt you," he whispered.

"Be very gentle," she said. "*She* is asleep in the cabinet and you could easily hurt her."

She came into his arms, rested against him, a warm young creature, a living, breathing shape.

"Is she real?" demanded Lyken.

"Absolutely."

"Then somebody had better look into that cabinet," he said, almost violently. "Reason is reason and a joke's a joke, God da—"

The *Other One*, passing near, closed his mouth with her slim hand, and Lyken nearly fainted on his chair.

"Get out if you can't control yourself," said Sadoul coldly. And, to Pockman: "Take their pulse and temperature."

The slender figure in Sutton's embrace released herself, rested one hand on his arm and leaned down to re-open the book. The page that interested her was printed solid with mathematics.

"Do you understand that?" whispered Sutton.

"Yes. How simple and interesting."

Pockman came with a clinical thermometer and Sutton stepped back.

He watched nervously the procedure—the tests made with this radiant being—the weighing, the stethoscope, the vial for saliva, a microscopic paring from a finger-nail, a few red-gold hairs, a tear duct excited and the secretion caught and bottled while the lovely creature laughed.

Pockman and Sadoul, camera-man and electrician, and the stenographer, Miss Parry, were busy for hours, it seemed to Sutton.

Gradually the lights had been increased to an intensity where photography required nothing else to aid it. Lyken, inert on his chair, slack-jawed and pop-eyed, merely stared and stared, utterly valueless as any assistance. The *Other One*, who had come curiously to look at Sutton once or twice, and who did not seem very friendly toward him, now smiled at him for the first time, rather shyly. "I am glad you did not touch me," she said. "Someday, perhaps. We are going now. Good-bye."

Sadoul turned from the camera: "Have you got to go?"

They nodded smilingly.

"I want to ask one more thing of you," he said, following the two figures toward the cabinet. "I beg you to let us see you both, with Gilda lying asleep at your feet. Will you do this?"

They seemed uncertain, whispered together for a moment. Then the *Other One* nodded.

Pockman and Sutton joined them; Lyken lurched up from his chair and stumbled toward the cabinet.

It was very dark inside.

Sadoul reached up and turned on a flood of light.

Gilda lay as they had left her, her face in her hands. Beside her the two white figures looked down at her, gravely.

"Camera!" said Sadoul, with an effort. "Pull that curtain wide, Sutton!" In the silence they heard behind them the grinding of the machine.

"Turn off the light," said the *Other One* to Sadoul.

"Must I?"

"Yes."

He closed and bolted the door, lifted a bony arm and plunged the cabinet into darkness. Nobody moved for a few minutes except Lyken, swaying on legs that scarce supported him. Then Sadoul turned on the light. Both white figures were gone.

On the rug at their feet Gilda sighed and stirred and opened her eyes.

CHAPTER XXXI

The daily grind down town was beginning to wear on young Sutton. It was not the routine of business, not the new responsibility that dragged him; it was the constant depression, the interminable whining. Gloom possessed the canons of the district like a dirty fog from the bay. Nobody did anything except snivel about the rottenness exposed by the several investigating committees, Civil, State, and Federal.

The interminable jeremiad set men's nerves on edge; nothing was to be looked for from the moribund Administration and only mischief came from it—the last spiteful and convulsive clawing at the people who had done it to death.

Pygmy wrath, miserable bunkum, sullen inertia—these were to be endured until March. Then the rat-pit would be empty and ready for fumigation.

Meanwhile, those joyless bacteria which feed and propagate on gloom became noisier in their bigoted zeal, boasting of their ability to blackmail a cowardly Congress. Paul Pry was at the keyhole; Mrs. Grundy at her window; Torquemada junior, an itinerant advance-agent, notifying a half-educated people from the Gulf to the Lakes that the incredibly cruel and stupid old god of Sabbath had come back to burn all heretics.

"Believe as I believe or I'll roast you," bawled Torquemada junior. "It pleases me to twiddle my thumbs on Sunday; and you'd better twiddle yours or I'll know the reason why!"

Time's great pendulum was being swung by fools too violently and too far forward. The backward swing was nearly due. A patient people, mostly ignorant or semi-educated, looked on, confused by the din of the fools and the Talkers.

But they were the people who had suddenly arisen in spite of the Administration and battered the face of Destiny out of all recognition.

The people who had burned for a space, transfigured in the blazing beauty of their Flaming Sword. And had dulled to a cinder, and returned to their millions of wallows, grunting of grandeur—the wonder, laughter, and sorrow of the world they saved for the sake of Jesus Christ.

The lumber business, in common with all affairs, remained in the doldrums.

Financing anything through old and accustomed channels was now the idlest of dreams.

Also an open winter in the Northland did not help. There was little snow. Logs were difficult to move. And when, late in January, arctic cold settled over a naked North, it was not good for forests.

Stuart Sutton worried a great deal. He worried about logs; he feared for the new plantations unprotected by snow. They sent him reports of depredations by deer—miles of browse—balsam, hemlock, Norway spruce cleaned out.

Slashings and danger of fire in reforested regions were ever in his mind; the weevil was a nightmare, too. But most terrifying of all to him was the white-pine blight—that dreadful, leprous thing out of the Orient. And he turned the ledger pages devoted to extirpation of wild and cultivated current and gooseberry, and figured out the cost of saving from extinction the noblest tree that ever grew in North America.

Only less noble was the chestnut, now, from another leprous blight, almost extinct. And upon the lumber-men of the land lay the responsibility for the survival of the white pine.

Letters from his father and mother in California were a trifle disturbing, too. They had heard that their son and heir infrequently decorated those social circles wherein, since Colonial days, the Hudson River Suttons were accustomed to gyrate. They confidently laid it to the exactions of business, fatigue from overwork. And cautioned him against it.

Which tender admonition hurt his Sutton conscience; in a rush of remorse he accepted a number of invitations; reappeared among his kind for a few weeks, bored and impatient at losing all that time away from Gilda; and then dropped out again—Gilda and the lumber business being all he could possibly attend to in life.

Suspecting this state of affairs, the girl chided him.

"You mustn't give up your family's friends," she said. "Such ties are generations in making. They are worth something, mean something. If one has an undisputed place in the social fabric, one should not vacate it without a reason. I know how that is," she added with a light, unconscious sigh.

They were seated before the fire in her living room. He reached over and rested one hand on hers.

"Do you care to tell me a little, dear?" he asked.

She did not misunderstand him, though not prepared for a demand of confidence so intimate.

After a short silence, and absently caressing his hand where it lay on her lap:

"There was domestic unhappiness when I was a child. My parents separated. Mortification made my father a recluse. My mother spent the remainder of her life in Europe—until the tragic end."

She took his hand between both of hers, pressed it, clung a little:

"The courts," she said, "left me under joint control.... I understand, now, that my father's attitude toward me was not aversion; it was that the sight of me made his shame and grief unendurable.

"My mother was much younger. She cared for gaiety and the brightness of things. She was very pretty; she had ample means, friends ... a position, once.... And still a position on the Continent.... It was obvious that my place was in boarding school. Under the court's ruling I could not remain more than a fortnight with my mother. I could have gone home to father, but he did not want me.

"So—you see what position in the world we had was vacated. There was no longer any circle; no longer a family; nor family friends.

"There were—and are—relatives. They write to me, still. They are very kind.... But I prefer liberty—the liberty of reserving my parents' affairs for my own private attention. Kinship can be a burden.... I could never endure being accounted for, explained ... at the expense of family privacy ... and the domestic misfortune of two dead people who gave me birth ... and whose sorrow is no concern of strangers."

Presently he said: "It is for you to decide, of course. And yet, presentable relatives mean almost anything to a girl alone."

The Hudson River Suttons who spoke out of his mouth were right. Perhaps Gilda Greenway was righter.

"I can't, Stuart. I am not very discreet, not even cautious. You know that. I'm not fastidious. You know how we met. But whatever else I do—whatever I condescend to, unworthy perhaps—I can't go back and let my relatives account for me at the expense of my father and mother."

He made no attempt to discuss the matter. Perhaps he felt that, when the time came, it would smooth their way with his own relatives and friends if Gilda had somebody presentable to account for her.

However, he said nothing further on the subject, nor did she.

Also, it was time to change her gown, for she had persuaded him to go to a reception at the Creative Arts Association with her—the girl refusing to neglect any opportunity to enlarge the pathetically small and badly mixed circle wherein she had her only social exercise.

It was a tea in aid of a drive to provide the starving inhabitants of Roumelia with fezzes.

Stuart usually lent himself to this sort of thing when she asked him, speculating uneasily at times upon his own future and unaided ability to lead her into a duller, more respectable circle—the sacred water-hole, trodden deep, hatched up, and trampled by generations of social pachyderms and gazelles.

"Or we'll make our own wallow," he concluded. But the alternative caused him a slight pang when he remembered the family corral on the Hudson, the old-time gardens, the ancient domain, tradition, tenantry, dirty window-panes and all.

They arrived at the Creative Arts Association in Sutton's car.

The function was in full blast; the Talkers were talking; big lions, little lions, fat lions, meagre lions, mangy lions, all were roaring. Potential pup-lions, pathetic, lovable adolescents, yapped shyly when noticed and patronised. There was the Fifth Avenue matron with a home on the Hudson and stringy hair, who condescended for charity's sake. Other fashionables were there, gracious, profusely democratic, patiently ready to endure, for the sake of Roumelia and half a million red fezzes.

The Creative Arts were there, physically hungry, mentally ravenous to filch material, but mostly bursting with necessity for vocal self expression.

Listeners were few, Talkers dominated. Here an intimidated world was told where it got off sixty times every minute.

On the edge of this milling mess of mouths Gilda stood, unconsciously holding tight to Stuart, who good humouredly identified for her the fauna:

Mrs. Marmot de Grasse, prominent at Newport and in Greenwich Village. Her Article in *The Post*, "Should an Art Student Pay $10,000 for a Studio?" was shaking Fourth Street to its profoundest cabarets.

Miss Smith-Durian, the wealthiest maiden lady in Tuxedo, had offered a prize of $300 annually for the best novel by a New Yorker. The novel to remain the property of Miss Smith-Durian.

Harry Stayr came up grinning like Silenus, and shook hands with Gilda.

"Heavens," he said, "what food. All squashy; and a fake punch to add the classic insult."

"It's so interesting," said Gilda, "—and one doesn't think of food."

"*One* does!" retorted Stayr with a grimace. "Mrs. Bazelius Grandcourt swindled me into coming, promising booze. I gave up ten bones. You're stung, too, I suppose."

"Mr. Derring sent me tickets," said Gilda. "Who is that preparing to sing, Harry?"

It proved to be the lovely Farrar, immortally young, always generous in charity.

The Talkers ceased for a while: Heaven opened; then the celestial transformation faded, drowned by the "noise of the storks."

Julian Fairless presented himself, saluted Gilda's hand, turned to interpret and identify at her eager request:

"They're all there. That's the new novelist, Theodore Howard Belper—small-town stuff, you know—wrote 'The Town Pump'—the last word in rube stuff."

"Why do you suppose he wrote it?" she asked with a distressed smile.

"Small towns want small-town stuff."

"But New York reads it."

"New York's the smallest of 'em all, only it doesn't know it," sneered Stayr. "That solemn guy, Gilda, is Horatio McPhoon, the sculptor. He has submitted a plan to make a bronze statue of the President a mile high, and erect it on top of Pikers Peak."

"Oh, dear," she said unhappily.

Fairless pointed out to her in rapid succession the bald, wide-eared editor of the *Daily Pillar*; Montgomery Skippy, the great publisher and platitudinarian; young Rawmore, the romantic actor, idol of the metropolis; Fitz-William Paunder, patron, director, founder, life-member of everything corporate in Gotham; Mrs. Charles Gilderling, a beauty once, socially formidable, and mother of several already notorious young Gilderlings.

And there were the Talkers, Leopold Pouncing, the critic; old Hunkerson, book-reviewer, brilliant as a spitting cat in the dark; his confrere, the ponderous gabbler on the *Daily Forum*, Seth Hawver; Scratchowsky, the Polish etcher; Sir Daniel Brunderby of the Embassy, worn and perplexed by Yankee and Sinn Fein alike, but talking hands-across, God bless him!—the only Talker of them all who had a word to say worth hearing.

Mrs. Gillately Gray fluttered up, always bright and birdish: and "How d'you do, Mr. Stayr, Mr. Fairless, Mr. Sutton — isn't it too wonderful for poor Roumelia? — How d'you do, Miss Greenway!—" fluttering to the presentation, *toujours oiseau*, preening the nearest feather, her own or another's—*vrai tête de linotte*.

After migration, Stayr said: "*Oiseau de flamme et bec de gaz!* Brrr! What a humming-bird!"

Fairless said to Gilda: "She has the social importance conferred by the social column. Her opera box drips diamonds. There's nothing else to her."

"Oh, come," said Sutton; "she's civil and anxious to please. Why the devil do you knock everybody, Julian?"

"You don't have to," retorted Fairless. "But your boosting is as snobbish as my knocking. I don't know which is the more sickening, after all—"

The greatest of living pianists began to play. It was an artistic mistake; the place was unsuitable; but it was a charitable success. Roumelia could be proud of her fezzes.

"If you'll shake this and come around to my place I'll shake something in a shaker that would shake a Shaker to—"

Julian's elbow in his stomach silenced him.

The most famous of string-quartettes was deliciously beginning.

But this, too, like all happiness, came to its own enchanting end. Again the place was clamorous with the talk of the Talkers.

Sutton whispered in Gilda's ear: "Who would you care to meet, darling?"

She ventured a preference or two, shyly. The men he went after, rounded up, and fetched. To the women he took Gilda, casually secure in his own self assurance.

And Gilda was too lovely to suspect—until she had gone—when the inevitable feminine reaction occurs, and any man is under suspicion who presents one woman to another.

She had enjoyed every moment. She said so to Stuart. "I know where you belong," he said glumly. "And you're going there someday."

He meant, of course, the sacred water-hole.

Gilda surmised it, looked at him tenderly, humorously, inclined to laugh, wholly inclined to adore him and his funny social instincts.

To certain English people there are no particular social distinctions to be expected in America. The only difference they notice is between those who are amusing and those who are not.

Perhaps Gilda's parents might have entertained some such idea—if they ever had troubled their heads about it at all.

They were going to the theatre that evening.

He took her home, went back to dress, returned to take her to dinner at the Ritz. And found her in her black evening gown, flushed, feverish from weeping.

But when, surprised and troubled, he took her to his breast, she wound her arms around him, strained him to her, kissed him, sobbing, stammering, warning him to beware. And gazing intently into her tear-wet eyes he saw the dark change coming, mirrored there in peril, trembling on her reddening lips, fragrant in her breath.

She turned, covering her quivering face with both desperate hands, sank down on the sofa.

He laid aside his overcoat and hat, seated himself near, and turned his altered face to watch her, grimly determined to see it through.

Freda had gone. But there was food in the refrigerator—a cold pheasant, salad, a bottle of claret.

When she heard him in the kitchen she rose and went out.

"I'll do all that," she said humbly.... "Do you really mean to stay with me?"

"Do you think I want you to call up Sadoul?" he said bitterly.

She had laid the cloth; she stood now, with a handful of silver, gazing at him. The *Other One* was rapidly possessing her. She gave him a lovely, flushed look.

"It is always one kind of hell for Sadoul," she said. "It will be another kind for you if you stay."

"Don't worry," he said, reddening with anger at the maddening hopelessness of it all.

She laid the knives and forks on the cloth and came close to him.

"You had better let me call up Sadoul," she said. "I am safe with him."

"You are safe with me," he said with an oath.

They both reddened painfully. He caught her hand, asking pardon—but released the burning palm.

"It is destruction for you to stay.... I still know what I'm saying."

"I'm going to stay. We'll have to win out together, Gilda.... Do you understand?"

She made no reply. And, looking at her, he realised that she no longer understood.

Toward morning the girl had cried herself to sleep, lying flung across the bed, face buried in her dishevelled hair, and one little hand so convulsively linked in his that the boy could scarcely manage to release himself.

He sat on the chair beside the bed for a while, gazing at her out of haggard eyes. Then, when he saw the dark change fading from her burning cheeks he got up, took his hat and coat and went out into the grey light of a foggy morning.

CHAPTER XXXII

Sadoul, playing with his cobra—or rather tormenting it—said to Pockman:

"Take the case mentioned by Chevreuil among scores of others. It is certain that the 'sensitive' experiences terror and anguish when any materialisation in which he or she has been concerned is subjected to brutal handling."

Pockman looked around from his microscope at Sadoul, then at the cobra in its glass-faced double hutch. It was a black cobra, not a spectacled one.

Sadoul ran his gaunt forefinger up and down the glass. Inside, the snake, erect in its coils, followed every movement.

Sadoul said: "The sensitive seems to be physiologically anemic. It is her own substance of which the phantom is composed. There are other cells, too, but the structural emanation is from the sensitive. And when anything excites or shocks, the sensitive begins to recover her own cells."

"What's your deduction?" inquired Pockman.

"This: that any common identity of sensitive and phantom is largely material; that this mutual sharing of substance accounts for bodily and mental injury to the sensitive if the materialisation be injured."

"Logically argued," nodded Pockman. "If one knew how to sever the natal cord between medium and phantom, the former would die, probably."

Sadoul stood absently teasing the cobra. "Yes," he said. "But in a case of dual projection, what?"

"A case of Siamese twins, I suppose."

"I wonder."

"You have in mind the case of Gilda Greenway?" Pockman spoke, leering into his microscope.

Sadoul no longer cared what Pockman thought—no longer took the trouble to conceal motive or purpose. He said, coolly:

"I've concluded it would endanger her if I attempted to rid her of one of these phantoms."

"Rid yourself, you mean—don't you?" tittered the other.

Sadoul's silent glance, full of effrontery and contempt, measured Pockman from head to foot.

"Yes, rid myself," he said. "But I don't know how."

"Your cobra was a premature investment," remarked Pockman, agitated with a sort of whispering laughter which hunched his shoulders to his ears.

"No," said Sadoul, "I got the snake too late, I'm afraid."

"What do you do with your hypodermics full of venom?"

"Try them on sputum."

"Whose?"

"Mine."

Pockman looked up incredulously. "That's a new one, isn't it?" he asked with a ghastly smirk.

"Quite new."

"Does it do the business?"

"Absolutely."

"I see. You mean to attenuate it, gradually attempt to render yourself immune. Then—what? Inject it?"

"That's the idea," said Sadoul tranquilly.

Pockman skeptical, disdainful of any amateur, yet intelligent enough to be interested, stared at the other in silence.

Sadoul's hand, moving rhythmically on the glass, seemed to hypnotise the snake which, towering from its coils, hood dilated, swayed gently with the moving hand.

Suddenly Sadoul made an abrupt pass; the cobra struck like lightning; a stream of venom clouded the glass and ran down inside.

The cobra seemed to collapse like a punctured rubber tube, falling limp in a flattened coil.

Sadoul took a bamboo rod, went to the rear of the hutch, opened a small panel, and, with the rod, flung the snake into the adjoining hutch and lowered the dividing screen of glass.

Then he opened the entire back of the hutch, stepped in and filled a small syringe from the cloudy pool gathering in the cup-shaped glass sill.

Pockman watched the proceedings with a sort of horrid, mocking intentness. To play with death was part of his profession. To watch an amateur do so approached the levity of a sport. Here was a man who might easily have abrasions on his skin, handling without rubber gloves the most deadly and rapid poison known to man—a poison for which no known antidote exists.

"Keep the damn thing away from me," he said as Sadoul came toward him with his syringe. "If you get any of it in your skin it's going to act like lightning."

Sadoul made no comment, and Pockman realised that perhaps he didn't care very much what happened. Which discovery did not particularly affect Pockman, except that if Sadoul died he might as well die a victim to research as die a jackass.

He said as much with a hunch and a shrug, but the other replied with a sneer: "Quand même, on ne meurt pas; on s'addresse, tranquilment, gentilement, au pays de l'ombre."

"If you want to, you can stop that murderous cough," said Pockman. "And if you're so fond of snakes there are plenty in Arizona and New Mexico."

Sadoul laughed: "You think I'll leave those two together?"

"Better than to leave them together permanently. You had another hemorrhage this morning—"

"You lie, Pockman."

"Why, you damned lunger," shouted Pockman, "I saw you in the wash-room. Don't tell me I lie or I'll fire you out of my place."

"You'd better not try," said Sadoul, his indifferent eyes on the angry man.

He went away presently, to his own quarters, carrying the syringe carelessly in one hand.

At the further end of the two rooms which Pockman had allotted to him for his experiments, was a third and smaller room. This he had fitted up as a combination of bed-room and study, and here he now did his writing.

To this place he had removed various articles from his apartment—some books, clothing, photographs of Gilda taken abroad, small personal possessions, letter-files, private papers, even the canary birds that never sang, for some reason or other, and that hopped and hopped and cracked seeds all day long in the tarnished tinsel cage.

As for the big, lonely apartment which he had taken nearly a year ago, he went there rarely. The Japanese servant remained as guardian of the furniture—all the dreary accumulations necessary to equip a housekeeping apartment for married people—furnishings for living-room, bed-rooms, dining-room, kitchen—pictures, mirrors, curtains, linen, carpets, silver, glass, china, batterie-de-cuisine—the whole appalling outfit.

That apartment had become a horror to him; there were no recollections connected with it except painful ones; no phantoms haunted those dusky rooms to evoke in him even the wistful pleasures of sadness; no memories clung to the unused, desolate place.

Except by a tuner the piano never had been touched; the brocaded chairs had never known the caress of her slender body; no lovely ghost looked out from the dim depths of gilded mirrors; there was nothing anywhere of her for whom, because of whom, he had cabled to Pockman to lease a home.

He might have sub-let it for the remainder of the year, but, sullenly determined upon her return, he had hung on.

Now it was not worthwhile; storage charges would more than balance any advantage of sub-letting. So he let it go with a final auction vaguely in mind, and established himself here on the East River. It was less lonely. He could sit, when feeling ill, and gaze out on the grey stream; on barge, schooner, steamer; on the forbidding prison in mid-stream; on the vast and dreary bridge overhead.

Here, when very tired—perhaps with a towel wetted crimson in his clutch—he could lie in a morris chair and follow the gulls in their interminable flight; or mark the mile-long convolutions of smoke from some lofty chimney, tinged with sombre sunset hues, or see the diamond blaze of light flash out across the bridges as the red west smouldered through thickening mists.

And, lying here, he could ponder the eternal problem—the only problem that preoccupied him since he first laid eyes on Gilda Greenway. Ways, means, methods, chances, how to win her, hold her, dominate, possess—always the dull fierce searching in his fevered mind—always the fixed idea, sleepless, burning, eternal.

All else was but an incident in the unaltered problem—the aborted marriage, the domestic debacle, the advent of Sutton—even the girl's death—all were merely incident to the main never-changing, never-ending problem.

His own physical condition, so long and sullenly unrecognised and unadmitted, merely enraged him with impatience. Yet, far in the sombre depths of his mind he was conscious of an ominous mental stillness.

It was the stillness of fear, awakening to the advent of the Future—trying to estimate its approaching speed—watching in a sort of stunned apathy the swift coming of something which had not existed yesterday.

Along with his daily free-lance work—always in demand, always profitable and to be depended upon to give him competence—he carried his psycho-hypnotic research. There was a road, that way, leading toward something—recognition, perhaps, authority, fame, as much of Fortune as the jade carries in her stuffed purse, perhaps.

Also, it was something to do—food to feed fever—possibly a key to unlock the Problem—the only problem existing for him.

He filled a phial with his cobra venom, washed the syringe without precaution, pocketed it, sealed his phial, stood for a while staring absently about him; then, very tired, lay down by the window and crossed his arms behind his dark head.

Presently his thoughts began to hover around death—but not his own—like grey dusk-moths round a ghostly blossom.

Long since satisfied of the incidental unimportance of human dissolution, he had left that conclusion as a starting point for research; for speculation, too.

For the exploring mind, impatient of proof, wanders on out of bounds. And Sadoul's idler thoughts roamed at hazard among scenes peopled by surviving identities—entered vast regions thickly inhabited, stirring with colour and energy and life in its every and illimitable aspect.

And now, finally, he thought of himself. How would it be with him and *her?* His passion must survive if he died.... Would her indifference survive with her? Was the pursuit endless as a star's course in orbit— endless as the drift of the universe?

If it must be, it must be. Eternal or not, it was a part of the scheme of things, irrevocable, inalienable, eternal.

A fog gathered on the river. Tall masts passed like shrouded spectres; the deep vibrations of the fog-horns grew in the thickening stillness; dock lights burned from every pier; long rows of windows glittered dimly in Astoria; a melancholy bell tolled incessantly.

Sadoul closed his heavy-lidded eyes, then opened them with an effort.

River whistles were blowing; the hour struck on some phantom ship; one by one the giant bridges festooned themselves with gems, veiled in the cerements of the fog.

A chill sweat grew on Sadoul's forehead, dampening his thick black hair, but in his hollow cheeks dull fire burned.

He awoke in the dark, coughing, ensanguined, wet to the skin with icy sweat.

CHAPTER XXXIII

There had come into Stuart's voice a hint of anxiety in these days when he greeted Gilda over the telephone. It was always the same eager, boyish question: "Are you all right, dear?" And a swift breath of relief when reassured.

The girl had taken up her music again, vocal and piano, and, three times a week, she had an Italian lesson as corollary to vocal cultivation.

A visit with Stuart to an exquisite loan exhibition at the Metropolitan Museum gave birth to an artistic impulse in the girl. The needle-work on the French renaissance furniture thrilled her; she ardently desired to learn the art; and she discovered a place on Fifth Avenue where instruction was given in *gros point* and *petit point*—where canvas was supplied, designs furnished and stamped.

Often, now, she sat by the window, her oval frame on her knees, an array of rainbow tinted skeins of silk at her elbow, embroidering with dull-tipped needle.

It was slow, minute, painstaking work, but Gilda, quite mad about it already, nourished a plan to tell in *petit point* the deathless story of Eros and Psyche.

The girl had copied designs filched bodily from every available source; and, determined upon covering two chairs, a sofa, and a footstool—none of these period pieces yet acquired—regarded her dismaying programme with mingled excitement and despair.

"After all," she ventured to Stuart, "we have a whole lifetime before us. Princesses used to sit in turrets and peg away at a lifetime's work without impatience."

She showed him the designs she had copied and tinted—delicate panels from the industrious Angelica, from Fuseli via Bartolozzi, even from Flaxman transposed into Bartolozzian terms—lovely, pastel tinted designs in regulation cartouches.

"You're terrifyingly clever," he said. "I wonder," he added, smilingly uneasy, "what you ever saw in a lumber merchant to attract you."

"Don't be silly, Stuart."

"I'm not going to be. But I'm wondering a little—"

"Piffle, darling. I was taught to draw by various teachers in various convents. That's where I learned to play, also. No girl could escape. Whether one wished it or not one was compelled to produce designs, tint them with watercolours. I could have learned *petit point* from the sisters; I did learn ordinary embroidery, crochet, the simple tapestry stitch. I don't want you to think me talented."

"Well," he said, "music, design—any artistic manual dexterity is utterly beyond me—any creative talent or any interpretive one."

"What I do is nothing," she said, smilingly occupied with her needle.

"You're better read than I am, too," he went on. "You've read more widely in standard literature. You're familiar with things I've merely heard of. I don't know what the devil I learned at Harvard. I've brought nothing away with me."

"You've brought away an unspoiled boy—with a blond head—and the perfect equipment of all that is ideal in manhood," she said, keeping her eyes on her embroidery.

He bent and kissed her where, at the nape of the neck, the hair grew soft as pale red-gold.

"I'd better read up on art and things," he said, "or there'll be silences at the breakfast table some of these days."

"I hope there'll be too many children for that," she murmured, intent on her needle.

The boy laughed and she flushed at her temerity, but the former, thrilled by the picture, took her small, smooth hand and rested his lips on it.

"All the same," he said, "I don't want to be the only dumb creature at breakfast, Gilda. You are far more cultivated than I and it worries me now and then."

She laughed: "I'm glad of it. I don't wish you to be too sure of me. You made me love you far too easily to suit my feminine complacency."

"Wasn't it inevitable, dear?" he asked, so seriously that the girl laughed again.

"Of course, blaming destiny softens the shameful fact that I no sooner beheld you than I seized you."

Her eyes sparkled, her colour glowed, her hair seemed a living flame enveloping the dainty head lowered above her embroidery, where the needle flashed in her white fingers.

Presently her expression altered; she said gravely:

"Love," she said, "necessarily originates in propinquity. But I do not believe I ever could have loved any other man."

Then, with a swift upward glance, and laughing again: "So you see, dear, lumber merchant or prince of the blood, it made no difference in my destiny. It was to be you. It is you. And I think you'd better tell me something about your pine trees and your business so that I may enjoy it with you."

He remained silent and preoccupied for a while, then: "Gilda, I've got to go to Heron Nest for a few days. Will you come as my guest?"

"Darling! I couldn't, in your parents' absence."

"Aren't we engaged?" he insisted stubbornly.

"How can we be when I'm already married?"

"I don't see why you can't come."

"It wouldn't be well for me if I ever marry you. It isn't going to be easy, anyway. I realise that."

He shrugged his indifference and impatience. The least conceited of men thinks himself sufficient compensation for troubles shared.

The girl looked at him sweetly but very soberly, her needle idle: the boy, boy-like, was busy thinking how he could have his way.

"It isn't your house, yet; it's your father's and mother's," she reminded him.

"And I'm going to marry you! What of it? If I wait a million years I'm going to marry you."

She shook her head: "It doesn't alter things."

"I want you to see the place—"

"I want to see it."

"Really, Gilda, it's rather nice in its way—nothing very grand, you know—but homelike. All my childhood, boyhood, was centered there.... Oh, come on up! There are only a few snuffy old servants at Heron Nest—"

"I'll go up with you if you like, but it wouldn't do for me to stay overnight."

"Why not! Good Lord, if we'd wanted to get into mischief—"

"I know. But I shall not sleep at Heron Nest until the master of the house asks me.... Even if I were unmarried I ought not to. But probably I would," she added.

"Do you mean to leave me there and come back alone to town?"

"There is nothing else for me to do, dear."

"I wonder," he mused, "if I hadn't better telegraph dad and mother that I'm engaged to you—"

"*Can't* you remember that I'm married!" she exclaimed in dismay.

"Oh, the devil! Well—" he drew a long, unhappy breath; "Well then, Gilda, I'll wire Heron Nest to expect us for lunch—"

"No, no, no! I won't touch your father's bread and salt in his absence and without his knowledge. Don't ask me, Stuart. A roof means something definitely personal to me.... My father's roof meant it.... The roofs of relatives offered to me as shelter mean more to me than I am willing to give for offered sanctuary. No! I'll go anywhere else with you. If it's indiscreet, reckless, nevertheless I'm not afraid. But eat and sleep, unasked, under your father's roof, I will not."

Again he remained silent, busy with another train of ideas.

"All right, Gilda. I know what we'll do. We'll go to Heron Nest, look over things, take the train that same evening for our timber lands, and have a wonderful two weeks together in the wilds!"

The girl gazed at him amazed and disconcerted, but enthusiasm was firing him; he was ravished by the idea, and he painted an enchanted picture of the trip.

"Why not?" he exclaimed. "I've got to go anyway. We know we're quite all right together. Nobody can misunderstand us because there'll be nobody there except lumber-jacks, bosses, river-drivers—a lot of Indians, Canucks, native mountaineers.

"I tell you it will be heavenly," he cried, "—just you and I, Gilda, and the forest. I'll choose your outfit for you; I'll wire ahead and make arrangements. I'll have Leggett put up a brand new log camp for us and stock it from the store."

"You are inviting me to disappear with you?" she asked, bewildered.

"For ten days, dearest. Can you stand me ten days?"

The girl nodded. "It isn't that I don't want to go. I do. I'm going with you. I'm just trying to comprehend our doing it."

"It *is* like an enchanting dream, isn't it?" he said, delighted. "I've been dreading it—not the work, but being away from you. It never occurred to me to ask you to go."

"Probably," she said, with faint sarcasm, "it would have occurred to me. All our improprieties seem to originate with me—"

He caught her in his arms.

"They *do*," she insisted, breathlessly. "So I'm rather glad that this imprudence originated in your own blond head.... Darling, be careful of my needle—"

It was something new to wait for, to plan for as the winter drew toward its end.

On Saturday afternoons they haunted those fascinating shops on Fifth Avenue and Madison which are devoted to sporting outfits—new and wondrous sources of delight to Gilda, who stood in ecstasy before racks full of skis and snow-shoes, hung over glass cases brilliant with trout-flies, glittering with reels and lures of metal and mother-of-pearl.

With Stuart she pored over the mechanism of guns, or compared fashions in hunting knives, or switched delicate rods of lance-wood or split-cane to test their stiffness, limberness, resiliency.

They looked at everything whether needed by them or not—at saddles, stirrups, polo mallets, golf-clubs. And as for sport clothes, he would have given her more costumes than the Empress of India, so adorable was she in knickers, in rough kilts and sleeveless jackets, in the hundred and one delightful confections invented for the outdoor convenience and adornment of healthy girlhood.

Those were sparkling, halcyon afternoons when he came uptown early and met her at the Ritz for luncheon. Nothing untoward marred them; of weather they were scarcely conscious, and it might rain or snow, or the sun might shine for all those two noticed such eccentricities of Mama Nature.

In those days late in winter another matter became apparent—more so every day they dared believe. And finally it became certain that longer and longer periods of time were elapsing between those dreaded hours when the dark change came over the girl and all the old unreal terror and bewilderment and despair overwhelmed them and left them exhausted, crushed, spiritually prostrate under the vast menace of destruction.

Such trouble seldom threatened them now. And, thinking of it, half fearfully, sometimes the boy wondered whether the grim vitality, now burning low in Sadoul, had anything to do with its infrequency—whether the will to suggest was becoming impaired.

For it was plain to him that Sadoul was ill. Even had he not witnessed that scene in the laboratory earlier in the winter, the physical alteration in Sadoul's features had now become sufficiently ominous.

Gilda noticed it, but attributed it to Sadoul's habits, not surmising the truth. She expressed her concern to Sadoul in a guarded, aloof way, never certain that her sympathy might not be mistaken by him and his ever smouldering and passionate tyranny blaze out anew.

But in these days she found Sadoul unusually silent, less saturnine, and frequently so tired that the weariness in voice and manner seemed a sort of gentleness which she was scarcely able to associate with the man.

But she soon learned of her mistake when she ventured an appeal to his generosity in behalf of their common and unhappy marital situation. For instantly the old passion flamed in his ravaged face and he swore that he would tolerate no legal separation, no other man as far as she ever could be concerned.

"You will come back to me someday," he said. "There is no other destiny for you. It matters nothing if we die. Ultimately you will come back.... Or I'll fetch you."

"You never had me, Sadoul."

"I shall have you absolutely. You'll come of your own accord or I'll go and get you.... Wherever you are.... Wherever I am."

"I am sorry you believe that," she said gently.

He muttered unintelligibly. He seemed suddenly fatigued. She had been writing automatically for him, sheet after sheet of matter which proved meaningless to her in a normal state.

For half an hour or more she had been sitting there at his desk in the part or the laboratory reserved for him, her head resting on a pillow laid on the desk, her right hand flying over the pad from which he removed each sheet as it was covered.

He, now that she was awake, had been reading over what she had written, striving to identify the controlling intelligence, certain that the written matter never originated in her or in himself.

Gilda never displayed any curiosity concerning what her subconscious self did for him. She displayed none now, tranquilly satisfied that she had helped him in accumulating data for future research.

Resting in her chair, idly playing with her pencil, she looked at the changed face of the man rather sadly. Already he was growing gray at the temples; his face, always thin, had grown unpleasantly bony; and his waxen hands were the hands of a big skeleton under a drawn membrane of colourless skin.

He continued to look over the sheets she had written, making marginal notes now and then. His under lip sagged. Noticing it, she also saw a fleck of blood on it.

Catching her eye, made suspicious perhaps, he wiped his mouth with a handkerchief already spotted with dark stains.

"Have you hurt yourself?" she asked.

He said he had bitten his lip, and went on reading, holding the handkerchief to his face.

Gilda consulted her wrist watch.

"I have a vocal lesson in half an hour," she said, rising.

"You mean an engagement with Sutton," he sneered.

"I mean a lesson," she retorted, disdainfully.

"A love-lesson?"

"No. But suppose I had," she said with cold resentment.

"It wouldn't do you any good. Or him. You're married and he's a snob."

"I am wondering," she said, exasperated, "whether I shall trouble myself any further to help your research work.... I need not sacrifice my time by coming here and enduring your bad temper. I don't know why I do it, either."

"I do. You belong to me and you know it."

The very devil gleamed in her eyes:

"I know to whom I belong," she said in a sort of whisper, "and he can have me any time—a word, a touch—a look from him is enough.... I don't know why I have any pity left for you, any feeling except indifference."

"You feel the tie," he said.

"That civil ceremony—when you confused me, used your power of suggestion on a bewildered, subconscious mind? Do you think that mockery of a marriage ceremony is any tie?"

"It is one strand in the occult bond."

"There is no bond!" she said violently, "—no accord, no sympathy, not a wisp or shred to tie me to you except brief memories of a brilliant mind perverted—rare intervals of mental pleasure—pity for you who might have been a friend and who so ruthlessly plotted my destruction!"

She turned and went to the door. He sat looking at her.

"I am deeply sorry for you," she said. "Good-bye."

He said in a weary voice: "So you must go to your love-lesson."

"That will be later, I hope," she flashed.

He nodded: "Later. Much later.... After you and I are dead.... Then, the first lesson. A lesson in love.... Our first.... Good-night, Gilda."

CHAPTER XXXIV

The Talkers were talking at the Fireside Club. The Talkers were talking of women. Fairless quoted Lombroso, Kraft-Ebbing, and Havelock-Ellis. Harry Stayr, who had been for years "half-way" in a "*new* novel," and who, like all Talkers, was taking out the remaining "half" in talk, laid down axioms, hard boiled, for his listeners to digest at leisure.

"*Si duo sunt idem*," he insisted in dog-Latin, "*non sunt idem*. But it's only in detail they differ," he added, "—finger-prints are still the prints of fingers. Like abhors like. There always is a latent antipathy between women. It is not so between men. Toward men women unconsciously but always cherish sex antipathy. There is no such fundamental instinct in men.

"Woman is a poor specimen of the species—if, indeed, she be not a subspecies. She is perfectly equipped to be the worst possible comrade for man. The normal woman is originally conservative, practically passionless. That is why it became necessary to invent the convention of marriage. That is why men are polygamous.

"In marriage she remains the congenital egotist. Necessity for beauty having passed, she becomes a slut. Like all animals she nourishes her young; fights for them. So do rats.

"What in God's name is there admirable about a woman except her beauty?

"Because she is soft, graceful, fine skinned, delicately limbed, men ascribe to her a sensitiveness which she is absolutely without.

"She is less sensitive physically than men; bears pain more easily.

"She suffers less spiritually than men. She has less capacity for real emotion, less mental potentiality, less physical sensibility.

"I'm sick listening to the cant of poets and novelists. They describe themselves and their own sensations when they try to write realistically about women. They ascribe qualities to her of which she is ignorant, virtues of which, constitutionally, she is utterly incapable; vices to which she is too lazy and indifferent to fall a victim.

"I tell you she's a tenth rate imitation of man, and man is a bum chromo of Christ.

"Now, go and tell that to the Great American Boob! Tell it to the American Aunty. Tell it to the Demagogue, the sissy sentimentalist, the pastoral crape-hanger, the national hypocrite, the dog-town fanatic!"

"Why don't you tell 'em yourself in your great novel, Harry?" asked Fairless.

Sam Warne said: "If you'd stop stuffing yourself, Harry, you'd reverse your argument. Your perversely sordid theories originate in that paté-de-fois-gras which you think is your liver."

The shrill cackle of Derring left Stayr with his mouth opening to speak.

"That's it," he said, "—livers talk, not brains! If you'd ever had a dear old mother you couldn't talk that way. Even a guy in Sing-Sing will admit that. Ask Lyken what they say when they're bumped off! Every damned one of 'em cries for his dear old mother. Isn't she a woman? Aren't there billions of mothers? Almost every man has had one. You ought to be ashamed, Harry—"

"Can't you love a thing that's imperfect?" growled Stayr. "It's the only thing man can love. If you're crazy about a girl it's because, in the back of your head, you know she's imperfect."

"Why don't the damned novelists say so?"

"Who cares," sneered Pockman, "what a novelist says? It never matters."

"That's where you're wrong, old Holbein," retorted Stayr. "Look what these slops have done to the country! Look what the 'good woman' stuff has done to the Middle West. Why, they're a race of chipmunks out there. 'The good woman' is running the country, knocking cigarettes out of your mouth, scaring a poltroon nation into prohibition, planning blue laws, re-gilding the old god Bunk to trot him out and scare a boob republic into Sabbath superstition again. That's what your women-praising novelists are doing. That's why the fanatics are raising the slogan of Christ and Kansas! Can you beat the blasphemous vulgarity? No, nor anybody else, including a Hottentot!"

Sutton, rather red, got up and started for the door.

"Am I right, Stuart?" cried Stayr. "Is there any difference in chickens except the colour of their feathers?"

Sutton said: "If we men really believed what you say, Harry, I think the decent ones among us would blow out our brains."

After he had gone, Stayr said: "What can you expect? He's acting up to the little Greenway girl as though he meant to marry her. He's the sort that would. There's your congenital celibate. There's your woman-worshiper for you! Why, Joseph was a lounge-lizard compared to that hick! Hell! He's spoiled as good a little sport as ever danced at Derring's!"

Sutton, nauseated with talk, and now, for the first time, utterly loathing the Talkers, shook the dust of the Fireside from his heels and drew in a lung-full of outside air.

All the pretense, tinsel logic, shabby intellectuality, pseudo-deduction—all the squalid impotence of these men who created nothing, produced nothing, meant nothing to the world, was becoming apparent to a young man who knew no more of modernism than to wish to be a decent member of the human family.

What was fundamentally right and what was wrong concerned him less than tradition regarding right and wrong—the tradition which had preserved the world through its development—the tradition which had proved wholesome to the human race, which had safeguarded his country, his family.

Whoever had framed the Decalogue, God or man, was the father of men. The records of the New Testament were chronicles of a God and his archangels, human or immortal.

Gradually he had been sickening of the Talkers. Now he was utterly sickened. Pockman had said they were mostly mouth and the remainder only an intestine.

More clearly, now, this boy whose business in life was to grow, cut, and sell timber, began to understand that there are only two kinds of men—Talkers and Doers. Some Doers are talkative; no Talkers ever do anything.

This great gabbling Mouth was the plague of the working world. It was the parasite of the people, a hook-worm to energy, a louse to humanity, breeding bacteria that poisoned all mankind.

He wondered, now, how the Talkers of the world had contrived to loosen his grip on Truth; how they had managed to emasculate his belief in God. Why, what pitiable imitations they were!—what mental dwarfs! And he thought of Vathek, and the "noise of the storks and the dwarfs." And he thought of the little daughter of Jairus, too. And of Gilda lying dead in her green mask.

The long, open New York winter had come to end. In the Park the grass was intensely green. Grackle and starling walked amid dandelions; thorns were white, yellow bell-flowers in bloom; some trees in sunny hollows and along the east wall were exquisitely green.

The gilded bronze General now rode his delivery-wagon nag behind a limestone balustrade—which he, his horse, and the winged servant-girl would be obliged to leap if they insisted on continuing down Fifth Avenue.

Proudly the expensive marble buildings looked down upon a new limestone quarry. Saucily the naked bronze jade across the way inspected the grim old warrior—who knew a pretty lass when he saw one, they say, and must have been bored to death with the winged domestic at his stirrup.

Sutton glanced up at the most classically uninteresting mansion in Manhattan, soon to be converted to business uses. Opposite, another and interesting commercial structure was rising almost overnight. Farther down, the most beautiful private residence in Gotham, doomed to pay tribute to Hermes, flanked the most lovely of all metropolitan churches—cool, calm, silver-grey façades in the feverish riot of architecture roystering away southward toward the tawdry horrors of Broadway.

What a city! What would it become if Faith died within its grotesque walls; on its crazy heights? What would these milling swarms turn into if belief withered—if conformation to custom, trust in tradition, perished?

If it were true, as Stayr said, that there are only two parties in the world—Conservatives, who are women; Liberals, who are men; then the salvation of the world is due to its conservatism—to woman, the perfect egotist, born respecter of custom and tradition—and not to Liberal man whose atavistic instinct is for an informality that would bring the temples of the earth crashing about his ears.

Stuart turned into Thirty-fifth Street. He was thinking: "The thing to do, the thing to believe, is what your father did, and what he believed. And *his* father. And *his*.... Not, of course, going too far back.... When they burnt witches...."

He ascended the stairs, stood a moment at Gilda's door.

"The thing to do," he concluded, "is to take what's coming to you within the law. Or fight it.... But always fight *inside* the law. You stand no show out of bounds."

Freda admitted him. He found Gilda pale, silent, seated at her satin-wood desk, a few sheets of scored music-paper before her—some task in transposition set her; the ink still wet on the heavily penned sixteenth notes.

"Are you all right, dear?" he asked uneasily.

She nodded, lifted her childish face; the long line of the neck so lovely that he kissed her throat.

"I have our transportation," he said happily. "Your luggage is checked and so is mine. Leggett wires that our shanty is ready—" He hesitated, looking at her. "What is the matter, Gilda? You *are* all right, aren't you?"

"Yes, I am all right."

"Anything to worry you?"

"No."

"You haven't had any unpleasant experience with Sadoul?"

"Not recently.... He's been decent since I relented and went back to help him. He looks so ill, Stuart—so emaciated."

The boy kept his counsel, sombrely, playing square with the man who was slowly losing out. For a while he sat gazing absently at the sheets of ruled paper, darkly lost in a mental maze. After a little he looked up; regarded her more intently:

"Gilda, what's the matter?"

"Nothing serious. I'm silly to be upset.... The surprise ... unexpected ... kindly intended, no doubt—"

He waited, perplexed.

She leaned over and blotted the wet score: "Fancy," she said. "I was in my bed-room—combing out my hair, I believe—when Freda came with her card!"

"Whose card?"

"A—woman's. A relative of mine."

Gilda drummed on the desk with nervous fingers.

"I supposed she was in England. I didn't know she was coming. And there she was.... In this room!"

"Was it not agreeable to have her come to see you?"

"I hadn't asked her. I have declined to visit her. Or any of them. I reply to their letters. I am civil. That seemed sufficient."

"Why does it upset you?"

"I don't know why it does.... For one thing, your sport-coat and stick were on the lounge where you left them this morning."

"Oh, Lord!" he said.

"It was all right. Being British she took them for mine. It wasn't that."

"What, then?"

"Oh, everything, Stuart. It was all well meant, you see, but I'd avoided it.... Didn't I once tell you that I couldn't endure being accounted for by my respectable relatives? Well, she is one of them and that was it."

"What did she wish of you?"

"She desired me to accept the respectable shelter of herself and the common family tree.... It's full enough of foliage without me. Also, she'd have to explain me.... No, no, no! A thousand, thousand times no! To explain me is to reflect on my parents. The British are not reticent in family matters. If they don't like anybody in their own family they don't hesitate to say so. I know how they regarded my mother. It's no use; they have nothing to offer that I could accept."

"She wished to take you back to England?" he asked, worried.

"To Calfornia first. She's travelling."

"And afterward?"

"She goes to Italy. Constantinople, too; and China and India, I believe. Ultimately to England. I couldn't endure it." She looked up at the boy: "Not that she's not presentable. I didn't mean it that way. There's nothing queer about her. You'd probably like her—" she smiled faintly—"your parents would quite approve, Stuart."

"That's just it," he said seriously. "It would make things so easy for us—"

"But *darling!* Can't you ever recollect that I'm married? I'd have to tell my relatives and your parents. How could I account for you to my aunt? How could you account for me to your mother?"

"Isn't it rotten luck?" he said fiercely.

"Yes, but listen, dear. Even if there were any prospects for my freedom, do you imagine my aunt and your mother would tolerate our companionship until the law unmarried me?"

"I suppose not," he said.

"Your supposition is painfully correct, monsieur.... I fancy that your people are rather conservative. My relatives are quite as rigid. They've had their nets and lines out angling for me from the day my father died. I thought they'd never notice me again when, after fulfilling legal requirements in London, I refused to remain to be cherished and explained.

"But my father was their idol. He died in battle. They continue writing to my dead father's only child—as in duty bound—or bound, perhaps, by something that may be more vital still to such gentle-folk as they."

"I can understand," said the boy.

"That is why I mentioned it—because you can understand."

An odd consciousness of the subtle but complete reversal of roles preoccupied him. This girl was, unconsciously, accounting to herself for him, a Hudson River Sutton. Evidently she expected, ultimately, to account to her relatives for him.

And what had always caused him anxiety for the future was that he must account for her to a family and a circle which was entirely equipped to make them miserable at will. It seemed funny. He smiled, then looked worried. "How long does your aunt remain in New York?"

"Oh, she left this afternoon for Denver."

"Then it won't make any difference about your going to the Forest?"

"No, darling. I said I'd go."

"But if you think—"

"I don't think! I won't think. There's no harm in it if we're not caught. I want to go; and I'm going to marry you sometime, anyway. And, oh! my beautiful sport-clothes, and my trout-rod, and you—*you*—O wonderful clairvoyant who looked into a muddy crystal and saw love on his knees to you!"

She looked at him humourously, tenderly, studying his features with the enigmatical smile hovering on her lips.

"At first," she said, "you naturally thought me depraved. I was merely queer. Not as queer as you very reasonably supposed. Not wanton. When you comprehended that you were sweet. Then I scared you.... And myself.... And went to pieces. You picked them up. You glued me together. I'm almost as good as new. I'll be quite new when we marry.... Your brand new toy."

After a moment he asked her if she had told Pockman and Sadoul that she was going away.

"Yes," she said, "I had to. Of course, I did not say I was going with you."

"Did they object?"

"Dr. Pockman grumbled. But I told him very gently that I didn't expect to be under observation indefinitely."

"Was Sadoul unpleasant?"

"No. He merely asked me to let him know when I returned."

"That's not like him, is it?"

"It's made me a little uneasy," she admitted. "But what could he do to us?"

Freda appeared to announce dinner.

It was late when the boy took his coat and stick, walked with his arm around Gilda to the hall, took her into his arms, then with a happy goodnight put on his hat and went out.

She waited till she heard the upper door slam, then locked herself in for the night.

Stuart crossed the lower landing. The place was rather dark. Half way down the stairs a tall shadow detached itself from the wall. The boy halted, instinctively. There was a moment's silence.

"Sadoul!" he said sharply.

Sadoul's first shot deafened him; then the pistol crashed again; but Stuart was already jerking the weapon upward, wrenching it free.

The bitter smoke strangled them both; he hurled Sadoul at the lower door, kicked him through it, kicked him across the sidewalk, saw him stumble, collapse, roll over on the asphalt.

He stood looking on as Sadoul got up on hands and knees, then staggered to his feet. His chin and collar and shirt were all over blood.

Stuart was still breathing hard. "Go home, you lunatic!" he managed to say. "Do you want a cop to butt in?"

Sadoul stood swaying slightly, fumbling toward his handkerchief. A passing taxi slowed up, interested. Stuart took Sadoul by the arm and looked into his deathly face.

"Where do you want to go?" he said in an altered voice. "Home?"

"Yes," whispered Sadoul.

To the driver: "This gentleman has fallen and hurt himself."

"I get you," returned the driver.

"Hadn't I better go with you?" asked the boy.

Sadoul, lying back in the cab, shook his head.

"I think I'd better see you safe, Sadoul. That was a nasty fall."

He got into the cab. It started with a buck and a jerk, ran skittishly to Fifth Avenue, rolled rapidly uptown.

Sadoul seemed exhausted, but when they arrived at the laboratory he descended from the cab without aid.

At the door of the building Stuart took the pistol out of his pocket, pulled out and threw away the clip, and handed the weapon to Sadoul.

"Here's your gun," he said in a low voice. "It wouldn't have solved our problem."

"Where are you going with her?" whispered Sadoul hoarsely.

"Only to look over our Forest. I'm playing square with you both, Sadoul."

"You'll bring her back?"

"Of course."

"When?"

"Oh, in a week or ten days."

Sadoul touched his bloody lips with his handkerchief: "In—in ten days?"

"Not longer."

"No.... Don't stay longer.... I am—ill, Sutton." He went up the steps, his shoulders sagging, carrying the empty pistol in his hand.

"What the hell did you hand that guy?" inquired the driver as Sutton went slowly back to the cab.

"What do you think it was, a ham sandwich? Drive back to Thirty-fifth Street and step on the tack!"

CHAPTER XXXV

It was the most wonderful week in Gilda's life.

They had stopped for an hour at Heron Nest. She would not cross the threshold; but inspected the big, dowdy old mansion from every outside angle, and the poor boy pointed out to her endless unwashed windows, describing eagerly what lay behind each. His room, his mother's, his father's, all were identified by windows; library, dining room, the two parlours—he spared her not a square inch of his natal roof.

But the girl adored it, tenderly desirous of making up for his disappointment at her refusal to enter the abode of the Suttons.

However, she went through the gardens with him, finding them quaint and lovely in the fresh brilliance of spring flowers.

Some young fruit trees still remained in blossom; hedges wore unsullied green, the warm aroma of newly turned earth where gardeners were working blended deliciously with the perfume of new blossoms.

There was an acre of glass. She went with him into two or three greenhouses, the grapery, melon shed—glimpsed the carnations, now in the sere and withered finis, accepted the violets that a gardener brought her, and then walked to the low, grey wall which overlooked the valley and its famous river.

Far below a train rushed by toward the metropolis, leaving writhing coils of smoke in the green ravine. Beyond, the Hudson sparkled under a blinding sun. Haze veiled the rolling heights to westward. Lagoon-like backwaters and bays were brimming with the flood-tide. From the south came a grey Destroyer speeding upstream.

The boy had possession of the girl's hand. He had a story to tell her of every inch of ground along the grey stone wall.

Here he had shot his first hawk; in yonder oak his first squirrel; among the distant reeds across that inlet he had pursued black duck and coots in a punt.

If she sighted along his levelled arm she could see a great blue heron wading out there in the shallows.

She laid her soft cheek against his shoulder and took aim with beguiling eyes. When, finally, she had discovered the dignified wader, she softly kissed her lover's sleeve. He touched her hair with his lips.

A squirrel derided them from the fatal oak.

That was her confused recollection of Heron Nest—the scent of spring, a squirrel shrilling in a lofty tree, miles of sunlit river, and her lover's cheek against her own.

And now they were on their way northward once more, thundering through short tunnels, roaring along rock-ribbed cuts, out into blinding sunshine again with the river a blinding waste of light quivering away into the magic North.

Sunset reddened the cars at Albany; starlight silvered their berths at Utica.

The boy lay awake, too thrilled to sleep. The girl, in her berth opposite, slept dreamlessly in supreme surrender to a destiny no longer questioned.

At ten o'clock the next morning the train stopped on signal at Fisher-cat Dam.

Dan Leggett, planting superintendent, awaited them in a Ford.

The road was awful; the flivver crawled as a dog negotiates an unsteady bridge, on its belly.

Pink-cheeked, glad of her fur coat, astonished to find the springtime just beginning here, excited by the heady air and the aroma of the pines, Gilda clung to Stuart and gazed fearfully from the pitching car.

She was full of breathless exclamations—now enchanted by a tumbling mountain brook, now in ecstasy as the blue view widened away over acres of forests accented by ridges of hard wood and set with steep little tree-clad hills.

Once, ahead in the bed of the brook which Leggett spoke of as "the road," a burly woodchuck scrambled over the stones and out of sight. And Gilda's excitement knew no bounds.

She stood straight up in the car when a ruffed grouse, "dusting," got up, leisurely, and walked on ahead with an irritated, reproachful air.

Wild birds called wistfully from thin depths of newborn foliage; pale blossoms starred the woods, clotted the twigs of slim grey shrubs.

In Gilda's breath the wine of the pines sweetened, intoxicating her; in her veins the fire of youth ran moulten. Solitude, and her lover! There was nothing else in the world. Nothing more to desire, beyond.

And all the while Stuart was talking—explaining trees, identifying pine, hemlock, spruce, and balsam, instructing her in the differences characterising each species, estimating "markets," guessing at "calipers," pointing out "ripe" growths, "cruising" in his mind's eyes as the creaking flivver crawled upward.

She only heard his voice as a celestial melody without words. Clinging to him in their lurching craft, her girl's eyes were as remotely lost as the rim of misty blue-green mountains on the horizon.

Once, in a gorge below, a stony river leaped into sight. But the river-driving was ended; the run of log was over. A few lay stranded here and there, or, caught between boulders crossways in mid-stream, lay massive and black, drenched with snowy spray.

A haze filled one valley where men were sawing. The wicked whine of the steam-saw came thinly to their ears.

Beyond, men were busy with slashings, preparing lumbered areas for reforestation.

After a while they began to pass panels of red pine and Norway spruce—the trees in various panels varying from eighteen inches to ten feet in height.

Acres of beautiful silvery grey-green trees were in sight, now—Scotch pines, soft as pyramids of moss to the eye, and prickly as briers to the touch.

He told her all about it. The weevil, curse of white pine and Norway spruce, also attacked these Scotch pines. It remained to be seen whether they were worth the planting.

Acres of emerald green, bushy, broom-like young evergreens clothed the hills ahead.

"Red pines," he explained, "immune to weevil and blister."

"So far," drawled Leggett.

"So far," echoed Stuart gloomily.

Gilda dreamed on blissfully, their voices vague as in a trance. A heavenly rapture possessed her through which her soul floated, drifted, slumbered on the wing, or swept the green earth below like the shadow of a sky-lark.

The sun's heat, waxing intense, distilled aromatic nectar from every stem and leaf and blossom, and delicate wild perfumes arose from black mould and rotting leaves.

"Hey, Mike!" shouted Leggett, as the car rattled across a log bridge.

Gilda opened bewildered eyes. Stuart was laughing at her.

On the edge of a flashing stream she saw twin log houses, and a faded man in formless, faded garments standing between them.

On a board over the door of one was painted *Villa Gilda*: over the other, *Hotel Sutton*.

In her ears was the golden melody of the stream; in her eyes the glory of the sun.

Eden!

"This is Mike Hanford, Gilda, who is going to look out for us. He tosses the finest flap-jack in the North Woods."

Mr. Hanford removed his cap and scratched his head to atone for such servility.

"Reckon you'll eat a snack," he surmised. And spat to readjust social conditions throughout the earth.

CHAPTER XXXVI

Never had Gilda known such delight. Their Eden was guarded by two sign-boards on the wood-road a hundred yards north and south of the log bridge.

The signs were painted and erected by Mr. Hanford. One read: "Keep offn this here privut rode. Ladies presunt." The other: "Don't go into them woods; there is ladies loose."

A cordon of infantry with machine guns might have failed to impress the sauntering timber-cruiser and lowly lumber-jack. But these signs routed them. Only the squirrel and the grouse invaded their leafy solitude.

The weather was perfect. The wonder-days waxed and waned.

Neither dawn nor the wild birds' choral awoke these two.

But when the sun gold-plated their glazed windows the boy and the girl stirred and awoke, and heard the fire roaring in the sheet-iron stoves behind the closed door of the only other room.

In bathing-dress, blanket-coated, they hailed each other from windows opposite. Gilda came out of her shanty, Stuart emerged from his. Hands touching they picked their way to the edge of the brook where Mike had damned it.

Here spread a long, green, transparent pool—"ungodly cold," they agreed—but if it was hell to go into it, it was heaven the next minute.

The thickets of bank ferns trembled under the rain of spray they dashed into the air. Outraged squirrels protested overhead; blue-jays exchanged malicious gossip regarding these shameless intruders; the affrighted trout fled up stream.

The girl's laughter echoed through the woods; distant wild birds answered. The boy dived and dived like a halcyon.

Then they ran glowing and dripping to their shanties, continuing conversation through open windows while preparing for the day.

When Gilda was ready, Stuart went out and dingled a cow-bell. Mr. Hanford, lurking within earshot, presently rambled into sight, bearing food.

"Mornin', ma'am. Mornin', Mr. Sutton. I jess heard some'n a-dribblin' onto a cow-bell, so, thinks I, I'll jess run over a spell an' help cook breakfast—*if* I'm wanted."

He always said this; always appeared uncertain that he was needed, always belittled his own culinary efforts, and hinted darkly of metropolitan gastronomic orgies in which, doubtless, they were daily accustomed to indulge.

Thus spake Mr. Hanford while tossing flap-jacks and frying brook-trout.

But he was secretly aghast at their capacity, and never before had two people compelled him to toss flap-jacks so fast.

His summons to breakfast was, "Coffee's bilin', ma'am." And that was the signal for him to toss with all his agility and skill against the rapid inroads on the brown and fragrant stack of cakes.

"My conscience," he said to Leggett, "I've seen feedin' in Canuck lumber camps but I hain't never seen nothin' like them two." He added irrelevantly: "Ain't she pretty, Dan? Say, when she sets curled up on the moss eatin' onto a hunk o' fried fish, I never seen nothin' prettier. She's cunnin' as a suckin' caaf, she is."

Halcyon days!—ecstatic hours along the stream, struggling to lift fat, heavy, lustily resisting trout from icy, foaming deeps; hours on the broader river with silk lines whistling out across pool and shallow, and the virgin wind blowing, and the fat trout splashing with a glint of rose and silver.

All day, all night the interminable song of the pines filled their ears.

In a depthless blue vault the sun glittered; stars jewelled the dark; and always the endless anthem of the pines.

She accompanied him when he went on tours of inspection. Everything in this utterly new world enchanted her.

She wandered through the seedling nursery, where rows and rows of oblong beds, raised and rounded above the trodden paths, bloomed like delicately tinted mosses. This flower-bed covered with pale blue velvet contained thousands of Coster's seedling spruces. This blue-green moss was composed of thousands of seedling white pines. Here were panels of silver-grey-green Scotch pines, panels of leaf-green red pines, misty stretches of spruce.

She saw acres of one year, two year, three years' transplants; acres of three foot, four, five, six foot trees; acres of new forests, ten foot trees, thirty foot trees.

Over the plowed "rides" she plodded, her hand on Stuart's arm. Once, dizzy, but trusting to him, she climbed a fire-tower, where the stolid lookout sat chewing tobacco and nursing a telescope.

She went afield with him after weevils, and saw the green terminal shoots ominously a-droop, or still upright clotted with white, or rusty and bent.

He peeled for her a terminal shoot and showed her the fat grey-white larvae in the heart of it, packed like cartridges in a rod-magazine.

Everywhere in some plantations men were severing and burning infected shoots. She heard Stuart swearing under his breath.

Another day she went with him on a graver errand.

No "blister" had appeared in the Sutton forests, and Stuart was determined that the leprous curse should never gain a foothold in the domain of his forebears. Yet, across the border, New England festered with it in certain districts.

She saw men in the woods working with grub-hoe, pick, and bush-hook; saw green fires burning.

Stuart showed her a sneaking growth of wild currant—tested the infernal toughness and resistance of the wretched shrub, turned the coarse leaves to search for the deadly rusty spores, and thanked God that he discovered none.

So she learned that the leprosy called "pine blister" begins as a rusty stain on the underside of a currant or gooseberry leaf. It can not originate on the doomed pine itself; it must have its loathsome birth on currant or gooseberry.

Winds or birds carry it to a pine. But the hellish spores must work quickly because ten minutes is their span of life unless they reach a white pine tree.

When they do the tree is as good as dead. Yet the diseased tree can not infect others of its species. Only spores from currant or gooseberry can do that.

Days came when Stuart remained in seemingly incessant consultation with Mr. Leggett. There were maps and deeds to consult, letter files to inspect—a never-ending mass of detail.

Gilda desired to listen, was gratefully encouraged by Stuart, understood as well as anybody could who had not been conversant with the operations of Sutton & Company for the last decade.

But there were intervals when clerical details formed the subject under discussion. And at such times the girl literally took to the tall timber.

The wild flowers of the Northland were a never-ending surprise and delight to her. She picked few, but was on her knees to every one—to the pink moccasin flowers on tall, slender stalks, to the white trilliums, to the violets, blue, white, yellow; to the scented wild lilies-of-the-valley, like patches of snowy foam in the woods.

Everywhere spread carpets of bloom, straw-yellow, purple, green-white.

The dull strawberry red of another trillium clotted the still places with an odour of death and decay—gloomy, unlovely flowers which drew carrion flies.

But the silvery shad-bush was in flower; witch-hopple, viburnum, squaw-berry, moss and fern were gay and lovely in their resurrection.

Into sunny glades flitted the Beauty of Camberwell on cream-edged brown-velvet wings, embroidered with violet-blue. Comma butterflies flashed to a resting spot on tree-trunks glowing like dull spots of fire; green-clouded swallowtails in floppy but rapid flight winnowed the dusk through wet woods.

She lay by the stream in grey shirt and knickers, pillowing her head on both arms crossed behind, and looked up through new leaves into a sky as blue as a cat-bird's egg; and saw squirrels in tiny silhouette, running along highways of tangled branches.

She rolled over on her stomach and looked down into amber water where trout lay stemming the current, their tails all waving like wind-blown banners above the golden bottom-gravel.

Strange little bluish grey birds creeked and cheeped and whined as they crept up and down mossy tree-trunks; chickadees found her and lingered, conversing with her in friendly levity; nearby, low in the sky, two hawks mewed querulously, and their broad shadows swept the trees.

But there were not many hours alone, for Gilda Greenway. Her lover was never far away, and he never left her long in solitude—if the forest silence could be called that—for forest solitude is in the soul, not in the still places of the earth—never in wilderness or desert or upon the grey waste of waters until man brings it with him into the silent places.

A week was gone before they realised it had fairly begun.

It worried them both. Gilda was washing out underclothes below the dam. Her full yet slender hands bore scratches where the little Ladies of the Briers had caressed her, and they were tanned to a creamy tint—which seemed to be the limit of sunburn on skins like hers.

They had mentioned the horrifying speed of Time that morning, surprised and disgusted that day and night should have played them so treacherous a trick.

Now, soberly soaping her intimate attire, Gilda felt inclined to mingle a tear or two with the suds as she watched the iridescent bubbles dance away on the amber current.

Never, never had she been so happy and free from care. Never for an instant had the dark change threatened her; never had the shadow of the *Other One* stirred in sunlight or lamplight or in the witch-light of the stars. Care slept; memory was kind; life an enchanted vision through which days burned like fire and every second was a flaming jewel.

She lived and moved in a sort of passionless ecstasy; the forest, the sunlight, her lover were impersonal miracles; and she herself a blessed, unreal, unfamiliar thing, born of the magic that enveloped all.

She had spread her wet and immaculate attire on bushes in the sun. Then she got up, slim as a boy and graceful as a girl in her shirt and knickers; and was carrying the soap to her cabin when Stuart came across the bridge waving a telegram.

"I've got to stay here!" he cried joyously. "They sent in a runner from Fisher-cat Dam. The office wires me that our deal has gone through; we take over the Lamsden tract; the lawyers are to meet at Chazy, and the surveyors are leaving Utica tonight!"

She flung the soap upon the moss and her wet arms around his neck.

"Oh, how divine!" she cried. "I never want to go back! —never, never. Tell me how long we have?"

"Nearly three more weeks. Can your linen stand it?"

"If it doesn't, I'll play Eve," she said, kissing him with abandon. Then she freed her sagging hair of the last pin, flung it wide and flashing, and danced away over the log bridge.

"Good-bye," she called, waving one hand behind her.

"I'm going to dance through the woods until I fall down! Good-bye—good-bye—good-bye!"

He was after her now; she dodged like a squirrel; and off she sped, a glimmering shape among the trees. He caught her at last and tossed her up into his arms, where she lay panting—her face a pink flower in a shower of gold-red hair.

And so he carried her back to Gilda's Villa, slowly through the wood, his blond head bent, his lips resting on hers.

CHAPTER XXXVII

The hemlock wore its honey-pale tassels; the white pine its waxen candelabra; the spruce its tender terminals; the balsam was veiled in misty blue. June had begun magnificently in the forest; but the dweller in the Villa Gilda and the boy with the blond head had taken their last dip in Mr. Hanford's pool, swallowed the last mound of Mr. Hanford's flap-jacks.

The only fishers in the pools were mink and otter; the only frolickers in the forest the red squirrels. In the Villa Gilda, wood-mice prepared to nest; a porcupine promenaded the porch of the Hotel Sutton.

They had come for a week and had remained a month. Not one shadow had fallen across their Eden. Yet, in that month the girl had learned definitely what manner of man she had to deal with; the youth began to discover in the girl her genius for comradeship.

She found that she had to do with the average American man, inartistic, unimaginative, capable, chaste by habit, law-abiding through custom, kind by inclination, brave through heredity.

There was no glimmer about him. The qualities he had, shone. To her they formed a steady aureole. His instinctive cleanliness of mind and person fascinated her. He was 28 but utterly a boy. Only the restlessly intellectual mature and age early, not this average, crisp-blond type with little imagination to worry it, no excesses to over-ripen it, nothing morbid to regret.

The boy-man was normal. He knew his mate when he saw her. And she knew hers. Subtler than he, she had realised it at their first encounter. Perhaps that was why, conscious of non-fulfilment, she had passionately returned his kiss.

Well, their destiny was clear to her now. Earth held for her only this man.

As for Stuart, her unfeigned interest in what interested him was a thrilling revelation.

Timber, the growing of timber, its cutting, its selling—these things had been the principal, the vital interest in his family for generations. It was his principal interest. He wished it to be his son's. And now, when his lips rested on this young girl's soft hand, he felt that it would be.

Mentally, to her, he accredited all that was to be intellectually sensitive and imaginatively fine in the visionary family which he so vaguely evoked.

Hers the aspiration of talent and cultivation. She the source of mental exhilaration, the medium through which he was to understand and care for those things of the mind to which he had been unresponsive.

But even so, what a stimulating and delicious comrade had he found to walk with him on his own plane, listen to him, understand him, labour with him, play with him upon the common playground of the average man.

Men of his race loved but once, married fairly early or never. There was no other woman for him. There had been none before her. His ability to love could not survive her. His only chance was this girl. And he must take that chance if it lasted a lifetime.

Thus their mutual conclusion after a month together.

But their journey back to town was not entirely a gay one. There was reaction, defiant, pleasurable, piqued by a sort of indefinable apprehension.

That they had shattered all canons of convention had something to do with their rather excited state of mind, no doubt. That they had nothing else to regret ought to have been a balm.

She said, laughingly, when they reached the Mohawk Valley: "I have a plaguey premonition that we're going to hear from this escapade."

"I don't see how," he said, forcing a smile but feeling a trifle uncomfortable.

"I don't, either. Gossip can't travel through a wilderness. Anyway, those nice men thought no harm of us."

"Fancy Leggett or Mike thinking scandal," he said, smiling at her.

"And there wasn't any," she added.

They ought to have been mutually reassured.

"I don't suppose your aunt came back to town?" he ventured.

"I don't imagine so. But she'll be coming very soon. She sails from New York.... I never thought to speak to Freda. Do you suppose that woman would tell anybody that I went away for a month with you?"

"Good heavens, no," he said, a little startled.

Gilda remained silent, her eyes gravely absent.

"What is on your mind, dear?" he inquired uneasily.

"Nothing. I was wondering, for the first time, what that woman really thinks of us."

"It doesn't matter, does it?"

"I suppose not.... Still, if she's got a mind she thinks with it.... I've had to write her. I've had to send her wages.... I wasn't concerned at the time but I suppose it would have been more sensible if we hadn't had the expressman check our hand-luggage from my apartment."

"Nothing will happen," he said, more carelessly than he felt.

"No.... Your people are not in town, are they, Stuart?"

"They're on their way back, I believe—"

A white clad negro bent ceremoniously beside her: "Dinner is served in the dining car, madam," he murmured; bowed again to Stuart, and continued his ceremonious progress through the car.

They arrived in town at noon on a cloudless day in early June.

Gilda had telegraphed Freda to prepare luncheon for two. No trace of uneasiness remained to cloud the gay excitement of their home-coming. Red-caps piled their taxi with luggage; their vehicle swung into Madison Avenue. It was but a five-minute drive.

Stuart and the driver carried up the baggage. Freda welcomed them with a pale Scandinavian smile.

"Oh, Stuart!" cried the girl, "it *does* look nice!"

She stood by the piled luggage in the sitting-room, unpinning her hat and looking happily about at the familiar place.

"It looks jolly comfortable," he admitted, tossing hat and light coat on the sofa. Gilda flung her hat after them, caught his hand, and walked him slowly about the apartment.

"Why shouldn't we like it?" she murmured. "You told me you loved me in this room. Every thing means you, here."

They looked soberly at the four walls which had witnessed already so much that had been happy and tragic in their brief existence together.

They walked into her bedroom and she seated herself before her mirror and began to unpin her ruddy hair.

"Scrub first, if you like, darling," she said; "and try to remember which tooth-brush is yours."

At luncheon it was arranged that he should go down town to the office, stop at his own house on the way back and dress, call for her and take her to the Ritz for dinner.

"I'll leave my luggage now, and carry it home tonight," he said. "I'm going to take the subway to the office.... You look wonderfully fit, Gilda," he added, lingering sentimentally.

"I'll have a fit if you don't go," she said. "I've simply got to look over my wardrobe if you expect me to dine out with you, darling."

But when he opened the door to go she detained him, wound her arms tightly around his neck.

"You have given me the most beautiful month in my life," she said. "I hope God will let me make it up to you—a year for every day of happiness you gave me...."

At the office of Sutton & Sons he nodded smilingly right and left in return for greetings.

In the outer office Miss Tower smiled primly upon him. "Mr. Sutton senior is here," she said.

"What!" he exclaimed.

"Your father is here, Mr. Stuart."

"Where?"

"In the private office, sir."

He found his father there talking with Mr. Connolly, department chief. Amenities were exchanged; Mr. Connolly left.

"Well, for heaven's sake, dad! I didn't expect you and mother until Thursday."

"We came on. We got here day before yesterday. When did you arrive from the forest, Stuart?"

"Just now. We—I got in about noon."

"Oh. You lunched at home."

"No—"

"Oh. You haven't seen your mother?"

"I had no idea she was home."

"She'll know you are by your luggage," remarked his father.

Stuart reddened violently, went over to his desk and fumbled the mail.

"Well," said his father, "you put over the new deal, I hear."

"I did. How did you hear, dad?"

"One of their surveyors from Chazy was in here a little while ago."

"Which?" asked the boy involuntarily.

"Anderson."

Stuart's face pulsated with hot, surging colour as he bent lower over the papers on the desk. His father, twirling his eyeglasses by the silk cord, was looking out of the window.

"Did you and mother have a good time in California?" the boy managed to inquire.

"Very.... Who did you take to the Forest, Stuart?"

"What?"

"Who was it you had up there?" repeated his father, not looking at him.

"I'm not quite sure I understand you," said the boy.

"Didn't you have some people as guests up there?" inquired Sutton senior, glancing casually at his only son.

"Yes."

"Do you mind saying who they were?"

"There was only one."

"Oh. I thought you had a girl or two in the party."

Silence was too nearly a lie. The boy said: "There was a girl."

"So I heard from Jock Anderson. Is she anybody your mother and I know?"

"No."

His father said carelessly: "All right. No doubt she was well looked after."

Silence, again, was conniving at untruth.

"There was nobody else," said the boy, "—no other woman."

After a silence:

"Well, old chap, wasn't that rather idiotic?" suggested his father calmly.

"It really wasn't, dad."

"It really *was*," retorted Sutton senior. "Do you care to talk about it, Stuart?"

"Yes.... Not now."

"At your convenience, my son."

He got up: "Glad to see you back, Stuart. Glad to be back. Heron Nest must be charming. I think your mother and I will go up this week. Will you be home to dinner?"

"I'll see mother. I'm dining out."

"Come in for tea then. We have a guest. It would be civil to speak to her."

"All right, dad; I'll be home by five."

They shook hands—his father dropped one hand on the boy's shoulder.

"Don't ever be afraid of me, Stuart."

"No.... Besides, dad, I have nothing to be afraid of.... I was going to tell you all about it anyway ... when the proper time arrived.... I'm all right, you know."

"Yes, I do know.... And if you'd been an ass, you're my son.... Also, you are Sutton & Son.... You talk to me when you're ready. That's what I'm for."

"You're a corker, dad.... What did Anderson say?"

"Well, to be plain, he said you had a very pretty girl up there named Miss Greenway, occupying the shanty next to yours."

"It sounds rather awful, doesn't it?" said the boy.

"Well—"

"Don't mention it to mother, will you?"

"I didn't intend to," replied his father drily.

"I'll tell her myself some day. It'll be all right. Don't worry, dad."

They exchanged a hand-grip. His father went out.

Stuart tried to read his mail, but couldn't. This business was going to worry Gilda. Not that it could matter, ultimately. But there had been obstacles enough without adding this one.

There seemed to be no point in telephoning her about the episode. They'd dine, then he'd tell her.

He turned again to his letters but the depression persisted. He was sorry his father had first learned about Gilda in that way. He felt a hot animosity toward Anderson. Probably the fool meant no mischief—yet he might have, too. He was just one of the vast brotherhood of Talkers—low in the scale because he had only petty gossip to detail—low enough to be stupid—too low to know, instinctively, when to hold his gabbling tongue.

He went up town about five and walked across to his own house, using his latch-key to enter.

From the east drawing-room came social noises—modulated voices, the clink of the tea cup.

He laid his hat on the console and walked in.

There were a number of people there. He kissed his mother, paid his compliments to her friends. One woman he had not met, but approached in his friendly, boyish way.

"My son, Stuart," said his mother, smilingly; and, to him: "Lady Glyndale, Stuart, with whom we came East."

He took a cup of tea beside Lady Glyndale.

"Do you like California?" he asked politely.

"Yes, excepting the natives," she replied with British frankness.

"I thought them rather nice," he said, smiling.

"I daresay there a few nice ones. The natives are a poor lot, poor farmers, slothful, stupid. The Japanese are far more interesting, better farmers, better tenants. It's rather extraordinary your wishing to get rid of them."

"I don't know very much about the squabble between California and Japan," he admitted.

"You should," she remarked.

Which was perfectly true, and the young man winced.

He talked to others, exchanged a few words with his mother, when opportunity offered.

Sideways he inspected Lady Glyndale and found her typical—arched eyebrows and small, flat feet; high bridged nose and little gouty hands; high-coloured and flat as a board at the back; and with that indefinable something that slightly irritates, slightly amuses, and wholly commands respect—the unmistakable aura of race and breeding.

He thought: "Whatever you think of them you can count on them every time."

He asked her if she'd had any tuna fishing at Catalina. She did not warm but became seriously animated. They discussed tuna and tarpon.

Then, having to dress, he made his adieux, regretted his inability to dine at home, and expressed his pleasure that Lady Glyndale was to be their guest.

"You shall tell me more about your tuna," she said. "I read late in your climate. I don't know how anybody sleeps at all in your American air."

When he was dressed he went out into the June evening and hailed a taxi. All the western streets were bathed in the rosy glory of the setting sun.

In dinner coat and straw hat he felt the happy relaxation of informal summer; lay back in the open vehicle to savour a cigarette and gaze at the familiar streets in their new June setting.

At the door of Gilda's abode he got out and told the driver to wait.

Freda admitted him. He caught sight of Gilda on the sofa, and went to her. She gave him a rather pale smile and a listless hand.

"Are you all right, dear?" came his invariable and anxious question.

"Yes.... Sit here near me." She took his hand again, absently, the faint smile still on her lips.

"You're tired from the journey," he concluded.

"No.... My aunt came in somewhat unexpectedly."

"When?"

"About two o'clock."

There was a silence.

"Well—did it upset you?" he asked.

"A little.... Our luggage lay there where we left it. Your overcoat, too."

"Oh, Lord!"

She touched his palm, lightly, reflectively, with each finger-tip in turn.

"It *was* awkward.... I had a bath. I was still in my bath-robe. The bell rang and I heard Freda go.... It was too late to instruct her.

"She showed my aunt in and brought me her card.... So I got into a boudoir robe.... There she sat—with all that damning luggage under her very nose—and your overcoat and stick.... I'd forgotten it. I turned scarlet-hot to my toes."

"What happened?" he asked, miserably.

"Nothing much. She'd arrived here three days ago. She'd been here every day. Freda forgot to mention it. But yesterday she told my aunt that a telegram had come and I was to arrive today."

"What did your aunt say?"

"She asked me where I'd been."

"Did you tell her?"

"Yes. But I didn't go into details."

"What did she say about the luggage?"

"Nothing. But I knew she had noticed it.... Stuart, she wants me to sail with her on the 6th."

He forced a smile: "Are you going to?"

"I was wondering.... I'd like to consult an attorney."

"Why?"

"About securing my freedom.... If it would help any for me to go abroad—"

The telephone rang on the table beside her. She picked up the receiver.

"Yes? ... Yes, this is Miss Greenway.... Oh, I didn't recognise your voice, Dr. Pockman.... Yes, I have been away nearly a month.... *What?* ... No, I had no means of knowing it.... Is he seriously ill? ... Do you mean he is not going to recover!!!"

For a full minute she sat with the receiver pressed to her ear, terribly intent on what she heard. Then:

"Yes, I'll come.... Who? ... Did he ask for him? ... He is here now.... You had better speak to him yourself, Dr. Pockman."

She passed the receiver to Stuart. Her hand trembled slightly.

"Sadoul is dying," she said.

CHAPTER XXXVIII

They had gone to the laboratory as they were, not delaying to dine, Gilda in her black dinner-gown, Stuart wearing his dinner jacket. For Pockman had advised haste.

They both were a little dazed—even Sutton, who knew what Gilda had not known. But he had looked for nothing like this—nothing swift—even nothing deadly, perhaps.

"Why does he want me," he said, partly to himself. "I can understand that he would desire to see you."

Her ungloved hand crept into his but she remained silent.

The June night was cool and spangled with big stars. It was deliciously cool near the river where a breeze was blowing from the Sound.

As they descended, Stuart said to the driver: "We may be here for some time. Don't go."

Miss Cross met them in the hall. She took Gilda's hand and caressed it; spoke pleasantly to Stuart.

"He's in his own room. The doctor is there, expecting you."

They followed her. Pockman rose and came forward in the subdued lamplight.

Sadoul, lying on his bed near the open window, did not open his eyes.

Pockman said to Gilda: "I've called up your house every day for a week."

"When did this happen?" she asked.

At the sound of her voice Sadoul's eyes unclosed. "Is that you, Gilda?"

"Yes." She went forward, slowly; laid one slender hand on the bed-clothes over his chest.

They looked at each other for a little while in silence. "If you don't come back to me, I'll have to go after you," he murmured.

He closed his sunken eyes, opened them presently, looked up at her. "Gilda, *t'en souviens tu?*—

> '*—Et quand, dernier témoin de ces scènes funèbres,*
> *Entouré du chaos, de la mort, des ténèbres,*
> *Seul, je serais debout; seul malgré mon effroi,*
> *Etre infaillible et bon, j'espérerais en toi,*
> *Et, certain du retour de l'éternelle aurore,*
> *Sur les mondes détruits je t'attendrais—encore—*'"

His breath came harsh, labouriously, obstructing the voice.

"Gilda, Gilda," he sighed.

She said nothing. He stared at her out of burning eyes, then, as his gaze wandered, he caught sight of Sutton.

"You damned liar," he said in a stronger voice.

"Is that what you wished to say to me, Sadoul?"

"It's one of the things. You told me you'd remain away only a week or ten days. You've been gone long enough to find me dying."

"I'm sorry.... I expected nothing like this. Business detained me longer than I expected."

"The business of making love to another man's wife," said Sadoul. And, to Gilda: "Well, what do you think of my marksmanship with an automatic, Gilda?"

"What?"

"My endeavours to—shoot up—your young man," he gasped, suddenly husky and shaken by his laboured breathing.

"What?" she repeated, bewildered.

"Do you mean to say he didn't tell you?"

"I don't know what you mean, Sadoul."

Sadoul looked at Sutton: "Didn't you tell her?" he barked.

"No."

The sick man lay gasping and fumbling at the covers, his fevered eyes roving from Gilda to Sutton.

"I guess you didn't mean to lie about coming back," he panted. "Sit down. I once showed you something. Do you remember?"

"Yes.".

"I'll show you something better than that. You'll be surprised." To Gilda: "Sit down. Are you in a hurry?"

"No."

"Have you a little time?"

"Yes."

"All right. I want to show Sutton something. But you'll have to make him see it."

"What is it you wish him to see?" she asked gently.

"I'm going to die," he panted, "and I want him to see me do it."

Pockman approached and looked down at him with a reassuring smirk: "While there's life there's—"

"Tell it to Sweeny," whispered Sadoul with a pallid sneer. "You know damned well I'm dying."

Pockman laughed: "You've plenty of vitality yet, I notice—"

"You tell 'em," barked Sadoul. And, to Gilda, with an effort: "I'm going after you when the time comes, if you don't come back of your own accord." To Sutton: "I want you to see what you'll be up against—someday—"

A terrible spasm of coughing overwhelmed him. Pockman and Miss Cross, beside him, supported his head. The nurse, presently, carried basin and towels away.

Pockman seated himself and placed his hand on Sadoul's pulse.

For a long while the room was very quiet. A river breeze blew the curtains. Stars looked in.

"Gilda," whispered the dying man.

"I am here, Sadoul."

"Is *he* here, too?"

"Yes."

"I want him to see. Will you let him?"

"See—what?" she faltered.

Sadoul's voice burst from him with startling violence: "I want you to let him see what you are going to see.... What you'll both have to reckon with someday.... The indestructible I! The surviving identity which is *I* myself! ... And always will be—eternal, deathless—"

He struggled to sit up, his eyes glittering with fever: "Will you do that last thing for me, Gilda?"

"I don't know," she answered, deathly pale. And to her lover: "He asks me to let you see his soul, when it leaves him."

"Sutton! Are you afraid to look!" gasped Sadoul.

"Not if you wish it."

Sadoul's glazing eyes were fixed on him: "I—want you to see—for yourself—what you'll be up against—someday— ... The hemorrhage was strangling him.... "On ne—meurt—pas—" he whispered.... "Je ne fais que—mon début—"

His voice failed; Miss Cross eased him back to the stained pillow. After a silence, Pockman turned partly around, his hand still on Sadoul's wrist.

"He's going," he said in a low voice.

After ten minutes: "He's nearly gone.... It isn't his lungs, either. It's that cobra serum.... I told him so. Hell! Cobra virus will kill Koch's bacilli. So will dynamite. So will jumping off the Woolworth building."

He released the pulse; laid his hand on Sadoul's heart. Miss Cross handed him a mirror and turned up the lights.

"He's gone," said Pockman.

Gilda, very pale, rose, walked to the bedside, sank to her knees.

After a while she averted her head, covered both eyes with her handkerchief, held out one hand, blindly, to her lover.

He lifted her, drew her back to their seats by the wall, retaining her hand.

Pockman drew the sheet over the dead man's face, nodded dismissal to Miss Cross, turned out all lights, teetered over to an arm-chair and sat down.

"Do you want a couch?" he asked Gilda.

"No."

"All right. Can you include me in this affair?"

"Yes."

"Very well.... Whenever you are ready."

The girl turned, rested her right hand on her lover's shoulder, palm upward; laid her cheek in the hollowed hand.

Sutton gazed at the bed. Over Sadoul's shadowy, sheeted face a faint light shone—starlight, he supposed.

After a few minutes he realised it was not starlight.

He gazed at the bony outline of Sadoul's face beneath the sheet, remembering what this dead man had said concerning the post-mortem persistence of consciousness.

Was Sadoul lying there dead, still conscious? The brain died last of all. Was Sadoul's brain still alive? What was that pale light, imperceptibly increasing above the shrouded head?

The girl resting on his shoulder was now breathing softly, regularly as a sleeping child.

He dared not stir; his eyes were fixed upon the outlined figure on the bed.

Suddenly the covered head became visible in silhouette, as though an electric bulb had been turned on under the bed sheet.

Steadily the glow spread to a radio-activity so intense that Sadoul's head itself seemed translucent, revealing the shadowy cerebrum and cerebellum slowly expanding within the skull.

The Senate of the body was preparing to adjourn *sine die*.

Now, the preparations for the spirit's departure from its worn out tenement were fully completed. The intense brilliancy of the head began to fade. A softly luminous atmosphere grew above the covered head, slowly assuming the contours of another head.

This new head developed more and more distinctly, more compactly, indescribably brilliant—

All around it spread a luminous atmosphere, seemingly in great commotion. This agitated pool of light penetrated like the white fire of an aurora; but, as the new head became more perfect, it waned, faded, disappeared.

Steadily, harmoniously, the neck, shoulders, chest, were developed in their natural progressive order.

The etheric body was slowly rising over the head and at right angles to the deserted body.

Now, about the feet of the etheric shape, a blinding vital light played like electricity, linking it with the sheeted head. For a few minutes this lasted, then the natal cord grew thin, fine as a luminous thread, parted.

All light died out on the dark bed. In the starlight a tall, greyish shape stood beside the dead—a figure like Sadoul, not quite as tall, with no mark of sickness on body or face; younger, tranquil of carriage, with vague, untroubled eyes that rested on the living without emotion, without surprise.

Leisurely, without effort, the figure moved to the open window and stood there gazing out into the starlight for a while. Then, turning, it passed Pockman, noticing him; passed before Gilda, sleeping on Sutton's shoulder, quietly observant, moved on to the open door, into the corridor beyond, where lights were burning on the whitewashed wall.

Here it became perfectly distinct, differing in no way from a living being.

The street door was open; the aged door-keeper sat in his box reading an evening paper.

Sadoul looked at him as he passed, smiled, and went out into the street.

In the death chamber Pockman got up on his rickety legs, pulled out his watch.

"Two hours, thirty-three minutes, nine and a fraction seconds," he said; smirked, wiped his sweating features, picked up a pencil and wrote down his observation on the chart.

On Stuart's shoulder Gilda was stirring. Presently she sighed lightly, opened her eyes, drew a deeper breath, sat upright.

For a few moments she sat gazing at the bed, her left hand still resting on her lover's shoulder.

Pockman came teetering across the room, holding out something that glittered in the dim radiance of the stars.

"He wanted me to give you this," he said with a sort of ghostly snigger.

She took the shining object. It was the gold-hilted misericordia.

The girl slowly stood up. There was a white rose at her sash. She drew it out, walked to the bed and placed it on Sadoul's breast. Beside it she laid the misericordia.

"Bury these with him," she said to Pockman. And to the still figure under the sheet: "Good-bye, Sadoul."

Pockman accompanied them to the street door, his arms twitching and jerking, the vague, habitual grin stamped on his flat and pallid face.

"He could have euchred old man Death in New Mexico or Arizona," he said with a mechanical snicker. "He preferred to take a chance with that snake. Hell!"

Sutton guided Gilda down the battered steps.

"I think," he said in a low voice, "that we'd better drive to the house and see my father and mother. I think we ought to set matters straight without delay."

"If you think it best.... What time is it?"

"A quarter to ten."

She stood for a moment close against him. He could feel her whole body trembling. Then she slowly moved forward, leaning on his arm.

He gave the driver directions, stepped into the taxi behind her and drew her icy hands into his.

The girl's eyes were glimmering with unshed tears.

Pockman, in his own lamplit study, touched the bell on his desk.

To an orderly who appeared, he said: "Send that damned snake to the Bronx tomorrow."

After the orderly had retired he sat thinking, mopping up the perspiration that drenched his hair. Then he opened a locked drawer in his desk, drew out a packet of blue-prints, examined them one by one, and, one by one, tore each into minute pieces.

There was a handful of these. He sat sifting them from one hand to the other for a long while. Finally he rose, went to the open window and scattered them in the pale lustre of the stars.

CHAPTER XXXIX

There were lights in both drawing-rooms when Stuart let in Gilda and himself with his latch-key. She let slip her evening wrap; he laid it on a chair by the console, with his hat and stick.

There were no traces of tears on Gilda's face, but she was rather colourless.

"It's dreadfully late," she whispered to Stuart; "do you think you should have brought me?"

"Father knows there was a girl with me as my guest in the Forest. That ass Anderson—do you remember I introduced him when we walked over to Fisher-cat Dam? Well, he's here and he mentioned my being there with a 'pretty girl.' That's why I don't care to lose any time about it."

Gilda's colour came back quickly. "No," she said, "it's better not to delay."

"I'm sorry I had to tell you," he said. "I hope it won't disconcert you."

She seemed a trifle surprised that the prospect of meeting his family under any circumstances should disconcert her.

"They're really not formidable," he added, seriously.

She regarded him blankly, suddenly melted into a bewitching smile.

"You're so sweet," she murmured, "and so entirely all that you should be. Take me to your parents and explain me, darling, and I'll try to be scared to death."

He was too nervous himself to notice her adorable but saucy levity. He glanced into the west drawing-room and saw his mother there alone, playing solitaire.

"Is it you, Stuart?" she said, busy with her cards. "I thought I heard your key in the door."

He took Gilda's soft hand and went in. When his mother raised her abstracted eyes she saw them standing before her in an odd, faintly smiling silence.

"Mother," he said, "this is Gilda Greenway. I'm madly in love with her. She has consented to marry me. We haven't thought much about the date—in fact, we haven't talked about it—but if she is willing I can't see any use in waiting—"

The flushed astonishment on his mother's face checked his nervous eloquence.

His mother arose. The manners of all the Suttons were perfect when they chose.

She held out a gemmed hand to Gilda. When the girl laid her own on it: "My child, what is this young man of mine trying to tell me?" asked his mother.

Under the calm scrutiny the girl's colour heightened to a lovely tint, but she smiled.

"He's trying to say to you that we are very much in love, Mrs. Sutton. We met this last winter. I'm sure it was love at sight with me."

She bent her charming head, hesitated:

"We have been spending the evening together. Stuart thought that perhaps this was the best way—"

"Mother," said the boy earnestly, "she's a perfect darling!—"

This is the moment in the lives of two young people when what is said and done by parents determines the future relations of all concerned.

These children did not know it, but the boy's mother did. She knew she could lose her son to this girl by a word or look—lose him in bitterness which never could be entirely forgotten. Every instinct in her was antagonistic to this departure from rule-of-thumb, from immemorial routine, from inherited conformation to convention.

Slowly she looked from her only son to this stranger. The girl was lovely to look upon.

She started to speak, waited to control her voice—the tremor of sudden tears in her throat—a throat all a-quiver with the protest of offended pride—of resentment, revolt indescribable.

But all the time she realised what this moment would mean to her and to her son, and to their future relationship.

She had her voice under control. She said to Gilda:

"If you love as I do, you understand Stuart's mother at this moment better than he can."

Gilda's face became beautifully grave.

"I do understand. It wasn't fair for me to come—I didn't realise how unfair, until now—"

She turned impulsively toward her lover, but his mother retained her hand:

"Don't go. My son's guests are welcome.... I think you would be welcome anyway. And if he is to marry you, this is your proper place, my child."

Gilda's eyes became suddenly misty: she averted them, turned her head slightly:

"It was not the thing to do," she said. "It was your right to be told, first—to talk to your son undisturbed. I—I've made a rather ghastly faux pas—"

"*I* have!" said Stuart. "I dragged you here—"

His eyes fell on his father who, hearing voices, had come from a game of chess in the other drawing-room.

With Sutton senior was his chess-antagonist, Lady Glyndale, wearing the complacent expression of the victor.

But when Lady Glyndale's satisfied gaze encountered Gilda, it altered radically.

Stuart, nervously retaining command of the situation, or supposing he commanded it, had already presented his father and Gilda to each other, and had begun in a determined voice:

"Lady Glyndale, my fiancée, Miss Greenway—" when his affianced interrupted calmly:

"Lady Glyndale is my aunt, Stuart. And how on earth we've managed to encounter each other here—"

"Are you engaged to be married, Gilda?" demanded Lady Glyndale grimly.

"Yes, I am, Aunt Constance.... If—I am—approved—" She looked at Sutton senior in a bewildered way—turned to Stuart's mother with the naive, involuntary impulse of a child seeking refuge.

In an overwhelming rush of relief that lady fully retained her aplomb.

"It appears," she said to Lady Glyndale, "that your niece and my son have chosen to surprise us."

She looked at Gilda. The girl went to her, took both her hands, pressing them convulsively.

"You odd, sweet child," murmured her lover's mother. "It's perfectly clear to me that this absurd, rattle-headed son of mine is to blame."

Lady Glyndale, looking at Gilda, said grimly: "So *that's* the reason you have declined to travel with me. Why didn't you say so?"

The girl's lips were quivering: "I don't know, Aunt Constance.... I seem to be a—a mindless sort—"

"You've no monopoly of mindlessness," said Sutton senior, staring hard at Sutton junior.

"For heaven's sake, dad—"

"Yes, for heaven's sake," said his father.

There was a silence. Then the boy's mother drew the girl to her, and the girl's red head dropped on her shoulder.

Sutton senior walked over, obviously pulling himself together.

"I'd like to have a look at my own daughter-in-law," he said to Gilda. "I'd like to see her smile, once—"

"Don't bother the child now," said his wife.

But Gilda lifted her head smiling, with wet lashes, and held out her hand.

"Good girl," said Sutton senior, and shook it gravely. And turned and shook the hand of his only son:

"It's easy to see she's much too good for you."

"Thank you, dad."

His mother smiled at him. He drew a swift, happy breath, went over to Lady Glyndale.

That lady was in two minds about this business:

"Your mother and father are charming people," she said frankly. "I hope you are."

The boy laughed: "I hope I am," he said, "and I'm sure you can be if you care to, Lady Glyndale."

"Well," she said, "I'm not at all sure. It quite depends, you see. Come and talk to me tomorrow."

"I shall, indeed," he said, fervently pressing her half-extended hand.

Then Lady Glyndale went over and resolutely kissed Gilda.

"Don't you think," she inquired with some sarcasm, "that you could find a few moments to talk over matters with me before I sail?"

"Yes, Aunt Constance," said the girl meekly.

Lady Glyndale took a brief, comprehensive sweep of the situation, the people, their environment. And into her absolutely British visage came an expression which seemed to mean: "Most certainly this is America and nowhere else, because these things never happen anywhere else on earth."

But aloud she said amiably: "Good night. I'm going to bed."

The men accompanied her to the lift. She graciously declined further politeness, got into the lift, started it, and hoisted herself bedward.

Sutton senior and Stuart exchanged an unpremeditated and crushing grip.

"Isn't Gilda wonderful?" said the boy.

"Absolutely," replied his father with every symptom of conviction. "So are you, by the way."

They laughed. Stuart went back to the west drawing-room. Gilda saw him, would have stepped back, but his mother retained her by the hand.

To her son she said: "Dear, I'm so glad you're happy." And held him wistfully a moment after they had kissed.

Then, smiling, she kissed Gilda, and went leisurely from the room, leaving her boy to his new love as must all mothers who bear a man-child in pain and travail and gratitude to God.

THE END

ROBERT W. CHAMBERS BIBLIOGRAPHY

In the Quarter (1894)
The King in Yellow (1895; stories)
The Red Republic (1895)
With the Band (1896; poetry)
A King and a Few Dukes (1896)
The Maker of Moons (1896; stories)
The Mystery of Choice (1897; stories)
The Haunts of Men (1898; stories)
Ashes of Empire (1898)
Lorraine (1898)
Outsiders (1899)
Cambric Mask (1899)
The Conspirators (1900; UK as *A Gay Conspiracy*, 1900)
Cardigan (1901)
The Maid-at-Arms (1902)
The Maids of Paradise (1903)
In Search of the Unknown (1904)
A Young Man in a Hurry and Other Short Stories (1904)
The Reckoning (1905)
Iole (1905)
The Tracer of Lost Persons (1906)
The Fighting Chance (1906)
The Tree of Heaven (1907; stories)
The Younger Set (1907)
The Firing Line (1908)
Some Ladies in Haste (1908)
Special Messenger (1909)
The Danger Mark (1909)
Ailsa Paige (1910)
The Green Mouse (1910)
Adventures of a Modest Man (1911)
The Common Law (1911)
The Streets of Ascalon (1912)
Japonette (1912; serialized as *The Turning Point*, Cosmopolitan, 1914)
The Gay Rebellion (1913)
The Business of Life (1913)
Blue-Bird Weather (1913)
Quick Action (1914)
The Hidden Children (1914)
Anne's Bridge (1914)
Between Friends (1914; novelette)
Who Goes There! (1915)
Athalie (1915)
Police!!! (1915; stories)
The Better Man (1916; stories)
The Girl Philippa (1916)
Barbarians (1917; interconnected war stories)
The Dark Star (1917)
The Restless Sex (1918)
The Laughing Girl (1918)
In Secret (1919)
The Moonlight Way (1919)
The Crimson Tide (1919)
The Slayer of Souls (1920)
A Story of Primitive Love (1920; story)
The Little Red Foot (1921)
Eris (1922)
The Flaming Jewel (1922)
The Talkers (1923)
The Hi-Jackers (1923)
America, or the Sacrifice (1924)
Marie Halkett (UK: 1925; US: 1937; serialized as *The Jolly Roger*, McCall's, 1923-24)
The Girl in Golden Rags (UK: 1925; US: 1936)
The Mystery Lady (1925)
The Man They Hanged (1926)
The Way of Dionysia (1926; only published as *Red Book Magazine* serial)
The Drums of Aulone (1927; serialized as *The Fear of God*, Liberty magazine, 1926-27)
The Gold Chase (1927; serialized as "Thalassa!", Cassell's Magazine, 1927)
The Rogue's Moon (1928)
The Sun Hawk (1928)
The Happy Parrot (1929)
Painted Minx (1930)
The Rake and the Hussy (1930)

Beating Wings (UK: 1930; US: 1936)
War Paint and Rouge (1931)
Gitana (1931; serialized as *Silver Knees*, *Liberty* magazine, 1931)
The Whistling Cat (1932)
Whatever Love Is (1933)
The Young Man's Girl (1934)
Secret Service Operator 13 (1934; UK as *Spy No. 13*, 1935; stories)
Love and the Lieutenant (1935)
The Fifth Horseman (1937)
Smoke of Battle (1938; completed by Rupert Hughes)

PLAYS/MUSICALS

The Witch of Ellangowan (1897; aka Meg Merrilies)
Iole (1913; musical comedy based on the novel)
Sintram and His Companions (opera libretto)

CHILDREN'S BOOKS

Outdoorland (1903)
Orchard-Land (1903)
River-Land (1904)
Forest-Land (1905)
Mountain-Land (1906)
Garden-Land (1907)

CPSIA information can be obtained
at www.ICGtesting.com
Printed in the USA
LVHW020033120222
710698LV00013BA/350